Every eye in the Control Room watched, riveted, as Myers's suited body flashed in and out of view, interspersed by static, appearing at crazy angles to the camera. A kinetoscope of flickering images—smashing, gloved fists, flailing legs and one shocking close-up of a mirror-visored helmet—reveled his likewise suited assailant. Abruptly, the audio kicked in, and clipped, garbled sounds that might have been shrieks filled the loop.

The image solidified for a few seconds. Myers's helmet was pressed up against the camera, his face absurdly large and curved. One terrified eye could clearly be seen, blinking rapid-fire, rolling around frantically to locate his attacker. The harsh rasp of the astronaut's breathing drowned out all other sounds.

There was just one moment more, in which Myers's faceplate could be seen to explode outward. Then, mercifully, the screen lapsed back into static. . . .

# COSMONAUT

## Peter McAllister

AN ONYX BOOK

ONYX
Published by New American Library, a division of
Penguin Putnam Inc., 375 Hudson Street,
New York, New York 10014, U.S.A.
Penguin Books Ltd, 80 Strand,
London WC2R 0RL, England
Penguin Books Australia Ltd, 250 Camberwell Road,
Camberwell, Victoria 3124, Australia
Penguin Books Canada Ltd, 10 Alcorn Avenue,
Toronto, Ontario, Canada M4V 3B2
Penguin Books (N.Z.) Ltd, Cnr Rosedale and Airborne Roads,
Albany, Auckland 1310, New Zealand

Penguin Books Ltd, Registered Offices:
Harmondsworth, Middlesex, England

Published by Onyx, an imprint of New American Library, a division of Pen-
guin Putnam Inc. Previously published in a Penguin Books Australia edition.
For information contact Penguin Books Australia, 250 Camberwell Road,
Camberwell, Victoria 3124, Australia.

First Onyx Printing, March 2003
10  9  8  7  6  5  4  3  2  1

 REGISTERED TRADEMARK—MARCA REGISTRADA

Printed in the United States of America

*For George, the master of craftsmen*

# Prologue

The astronaut froze, fingers poised clawlike over the laptop keyboard.

*What was that?*

He closed his eyes and listened carefully, but there was nothing—just the faint background hum of ISS's circulation fans and the tiny whine of the station's fluorescent lights.

He let his breath out in a short, nervous laugh. *Jesus, man,* he told himself. *You're getting really paranoid—you know that?*

He forced himself into a rhythm of slow breathing, inhaling the faintly sour air of the Hab Module in deep drafts that set him drifting, imperceptibly, in the tiny cabin. *In, wait. Out, wait.* That was better. His heart rate began to throttle down.

*Maybe I'm wrong,* he thought suddenly. Hope flickered in him.

*Please God, let me be wrong.*

His eye was caught by his own image reflected in the large porthole window to his left. ISS was still in the eclipsed third of its ninety-five-minute orbit; even his cabin's single fluorescent tube was enough to opaque the glass against the blackness of space. He was floating vertically in the upright closet of a cabin, the wall-mounted sleep restraint inches from his back. His legs dangled beneath him, crossed loosely. His hands hovered over the laptop strapped to the small ledge jutting from the beige, aluminum-panel walls. The blue flight suit floated around his wiry frame, ballooning from gathered folds at his waist and shoulders. Brown hair formed a weightless halo around his head.

As he watched, a needle of light pierced the image: the sun peeping from behind the suddenly visible Earth. Within seconds it had swung out to hang in front of the advancing station like a molten blob, its pale gold light dissolving his reflection and revealing the world below. He stared, mesmerized, as ISS drew level with the sunlit lip—just short of the long, buckled belt of the Rockies, he saw—here the Earth was rushing into dawn, then shot past it.

Morning would be breaking in California soon.

He looked away from the window, a sudden pang of homesickness threatening to overwhelm him. God, what wouldn't he give to be back down there now. Or even to have another American on board. That was the worst; being the only one. There was no one to turn to, no one to tell. The handover crew was not due on ISS for another twenty-four days. He counted back. Over five weeks had passed since Bud's arrhythmia had forced the expedition commander to return to Earth. That meant nine weeks . . . What was the joke Leonid had made? The only American on a mostly America-built station?

He shivered, despite the Habitation Module's evenly maintained seventy-two degrees. Somehow, it didn't seem a joke anymore.

He turned back to the laptop and started typing again. He *had* to get the message finished, quickly. Any moment now, Boris would be knocking at the cabin door. He wrestled with the wording; he didn't dare give too much away. *God, if it gets out . . .*

As if on cue, he heard the scraping as the Russian commander came hand-over-hand towards him through the module. The astronaut swore silently, forcing his fingers to speed across the keyboard. The clang of Boris's wrench on the aluminum, right beside his ear, nearly made him cry out, though he had heard it most mornings the past few weeks. *That goddamned wrench,* he thought distractedly. *Why can't he ever just knock?*

*"Vstavai posnymaisya, Americanyets,"* Boris's muffled voice called through the thin metal. "Gary! Rise and shine, *da*?"

*"Podozhdyte secan . . . secundoch . . .* oh Jesus . . . just a moment," he called, his fingers picking the transmission script out hurriedly. He winced at every tap, imagining Boris on the other side of the door, head craned, hearing everything. He held his breath as he tapped out the final characters of the address sequence; all he had to do now was hit the Send key. He hesitated, finger poised over it.

*Maybe I am wrong,* he thought, assailed by sudden doubt. His finger drew back slightly. *Mabye I should wait, check things out . . .*

*"Americanyets!"* Boris repeated humorously, hammering the door again. "What goes on? You have a woman in there?"

He stared at the key a moment more then jabbed it, releasing the breath as he did so. *There.* The message began coding; it would slot into the queue and be relayed to the Ground Terminal at White Sands at the next e-mail downlink. He snapped the computer shut and twisted around to the door, yanking it open to reveal Boris's grinning face, upside down.

"You bet, Commander," he said smoothly. "It just took me a minute to hide her in the *kladovka*." The Russian laughed uproariously and pushed himself off the module wall towards the galley, where breakfast, and the other cosmonauts, would be waiting. The astronaut followed, fighting down the fear and revulsion that threatened to overwhelm him. *God, to have to sit there and pretend. When I know . . .*

He shoved the thought away, visualizing instead his message, by now streaming through space towards Ground. He felt a semblance of confidence returning. At least now he'd be able to *tell* somebody. That would be a relief in itself.

He was almost calm as he followed the Russian captain through the module. *Besides,* he reminded himself as he glided through the ninety-degree turn into the station's central corridor, *maybe I'm wrong.*

11:13 A.M., Central Standard Time, 9 March 2005
Space Station Control Room One, Johnson Space Center

Flight Director Dr. Wayne Calden swept angrily into the
Flight Control Room, acknowledging the greeting from
Louie, the security specialist standing guard, with a mere
nod. His ears were still burning too hot for pleasantries,
ringing with the dressing-down the judge had give him.

". . . your failure to work at your marriage with Ms.
Wellers . . . your failure to pay child support . . ."

*Bitch,* Calden thought sourly, though whether he
meant the judge or his ex-wife even he couldn't have
said. He wondered if the judge was a friend of Helen's.
Some buddy from her "Power Breakfast" group maybe.
She certainly talked like it.

Calden halted at the base of the ramp that led into
the Flight Control Room, surveying the scene. As always, the FCR—"ficker" in NASA parlance—was humming. His team of flight controllers were mostly at their
places in the five zigzag banks of workstations: checking
incoming data with projections; calculating revisions;
tracking the satellites which kept ISS in touch with Mission Control. A few gathered in knots, discussing problems animatedly; one or two, noticing Calden, waved
greetings. Support staff glided around the room's edges.
To the right of the center aisle in the second row, Calden
could see the Russian Interface Officers, immediately
identifiable by their Cyrillic nameplates and additional
television monitors, uplinked in permanent videoconference with Mission Control, Moscow.

A soothing sense of power washed over Calden as he
took in the scene. His irritation began to dissipate. This
was *his* place, damn it. This was where he was king.
At least until one of the three other ISS control teams
took over.

His eyes swung to the front of the room, to the three
huge projected displays covering the wall there. The center screen, the largest, showed a world map overlaid with
a pattern of sine waves—ISS's wandering, fifty-one degrees to the equator orbit. A selection of data tables
glowed, yellow on black, on the left-hand one. The right,

Calden noted with satisfaction, was cycling through shots from three sides of ISS's photovoltaic array number three—calibrating camera angles for the EVA, the extra-vehicular activity that was to take place that day. Every now and then Gary Myers, currently sole U.S. astronaut aboard the station, would appear in-camera, barely recognizable in his bulky white space suit. Calden noted approvingly the signs of Myers's preparation for EVA: umbilicals busy pumping consumables into the astronaut's suit-mounted life support; the zero-reaction tools floating nearby, ready for packing into the mobile tool platform the astronaut would wear.

Calden's ill humor dropped another notch. Things were evidently proceeding to plan.

A movement at the far corner of the control room caught his eye: his Flight Activities Officer, Steve Lyan, was waving to him from within the gaggle of CNN cameramen. Calden returned the wave, suppressing the frown he felt returning to his face at the sight of the TV crew. He turned and headed to his office in renewed irritation. *Christ, I forgot all about the CNN thing,* he thought, pushing the door of his tiny, glass-walled office open.

Not that *that* surprised him. He hated this kind of junk.

Calden tossed his battered briefcase onto the visitor's settee, toppling the stacked reports already in residence. He bent to retrieve them, cursing, and heard the door swing open behind him. "Steve," Calden grunted, knowing it would be the FAO. He straightened to face him. Not for the first time, Calden thought how ill fitted his second-in-command looked for the position he held. A slight, nervous man with a shiny, bald pate and weak, perpetually watering eyes, Lyan looked like nothing so much as a low-order bank executive. There was no doubting his efficiency, though. Steve Lyan kept Mission Control humming.

"Wayne, where've you been?" Lyan said, eschewing a reply in favor of a rapid-fire launch into business. His voice betrayed an edge of exasperation. "I've been paging you all morning."

Calden scowled, dropping the papers back into place. "I've had my tit in the wringer at court," he said. "You wouldn't believe it. A 'no fault' divorce, but you still gotta spend a session listening to how Ted Bundy was a better guy than you."

"Uh huh," Lyan said absently. "They don't give a guy a break, do they?" The Flight Director's marital imbroglios—he was on his third divorce and counting—were so routine as to have ceased raising eyebrows. "Can we discuss the flight plan now, please, Wayne? We're on in five minutes."

"Sure," Calden replied, tugging the legs of his chocolate-brown trousers up and seating himself on the edge of the desk. "Fire away."

"Well, you saw Wes Jones and the CNN guys, right? They're going to shoot the comm session live, all the way up to the unfurling of the flags. Then they'll probably want talking heads from you and Sergei. You know—leader of U.S. Mission Control and Russian Interface Team on this historic occasion . . . blah, blah, blah."

Calden wrinkled his nose in disgust. Mindful of how near impossible it was to get Americans watching ISS events, NASA had started cooking up spectacles to make them. Like today's—the unfurling of gigantic, foilfilm U.S. and Russian flags in honor of the tenth anniversary of the space alliance. Gary's first act on the EVA would be to jettison the two aluminum cylinders and remote-detonate their pyrotechnic units, spreading the football field–sized flags across the black backdrop of space—totally visible to any kid down on Earth with a sixty-millimeter telescope.

Scientific value of the exercise? Nil. But Calden knew the stunt would send TV ratings through the roof.

Lyan cocked his head at Calden mistrustfully. "Now, Wayne," he said, a lecturing tone creeping into his voice, "live means live, okay? Eighty million households, coast to coast?"

"No problem," Calden said, grinning. "I'll be sure and profane only in Russian." He dropped his voice mockingly. *"Igrat na kozhanoi fleite,"* he intoned. Lyan winced. "You like it? Yegor taught me. It means . . ."

"Go play the leather flute," Lyan said hurriedly. "I know. And that should be *'igraite,'* by the way. *'Igrat'* is the infinitive. Just keep it clean, okay?"

Calden laughed. "Don't sweat it buddy," he said. "I'll be good. So how's our schedule sitting?"

"Let's see," the FAO said, running a finger down the sheet atop his armful of paper. "First up, Phil wants to talk to Gary about that shoulder."

Calden nodded. Some time before, Gary had reported a pain in his shoulder; the flight surgeon had diagnosed mild bursitis aggravated by muscle atrophy and prescribed anti-inflammatory medication and mild exercise. "What's our boy said about it?"

Lyan shrugged. "He hasn't complained." His mouth quirked in a nervous smile. "Maybe the Russians are rubbing off on him after all."

"Christ, let's hope not," Calden winced. "Four of the bastards is too many already. What else?"

"Next up there's a selection of grade-school letters to read out. I've got those somewhere here . . ." Lyan said, delving into the sheaf of papers he was holding and emerging with an untidy handful of crayoned and pen-written letters. "Here they are."

"Do I have to read the goddamned things?" Calden growled.

"No, we'll get Suzanne to go through them," Lyan answered, shuffling the letters back into the pile. "Then we're onto the checklist run-through for the EVA."

Calden nodded, running a loosening finger between his shirt collar and neck. The real purpose of the EVA, giant flags aside, was to change a faulty servomechanism on ISS's number three photovoltaic array. It would take Gary Myers outside the station, solo, for almost five hours. Calden glanced at the front-room screens; the cycling shots of ISS's solar panel, cobalt blue against the brilliant blue of the Earth beyond it, had disappeared, leaving only the grainy image of Gary in the gray metallic surrounds of ISS's primary airlock. The astronaut was now working methodically through the steps to disengage the umbilicalis. "How's Gary with the procedure?" Calden asked. "He feeling good about it?"

There was no reply. Calden looked back at Lyan in

surprise; the FAO was standing there, frowning, apparently preoccupied. "Steve?" Calden repeated. "How's Gary with the EVA procedure?"

"Uh . . . what?" Lyan replied, flustered. "Oh . . . he should be okay. The cuff checklist was teleprinted to him last night, and he had a couple of hours to run through the sim data yesterday." For a moment Calden thought the FAO was about to add something, but all he did was repeat the assurance. "He should be fine."

*What brought that on?* Calden wondered. It wasn't like Steve to get distracted by anything.

"Good," he said, standing up and tugging the creases out of his trousers. "Is that everything then, Steve? Guess we should get out there and do it, huh?" He extended his hand towards the door, inviting the other man to exit.

To his surprise, Lyan didn't move. He stood in front of Calden, the same worried frown on his face, his hands shuffling paper nervously.

"Well . . . no," the FAO said hesitantly. "There is something else, actually."

Calden regarded the man curiously. "What else?"

Lyan swallowed. "Just a moment," he said quietly. To Calden's surprise, he turned and shut the door. The babble from the Control Room cut off abruptly, leaving the two of them in silence. Lyan looked up at the Flight Director nervously. "I got a call from Crawzcyk about an hour ago," he said, after a moment's pause. "He wanted to speak to you."

Calden appeared puzzled for a moment, then his eyes widened in surprise. "*Bob* Crawzcyk?" he asked. "Security Directorate?"

Lyan nodded. "Uh huh. He says he got an e-mail from Gary this morning."

"An e-mail from Gary?" Calden frowned. "Why? What can Gary want with SD?"

"That's what Crawzcyk wants to know," Lyan replied. "He called us to find out."

Calden shrugged. "I don't know anything about it. What does the e-mail say?"

"According to Crawzcyk, Gary requested a videocon with him for sleep-shift tonight. On an isolated channel."

Calden's frown deepened. *A videoconference. On an isolated channel. What the hell?*

He tried to think it through. *Why would Gary contact Security Directorate?* SD was responsible for NASA's security programs: counterintelligence; technology evaluation; liaison with Defense and national security bodies. They also ran the physical security programs at NASA facilities; Louie was a Security Directorate employee. Calden couldn't think of any reason Gary would want to talk to them. Not a good one, anyway.

"I don't like the sound of this," Calden muttered. "Is he in some kind of trouble up there?" He looked at Lyan sharply. "Did you check with Sleep Team? Maybe something happened last night."

Lyan shook his head. "Makerson didn't say anything about it at handover. I called him again, after I spoke to Crawzcyk, just to make sure. He swears everything was quiet as a mouse."

Calden tapped his lip. "An e-mail direct to Crawzcyk . . ." he meditated. "Why do that, do you think, Steve?" he asked. "Why didn't Gary route the request through us?" Lyan raised his shoulders mutely. His eyes strayed in the direction of the Flight Control Room, then dropped guiltily. Calden stared at him a moment, then swung his gaze out to where the FAO had looked. He let out a heavy, whistling breath. "Jesus, Steve," he said softly. "I hope you're not thinking what I think you are."

Lyan shrugged. "Well. Gary *is* watch for sleep-shift tonight. He'll be the only one on duty—all the Russians will be asleep. And with an isolated channel . . ."

Calden nodded thoughtfully. An isolated channel meant the signal would be barred to the international control centers that usually received it simultaneously with Houston: SSIPC in Japan; APM-CC in Europe; and MCC-M in Moscow. Calden had to admit Steve's unspoken thought had the ring of logic about it. It would explain the e-mail—cutting Mission Control out of the loop. *He wouldn't want to risk giving whatever it is away.* He studied the three Russian Interface Officers, Sergei, Nikolai and Pavel, hard at work adapting incoming telemetry for upload to Mission Control, Moscow. "What about the RIOs?" he asked in a low voice. "Are they rostered on Sleep Team tonight?"

Lyan fished a roster out from his armful of paper. "Vadim is," he answered, consulting it, "but not any of the others."

Calden nodded, deep in thought. "Okay," he said finally, turning back to Lyan. "Get him off then. Our boy wants a private conversation. That's what we'll give him."

"Okay," the FAO replied. He hesitated. "What'll I tell him?"

Calden scowled. "Christ, I don't know. Tell him anything—tell him his goddamn visa's expired. Just get him the hell out of there."

Lyan nodded. "I'll come up with something. And what about Crawzcyk? Do you want to talk to him?"

Calden thought about that. "I don't think so," he said, after a moment. "Just tell him we'll have a line ready for him tonight. Say eleven-thirty local time." He shrugged. "Guess we'll just have to wait until tonight to find out what's on Gary's mind." He clapped the FAO on the shoulder. "Let's leave it at that, huh? What do you say we get down into the pit?" He jerked his head in the direction of the CNN team, some of whom were staring curiously through the glass at them. "Looks like the lions are waiting."

Lyan nodded and opened the door, flooding the office with the Control Room's hum. Calden followed him out, threading his way along the Command Row to his position in the top right-hand corner of the Control Room. He tried to put Gary's message out of mind, concentrating instead on the schedule for the day. But he found his eyes drawn to the astronaut's larger-than-life image. Gary was bent over the tool platform, clipping the finishing pieces of the kit into place; the angle meant Calden was unable to see his face. *Look up,* Calden found himself urging. Maybe something would be visible in his face . . .

But by now Calden was already at his station. "Okay, people," he said loudly, dismissing the image from his mind. He fitted his mike and earpiece, flicked the switch to line and heard the Control Room's command channel leap into chattering life. "This is FLIGHT. Let's get this session operational. CAPCOM, FLIGHT. How's our downlink?" He looked up at the left-hand screen.

The badinage on the audio fell silent, allowing the Communication Officer's voice through. "Uh . . . copy that, FLIGHT. Securing channel . . . verifying . . ." Jarulewski said. Seated directly in front of Calden in the fourth row, she punched a series of keys in the panel mounted beside her workstation screen. ". . . that's it, channel secured." She turned to look at Calden. "Downlink is go, FLIGHT."

Calden nodded. "Okay, thanks, CAPCOM. ISS, this is FLIGHT, Space Station Control. Do you copy?" He saw Gary, finished with the tool platform now and waiting patiently, nod as the message came over his suit radio. The two aluminum cylinders, stuffed with their furled flags, bobbed idly beside him.

"Roger, FLIGHT," the astronaut said, holding up a gloved hand, his thumb and forefinger forming a bulky *o*. "Reading you fine."

*Is that an edge of fatigue in his voice?* Calden wondered. It was hard to tell over the fuzzy suit radio. "That's great, Gary, great," he said out loud. "How're you feeling this morning?" He strove to keep the question neutral.

"Real good," Myers said, after a slight lag. "You can tell Phil the shoulder's coming along fine."

"That's good, Gary," Calden nodded. "Dr. Finnegan's going to want to talk to you about that a bit later on. Now, Gary, we've got a few things to get through today. First up, as you know, we'll be going out live through CNN today, for the flag ceremony, and we're all really looking forward to that. Is there anyone you want to send special greetings to?"

"Copy that, FLIGHT," Myers said dutifully. "I'd just like to say a big 'Hi' to my wife Kylie and my little boy Jason." He waved his hand slowly as he floated in the airlock. "Hi, Jason! You know, FLIGHT," Myers continued, reading, Calden guessed, from a suggested script from the FAO, "the cosmonauts here on ISS are also celebrating *Maslenitsa,* which means Spring Day, today, just like down in Moscow . . ." He pushed himself across the airlock and grabbed something off-camera, returning with a miniature Russian flag, ". . . so we've got these up all over ISS . . ."

*"Ura Rossiya!"* The Flight Control Room erupted with a loud cheer from the three Russian team members.

". . . and Commander Kalganin made blini pancakes for breakfast this morning. They're a special little round cake Russians make that symbolizes the sun. I have to say, you know, they weren't bad either."

Calden smiled indulgently. "Wonderful, Gary. I bet they were delicious. Now, as I said, Dr. Finnegan is going to talk to you for a minute about that shoulder, then the Flight Activities Officer is going to go thr . . . oh Jesus Christ."

The image on the huge display had broken up into static.

Calden placed his hand over the headset mike and cleared his throat. "Ah . . . Gary," he said, taking his hand away, "you're breaking up down here. Are you still reading us? I repeat, ISS, are you still reading us?"

Static hissed in reply. Heads began to look up throughout the Control Room.

Calden placed his hand back over the microphone and uttered a string of curses. "Ah, CAPCOM," he then said into the microphone, forcing the irritation out of his voice, "we seem to have lost transmission, could you confirm? Do we have a problem?"

The Communications Officer's hair swung from side to side as she checked the screens in front of her, comparing. "Copy that, FLIGHT," her voice came over the communications loop, "I'm switching through channels . . ." Her fingers danced on the keyboard. ". . . negative . . . wait a minute . . ." She paused a moment, finger tracing some data on-screen. ". . . wait . . . Ground Station White Sands reports loss of signal . . ." Her finger drew away from the screen uncertainly, then returned, as if to double-check something she had trouble believing. She looked up at Calden. "FLIGHT, it looks as if the communications array on ISS has been put out of alignment."

Calden frowned. "Computer error?" he asked tersely, though he knew that was impossible.

"Negative," the woman replied, returning to her screen. "It looks . . . it *looks* like a manual override."

"Manual over . . . ?" Calden's lip twisted in disbelief. That couldn't be right. It had to be some sort of glitch. "Well . . . okay, CAPCOM, switch from ISS Control to Ground. Realign the array from here."

"Copy that," replied the Communications Officer. "Recomputing now. It'll take a minute or two, though. It's gonna be patchy."

"Copy, CAPCOM," Calden said shortly. "Just as quickly as you can, please."

Calden was conscious of a movement beside him; the CNN reporter, Wes Jones, had materialized there, camera team in tow. "Yep . . . just a moment, Kirsty," the plump black journalist said into his own earpiece mike. He brought the on-air microphone up to his mouth. "It appears a problem has developed with communications to ISS; with me now is Dr. Wayne Calden, Flight Director at ISS Mission Control. Dr. Calden, good morning. Just what is the problem you are experiencing?"

"Good morning, Wes," Calden replied, cursing inwardly at the interruption. "We're not exactly sure yet, I'm afraid. We've had a minor system malfunction with the communications array on ISS, but our Communications Officer, that's the CAPCOM you heard me mention, is reestablishing contact for us now. We should be back up in just a few seconds."

"Uh huh. I see." The reporter nodded, but made no further comment, obviously inviting Calden to continue.

Calden, exasperated, almost swore. He cast around for something with which to fill the gap. "You know, Wes," he continued awkwardly, "that call sign, CAPCOM, actually dates back to the days of NASA's Mercury Program. The Communications Officer used to be called a Capsule Communicator because the spacecraft was a capsu . . ."

Calden's voice tailed off in surprise. The correspondent was no longer listening to him. Instead, the man's face had become a mask of dawning shock—his widening eyes and dropped jaw pushing the fat on his face

into folds over his brow and below his chin. He was
staring over Calden's shoulder at the front-room screen.
The microphone slipped from his hand, falling with a
soft thud to the carpeted floor.

*What the hell?*

Calden was suddenly conscious, as well, that a deathly
quiet had settled over the Control Room. He followed
the black man's gaze to the front of the room. And understood instantly.

The hiss from the audio channels had disappeared.
CAPCOM had obviously succeeded: a patchy image had
reappeared on the screen, flickering in and out of the
static. Even through the staccato images and dead audio
though, it was obvious.

Myers was being attacked.

Every eye in the Control Room watched, riveted, as
Myers's suited body flashed in and out of view, interspersed by static, appearing at crazy angles to the camera. A kinetoscope of flickering images—smashing,
gloved fists, flailing legs and one shocking close-up of a
mirror-visored helmet—revealed his likewise suited assailant. Abruptly, the audio kicked in, and clipped, garbled sounds that might have been shrieks filled the loop,
punctuating the ragged breathing and the renascent
background hiss. There was an odd absence of external
sounds to accompany the struggle; Myers's helmet mike,
of course, picked up nothing in the vacuum of ISS's airlock except the terrifying cacophony inside his space suit.

Calden's body twitched involuntarily as he watched. *I
don't believe this,* he thought, stunned. *There's something
wrong with the camera. It's some kind of joke.*

Abruptly, the image solidified for a few seconds. Myers's helmet was pressed up against the camera, his face
absurdly large and curved. One terrified eye could be
clearly seen, blinking rapid-fire, rolling around frantically
to locate his attacker. The harsh rasp of the astronaut's
breathing drowned out all other sounds.

Calden tore his eyes from the screen and looked
wildly around the Control Room, searching for something, anything, to explain the images he was seeing. But
the room was deathly still, every gaze locked on the

front of the room. Suddenly, a loud crack from the audio
made them wince collectively, comically, and forced Calden's attention back to the screen. Myers's helmet was
still pressed up against the camera, but now a blurred
something—Calden registered dimly that it was a rectangular metal object—was smashing down against the helmet faceplate. It flew out of vision, then smashed back
down again, accompanied by another earsplitting crack.
Myers's faceplate splintered, cracks crazing out across it
like sprawling spider silk. Through the suit microphone,
the faint hiss of escaping air could be heard.

There was just one moment more, in which Myers's
faceplate could be seen to explode outwards and red
gouts of his blood to spray forth and boil into the vacuum, then, mercifully, the screen lapsed back into static.

The silence in the Control Room held for a moment,
then erupted into pandemonium. Calden groped behind
him for his chair and fell into it heavily. Forgetting entirely his still-active mike, the reporter standing in mute
amazement beside him, and the eighty million viewers
patched in live through CNN, his lips formed around
the word.

"Fuck."

# 1

"**M**otherfucker!"

Detective Sergeant Mike Fitzwilliams banged a chunky black fist against the side of the small television. Its battered plastic shell cracked audibly. The coathanger aerial shook and nearly toppled. But the white noise cut out, zapping into the picture of a WDIV anchorwoman and painfully loud words that boomed through the tiny lunchroom.

"*. . . statement calling for calm. Meanwhile, NASA officials . . .*"

"Thank fuck," he muttered, turning the volume down and lolling back in his seat. He flashed a grin at the uniformed patrolman seated at the lunchroom table, a new recruit to the bureau's admin staff and one obviously still a little overawed. "Thought I'd have to fill out a goddamn maintenance report."

The patrolman gave an embarrassed murmur of support.

Images of placard-waving crowds pushing up against a chain-link fence filled the screen—teeth bared in shouting mouths, faces contorted in fury—accompanying the voice-over:

"*. . . violent confrontations outside Johnson Space Center for the third day running. Angry demonstrators protesting the shocking murder . . .*"

Fitzwilliams looked up as a shadow blocked the door-

way light momentarily—a man had entered the lunchroom. Another grin quirked the mouth of the seated
detective; he glanced at the uniformed cop again, as if
to check if the patrolman was up for some joke he was
about to pull. The new entry was a rangy Caucasian in
his midforties, dressed in the bureau standard suit and
tie. Graying hair was cropped close to the man's skull.
The road-metal gray eyes in his craggy, hard-bitten face
were distant, locked into concentration on some inner
problem. He busied himself at the coffee machine without a greeting, or any sign he'd seen the room's
occupants.

"Hey, Reynolds," the seated detective called over his
shoulder. "Yo, Microwave!"

A running joke that. Reynolds was Eight Squad—
Cold Cases. His job was to take old, unsolved murders
off Six and Seven—Felony and Narcotics Murder—and
rerun them, from beginning to end, working whatever
new angles he could. His uncanny success in reheating
dead cases had earned him the grudging nickname—
along with less flattering ones in private.

"Check this out," the detective continued, indicating
the television with a jerk of his chin. "They're talking
about NASA, man. Your people."

Reynolds glanced at Fitzwilliams briefly, then at the
television. Chaotic scenes—scuffles, blood, a fence collapsing under hundreds of climbing demonstrators—
flashed on-screen under the measured words of the anchorwoman: *". . . and the immediate expulsion of Russia
from the International Space Station Program. Meanwhile, in Moscow, more violence against U.S. . . ."* Reynolds stared at the TV a moment, then turned back to
the coffee machine without responding.

The black detective's mouth spread into a smile, savoring the joke. "What?" he said, trying to inject a note
of puzzlement into his voice. "They *are* your people,
aren't they? Reynolds? You hear me, man?"

"Eat me, Fitz," the man said without interest. He finished stirring, tossed the teaspoon into the chipped
enamel sink and turned to face the grinning detective.
"Okay?" He sipped his coffee then left, flipping Fitzwilliams the finger as he went.

The black detective turned back to the television, chuckling. After a few seconds had passed the uniformed patrolman leaned towards him hesitantly.

"Detective Sergeant?" he said. "Sir?"

Fitzwilliams looked over at him, the grin still on his face. "What is it, Patrolman?" he said.

"Is it true, then?" the uniformed man said, indicating the departed Reynolds with a jerk of his head. "What they say about him?"

Fitzwilliams glanced at the doorway. He snorted dismissively. "They say a lot of things about him, Patrolman," he muttered, his voice falling back to its normal bored tone. He lounged deeper in the chair, turning his attention back to the TV.

"You know," the uniformed cop insisted. "That he used to be an astronaut and all?"

The black detective looked over at the doorway once more. His mouth twisted as he chewed his lower lip meditatively.

"Yeah," he said finally. "That one's true."

5:51 P.M., Central Standard Time, 13 March 2005
The Coronado Motel, Cass Corridor, Detroit

"Oh my God oh Jesus I'm gonna die I'm gonna die . . ."

Investigator Maria Ramirez moaned the words through chattering teeth. She was on her ass, huddled into the far corner of the squalid motel room, feet kicking feebly against the painted concrete floor as if to cram herself further in. Her hands scrabbled at the dingy drywall, smearing it with a glistening red crescent of blood from her shattered wrist. The Glock that Benson had shot out of her hand lay uselessly at her feet. Plumes of plaster dust from the fusillade that had dropped her eddied overhead, settling in her hair and adhering to her lips, there to jiggle obscenely as she mouthed in terror.

". . . oh please no, don't kill me, I'm gonna die I'm gonna die . . ."

*Sliding into shock,* Reynolds thought. Ramirez was losing it, composure draining from her with every lost cc of blood. From his vantage point at the door, Reynolds could see another two spreading slicks on her stylish pantsuit; Benson had really nailed her good. Judging by her fixed, terror-filled gaze, Reynolds guessed she could still see the lowlife, just feet away in the bathroom, pointing the gun he'd cut her down with right at her.

" . . . oh fuck, oh please, I'm gonna die . . ."

"THAT'S RIGHT, BITCH!" Jimi Benson screamed suddenly, his voice muffled by the bathroom wall. "YOU ARE GONNA DIE!"

The pimp had obviously dived behind it the moment he'd heard the two of them at the door, holding his fire until Ramirez had walked into his line of sight. Long fingers of light poked through the wall where Reynolds had hammered it with return fire, though if Benson had been hit he wasn't showing it. In front, on the bowed double bed, was the prostitute Jimi had left as decoy, mutely shaking in wide-eyed terror worse than Ramirez. Scattered around her, on the threadbare quilt, was a lit-ter of drug paraphernalia—foils, baggies and a pipe with a scattering of milky pebbles of crack.

"YOU ARE GONNA DIE, BITCH!" Benson shouted again. "YOU'RE GONNA DIE RIGHT NOW IF YOUR MAN OUT THERE DON'T BACK OFF."

Ramirez shrieked. Her eyes squeezed shut in despair. Her feet beat a terrified, scrabbling tattoo on the floor. Her breaths turned to explosive, hysterical sobs.

"YOU HEAR ME, MAN?" Benson yelled, ad-dressing himself to the out-of-sight Reynolds this time. "BACK OFF OR YOUR BITCH DIES."

Reynolds nearly laughed out loud at that one. *Your bitch.* Under other circumstances, he knew, Ramirez would have been offended too. No doubt in Benson's twisted, pimp world any woman accompanying a man was his bitch—wife, lover, friend. Or partner. But Rami-rez wasn't even that. She was just temping at Homicide, on loan from one of the precinct bureaus, and Reynolds had only partnered with her for the day, on the lieuten-ant's orders.

"Reynolds, I want you to buddy up with Investigator Ramirez here, okay? Take her out. Show her the ropes."

*Well I did that, Dennison,* Reynolds thought grimly, listening to Ramirez sob. *I showed her the ropes all right.*

Benson's voice shrieked from behind the bathroom wall again. "FUCK YOU, MAN, DO YOU HEAR ME? BACK OFF, NOW, OR I KILL YOUR BITCH!"

Ramirez started crying softly. The shock was really setting in now. Her skin had gone chalk white and her voice had dropped back to a low, repetitive moan . . .

". . . I'm gonna die I'm gonna die I'm gonna die . . ."

"No, you're not," Reynolds said quietly.

The flat assurance in his voice hit Ramirez like a slap. She stiffened. Her words stopped dead. Her eyes flew open and she stared at him.

"You're not going to die, Ramirez," Reynolds repeated. "Not today anyway."

He stood immobile at the door, his body loose but ready. The Glock was back down at his side, held in an easy, almost negligent grip. Despite the adrenaline surging in his veins, the blood pounding thickly at his temples, he was calm. He was Zen; he was the eye of the storm; he was the hub around which the murderous impasse Benson had kicked into motion whirled.

And he would be the one to bring it down.

"YES, SHE IS," Benson screamed. "IF YOU DON'T BACK OFF. I WANT YOU OUT OF THIS ROOM, MOTHERFUCKER! NOW! OUT OF THIS ROOM OR I CAP YOUR BITCH."

Reynolds waited until a few moments had passed. "Okay, Jimi," he said evenly. "You win. I'm leaving."

Reynolds held his position, moving not an inch. Seconds ticked by. In the corner Ramirez watched him mutely, her face a mask of uncomprehending terror.

Behind the wall Benson lay quiet, listening. More seconds passed.

"Is he gone, Darien?" the pimp said finally, his voice low. On the bed the terrified prostitute, presumably Darien, moaned.

Reynolds lifted a finger to his lips, a silent *shhh*. The seminaked woman stared at him in fear. Her body was trembling; in the splotched ceiling mirror Reynolds could see the ludicrous shake of her buttocks. Her gaze locked onto the Glock in the rangy detective's right hand as it rose steadily, as if of its own volition, and settled into a two-handed grip.

"FUCK YOU, DARIEN, IS HE GONE?" Benson shouted.

Reynolds shook his head slowly, side to side, in warning. The prostitute gaped at him, mute, her hands clenched like rocks in the twined bedsheets. Reynolds squeezed the trigger guard on the Glock gently, taking it off safety again.

The seconds stretched out.

Reynolds could almost *feel* Benson's tortured indecision. Finally, the tiny sounds of a muttered oath and an unwilling scrape came from behind the wall. A shadow blocked one of the bullet holes in the wall momentarily. Benson was getting up to see for himself.

For one split second Reynolds had a vague impression of something that might have been an eye pressed to one of the bullet holes and rolling to locate him. But there was no time to say, for with his man fixed, the detective swung his weapon into line and opened fire. The Glock danced in his doubled hands as he jerked the trigger back and forth, shredding the wall and Benson behind it in a cloud of dust and sprayed blood. And drowning his screams in the noise.

**6:43 P.M., Central Standard Time, 13 March 2005**
**The Coronado Motel, Cass Corridor, Detroit**

Reynolds leaned patiently on the hood of the unmarked Chevy Lumina, ignoring the cold, as Hanahan took down his words. The Coronado's central court—if you could call the potholed asphalt wasteland the motel enclosed that—was a hive of activity. Pulses of red light from the EMS trucks strobed the seedy rooms. White-uniformed paramedics bustled. Cops swarmed the scene—staking out tape, knocking on adjoining doors for witnesses. The only things missing were the onlookers.

*That much figures,* Reynolds thought. The Coronado was a short-stay joint—renting rooms by the hour to whores or crack users too upmarket to smoke in one of the Corridor's numerous crack houses. Anybody trapped in one of *these* rooms when a hundred cops poured through the front gate would be too busy sweating to rubberneck.

Hanahan finished writing and looked up at him. "That it, Edge?" he asked, pen poised in chunky white fingers over the injury report.

Reynolds thought about the irony of that. *The injury report. They call it that even though the guy's dead.* Well, Benson was injured all right. As in pulped. Reynolds had looked in as he was being bagged.

"Just about," he answered. "You might want to organize a homestay for Ramirez when she's released, though. I think she told me she's on her own at the moment."

Hanahan glanced over at the knot of activity at the back of the second EMS truck, where Ramirez was being loaded. The paramedic team had quickly found her wounds, though bleeding profusely, to be all muscle trauma—noncritical. With the blood loss stemmed, and the danger of distributive shock averted, they had elected to wait for another EMS truck, to save her making the trip back to Detroit Receiving Hospital in the company of Benson's corpse.

Hanahan nodded. "Oh-aight," he said, passing the clipboard to Reynolds for signature. Reynolds signed, barely registering the incongruity of a third generation Irishman's use of that African American patois. Hanahan hitched up his uniform pants as he accepted the clipboard back. "Well," he said, consulting his handwritten notes, "Headquarters says Cooper's coming down to act as 2400—Chief's out of town today. You going to stick around?"

"Nah." Reynolds shook his head, gritting his teeth against the lie he was about to let slip. He pushed himself off the car and rolled his shoulders as if to relax them—all fake nonchalance. "I'm going back to Beaubien Avenue myself. Fix up the PCR and 'Shots Fired.' "

Hanahan nodded. "Oh-aight. We'll get things wound up here." He turned to scan the gaggle of patrolmen grouped around the EMS truck. "I'll get Dubois to ride along with Ramirez. Dubois!" he yelled, locating the object of his search. "Get over here!" He looked back at

Reynolds, as if in afterthought. "What about you, Edge?
You gonna be okay?"

"Sure," Reynolds nodded. He turned to go, jamming
his hands into the deep pockets of his overcoat and
wrapping it around himself against the cold. He left
quickly, stepping through the gathered cops with his
head down, avoiding eye contact.

That was two lies now. He had known for several
minutes now he wasn't going to be okay. And he wasn't
going back to Homicide to fill out paperwork either.

He was going for a drink.

9:07 P.M., Central Standard Time, 13 March 2005
The Sergeant's Arms, Rivertown, Detroit

*Oh God, for the sins we are about to commit we beseech
thy forgiveness.*

Reynolds let the cheap scotch slide down his throat
and burn his stomach in completion of the ritual.
Warmth spread from his gut through his body. Deaden-
ing molecules of alcohol started the climb up his nervous
system to his brain. He closed his eyes, savoring the
feeling.

*Jesus yes. That's the stuff.*

Reynolds downed another shot, grimacing at the taste.
He was starting to regain composure now, the liquor
rolling through him like calming oil. The crowd's rau-
cous babble began to recede. Reynolds opened his eyes
and surveyed the patrons: blue-collar blacks, most of
them, with a leavening of shores and solitary booze
hounds, *like you, pal, ha ha ha.* No cops though—despite
the name, Sergeant's wasn't a police haunt. Even precinct cops tended to shun the bar's dingy ambience and
low-rent clientele, joining their Bureau colleagues instead in the upmarket Greektown joints. That suited
Reynolds. He *wanted* solitude when he was there, damn
it. Sergeant's was his church. Where he worshipped.
Where he committed his sins.

*But not too often, Lord. Grant me that.*

Reynolds snorted, sucking down another mouthful of
the crude scotch. *Every doomed sinner's cry,* he thought,
placing the tumbler on the bar. True enough these past

few years though. He drank himself into oblivion infrequently these days—no more than once or twice a month. Not like in the old days, just after she'd died, when he'd first discovered the soul-destroying bliss of alcohol. When the binges would blue into uncounted days, weeks or even months—calculable only by the length of his wino stubble or the weight he'd lost. When the only way to keep ahead of the demons was to drink himself out of their reach, like Superman in front of the train—running, running, running—mere inches in front of that oily, black terror screaming in pursuit . . .

These days Reynolds didn't need to do that. He'd worked out a compromise.

*You grind yourself down through unrelenting work. You lose yourself in the rats' maze of unsolved murder. You soak yourself in the everyday blood and horror and never, ever, give yourself time to think.*

That was usually enough. Enough to leave the demons behind, temporarily, somewhere out of sight. Enough to lock them down so tight you could hardly even hear them howl.

Except . . . sometimes.

Sometimes when something—some *little* thing—would sneak through his defenses and upset the razor-wire equilibrium. Then that chasm would yawn open in him again, wide as the pit of hell, the demons would give voice and the flames would burst into life again and start to lick higher and higher. Those times, there was nothing for it but to throw a snaky old ladder of scotch across and crawl over on his belly, eyes closed, never looking down for fear of what he knew was down there, what he knew he'd see . . .

Reynolds reached for his drink automatically. The AA intro went through his mind, inverted.

*Hi, my name is Edge Reynolds and I haven't had a drink for thirty-five seconds. But I'm about to rectify that.*

He drained the glass and laid it back on the bar with a note beside it. The barmaid took it, hands materializing out of the forest of arms and elbows at the bar, without comment. A half-minute later another triple appeared, change beside it, again without a word.

They knew his habits here.

Reynolds took it and sipped deeply. Seeing Ramirez like that was what had done it this time. On her ass, hands in the air, pleading for her life. He'd known he was in trouble when the image kept flicking into his mind while he was talking to Hanahan. With a little rider attached to it.

*Alicia must have looked like that.*

Flat on her back. Kicking her way up the hallway, hands in the air to ward off the blows.

*Please don't kill me . . .*

Thwack.

*Please don't . . .*

Slash.

Reynolds upended the glass, slamming another shot. Riding the train now, desperate to keep ahead. But he knew it was no good. Once the memories kicked in there was no stopping them. All you could do was sink one drink after another to turn the volume down and let the images unfold.

*The moment they told me.*

Actually, there'd been no need for them to say anything. He'd known instantly something was wrong. The mere appearance of county cops on Johnson Space Center grounds, where you normally never saw them, told him. He'd been working one of the Shuttle's Single System Trainers at the time. Connor had called him off. Reynolds had walked towards the two patrolmen with fear chilling his heart. He could still *see*, with crystal clarity, every detail of those brown uniforms. Hear every nuance of those words.

"An incident at your home . . ."

"Your wife . . ."

*The blind, crazy drive home.*

They had wanted him in the patrol car. He hadn't listened, just jumped straight into the Mustang and torn off, lead-footing it all the way to the Clear Lake house. Heart hammering all the way, mouth dry with despair because he *knew*. It was already too late. They had refused to tell him, but he knew.

She was dead.

*Entering the house. Finding her there.*

That was another good thing about booze—it even damped down the *color* of memories. He could sit here and remember the yellow of the police tape without it burning into his mind's eye, like it did in nightmares. The white of the tiled laundry floor. The red of the blood, all over the floor and walls, pooling in the tiny alcove into which Elwood had stuffed Alicia—*like a rag, like a fucking dog*—when he'd finished with her. The dark purple contusions and stab wounds, all over her skin.

Impossible to fool yourself about what had happened. The story was written indelibly on Alicia's body.

Someone—he didn't yet know about Elwood—had had a good time with her. Raped her. Tortured her some, for sport, all the way from the living room where he'd caught her, through to here. Probably raped her some more. Bashed her.

Then cut her throat to finish the job.

Reynolds drained the glass and dropped it to the bar calmly, another note beside it.

*Better get another.* He was in for some heavy-duty drinking tonight.

*Elwood.* Reynolds turned the name over meditatively in his mouth, along with the ice cube he'd sucked in, as he waited for the next scotch. *Duane Elwood.* He cracked the cube slowly between his teeth. It was funny how a name like that, a name that had meant *nothing* to you, could become emblazoned on your brain. The most important set of letters in your life. Reynolds's drink materialized; he reached for it automatically.

*Well,* he told himself, taking a healthy slug, *that's what a man murdering your wife will do for him.*

*Make him really someone.*

*No!* Reynolds slammed the glass down on the bar, so hard the liquor splashed his hand. He sucked it off absentmindedly, ignoring the glare from the woman beside him at the bar, whom he'd also splashed. He still couldn't accept that, even after all these years. What made Alicia's death hurt so bad was that Elwood really *was* a nothing. A loser. Psycho flotsam. When they collared him, the police had been surprised to find that despite a revolving-door history at Harris County Psychiatric, Elwood didn't even have priors.

*Priors.*

Reynolds smiled drunkenly at *that* part of the memory. Back then the cops had to explain the term to him. Who'd have guessed he'd be using it himself one day? That he'd one day *be* the cops?

Anyway. The point was, before Alicia, Elwood had never done *anything* like what he did to her. It was a random eruption of psychotic violence, inexplicable and unpredictable. If Ally hadn't chosen that particular day to weed the tiny garden she'd started, it might not even have happened. Elwood had told the arresting detectives it was the sight of the pruning shears and scarf that set him off. They reminded him of an aunt or something. Some aunt who abused him as a kid.

*Well, boo hoo, Elwood. Boo fucking hoo.*

Reynolds downed the remaining scotch and signaled for another, suddenly grateful for the anonymity of the pressing crowd. He could feel his face contorting, despite himself, into the familiar mask of hatred and grief. Inside, that old cyclone wind was blowing again—ancient, bitter rage howling uselessly round and round. Reynolds felt it build, mixing with the booze-fueled spin of his head, to a sickening climax. Then, suddenly, it was gone, leaving him drained, like always, but for the aftertaste of despair. He sagged against the bar and let his head fall into his hands.

*Oh God. What the fuck am I doing here?*

The scotch appeared under his nose; Reynolds pulled himself together enough to acknowledge it with a slight jerk of his head. He took the tumbler and drank, steadying himself as his mind returned to the question. He tried to concentrate.

*Well? What the fuck are you doing here?*

He knew what it really meant. Not what was he doing here tonight, at Sergeant's, drinking himself stupid with hookers and roughnecks. But what was Edge Reynolds—aero-engineering graduate, ex-Blackbird pilot, ex-astronaut and space-shuttle stick-jockey—doing as a Motor City homicide cop in the first place? Chasing down murderers and lowlifes as if the only stick he'd ever had in his hand was the shift of an unmarked squad car or the butt of the Glock currently nestled under his left armpit?

Reynolds swirled the scotch around in the glass, lost in thought. He often sensed that Dennison secretly wanted to ask him that too. *What the hell are you doing here, Reynolds?* The lieutenant was happy enough to use him—turn his sharp intelligence and savage drive loose on the cold, dead cases that were Eight Squad's stock-in-trade, then sit back and take credit when the figures came up shining. But Reynolds knew Dennison also shook his head, privately, over someone with his subordinate's talents choking up a shitkicker DT's office in one of the worst paid, bloodiest jurisdictions in the country. And wondered where the drive came from.

*Revenge,* Reynolds thought. *Revenge is what Dennison thinks it is.*

He took another sip, acknowledging the insight. He guess that *was* what Dennison thought; the lieutenant knew those parts of Reynolds's history others in the Bureau didn't, after all. And it was logical enough. It was what Reynolds himself had long believed, ever since he'd arrived in Detroit.

Back then, in '91, Motortown was cutting a name for itself as Murdertown, the most violent city in the USA. When Reynolds surfaced from the two-year tailspin Ally's death and his resignation from the Corps had sparked, he'd felt himself strangely drawn here. *Revenge,* he'd thought. He couldn't fry that piece of shit Elwood himself—Texas was going to handle that, and take years at it—so he'd go where he could get his hands on some substitute lowlife. Murdertown was making headlines, so that was the academy he applied to. Became a beat cop, worked his way up to Homicide. Into position to start handing it out to the scum.

And he had. For nine years now he'd been collaring them, busting them, taking them down. Collecting a hell of a reputation for himself. All the while seeing the faces of the lowlifes he put away and thinking, *This is what it's all about.*

Watching *them* suffer.

It was only now, in the flash of drunken illumination—dim bar light filtered through amber scotch—that he could see he'd been wrong.

*It's not the perps' faces you need, bud. It's the victims'.*

Reynolds stopped short at that, glass arrested halfway to his mouth. He frowned.

*The victims? Jesus. That's fucked up.*

He tried, uneasily, to laugh the idea off—*just another alkie fantasy*—but it had its teeth in him now and wouldn't let go. He could see it was true; that *was* why he'd come here, all those years ago. Why he stayed.

It was the *place* he needed. A place where other people were suffering too. Where he wasn't the only one.

Reynolds swallowed the last of the scotch and pushed the glass away. *You're all fucked up, bud,* he told himself thickly. He climbed unsteadily to his feet, shrugged his overcoat on. *You're drunk, you're fucked up, and it's time to go.* Part-time booze hound he might be but he knew better than to drink himself blind down here in Rivertown. He'd brown-bag one home to finish the job.

Reynolds pushed his way through the blurred crowd and out into the street. His breath billowed in the late-winter cold. No snow, but the Rivertown streets—ribbons of buckled asphalt leprous with patches where it had worn down to nineteenth-century cobble—were slick with the residue of the day's freezing rain. The lights of the isolated bars and restaurants nestled in the decrepit industrial area shone off it like neon sabers, pushing back the surrounding darkness.

He hit the liquor store across the street from Sergeant's for the bottle, then turned his collar up and headed for home.

Reynolds walked the ten blocks by rote. Following the old railway tracks for part of the way, then cutting by the garbage-strewn vacant lots that took him through to East Jefferson. Weaving his way down the avenue blindly. Counting out the stairs to the lobby of his drab apartment block, not even having to look.

Just another early-evening drunk. Zeroing home on autopilot.

He shouldered his way into the lobby through the

swinging metal and glass doors, unsecurable since their locks—standing incitement to smash the glass—had been abandoned some years before. The intercom was likewise unusable, burned out years ago.

This combination of factors made the lobby, of course, extremely vulnerable to intrusion from street life. It was nothing to come down in the morning and find mounds of filthy clothing—winos, junkies or other bums—clumped here and there. Bottle-glass and syringes often crunched underfoot. A junkie had even been shot there once. The bloodstains, brown and faded, were still on the painted concrete—red badge of indifference and neglect.

The residents—students, blue collars, some low-income assistance families and the occasional street-walker—had learned to just shrug. Wear thick-soled shoes and pick their way through the lobby with unseeing eyes. Got used to it.

Reynolds included.

Guys at squad were always ribbing him about it. Just last week Davis had taken time out from big-talking himself in front of his Baby Squad acolytes to rip on him over it.

"Hey, talking about houses," he'd said, noticing Reynolds walking by, "you guys oughta see where Microwave here lives. Down on East Jefferson. Man! No doorman. No security. Lobby full of junkies. Worse than living in the projects, I tell you."

Then, addressing him: "Hey, Reynolds! You still in that damn crack-house apartment? Huh? Man, you're a cop. Aren't you afraid some mother you put on ice is gonna get out and blade you? Why don't you get a *real* house? Move out to Copper Canyon and get yourself a bungalow with these fine gentlemen . . ."

At the time Reynolds had said nothing, just flipped Davis the bird, provoking laughter from the groupies. But standing there now, in front of the scuffed metal elevator doors with his finger heavy on the button, the words were harder to ignore.

He had to admit it. Some nights he worried. Nights he hadn't been able to drink enough, usually.

Those nights, he'd stand here staring at the dim shine

from the lobby's few remaining lights and imagine he could *see* something in the cloudy metal. A blurred shadow, darkening into a long, vertical bar. Moving slightly, thickening, as whoever, whatever it was, stepped closer . . .

Reynolds blinked in confusion.

*Wait a minute. There* is *a shadow.*

He watched, fascinated, as the dark bar jiggled and grew. Just like he always fantasized it. *Something different about it this time though,* Reynolds realized.

It was more defined somehow. More real.

As if there really *were* someone behind him, hiding in the lobby's shadows, stepping out to take him at the door, now his back was turned . . .

The sudden crack of a foot on *something*—a fit, some glass or one of the wine-crusted plastic cups Reynolds sometimes found down here—snapped him out of the daze.

*Fuck, there is someone there.*

*Coming up behind me. Fast.*

Even drunk, Reynolds's movements were fluid. He opened his hand to let the scotch fall; it thudded to the ground a split second later, miraculously unbroken. He jerked his left shoulder back to deflect the blow he sensed descending, following it with a clenched, sweeping fist. Kicked himself off his right leg to drive his body back, into the man, and throw him off balance. Plunged his hand into his opened overcoat, locking onto the Glock's butt and flicking the retaining strap clasp open in one easy motion. He yanked the gun out, using the twist of his body to free it from the holster.

He was so quick his fist struck at the moment the man's hand hit his shoulder.

Reynolds felt his knuckles bite bone at the man's temple. He was rewarded with a muffled cry. *That's gotta hurt,* he thought wildly, but there was no time to crow—there would be a blade, or a gun maybe, swinging up towards Reynolds's back at this very moment. He had to get his assailant disabled.

Then disarmed.

Reynolds let his fist unfurl and drop to the man's col-

lar as his own body continued the roll around. He scrabbled for a hold, getting one on the collar of the man's
lapel-less jacket, and used it to anchor the man in place
as his right hand smashed the Glock into the temple his
fist had just hit. The man howled as the pistol smacked
his skull. His body sagged, held up by Reynolds's hand.
Reynolds felt blood spurt warmly over it.
*So far so good.*
He drove the stunned man in front of him, before he
had a chance to recover, hauling him by the twin contact
points of his clenched hand and the barrel of his Glock,
now jammed into the attacker's cheek. He listened for
the clatter of whatever the guy was carrying slipping
from his limp hand, but nothing came. However stunned,
the man was obviously keeping a tight grip.
*Well,* thought Reynolds, *soon fix that.*
He slammed him up against the far wall. Pinned him
against it by driving the Glock harder into his cheek and
jamming his left knee into the man's thigh. Reynolds's
left hand dropped and groped for the man's right one.
"You carrying, asshole?" he hissed, running his hand
down each of the man's arms. "Huh?" But there was
nothing there. The man's hands, hanging limply, were
empty.
*What the fuck?*
Reynolds was suddenly aware there was something
odd about the man too. He appeared to be a middle-
aged, old even, Caucasian, dressed moderately well in a
peculiar white Windcheater with some kind of symbol
at the breast. Reynolds dragged him, by the throat, along
the wall to one of the surviving fluoros and peered at
him in its weak light.
*What the hell is this?*
The man was stocky and somewhere in his early sixties, Reynolds estimated. His seamed skin was stretched
taut by the gun barrel at his cheek, giving the left of his
hard, dark green eyes a ridiculous, floppy-lidded appearance. The right side of his face was mashed against the
stucco concrete wall. In profile, the man's nose was impossibly pug, and his bald forehead bulged out, high and
broad, from his head. A stubby chin completed the pic-

ture, jutting out from the fat of the man's neck in two knobs of bone. Graying stubble rasped against Reynolds's grasping hand.

*I know that face,* Reynolds thought, bewildered. *But from where?*

His hand loosened fractionally on the man's throat. His eyes fell to the round, blue symbol he had noted, then widened when he saw what it was.

*NASA. Oh my God . . .*

The words the man had been trying to get out were released by Reynolds's partially relaxed grip. "Jesus Christ, Edge," he gurgled. "Do you treat all your old buddies this way? Or just me?"

Reynolds nearly jumped at the sound of the voice, instantly recognizable even through its choked tones. It was his turn to sag. Both his hands loosened their grip and dropped away, so quickly the man nearly fell.

"My God," he said softly. "Matt Connor."

# 2

Connor sipped scotch and flat soda from the coffee mug Reynolds had given him. He winced, at the taste, but also from the pain at his temple. His hand went to the cut, tracing it through the sticking plaster Reynolds had dug up for him. There was a quail's-egg-sized lump there. The cut was a ragged crease bisecting it.

*Goddamn it. That'll need stitching tomorrow.*

Reynolds, pouring his own drink, noticed the movement. "Jesus, Matt," he said. There was no slur in his voice; the adrenal confrontation in the lobby had sobered him instantly. "Once again, sorry for the pistol-whipping. It's just . . . well." He waved his glass at the walls of his dingy apartment and shrugged. "You know." He upended it and swallowed a mouthful. Straight, Connor noticed. No mixer at all.

*Still putting it away,* the older man thought. He understood the unspoken gesture. *This is a world away from NASA,* it said. *A different world. With different rules.*

"Forget it, buddy," he growled. "My fault." He took another pull of scotch. "I should have known better than to try and lay a hand, even a friendly hand, on a goddamn cop." Connor laughed, this time without pain. The liquor was already starting to dull the receptors. "I'm just glad I didn't try and goose you. Probably would have shot me."

It was Reynolds's turn to laugh.

Connor leaned back, carefully, in the flimsy kitchen chair. He sipped his drink and studied the younger man, opposite him on the tatty sofa. *Is this really Edge?* he wondered. Had to be, he guessed. He was seeing him, wasn't he?

But he sure as hell wasn't believing.

Back then, in '89, Reynolds had been a hotshot young pilot candidate in the Astronaut Corps. The best Connor had ever seen actually, and he'd seen a few in his ten years at Crew Training.

Connor had nursed him, ridden him, driven him, through the program and had him emerge as a top-grade shuttle pilot, one of the new breed who were to spearhead NASA's return to space after *Challenger*. Reynolds had been locked in for STS-30, the mission to launch the Magellan Venus probe, when tragedy cut him down.

His wife's murder. That sick asshole . . . what was his name? Elwood?

Connor had tried to persuade Reynolds to stay, to ride it out. "Quitting is letting the bastard win," he'd insisted. "Letting him rob you of *everything*." Maybe STS-30 had to be passed up, but there were still years of missions Reynolds could fly. At one stage Connor had even begged him.

"Please, Edge. For my sake as well as yours."

But it had been hopeless. Reynolds had taken deferred leave—a farce that; both of them knew he wouldn't be returning. Cut loose from the Corps, the young astronaut had fallen into an alcoholic mire, becoming such an appalling drunk Connor had to push through a termination, just to keep Reynolds's NASA file clean.

Connor had tried to maintain contact, but watching Reynolds tear himself apart eventually became easier from afar. They fell out of touch. Connor only even found out his protégé had left Houston from the NASA grapevine.

*That* Reynolds had been an Adonis—a thickly haired young powerhouse with lively eyes, handsome, chiseled features and a lean, muscular body that caught many an admiring glance from female staff. Even the alcohol hadn't ravaged him—at least, not the last time Connor had seen him.

But this man was different.

The leanness was still there, though now Connor would have called Reynolds wiry. And hard. The brown hair was gone, receding back from a long widow's peak to a cropped mass of mostly gray stubble. The chiseled features were there, but the skin was rougher, and drawn in on them so tight that what had been handsomeness had slid into cragginess. Still handsome, Connor supposed, but hard. So very hard.

It was the eyes that sealed the deal though. The same gray, and with depths to them, as before. But different depths. *Depths of suffering,* Connor thought. Of things endured.

Reynolds smiled wryly, noting Connor's interest. "You tell me I haven't changed, Matt, I'll throw you back out on the street," he said.

Connor chuckled. "No, you've changed, Edge. No argument there." He shook his head. "Goddamn it," he continued, "I've thought about you so often these past few years. Wondered how you were. What you looked like now." He waved *his* glass in a repeat of Reynolds's earlier gesture. "I knew you were here, of course. I guess if I'd known shit from shinola I would have figured this is exactly what you'd be like."

Reynolds shrugged. "That's the good thing about being a cop," he said, sipping scotch. "The worse you look, the better you get at it."

Connor was silent a moment, then gave another low chuckle. "Goddamn you, Edge," he said. "You always were a hard-ass. Even back then. So, what? You like being a cop?"

Reynolds wrinkled his nose. "It's okay. Most of the time it's just boring. People screwing each other over in exactly the same ways." He frowned, thinking back to the "Karl" case he'd cracked the year before. The Grosse Point doctor with the nasty sideline in serial mutilation of his female patients. "Every now and then you get a genuine hard case. A dangerous nut with brains. Then it gets interesting."

"Uh huh," said Connor. His eyes flicked around the apartment. "A woman?"

Reynolds grinned wryly. "Take a look around you, Matt. Then tell me what *you* think." He shook his head. "Not really. There *was* . . . someone," he said, and Connor could tell the question made him uneasy. "We were thinking of getting married . . ."

Reynolds's voice tailed off. He was lost, momentarily, in the memory of those two bittersweet years with Luce—Dr. Lucy Chang, Senior Pathologist with the Wayne County Medical Examiner.

*More bitter than sweet, though,* he thought, stung. *Towards the end.*

Luce had been unable to cope with the nightmares, the memories—the constant intrusion of another woman, even a dead one, into the life she was trying to build with him. The fights kept getting worse, the words harsher. Until the inevitable happened.

She left him.

Reynolds could still remember the scene. Five years ago now, nearly to the day. Luce flinging her stuff into her bags, tears making rivulets through her makeup. Lamps smashing as she stormed through the house, him shouting. And her parting shot at the door as the cab waited.

"Edge, you bastard! Don't you go coming around for me." Choking back tears. "If I want a fucking polygamous marriage, I'll move to Utah . . ."

He couldn't blame her, he guessed. That didn't make the memories sit any easier though.

Reynolds frowned, attention returning to Connor. "Anyway. It didn't work out. You could say. So, no. No woman." He took another slug of scotch. "What about you, Matt?" he asked, changing the subject. "How's Carol?"

It was Connor's turn to grin. "Touché," he said. "Ask me in a few months and I might be able to tell you." His voice grew sober. "She left me, Edge. Six years back now. Got divorced and everything. The whole shebang."

Connor shrugged.

"You know what it's like in the Agency, Edge. That's

who you're married to. Your wife is just someone you
sleep with once every six months. If you're lucky. Carol
got tired of it. Can't say I blame her."

He emptied his mug, paused while Reynolds refilled it.

"I stuck it out a few years," he continued, when the
cup was back in his hand. "Lived like this," he said,
waving the cup at the apartment walls. "Got along. Told
myself it was *her* problem. Then one day . . ."

He broke for a sip of scotch, swirled it around in his
mouth.

"I had a car accident," he said, swallowing. "Nothing
major. But enough to make me take a good, hard look
at myself." He shrugged again. "I decided I wasn't going
to die alone without making at least one more attempt
to get her back.

"So I rang Carol and told her I'd changed. She didn't
believe me at first, of course. Why the hell should she?
But I did all the right things. Bought a frame house in
Clear Lake. Set it up for her. Transferred out of Crew
Training into a soft option at Security Directorate." He
chuckled. "Hell, no fun pushing sorry-ass flyboys around
since *you* left, anyway."

Reynolds cocked an eyebrow at the older man. "Security Directorate?" he said. "I wouldn't have thought that
was one of the Agency's softer options."

Connor snorted. "It goddamn is where I am, believe
me," he growled. "Lunar Materials Security. Fielding
calls from eggheads all day about whether they get to
fondle the pretty moon rocks or not. It's all paperwork.
Pure nine-to-five time clock."

He took a pull of the scotch.

"Perfect for what I wanted. Almost worked too. I had
Carol *this* close to moving back in, patching things up.
She was starting to believe me." Connor grimaced.
"Until last week."

"Myers," Reynolds guessed.

Connor nodded. "Uh huh." He looked up at Reynolds. "You been following it?"

Reynolds looked down at his glass. It was good to see
Connor, but this NASA shoptalk, coming on top of what
had happened today with Ramirez, disturbed him. He

tried to stifle his unease. Normally he refused to talk anything to do with the Agency, ignoring hints from curious Bureau colleagues or the baiting of assholes like Fitz. Doing so just stirred the ghosts up worse.

The furor over Myers's death, though, had been inescapable. The papers were full of it, the networks blasting out saturation coverage. Folksy stories of Myers's hometown, specials on Space Station Program history. Ad nauseam reruns of that grainy, terrifying footage—Myers's helmet caving in. Coverage of the demonstrations sweeping Russia, murders of U.S. businessmen, the apparently retaliatory killing of that Russian diplomat.

Even a statement from the President.

*I want to tell the American people that the Government, and NASA, has this situation in hand. I want them to rest assured—this killing of a United States astronaut will not be allowed to pass . . .*

All totally understandable, of course—it wasn't every day an astronaut got whacked.

An *American* astronaut. On a station full of *Russians.*

For a few dizzying moments, it had even seemed the cold war was about to reignite. Demands from congressional Republicans for the Russians' expulsion from the Space Station Program. Threats of nuclear retaliation from nationalist hotheads in the Duma.

Reynolds had frozen it out, as much as he could. Tried to ignore the blanket coverage. He didn't want to think about Myers. Or who had killed him. Or ISS, or NASA, or any of that shit. That was all another world.

A world he had left behind.

"You'd have to be living on Mars not to, Matt," he said, noncommittally. He swirled the scotch around in his glass before taking a slug. "So what, they give you poor saps the job of handling it?"

"We lobbied for it, as a matter of fact," Connor said quietly. "NASA. Security Directorate. Sold the Attorney General and the President hard on appointing us the investigating agency." He looked down at his cup. "We got it too, luckily. The announcement is going to be made tomorrow. South Texas as U.S. Attorneys and Security Directorate as Investigating Agency."

Reynolds nodded. The Agency *would* want to handle the investigation, he supposed. Keep it under wraps. Control collateral damage.

"Keeping it in-house, huh?" he said, out loud. "The FBI won't like that."

"You goddamn bet they don't," Connor rasped. "They've been complaining all the way up to the AG to get it overturned." His jaw set hard. "But we're damned if we're going to let anybody in there to screw this up for us. We had to fight too hard to get the Station flying for that."

He shifted uneasily on the seat.

"And now we've got another fight on our hands to keep it there. Trouble is the jackals are circling. On the one hand we've got Coleman and his goons in Congress, who want the budget cut, no matter what. They know that means grounding ISS, but they don't care. An incident like this is just gold to them.

"And on the other we've got the Russians, already pissed we made them dump *Mir, extremely* pissed about being junior partners in the ISS program and going goddamn ballistic about the possibility of one of their cosmonauts being tried in an American court."

Connor shook his head. "I tell you, we're going to have to be more careful than a dog pissing razor blades. If we don't play it right, we could lose the whole goddamn program."

"So what's NASA gonna do?" Reynolds said, throwing down more scotch. "You know which one's the perp? Sorry, the mur . . ."

"That's okay, Edge," Connor interrupted, grinning. "I understand." He shook his head again, ruefully. "Unfortunately no. Not for sure. Just that it was one of the Russians. They've all denied it, of course."

Reynolds shrugged. "So bring them all down and put them through the wringer. Polygraphs. Interrogations. Christ, there's only what . . . four cosmonauts? It'll be like shooting fish in a barrel."

Connor shifted uncomfortably again.

"I'm afraid that's impossible, Edge," he said. "We can't afford to leave ISS unoccupied like that. Not for a

moment. You know the deal, Edge. ISS is our ticket to
Mars. If ISS goes, so does Mars."

A bitter note crept into his voice.

"Christ, it's not like the old days anymore. The country's not behind us. They don't care about Mars, they
don't care about space exploration. They don't give a
shit about anything on ISS except how much it costs.
The program's hanging on by its fingernails. A long period unmanned would be just what Coleman needs to
wind it down."

His eyes slid from Reynolds's guiltily.

"We can't allow that, Edge," he said, shaking his
head. "There's nothing for it. We're going to have to
send someone up there."

Reynolds pursed his lips, sucking scotch through his
teeth. He swallowed and put the glass down on the table.

"You should have told me this was a work call, Matt,"
he said calmly. "I would have made you pay for the
drinks."

Connor looked at him a long moment, his eyes troubled. He snorted. "Okay, buddy," he said. "Let's get
things all out front. We want you to go up to ISS and
find Gary's killer."

Reynolds nodded slowly. When no more was forth-
coming he spread his fingers in a questioning gesture.
"Well, what?" he said. "Am I supposed to say no now?
Or after the spiel?"

Connor held up a hand. "Just hear me out, Edge,"
he said, his voice tinged with sadness. "Okay?" Taking
Reynolds's look away for assent, he hurriedly sipped
some scotch and continued. "One, you're the only detective or investigator anywhere in the country who has
gone through the Shuttle training program . . ."

"Twenty years ago, Matt," Reynolds said quietly.

"Sixteen," Connor corrected. "And you're still the
only one. Two, we haven't got time to screw around
with training somebody. Goddamnit, Edge, you've heard
them! The American public is baying for blood on this
one. They want something done about it. Now! Matter
of fact, what they *really* want is for us to kick the Russians the hell out of the ISS program, even if that means

sinking it. But we might just be able to head that off and save the Station if we throw 'em an investigation and an indicted cosmonaut. I say we *might*. If we jump quickly."

He paused to suck in a deep breath. "Hell, I know it's dangerous . . ."

Reynolds opened his mouth to say something, but Connor overrode him.

"Please, Edge," he said. Even in the dim light Reynolds could see the perspiration beading his old trainer's forehead, hear the desperation in his voice. "Let me finish. It's dangerous in ways you can't imagine."

Connor shook his head in exasperation. "You should see JSC at the moment," he said. It took Reynolds a second to place the half-forgotten jargon. *JSC. Johnson Space Center.* "State Department types crawling all over the goddamn joint. Going apeshit about World War Three." He dabbed at the perspiration on his forehead. "They're right though. They've shown me stuff. CIA reports. Defense Intelligence briefings. Stuff you wouldn't believe."

He looked up at Reynolds. "What do you know about the Nunn-Lugar programs?" he asked.

Reynolds frowned. He'd heard of them, of course. They were programs run by the State Department and Defense, funded by Congress, to maintain security at nuclear- and chemical-weapons sites in Russia. Make sure Dimitri the security guard didn't walk off with a kilo of plutonium and sell it to terrorists, Reynolds supposed. Stop Libya and Iran buying Russian SS-25s wholesale and launching them at the States. He presumed the programs were still in operation. Leastways, he hadn't heard of any incoming renegade ICBMs.

"Not much," he admitted. "Something to do with weapons security in Russia, aren't they?"

"You got it," Connor replied. "The Nunn-Lugar programs are about the only things keeping the lid on Russia's strategic rocket forces right now." His mouth quirked dismissively. "Hell, I know the public doesn't give a shit about the nuclear problem these days. They think the Russians are all drunks and fools, and maybe they're right. But they're dead wrong there's nothing to be scared of anymore. Dead wrong."

Connor laughed hollowly. "Goddamn, how frightening is that? Drunks and buffoons in charge of the world's second-largest nuclear arsenal? With any number of anti-American lunatics running around, inside the Duma and out, just itching to get their hands on them? And the only thing stopping them a handful of underpaid U.S. techs nobody wants there?"

Connor swigged from the mug. His mouth set grimly.

"That's the problem, of course. The programs aren't secure. The Russians hate them. Even the bastards supposedly on our side. But our own people aren't keen on them either. The Republicans usually put two or three bills up a year to dump them. There's one before Congress right now, as a matter of fact."

He hesitated, swirling scotch around in the cup.

"Anyway, State is afraid Gary's death might be a conspiracy to destroy Nunn-Lugar. You know. A dramatic, public killing to get John and Jane Citizen worked up against Russia. Have them stampede Congress to cut off all aid. Including the Nunn-Lugar programs, which technically qualify as U.S. aid to Russia."

Reynolds shrugged. "What for? And by who?"

Connor grimaced. "That's where it gets scary. Ever hear of a man called Lavrenti Korbalov?"

He nodded at Reynolds's blank look. "Uh huh. Neither had I, until they showed me this Defense Intelligence stuff. He's this Russian general, a real piece of work from the sounds of it. Ex–Strategic Rocket Forces Command, until he was cashiered for refusing to obey orders on the START II missile cuts. Currently heads a terrorist organization called the Patriotic Union, though he disavows them publicly. Their big trick is murdering army officers and Duma members they deem 'traitors'— which means anyone friendly to the U.S. Their program is supposedly 'Renovation of Mother Russia,' but what it amounts to is reinvading the old Russian Empire, supreme power for Korbalov and jackboot rule for the rest of the country." Connor waved dismissively.

"No surprises there," he continued. "Russia's crawling with protofascists like that, waiting for democracy to fall on its ass so they can seize power. What's different about Korbalov is the plan he's got to make it happen. And the lengths he's prepared to go to."

Connor sipped the scotch-soda mix, shaking his head in disbelief.

"Two years ago, according to DIA, Naval Intelligence intercepted one of Korbalov's henchmen en route to San Juan, Puerto Rico. He got away, but they retrieved the package he was carrying. It was a one-kiloton plutonium 'briefcase bomb'—a little terrorist treat dating back to the KGB era. Apparently, the plan was to detonate it and flatten the city, leaving enough pointers to implicate the Russian security services. The idea was to provoke a U.S.-Russian confrontation, maybe even a retaliatory strike on a Russian provincial city. Destabilize the Russian government and military leadership so Korbalov could carry out the coup he's itching for, no questions asked."

"That's insane," Reynolds muttered.

Connor shrugged. "That's Russia. You and I both know it's not a normal democracy. The man at the top rules it with an iron fist, like Putin did, and like Molodin does. And behind him are the thousands of dictators-in-waiting, hot on the trail of their chance to do the same. The only difference with Korbalov is he's prepared to dick around with limited nuclear war to get his."

Connor leaned forward. His voice was feverish, his forehead wet again with perspiration. "You see why State is so worried about Gary's murder? Christ knows, it's bad enough as is. But what if it *is* a conspiracy? DIA is adamant Korbalov hasn't given up his plan to try to spark a tit-for-tat exchange with us. The only thing stopping him is the Nunn-Lugar programs, which are choking off his access to any more of Russia's weapons stockpiles. So far. If he gets them lifted . . ." Connor broke off, shaking his head.

"Could be this is more than just bringing Gary's killer to justice, Edge," he continued. "Could be it's a matter of stopping a war . . ."

Reynolds's reply came out of the half-light. "They tell you to tell me that, Matt?"

Connor stared at him a moment, then dropped his

eyes. "They wanted worse than that, Edge," he muttered. "Believe me."

Reynolds nodded, downing a mouthful of scotch. "Let me guess," he said. "Threats?"

Connor's eyes found his; for a moment he seemed on the verge of saying something. Instead he relaxed visibly, settling back on the chair.

"We're none of us our own people in this thing, Edge," Connor said deliberately. "For Christ's sake, look at *me*." He lifted his hands in despair. "Sixty-two goddamn years old this year. I should be laying in the adult diapers and getting ready for senility. Instead they got me in charge of our end of this thing. I . . . I got a wife I'm trying to win back, she won't return my calls . . ."

Connor downed a shot of scotch angrily, then looked up at Reynolds.

"We got no choice, Edge, is what I'm trying to say. *I've* got no choice. It's not just this State Department bullshit. Despite everything, I still believe in the Agency. In ISS, in Mars—the whole shebang. *I* think the program is worth saving. And I still believe the country *needs* us, even if they don't goddamn think they do."

He hesitated a moment, then because the scotch was spreading warmly from his stomach and three more were already in his bloodstream, pushed on recklessly. "But I'm not asking *you* to do it for those reasons, Edge. I'm saying you should do it for yourself. Not for me, or for NASA, or even the goddamn country. For you."

Connor took another shot of Dutch courage. "It's been a long time since Alicia died, Edge," he said softly.

"Oh, come *on*, Matt," Reynolds said. He looked away in disgust.

"Sixteen years," Connor persisted. "That's a long time in anyone's book."

Reynolds nearly hit him again, there and then, for daring to talk like that, but Connor was already going on, his words tumbling out feverishly.

"Listen to me, Edge," he said desperately. "The Directorate didn't just send me here cold tonight, you know. We've been checking on you these past few days. Digging into your files. Talking to your colleagues. Your boss . . ."

Reynolds snorted at that. *Fucking Dennison,* he thought. *Two-faced bastard.* How long had the lieutenant known what was in train?

"They tell us you're a king-hell detective. The best on the force. They say you don't let up, you just keep coming. They say they wonder sometimes what drives you. They don't know." Connor paused. "But I think I do."

"You're out of line, Matt," Reynolds growled, warning him.

"Am I?" Connor asked, dabbing at the sweat beading his forehead. "I'm sorry if I am. But I think it's true. I *do* know what drives you. You've never forgiven yourself for Ally's death, have you, Edge?"

He rushed on, not giving Reynolds time to interrupt. "Listen to me," he said. "Please, Edge. Goddamn it, I should have said these things to you a long time ago. When it happened. I'm sorry for that. I didn't know how to get through to you back then. But if I could have, I would have told you what I'm going to now."

Connor dragged in a deep breath. "It wasn't your fault, Edge. That goddamn asshole . . . that . . . Elwood. He was just one of those random things. One of those shit pieces of luck that rains down on you from out of the blue. Hell, you can't plan for sickos like that," he said adamantly. "You can't. You couldn't. Nobody could."

His voice softened. "Don't you see you have to forgive yourself, Edge? That it's what Alicia would have wanted? Goddamn, can't you see she would have wanted you to do *this*?"

But Reynolds was no longer listening. The walls of the claustrophobic, one-bedroom apartment had receded and he was suddenly back *there,* where Connor's words had thrown him. Those desperate days immediately after Ally had been killed. Tearing himself apart. Drinking himself into a stupor day and night to try and drown the knowledge burning in his guts.

*I killed her.*

Connor wasn't to know, then or now, that he was wrong. It *had* been Reynolds's fault. Connor couldn't know about the fights, the shouting matches between Ally and him because she wanted to go out and work, and he wouldn't let her.

"Fuck you, Reynolds," he could still hear her screaming. She only ever called him that when she was mad.
"I'm sick of being a trophy wife. I never see you. Why
can't I go out and have a life of my own?"

Because he'd been a selfish prick who didn't want anything to take her away from him. That was why. He'd
invented a hundred other reasons, but that was basically it.

Connor couldn't know that, in the end, the sole reason
Ally was even home that day for Elwood to go to work
on was because Reynolds had persuaded her to get pregnant. The ultimate way to squash her desire to make a
life for herself—Reynolds had soon worked out that that
had been his motive—and in his blackest moments, after
she died, he had used the knowledge to torture himself
sick.

*Well, you did that, boy,* he told himself sickly.
*Squashed it good and proper. For keeps.*

Reynolds's hand tightened on his glass. He was losing
it, he could tell. Despite the scotch, despite Matt's presence. The demons were howling again. Flailing at his
temples—hammer blows of the awful memories of what
he had done.

*Oh Ally,* he murmured wordlessly. *Forgive me, darling. Please.*

He heard, somewhere through the blind swirl of emotion, the scrape of Connor's chair as the older man
stood. Suddenly, a card was being thrust into his fingers.
And Connor was talking.

"I'm sorry, Edge," Reynolds's old trainer said. His
voice seemed miles away. "I have to call it as I see it.
That's the number of the hotel I'm staying at. Give me
a call when you've had a chance to think things over."

There were steps and a slam of the door somewhere
in the haze too, but Reynolds registered them only distantly. He sat on the cheap sofa, doubled over, head
cradled in hands whose powerful fingers bore down on
its temples like vices. As if memories were matter, and
flesh and bone the metal that could drive them down
to silence.

\*     \*     \*

Later that night Reynolds woke, drenched with sweat, twined in the bedclothes and gasping for breath. He lay there panting, eyes adjusting to the early-morning dark.

The dream of course. As always.

He'd known it would come. He'd crawled drunkenly off to bed, after Connor had left, expecting it. No way he was getting off tonight without the full treatment—sweating horror, soundless cries and the whole high-definition, technicolor nightmare trip.

But when it came he was surprised to find it different.

It started off the same. Pulling up to the house, the yellow police tape cutting into his retina like garroting wire. Leaping from the car and running into the house, like always, with that incredible dream motion—panicked, rushing, yet molasses-slow and utterly silent.

Swinging open the front door to reveal the cops and EMS personnel, expressionless and unmoving but for the eyes tracking his progress through the house. Striding dreamily, yet with mounting horror, through to the laundry, following the trail of blood. Heart rocking in his chest, the terror building so bad that by the time his hand reached for the door handle he was nearly paralyzed, begging the hand to *please stop, please don't open the door and show me what I know is there.*

Amazing how little difference that made. How undiminished the terror was, no matter how many times he . . . saw her there.

But this time the door opened on a bright, sunlit scene. A lovely park, somewhere—trees, a children's playground, a small lake. Ally was there, but *alive.* Fresh and beautiful, her long brown hair contrasting attractively with the light print dress she had on. She beckoned Reynolds over sunnily and he went, feet springy on the luxuriant grass, eyes full of brilliant blue sky.

She took his hand. Her touch was cool and beautiful.

He was suddenly conscious Ally was saying something. Reynolds bent forward to listen. He could hear her perfectly, but try as he might, he couldn't make out the words. What was she talking about? Reynolds couldn't tell—just that whatever it was it must be all right because Ally's voice was soft, carrying not a hint of recrim-

ination. And she was *smiling*—an easy, *forgiving* smile
that burned itself into his brain so that it was the only
thing that stayed when he woke a split second later,
wringing with sweat, his mouth dry from sleep-uttered
cries.

*That,* at least, hadn't changed.

Reynolds swung his feet over the edge of the bed and
shrugged on his robe. He stumbled into the bathroom,
flicking on the light that overhung the washbasin. That
same post-dream face greeted him in the mirror—hag-
gard, drained of color, slick with sweat. He turned on
the tap and splashed his forehead. Cupped a hand under
the stream and sucked down a few mouthfuls of cold
water. Then screwed the tap shut and slumped down on
the basin, weight on his outstretched hands.

When he was able, Reynolds made his way back to
the bed and switched on the bedside lamp. Grabbed the
telephone handset and reached for the card Connor had
given him.

He dialed the penciled number.

The phone was picked up almost immediately; Matt
was sleeping light. Connor's voice was sleep-blurred,
but alert.

"Yep. Connor," he said.

Reynolds was silent a moment. Then he broke.

"Just tell me one thing, Matt," he said. "You'll be
there, right? Through the whole thing. You'll be my
controller?"

For a moment Reynolds thought the older man hadn't
heard. Then a low chuckle came down the phone.

"You bet, Edge," the voice in his ear rasped. "You
just try to keep me away."

Reynolds found himself nodding. "Okay," he said, his
voice clipped. "I'll do it."

He dropped the handset down, though he could hear
Matt still saying something at the other end. He sat there
for some time, staring at the opposite wall. Finally, as if
recollecting himself, he stood up, pulling the robe tight
around himself, and padded through to the kitchen.

To get started on some strong black coffee.

3:53 A.M., Central Standard Time, 14 March 2005
Room 153, Pontchartrain Hotel,
West Jefferson Avenue, Detroit

Connor clicked the receiver button down, once he realized Reynolds was no longer there, and let it rise again.
He punched in the number and listened to the phone
ring, glancing at the LED clock by the bed.

It was 3:53 A.M. The Director would be in bed, but
that was okay. He'd said to call. Whatever the hour.

The phone was picked up. The Director's voice came
down the line. "Abraham. Is that you, Matt?"

"Yes, sir," Connor replied. "Good news. Reynolds
has agreed."

The Director was silent a moment. Connor heard him
exhale a worried breath. "That is good news," he said.
"Good work, Matt." He hesitated. "Did you have
to . . ."

"No," said Connor, deadpan, cutting him off. "There
was no need for that, sir. He wants to do it."

The Director was silent once more.

"Okay," he said finally, and Connor was glad Abraham had the grace to at least *sound* relieved. "That's
very good, Matt. Well, you know what to do. Get your
boy over to Selfridge Air Base as soon as possible. We'll
have the transporter standing by." And with that the
Director was gone, leaving Connor holding the dead receiver. He placed it back in the cradle, went to move off
the bed, but hesitated. He looked back at the telephone.

*Should I call?*

Carol would be asleep of course, but Connor suddenly
had the most powerful urge to speak to her. His hand
moved to the phone, but he withdrew it, reluctantly. It
wasn't so much the fear of waking her. It was the disbelief he knew he would hear in her voice.

*Of course, Matthew. It'll be different now. I understand
that. Thank you so much for breaking your work trip to
call and tell me. From one thousand miles away, at four
o'clock in the morning . . .*

Connor wished he had the words to tell her. To make
her believe him.

*These things are not always within a man's power to change, Carrie,* he would protest, if she were there. *Sometimes the only thing you can do is ride the river God throws you in.*

*And hope to stay afloat.*

That was one thing he hadn't included in the potted history he'd given Reynolds. That he'd sunk so goddamn low, those years with Carol gone, that at one stage he'd even got religion. Fallen in with a bunch of Pentecostals—the whole charismatic, arm-waving, tongue-gibbering deal. Become Brother Connor—"the latest of our flock to bathe in the blood of *Christ,* do you hear me? To have his sins washed away in the sweet, sweet blood of the *Lamb . . .*"

It hadn't stuck of course. Connor couldn't get the voices right, and he'd never felt anything but a goddamn fool whenever "Pastor" Munoz laid hands on him and pushed him on his ass. He'd split from the group after a couple of months. Set his dog on the congregation members when they came around the goddamn house, pestering him not to backslide.

But Connor hadn't been able, ever since, to shake the idea that maybe there was a God there after all. He'd started seeing *His* hand everywhere.

That had been his first thought when he saw how things were shaping up in the immediate aftermath of Myers's death. The panicked talks on how to keep the investigation under Security Directorate control. The desperate search of the files that brought up only one astronaut with investigative credentials.

*Ex–Pilot Candidate Reynolds. Now Detective Sergeant with the Detroit City Police Homicide Bureau.*

And only one contact still working at NASA, incredibly right here, inside Security Directorate.

Security Adviser Matthew J. Connor. Ex–Crew Training Division.

*This is His work,* Connor had thought, awed. *His way of bringing Edge and me back together.*

And now it was all coming true. Edge had agreed to go. Connor was finally going to see all the work he'd poured into the younger man pay off.

Connor shook his head in amazement.

*Who would have believed it?* he thought. *After all these years. I'm finally going to see that boy I trained up in space.*

And because he was alone, he slid to his knees and, there on the thick carpeting of the Pontchartrain Hotel, did something he hardly did at all anymore. He prayed. But whether it was from gratitude, or for strength to face the coming ordeal, even Connor couldn't have said.

11:15 P.M., Moscow Time, 14 March 2005
Simulations Center, Zvezdny Gorodok (Star City),
Korolev, Moscow

Lyudmila's head shot up at the noise. What was that? She peered into the semidarkness nervously, the broom in her hands gripped like a cudgel. She listened carefully. Had she really heard it? The scrape of feet on the concrete floor?

*"Kto tam?"* she said finally, when seconds had passed without it repeating. *Who's there?*

Her words echoed through the vast, deserted building. Around her, the various spacecraft simulators loomed out of the darkness like sinister behemoths. Lyudmila shivered at the sight of them. She bent back to her work with renewed urgency.

Nobody there, of course. Just a silly old *babushka,* afraid of the dark and jumping at shadows. Still. The sooner she was finished and out of here, the better.

Lyudmila shoveled the last load of trash into the compactor's maw, using the broom as a spade, then climbed in herself. The compactor was a Soviet-era relic—a rectangular chamber of twenty-by-ten feet with a massive, movable plate for one end wall and noisy electric motors that crushed it in hydraulically at several tons of pressure. Over the years the plate's edges had ground so far down that pieces of trash sometimes slipped through the gap and fouled the driving mechanism. Which was why poor, stupid *babushkas* like Lyudmila had to get in there, with the stinking trash, and tamp it down a bit first.

Once inside, Lyudmila got to work piling the garbage
up against the compactor's far wall with her broom. In
truth, she didn't really mind having to climb inside. It
was safe enough. The motors could only be activated by
the lever on the control panel; you couldn't accidentally
trip them from inside. And it was better in here, in some
ways. At least you didn't have that huge, dark building
around you—all that empty space with just dim shapes
and imagined noises to fill it . . .

Lyudmila frowned, jabbing savagely at the garbage.
She really hated working here at night. All alone. She
only did it because jobs were so short right now. You
had to be grateful for what you could get, even a shitty
cleaning job.

She giggled suddenly at the thought of Mikhail Vissarionovitch hearing his precious job described thus. The
supervisor was always telling them they should be proud
to work for such an historic organization. Always trying
to interest them in what went on at the Space Agency.
But Lyudmila didn't hold with that. Poking your nose
into things that didn't concern you.

You only got into trouble that way.

*Like last week,* Lyudmila thought. Those people she
had inadvertently stumbled in on. She shivered again, at
the memory. Four of them, three men and one woman—
two of the men, Lyudmila was almost certain, what she
called spacemen. Cosmonauts. Lyudmila knew instantly
she'd seen something she shouldn't have. She didn't
know what, but there was something *wrong* about the
scene. Something . . . unnatural. The spacemen inside
that huge machine, naked as the day they were born,
though it was easily minus twenty in the unheated building. And those eyes! One of them had looked at her,
through the glass, and Lyudmila had nearly died of
fright. They were like . . . nothing. Nothing she'd ever
seen.

But it was the hostility that really scared her. Arcing
towards her in thousand-volt blasts of hatred and fear.
For a moment she'd thought they were going to attack
her, there and then. She'd wanted to protest, tell them
it was all right—she was just stupid Lyudmila, she didn't

know anything about anything. But her *babushka* tongue betrayed her, frozen with terror, so that all she did was bob timidly and back herself out of there, fast as she could.

Lyudmila shuddered. Thinking about things like that made her nervous. She pushed at the trash with redoubled energy. *Maybe I should talk to Alexei about that department store job,* she thought. Anything would be better than working here. On her own, late at night like this.

A carton slipped from the pile, dislodged by her prodding, and rolled to her feet. Lyudmila dropped her broom and bent to retrieve it, holding her breath against the stink. That was why she was able to hear the noise clearly, when it came again, despite the surrounding metal walls.

The scrape of feet on concrete. Unmistakable. Coming towards her.

Lyudmila straightened in terror. Her heart thumped at her sternum. The steps were still audible, moving steadily closer. She peered through the access hole in fright. It was impossible to make out anything in the half-light.

*Who can it be?*

Masha, returning for something she'd forgotten? But Masha was hours gone; she was taking her time if it was her.

*"Kto tam?"* Lyudmila said again, trying to make it a rough command. Instead, it came out a squeak, forced through her terror-constricted throat. "Masha?" she added, whispering fearfully. "Is that you?"

No answer. Lyudmila was about to ask again, when a figure moved into silhouette against one of the night windows, drying her voice in fear. Even in the dim light she could see it wasn't Masha.

It was a man.

*Mikhail Vissarionovitch,* Lyudmila thought wildly. It didn't look like the supervisor—too tall and thin, for one thing—but it had to be. She opened her mouth to ask him, *What is it, Mikhail Vissarionovitch, what's wrong?,* but the figure's silhouetted arm flashed in movement, cutting her off. A second later came a chilling, unmistakable *clunk*.

The trip lever. The man had rammed it home.

The chamber shook as its electric motors thrummed into life. Bass vibration rippled the walls. Metal groaned as hydraulic cylinders filled, then squealed as the plate ground against the floors and walls, starting its journey. Through it all, Lyudmila stood rooted to the spot, her stupid *babushka* mouth open in a perfect, horrified *o*.

That was what really killed her. For there was another thing Lyudmila could have said about the compactor, this old dinosaur, if she'd been thinking straight. It was stupidly designed so that the access hole was at the end the plate started from. So if you *did* get trapped inside, and didn't make it out in the first three seconds, that was it. There was nothing left for you to do but die. As Lyudmila shortly did, brawny arms beating at the walls, the bellows of terror she finally found voice for twining, unheard, in the mesh and grind of hydraulic gears.

# 3

Reynolds levered himself through the hatch and sailed through the Laboratory Module, ducking to avoid debris shaken loose by the collision. He felt, rather than heard, a crack as he collided with a spinning oxygen cylinder. He ignored it. His whole being was focused on getting through the Lab Module and Cargo Block, then up into *Soyuz* in time. ISS's depressurization alarm was squealing in his suit headset. The Atmosphere Control System's automatic warning—cabin pressure critical; 35 kilopascals—was scrolling down the head-up display on the inside of his helmet faceplate. Beside it, his suit's depleted oxygen readout counted down.

*Fifty-five seconds left.*

Another line of glowing blue type appeared as Reynolds shot through the Cargo Block's narrow corridor—Soyuz Commander, prepare crew for emergency ingress. *No chance of that,* Reynolds thought grimly. The *Soyuz* commander was no doubt dying, somewhere back there with the other Russians. All trapped in the depressurizing Hab Module, doomed to Myers's grotesque fate.

Reynolds would have to make it to the escape vehicle on his own.

He kicked the last few yards through the Cargo Block, readying himself for the abrupt right-hand turn that led through the Mating Node up into *Soyuz*. Maneuvering in the Titan Hardshell suit took some getting used to.

"You have to move the way the joints allow you to," Allison had urged him. "Otherwise you'll exhaust yourself and get nowhere." He was right, Reynolds had found, but the technique was unnatural and took some effort. In the event, he bucked into the connecting passage flawlessly, bending at the metal-banded waist like a pro.

*Perfect.* He had forty-six seconds left.

He resisted the urge to push himself up into the *Soyuz,* instead using the passage to wheel around and enter feet first. It would be impossible to turn in the first of the module's three capsules, he knew, and he'd need his hands in position to seal the hatch immediately. He backed through as quickly as he could. His gloved hands scrabbled for the lever handles as his eyes shot back to the flashing countdown.

*Thirty-eight seconds.*

He forced himself through the closeout steps calmly; the hatch had to be securely shut before the atmosphere in the *Soyuz* could stabilize. He locked it down to a tight seal then hit the detonate button to initiate separation. Relief surged through him as he felt the explosive bolts fire, freeing *Soyuz* from ISS's deadly embrace.

So far so good.

He backed through the *Soyuz* into its descent capsule. Entering the tiny, acorn-shaped capsule, he maneuvered himself into the commander's seat, trying to ignore the spiraling countdown. Designed for a Russian cosmonaut wearing a thin Sokol pressure suit, the seat, even after NASA's modifications, was a cramped fit. By the time Reynolds had strapped himself in and could look up at the instrument panel, nearly a quarter of a minute had passed.

*Seventeen seconds left.* Then his secondary oxygen tanks would cut out. *Say another minute after that, if I breathe shallowly.*

He had to get the atmosphere inside *Soyuz* stabilized. Quickly.

Reynolds studied the panel calmly. It was a masterpiece of archaic simplicity, like all Russian instrumentation—chunky Bakelite buttons, hand-etched glass gauges

and an ancient cathode-ray display. He punched the incomprehensible Cyrillic keys from memory, initiating the
cabin-pressurization sequence, and was rewarded with a
blinking light on the Programs Indicator. The cabin-
pressure gauge began to climb; when it reached 101 kilopascals it would be safe for Reynolds to remove his helmet. In the meantime, he had to get *Soyuz* away from
the doomed ISS, out to where he could reestablish contact with ground via the module's communication
system.

He punched in the undock sequence cautiously,
double-checking everything. There would be a mistake
somewhere, that was the thing. He had to pick it up,
quickly, *had to,* otherwise he would have failed. He
watched the Programs Indicator like a hawk, but it never
wavered. Everything looked smooth, until the thrusters
fired, starting *Soyuz* on its gentle trajectory away from
ISS.

And all hell broke loose.

Suddenly *Soyuz*'s depressurization alarm was screaming, and the cabin-pressure gauge was going wild—dipping to fifty kilopascals, hovering, then plunging . . .
forty-five . . . forty . . . thirty-five. Goddamn it, *Soyuz*
was losing her guts, her atmosphere somehow *pouring*
into space. For a moment Reynolds put up a desperate
resistance—running through the key sequence frantically
from beginning to end—then, realizing it was hopeless,
sat back sourly and waited for the end.

It was over. He'd croaked again.

As if in confirmation, the wall lights of the Neutral
Buoyancy Pool snapped on, spilling bright light through
the water into *Soyuz*'s tiny porthole. The type on Reynolds's helmet display dissolved, replaced by one line, repeating over and over.

Red or black roses for the funeral?

"Smartasses," Reynolds muttered, then looked up at
the porthole as a dull thud sounded. One of the divers
was at the glass, hair a floating blond halo around his
head, lips grinning around his chunky mouthpiece. He
waved his fist in front of the window, thumb pointed
downwards. "No shit?" Reynolds mouthed. He waved

the man away. "Okay, Allison," he said, out loud. "Where did I screw up?"

His suit radio crackled. "Whoa, don't take it so hard, big guy," the Chief Sim Control Tech chuckled. "The malfunction was in one of the pyrotechnic units in the module separation bolts. Number three shot, but failed to unlatch. When you listen to it on the tape you'll hear it; there's three clicks rather than four. When the thrusters kicked in you were still hitched to ISS at the hatch. You tore the ass out of *Soyuz* as you moved away."

Reynolds shook his head in exasperation. He'd been concentrating so heavily on software errors he'd forgotten to listen for external cues. "Okay," he said. "Let's give it another run-through then."

"Uh, that's a negative, champ," the reply came over his suit radio. "Remember, not everyone's wearing a suit down there. We've gotta give those divers a break. Why don't you just sit back and enjoy the view, okay? Dive Team Two'll be down in just a minute. By the way, how's the suit? Comfy?"

Reynolds's scowl was almost *audible* over the suit radio. "No comment," he answered. "Let's just say I've felt more comfortable in evening dress."

Allison laughed. "Copy that, Reynolds," he said. "I'll get you an inflatable tux to wear down there, okay?" With that the technician signed off, closing the channel to wait out the changeover.

He leaned back in his chair, chuckling. A baby-faced man with a lone kink of cherubic blond hair gracing his baldness, Doug Allison's affability was renowned among staff at the Sonny Carter Training Facility—NASA's huge Neutral Buoyancy Pool, where astronauts trained underwater in simulated weightlessness. In all but one respect. As two partying juniors had found when caught in an out-of-hours skinny dip, Doug Allison did have one hard-and-fast rule. *Don't mess with the pool.* Allison had scooped the naked couple out with one of the jib cranes at the pool's edge, normally used for hauling suited astronauts in and out. And left them hanging there, fixed in the arc lights, until security staff arrived.

Allison reached for his coffee, simultaneously running

a proprietorial eye over the facility, refracted through
the bank of TV monitors. God, she was beautiful: 202
feet long, 102 wide and forty deep. Big enough to fit
full-sized mock-ups of nearly half the International
Space Station at once, lifted in and out by the ten-ton
bridge cranes overhead. Filled with 6.5 million gallons
of the purest, clearest water—sand-filtered, completely
replaced every nineteen hours and temperature-constant
to protect the support divers from hypothermia.

Even so, dive teams had to be rotated every two
hours. Allison watched One Team tread water as they
slowly ascended. Even with the special, oxygen-rich Ni-
trox they used, the pool was deep enough for divers to
get the bends if they came up too quick. Above water,
Two Team readied themselves for the changeover: donning tanks and wet suits; those with bulky equipment
mounting the jib-crane platforms that would lower them
in. The pool's surface shimmered from the overhead
lights. The thick, white umbilicals carrying oxygen and
cooling water to Reynolds's suit coiled atop it like surreal entrails—glowing superwhite in the brilliance.

*Pretty as a picture,* Allison thought again, sipping his
coffee.

A sliver of light appeared on the glass of one of the
monitors; someone had opened the Sim Control Center's
door. A bulky shadow appeared that Allison recognized
as Security Adviser Connor, Reynolds's controller. He
didn't look around. He was used to Connor's intrusions
by now. The adviser had been visiting four or five times
a day, like a mother hen, since Reynolds's pressure-
cooked neutral buoyancy training had begun.

"Matt," he said, tossing the greeting over his shoulder.
His hands went to the keyboard and began typing. Little
hiccup in the anticontaminant program's flow, he'd just
noticed.

"Doug," Connor replied, materializing beside the
technician's chair. His eyes sought out Reynolds's image
on the bank of monitors. "How's he doing?"

Allison shrugged. "Great. Like always." It was true
too. Allison was jumping Reynolds through the hoops—
running the simulations at a 120 percent intensity, back-

ing them up on one another so fast he'd had to pull in an extra dive team to cope. But Reynolds had taken it all, with no sign of flagging. Yet.

Allison looked up at Connor, grinning.

"You *sure* he's been out of the loop sixteen years, Matt?" he asked. "He's eating this stuff like he was made for it."

Connor suppressed the swelling pride he felt, enough almost to override his anxiety. "He's gonna need to," he replied tersely. That was no lie. The jury-rigged program Crew Training was putting Reynolds through was a joke really, not enough to qualify him for half the critical scenarios he could face on ISS. Reynolds's ability might just make good the difference and keep him safe.

Maybe.

Connor frowned. "Wait a minute," he said, peering at the underwater image of Reynolds crammed into the tiny seat. "What the hell's that he's wearing?" It wasn't the normal baggy, white EMU suit—Extravehicular Mobility Unit—used on ISS and the Shuttle. It was slimmer, tighter, and its smooth, rigid surface *gleamed,* even through the blue water.

*Metal,* Connor thought, surprised. *What the hell?*

"It's something, huh?" Allison chortled. He manipulated a tiny joystick, zooming the camera into tight focus. "That's the new Titan Hardshell. One hundred and twenty pounds of superstrength, aluminized carbon-fiber shell with metal-banded joints and high-pressure gloves. She's a one-step suit—rated to one atmosphere pressure. Reynolds can jump in and out of that thing like putting on a sweater."

Connor barely heard him. Anger thrummed at his temples. He knew the principle, of course. The problem with EMU suits was their low pressure—even the new generation ran at a mere forty kilopascals, less than half an atmosphere. Like ascending divers, astronauts donning them too fast suffered nitrogen bubbling in the blood and brain—caisson disease, or decompression sickness. The only solution was a forty-minute prebreathe of pure oxygen, to get the nitrogen out of the body before pressure was reduced. But that was dangerous in emergencies, not to mention a pain in the ass at other times, and Connor was aware NASA had been working for some time on high-pressure suits that would eliminate the problem. He wasn't surprised to see one finally appear. But he was furious to see it on Reynolds.

"Goddamn it, Doug," he said testily. "Edge is gonna be on ISS in six days. He has to know that goddamn EMU backwards before then. Who the hell told you to screw around and put him in a nonissue suit?"

Allison cocked an eyebrow.

"They didn't tell you?" he said. "The Titan's man-rating came through last month." Man-rating was NASA's term for safety approval. "Mission Operations decided to integrate the suit's first operational test with Reynolds's mission. That's what he's going up in."

Connor's skin reddened. He struggled to contain his temper.

"The hell he is," he said hotly. "Jesus, Doug, that boy's got enough on his plate as is. Goddamned if I'm going to let Mission Operations make him a guinea pig for their systems programs too."

Allison laid a hand on Connor's wrist. "Easy, Matt," he soothed. He understood the security adviser's anger. Trainers and controllers developed strong protective feelings for the astronauts in their charge. Beneath the man's bluster, Allison sensed, he was genuinely worried.

"The orders came through this morning," he continued. "Surprises me they haven't told you yet—somebody fucked up, I guess. But I tell you, Matt, I bet safety was a big part of the reason for the change." He shrugged. "The Titan's a good, simple suit. It's designed for contingency use. And God knows it's safe. It's been tested up to the ass down here."

He looked up at Connor.

"Trust me, Matt," he grinned. "The Titan'll keep your boy safe up top. Promise."

Connor didn't reply. His anger was fading; Allison was right, after all. Systems Division *would* have tested the suit to the nth degree. He'd have to go over the specs himself, but Allison was probably right about that too—the Hardshell would be a better option than the EMUs

in an emergency. But, unlike Allison, he knew Edge
faced worse than just the critical situations most astronauts had nightmares about.

Maybe much worse.

Connor had seen the "eyes only" Security Directorate
estimates—the analyses SD headquarters had drawn up
on likely scenarios for the conclusion of Reynolds's mission. They were all premised on Reynolds finding the
killer, which was something, Connor supposed. A vote
of confidence, at least. Or wishful thinking. But it was
the calculations of what would happen next that had his
guts churning so bad he could hardly bear to look at
Reynolds's image on the monitor—blue-tinged and
placid in his underwater surrounds.

The *best* news was the one-in-five chance the killer
would suicide upon discovery. That was the best. The
other options were where it got scary.

A one-in-twenty chance the guilty cosmonaut would
try to silence Reynolds violently to avoid discovery. A
one-in-*ten* chance he, or she, would engineer a critical
situation and try to destroy ISS.

*One in ten. Jesus Christ.*

Connor turned away from the monitors and took his
leave of Allison with a bitter taste in his mouth. It was
a goddamned dangerous game Security Directorate was
playing. Sending Reynolds up there like that, bargaining
they could manage the confrontation and bring him
home safely. And Connor was caught right in the middle, torn between his loyalty to the agency and to the
friend he was helping send into the lions' den.

Allison was wrong about one thing, at any rate. It was
going to take more than the Titan to see Reynolds
through.

A lot more.

11:12 P.M., Central Standard Time, 25 March 2005
Crew Block, Johnson Space Center

Reynolds sat locked in concentration, face bathed blue
in the light of the laptop screen. His fingers skipped on
the keyboard as he checked and dismissed documents—

reviewing the investigative database Security Directorate had assembled on Myers's murder. His eyes were red and his hair plastered down with drying sweat from the day's exertions. He should have been asleep—God knows there was already little enough time for rest in the punishing schedule Connor had him on. But, though tired bodily, Reynolds's mind hummed with alertness.

This was what he did, damn it. What he was good at.

He clicked through the blizzard of words and images with increasing unease. Normally, he loved this cerebral stage of investigation—sifting and analyzing evidence for those few threads that, properly picked, would unravel the case. The harder to find, the more obscure the case, the better he liked it. By rights, Myers's killing should have had him salivating. But it didn't. It had him *rattled*.

Myers's murder wasn't just obscure. It was impossible.

At first sight the problem was simple. Where else did you get a murder scene physically confined to a single chamber, the airlock, less than twenty-five feet in diameter? Where all possible suspects were bottled up in the same "sausage string" of modules, 350 feet long and just a few yards wide, barring the odd module jutting to the side. All never more than forty yards from the scene of the crime, the whole time Myers was being bludgeoned to death. With their every move under the round-the-clock scrutiny of hundreds of flight controllers in centers all around the world.

In fact, it should have been even simpler than that. Of ISS's five other occupants, one could be discounted immediately. He was Doctor Kutashita Akira, a medical researcher from Tsukuba Space Center's astrobiology department. A number of factors ruled the Japanese out. One, for what it was worth, was his personality inventory: Akira's MMPI rated him normal on all ten scales with just a slight inhibition of aggressive drive and a minuscule tendency to psychasthenia—compulsion and phobia—to mark him out. Hardly the stuff murderers were made of. More telling was the fact the Japanese was physically incapable of wearing the EMU suit the killer had been in. A violent allergic reaction to the spandex used in the inner cooling garments of the American suits restricted Akira to his own, Japanese-modified EMU—definitely *not* the one visible in the terrifying footage of Myers's murder.

But the crowning exculpatory fact was Akira's alibi. He was the only suspect whose position could be independently verified. Akira was on ISS to run experiments on metastasization rates of tumor cells in microgravity—NASA's technical term for weightlessness. At the exact moment of Myers's murder, he had been in the Japanese station module, Kibo, entering figures on those experiments into the lab computer. The data log, radioed to Tsukuba in by-the-millisecond packets, proved it. So, whoever it was on the tape coldly bludgeoning Myers to his bloody, explosive death, it wasn't Akira.

No way.

But therein lay the problem. The killer, as Connor had said, had to be one of the four Russians. None of their whereabouts at the time of death, however, *was* verifiable. It was clear where they were supposed to be—where they all said they *were*: Commander Boris Kalganin in the Cargo Block, performing inventory; Flight Engineer Matchev working on the Russian Segment computer system; *Soyuz* Commander Kostia Drupev running maintenance routines on the *Soyuz* module; and Mission Specialist Irina Ruskaya setting up a crystallization experiment in ISS's centrifuge. Unfortunately, because of the EVA that was to take place that day, the channels that normally carried signals from ISS's internal TV cameras had all been reassigned to externals.

Hence there was no way to tell which cosmonaut was lying.

Reynolds brought up the schematic Security Directorate had prepared—a colored diagram of ISS with the claimed location of each Russian marked in red. He studied them in mounting frustration—calculating approach routes to the airlock, counting the number of hatches and estimating the time to open and close each. Actually, he knew, all that crap was meaningless. How long it would have taken each cosmonaut to get there, how well they could conceal their actions. The plain fact was, none of them could have done it either.

None of them.

The problem was one of time. The insignificant distances separating each red dot from the soon-to-be-murdered blue dot, Myers, also represented an insurmountable barrier—the mere twenty-eight minutes the killer had had. The video channels had been switched over to the external cameras at 11:06 A.M. ET, Expedition Time. That was the last moment at which Space Station Control was positive each cosmonaut *was* where they said they were. Myers had died at 11:34 ET—that left twenty-eight minutes, max, for the murderer to don a suit, disable the communications array, then infiltrate the airlock and attack Myers.

But that was nowhere near long enough. As Reynolds well knew.

The suit, that was the trouble. If Reynolds had been privy to Connor's thoughts earlier he would have agreed—the low-pressure EMU was a deathtrap if you got into it too quick. Without that forty-minute prebreathe, nitrogen would just *boil* out of your blood, muscles and the fatty tissue of your brain and spine the moment you left ISS's high-pressure environment for the vacuum of space. Or the airlock, in this case. If you were lucky enough to escape brain damage from gas embolism you'd still suffer, at least temporarily, crippled limbs from nitrogen bubbling in the joints, severe muscle trauma and choking nausea.

Yet the killer had a twenty-minute prebreathe, at most. The guilty cosmonaut should have been instantly identifiable by the symptoms—drooling, limb paralysis, slurring speech and disorientation. But the postmurder interviews showed nothing. Reynolds had got biomedical to prepare tests he could run ISS's occupants through once he was up there—coordination, speech and mental exercises to probe for subtle signs of cerebral or nervous damage. He wasn't holding out much hope, though.

If the murderer had been a tough enough son of a bitch to endure the agonizing pain of decompression sickness without betraying himself, it was unlikely Reynolds would catch him that way now.

Other anomalies jangled Reynolds too. Usually homicides fell neatly into the premeditated vs. unpremeditated divide. Myers's murder, though, was a weird mix of both.

Specifically, why kill Myers so publicly? If the State Department's nightmares were true, and the killing *was* a conspiracy, that was deliberate. The killer had bludgeoned the American to death in the most brutal, open fashion possible—to maximize U.S. outrage. But why take the enormous risks of such a physical assault? It struck Reynolds there were hundreds of trouble-free ways to murder fellow astronauts: tamper with their suit, cut their umbilicals on EVA, trap them the wrong side of a hatch in a depressurization incident, just to name a few. Any one of which would still spark outrage when it became apparent it was deliberate. And at far less risk of injury or exposure, too.

That was another thing. If the killer *wanted* to be observed, why had he dealigned the communications array? That argued desire to hide the crime: premeditation. Yet it was such an inept cover-up—Space Station Control's successful recontact showed how nearly it *hadn't* worked—you couldn't imagine an intelligent, murdering cosmonaut relying on it.

*Unless,* Reynolds thought suddenly, *he'd had no choice.*

*Unless he'd just decided Myers had to die,* right then, *and had to improvise.*

But that was a prime indicator of nonpremeditation— what cops called "mission orientation." The killer was overwhelmed by such a violent emotional *need* to commit the crime that he just went ahead and did it. There and then. Regardless of the consequences. Without much of an escape plan, and with minimal, if any, attempts to cover up.

Homicide cops saw it all the time. The father who goes into his ex-wife's workplace, guns her down, then finds his only way out is at the end of his own bullet. The loser who takes a Tec-9 to work and plugs ten or twenty imagined causes of discontent before taking out the real problem—himself.

*The cosmonaut who dons a U.S. space suit, forces his*

*way into the airlock and bludgeons his fellow astronaut to death.*

Reynolds thought about that. In some ways it fitted. There was Myers's message too; he had to remember that. If there *had* been tension, some violent upsurge brewing, it was possible Myers had caught a whiff of it. Sent his message, suddenly aware of the danger he was in.

*Or the message itself was the trigger.*

Reynolds tried that one out. He had to admit it made sense too. Could be the killer had learned of Gary's e-mail somehow—the systems weren't that secure. And he was so afraid of what Myers was going to say he put him out of the way. Immediately.

*What, though?* Reynolds thought. *What could Myers have said that was so important the murderer would risk everything to silence him?*

He clicked through windows on his laptop thoughtfully, bringing up the video-stream of ISS's airlock. NASA had left Myers's corpse in there to freeze—partly for hygiene, partly to preserve the crime scene—sealing the airlock under twenty-four-hour camera scrutiny. Reynolds could access it live through the "Investigations LAN" NASA's data engineers had established.

He studied the tableau. Myers's suited corpse was circling endlessly through the chamber, the way things do in weightlessness. Bumping stiffly off the walls, spinning away into the darkness beyond the cone of the airlock's standby lights, then reappearing—a ghoulish mannequin locked into eternal, purposeless motion. Accompanying it were drifting clouds of glittering crystal—frozen blood, fluid and shards of clear polycarbonate from the smashed helmet—with tools and larger pieces of unidentified flotsam wheeling throughout.

Reynolds watched the corpse's ceaseless, hypnotic roll, frowning.

What secrets was it keeping? Which of the cosmonauts had hated Myers, or feared him, enough to turn him into this?

He closed the window on the circling phantom and brought up the cosmonauts' biographies instead. It was almost the first chance he'd had to have a look at them, he'd been so busy with the training program. Reynolds went through them, one by one.

The men were Russian carbon copies of U.S. astronauts—or Reynolds himself, in fact. Commander Boris Kalganin, for example, was a graduate of Chernigov Higher Air Force College in Ukraine, and had flown Sukhoi 24 interceptors before joining the cosmonaut program. Reynolds noted he'd been shot down in Afghanistan and survived eighteen months in Mujahideen hands. The accompanying head-and-shoulders shot showed a virile, athletic man whose hawk nose, angular features and bristling shock of dark, Slavic hair were softened by the smile quirking his mouth and by his jovial eyes. The Russian Space Agency, RKA's, personality inventory rated him "self-confident and durable, suited to command." Which probably accounted for his RKA record: stints of command on *Soyuz* T-11, TM-7 and two on *Mir*.

Reynolds thought about that. *A commanding personality, used to being top dog in his own country's space program.* That couldn't have been easy on ISS, where for all their long-duration spaceflight experience, the Russians were definite junior partners. Constantly under the irritating thumb of their NASA financiers and controllers.

Reynolds shrugged, closing the biography. *Sure, it would rankle. But enough to kill for?*

He brought up the next file—Flight Engineer Leonid Matchev. Reynolds skimmed through the notes. The same deal: top-shelf engineering graduate from Leningrad Mechanical Institute; a few years at NPO Energia, the Russian space-launch corporation; two missions to *Mir*. His photo, when it loaded, showed a Nordic blond with square, severe features and cropped hair. Matchev was big for a cosmonaut, Reynolds noticed— six three. His inventory called him "independent and self-reliant," which Reynolds guessed was RKA-talk for a pain-in-the-ass at times.

Well, that *could* rub people up the wrong way. Especially across the cultural divide.

But again, hard to see how it might have put Myers where he was today.

An item of minor interest was that Matchev was one of the "space orphans"—the parentless kids taken into Soviet space-program crèches and purpose reared for cosmonaut training. Reynolds had heard of this. It was one of the crazier Communist space-race schemes—the idea that children brought up in-house would somehow become "super cosmonauts." Ceausescu had done the same thing in Romania, with the Securitate, to infinitely more savage effect. Reynolds wasn't surprised by such excesses; anybody who'd checked the period's history knew about them.

But he *was* amazed to find any of the unfortunate orphans *had* actually gone on to become cosmonauts.

Reynolds dismissed the biography and opened that of the last male cosmonaut, *Soyuz* Commander Kostia Drupev. The *Soyuz* module was basically a primitive, wingless equivalent of the Shuttle—a three-capsule workhorse the Russians had used to ferry men to space and back since the sixties. It was a measure of the importance the Russians placed on the vehicle that they designated its command an ISS position.

Drupev, if anything, seemed an even worse candidate for murderer. The bio's photo showed a short, bearish man with the Tatar "moon face" of southern Russia— Kazakh, Kirghiz or something, for sure. His Asiatic eyes were narrowed further by his placid, unassuming grin. He'd been a pilot too, Reynolds noted, only Navy this time—flying YAK-38 vertical takeoff jets for the old Soviet Pacific fleet. His RKA record was exemplary, a smooth transition from cosmonaut training to joint RKA/NASA Shuttle missions, then onto backup missions for *Mir*. His personality inventory, likewise, confirmed the message of the man's face, rating him "self-effacing, efficient . . . a good team player."

Reynolds closed the document, grimacing.

*Not much there to turn into a vicious killer, either.*

Yet *somebody* had been turned into one. *Somebody* had been inside that faceless suit. That was the exasperating thing about the footage of Gary's death. His assail-

ant's use of an American EMU suit made it impossible
to judge who was inside. It wasn't just the gold-filmed,
UV-opaque visor that hid the killer's identity. The problem was the "one size fits all" policy NASA had adopted
for the new-generation EMUs. Though still assigned to
individual astronauts, the new suits were externally almost identical, thanks to modified inner garments that
stretched or shrank to the occupant's size. Russian
"Orlan" suits, which ISS residents were also provided
with, were a different story. They were fitted by shorten-
ing or lengthening limb lengths at the shoulder, elbow
and knee joints, leading to identifiable discrepancies. No
doubt that was why the killer hadn't used his.

Reynolds scowled. What cop could believe it? A situation where you had the offender, *on tape* for Christ's
sake, committing the crime. And you still didn't know
who he was.

It could have been any one of the cosmonauts inside
there. The EMU would hide the most elementary details
of physique, even the difference between Drupev's five
feet eight and Matchev's six three. It could even have
been the woman, Irina Ruskaya, of course, and Reynolds
brought up her biography to complete the set.

He read the woman's bio as her picture loaded. Mission Specialist Ruskaya was an astrobiology graduate
from the Moscow Institute of Biochemistry. She'd passed
cosmonaut training at the Yuri Gagarin Training Center,
Star City, with "one pluses," which Reynolds presumed
was top ranking. Her subsequent career seemed as dis-
tinguished. Reynolds skimmed the details: Shuttle *Mir*
mission STS-84; a 200-day stay on *Mir*; first female recip-
ient of the CIS "Long-Duration Spaceflight" medal.
Then her image came up on-screen, driving everything
else temporarily out of mind.

Reynolds's breath caught in his chest. He stared at the
woman's photo stupidly a full few seconds.

Then he recovered himself. He frowned at his reaction. It wasn't just that Ruskaya was beautiful, though
she was. Strikingly. The image was that of a young
woman—twenty-nine, Reynolds noted—whose fine-
featured face rose from a slim neck and ended in a tum-

ble of rich, dark hair. Brown eyes with the merest hint
of a Slavic slant completed the picture, looking out from
the woman's unblemished, milky complexion. Beautiful,
all right, but that was nothing. That could be dealt with.

The real problem was who she reminded him of.

For one shocked moment, Reynolds had thought he
was somehow looking at a picture of Alicia, one he
didn't know about, taken back when *she* was twenty-
nine. The year she died, that was, and Reynolds supposed the coincidence of ages was what had triggered
his confusion. For though Ruskaya resembled Ally—
both dark-eyed brunettes, both delicately featured, both
*beautiful*—the resemblance wasn't close. It was more a
similarity of *manner*. There was something in the challenging tilt of Ruskaya's head that reminded him dis-
tressingly of his dead wife.

Except with Ally, of course, it would have been accompanied by a mischievous grin. Not the firm mouth
and smoldering eyes of the female cosmonaut in front
of him.

Reynolds closed the document, disturbed. The momentary lapse had thrown him. He wondered uneasily
how he would cope with seeing the woman live, face-to-
face, when he got up to ISS.

*When this is how just her photo affects you . . .*

Reynolds took hold of himself. He'd cope, all right.
He'd cope because he had to, because it was true—it
*could* just as easily have been Ruskaya in that suit.

*A suspect in a homicide case, pal,* he told himself
roughly. *That's all she is to you.*

To shake himself out of the moment, Reynolds called
up the innocuously named <dump 61_43281. mpg>
video clip, the two minutes either side of Myers's death,
and watched it through. He ran it at half-speed, patiently
scanning the frames, though by now he'd seen it so many
times he knew it almost pixel-by-pixel.

Myers floating, listening to Ground's last words before
communication is cut . . . long lapse into static as the
array goes off alignment . . . grainy, staccato images as
it kicks back in . . . the killer's arm hammering, Myers's
terrified face . . . eerie silence on the control channel . . .

then an explosion of sound from Ground staff, delayed counterpoint to the blood erupting from Myers's breached skull and helmet . . .

Reynolds played it through, over and over. He was searching for something, anything, to give him a handle on the mystery of who had killed the astronaut. Any leverage he could use to force his way in.

He didn't get it. Instead, he got something else.

In frustration, he'd started playing the file backwards, searching for a different angle. It was on the third run through that it clicked.

*Wait a minute.* He frowned. *What was that?*

Reynolds went back to the spot, played it again. *There!* Frames 346 to 358. No mistaking it.

A sudden jerk of Myers's head.

Reynolds ran the frames again and again, fierce exultation gripping him. He couldn't see what it meant, but it shouldn't be like that, it was wrong, and that was something at least. He was so carried away that before he knew it he had the phone handset cradled against his shoulder and was tapping out the internal number for the room in Crew Block where Connor, like Reynolds himself, had been assigned.

"Connor." Matt's sleep-weary voice came down the line.

"Matt?" Reynolds said excitedly. "It's me. Sorry to interrupt your beauty sleep. I've got something here. Something to run by you."

"Edge, you bastard," Connor groaned. "What is it? Why aren't you asleep, for Christ's sake? We're leaving for Moscow in . . ." there was a pause as Connor checked his clock, ". . . four hours."

"I've been . . . what?" Reynolds said, arrested mid-sentence. His eyes automatically sought out the schedule SD had given him. In truth, the program had been so hectic he'd stopped looking at the damn thing, instead just taking what was thrown at him. But he was sure he hadn't overlooked a trip to Russia. "Moscow?" he continued. "When was this decided?"

"At the Task Force meeting," Connor grunted. "I told you about it yesterday. Two days' training on Russian

ISS systems at Star City. Never mind. What did you call for?"

Reynolds shrugged. Working his ass off in Moscow, working it off in Houston—what difference did it make? And at least he wouldn't have to spend six months there training. Like most ISS astronauts did.

"There's something on that goddamn video file," he answered excitedly. "The footage of Gary's death. I only just saw it. Bring up frames 346 to 358, you can see . . ."

He hesitated, remembering. *Shit, Matt won't have his computer.*

His old trainer was a dyed-in-the-wool Luddite, without even the elementary Windows training Detroit City cops got. Connor's laptop, when last seen, was weighing down a pile of reports on his office desk.

"Never mind," Reynolds continued, "I'll describe it to you. Frames 346 to 358 Myers jerks his head suddenly. It's a tiny movement—I only noticed it because I played the file backwards a couple of times. But it's almost as if he *sees* something."

"Uh huh," Connor said tiredly. "Like what?"

"That's the thing," Reynolds said, the words tumbling out. "It happens just before the array goes off and the image breaks up. Fifty-three seconds later it kicks back in and he's getting hammered. I counted it out—that's about enough time for the murderer to enter the airlock and blitz him."

He paused a moment, checking his reasoning. "Uh huh, fifty-three," Reynolds confirmed. "That's about right. My point is this—what if that twitch was Myers noticing the killer entering?"

The phone was silent a moment, save for Connor's labored breathing. The older man was thinking it through. "Okay," he said finally. "I'll buy that. So what about it?"

"Just this," Reynolds said tensely. "The murderer had to enter the airlock through the internal hatch, using the Equipment Lock Compartment behind it as a rudimentary airlock, right? That's the only way into the airlock from inside ISS. Now that hatch was at Myers's left in the airlock, looking at it from his point of view. That means Myers should have first sighted his killer coming from his left."

"Uh huh," said Connor, when nothing more was forthcoming. "So?"

"So . . ." Reynolds said, his voice dropping for the first time to a note of puzzlement, "why does Myers look right?"

# 4

"Sirs?"

Reynolds and Connor both looked up. The flight attendant, a wiry African American in pressed NASA whites, was leaning over the broad, white-leather seats.

"Sirs, the pilot has asked me to request you buckle up. He says we may be in for a few minutes rough traveling."

Reynolds looked out the large porthole. Thousands of feet below, the black North Sea ran into the jagged Norwegian coastline, pushing dark fingers deep inland. Ahead, beyond the coastal patchwork of human habitation, the terrain climbed up to the far-off towers of the Kjölen Mountains. He nodded sagely. "Uh huh," he said. "What is it, clear-air turbulence? He probably thinks we're going to run into a breaking wave over the Kjölens, right?"

"That's right," said the attendant, taken aback. "Are you a pilot, sir?"

"Pilot?" growled Connor. "Steward, this is 'all the way to the Edge' Reynolds—the best goddamn pilot in the U.S. Air Force. This man flew SR-71s for Strategic Air Command!"

"Really?" said the man, awestruck. "You used to fly Blackbirds?"

Reynolds nodded uncomfortably. For a moment his

mind slipped back and he was *there*— sitting in the cockpit of the super-slim spy plane, the molded joystick grasped in his right hand as he sped down the runway, the thump of the engines pounding his body as he pushed the throttle through the gate into afterburner. He pushed the images away. The Blackbird, and his time at SAC, were a world away from him now. A world he had left behind.

"Goddamn right," Connor continued. "This hombre is the only man to take a Blackbird over 100,000 feet and live to tell the tale. Read the history books if you don't believe me. He would have made Mach four too, if he hadn't been hit with a simultaneous flameout in *both* engines—right, Edge?"

The attendant looked at Edge in mute amazement, awaiting confirmation.

"C'mon, Matt," Reynolds muttered in embarrassment. "You know that isn't the whole story. My fuel controls stuck, remember? The bird took itself over 100,000. I was just along for the ride."

The steward let out a whoop. "Goddamn!" he said, shaking his head and laughing. As if to remind them of the pilot's warning, a tremor ran through the aircraft, throwing the man up against Connor's seat. "Well, gentlemen," he said, levering himself back up, "I have to get up front myself and buckle up. But you can be sure I'll tell the pilot he's got a Habu on board."

The man moved off, still shaking his head.

Reynolds looked out the window, trying to stifle his unease. *Habu*. The old Air Command nickname for the SR-71, derived from her supposed resemblance to an Okinawan snake. That *really* took him back.

Back to places he didn't want to go.

Kadena Air Base, Okinawa, Japan. That was where he'd met and wooed Alicia, all those years ago. Where he'd proposed to her, one crazy summer day out on that tiny boat in Naha Bay.

Reynolds turned his attention back grimly to the report he'd been reading, dispelling the memories. It was a dossier on Myers's life—a 1,000-plus-page summary of everything the astronaut had done, or had done to him,

right up to his brutal murder. Everything was there: birth
certificate, academic reports, psych assessments, employ-
ment records. Even his tax returns, for Christ's sake.

Reynolds scanned the bound pages patiently, ignoring
the jolting as the little jet, true to prediction, hit the
shearing mountain winds. He was trying to build a picture of the dead man. In Reynolds's experience, the first
step in solving a murder was not asking why the victim
had died. It was to get inside him, find out why he had
*lived.* Somewhere in the biographical maze would be
something—an insignificant detail maybe, something easily overlooked—that would hand Reynolds the tool he
needed to start picking apart the seams of Myers's death.

Insight.

His search for it wasn't helped by the cookie-cutter
normality of Myers's career. An honor-roll student and
chess champion at high school, Gary Myers had, according to the documentation, moved smoothly through
a bachelor's, then a master's, in Computer Science at
California State University, to a position in NASA's
Software Engineering Laboratory at Goddard Space
Flight Center. Acceptance as a candidate for the astronaut corps in 1999 had led to completion of basic training at Johnson and two Shuttle missions during the
construction phase of ISS, with predictable regularity.

Myers's selection for the fourth resident crew was a
little more unusual. At twenty-nine, he was the youngest
U.S. astronaut to have flown the mission. The discrep-
ancy was, however, explained by his designation: Mission
Specialist for Onboard Computer Systems. The International Space Station was the most complicated gadget
NASA had ever flown; Reynolds guessed Crew Selection
had been happy to bump Myers up the queue on the
strength of his software engineering background.

Reynolds chewed through the stultifying mass of
paper methodically as the C-20 winged them towards
Moscow. His patience was rewarded some half hour out
from landing, over Riga, when he flicked past a document whose format looked vaguely familiar. He
thumbed the few pages back to it.

*There.*

Reynolds stared at the document. Christ, he hadn't been mistaken; it *was* a court memorandum. He scanned the details . . . Central District Court of San Francisco . . . Gary Austin Myers . . . a nonrecorded conviction for "unauthorized access to a computer." He checked the date—17 May 1993. Myers's sophomore year at California State.

Reynolds leaned back in his seat. *A hacking charge? Myers?*

At that moment Connor, who had taken advantage of the subsided turbulence to visit the plane's communication suite, materialized in the aisle. In his hand was the loop of paper he'd retrieved from the fax—Reynolds's updated Moscow itinerary. The older man let out a low whistle, studying it. "You better hope you don't itch for the next couple of days, Edge," he said, lowering himself into his seat. "You're not going to have time to scratch, according to this."

"Who said the gulag was dead?" Reynolds replied, perfunctorily. "Lookit, Matt, what the hell is this?" he asked, passing Connor the open report.

Connor took a look at the document, then nodded in satisfaction. "Thought you'd be interested in that," he answered, working himself into a more comfortable position on his seat. "We dug that up in the background check for Gary's Personnel Security Clearance. If you look a little further, you'll see there's a deposition in there too."

Connor grinned.

"Seems Gary was something of a hacker in his youth. Nothing heavy, of course. Just kids jerking around. Well, unfortunately for Gary, not everybody saw it that way." He grimaced. "You remember the AT&T crash in the early nineties?"

Reynolds frowned. "What, Martin Luther King Day? Don't tell me Myers was involved in that?"

"No, not exactly. You remember how apeshit the Secret Service went over it? How they started rounding up all those teenage hackers on the West Coast? Well, it so happens Myers chose that particular time to play a little trick on the San Francisco Pacific Bell office." Connor shrugged. "He had a girlfriend working there apparently. So he cracks, or whatever the hell they call it, into their system on Valentine's Day and ties their terminals up running 'I love you, Jemima May,' or whatever her name was, over and over."

Connor laughed.

"There was no way the judge could let him off; he'd even put his name in the message. So he gave him a nonrecorded and left it at that."

"A romantic, huh?" Reynolds said. "So . . . what? He ever do it again?"

Connor shook his head. "Not as far as we know. Seems the court scared the piss so much out of him he never dared." He shrugged again. "Lucky for us too. Shit, Myers *wrote* a hell of a lot of ISS's command software. That's why he was up there in the first place." He looked at Reynolds. "What are you thinking?" he asked. "There's an angle?"

"Not really," Reynolds replied. "Just interesting, is all."

Connor nodded, opening his mouth to add something, but was interrupted by the appearance of Jacobson, the Security Directorate agent heading the detail that would guard Reynolds and Connor in Moscow. The tall, spectacled agent wore a perturbed expression.

"Adviser Connor," he said tersely. "Apologies for interrupting. I'm afraid there's a change of plans, sir. Doesn't look like we'll be able to land at Sheremetyevo after all. I've instructed the pilot to reroute to Khodinka military air base instead."

As if to confirm his words, Reynolds and Connor felt the aircraft bank left.

Connor frowned. Sheremetyevo was Moscow's main civilian airport. A gaggle of Russian dignitaries and press was supposedly waiting there at this very moment to photo-op the hasty induction of NASA's detective into the Investigations Directorate of Russia's Federal Security Bureau. A pathetic farce, Connor knew, aimed at fabricating a nonexistent solidarity between RKA and NASA over Myers's killing.

But a necessary one, nonetheless.

"Goddamn it, Max," he said testily. "That'll throw everything out. What's the problem?"

Jacobson shook his head. "Word's come through from the Militia Liaison Office. It's hairy down there, Adviser. Demonstrators are ripping the place to shreds."

He hesitated, glancing over at Reynolds. "They say there's no way they can guarantee Detective Reynolds's safety," he continued. "I'm afraid there's no choice, sir. Militia Liaison are adamant Khodinka is the only facility they can secure."

Connor swore.

"Okay," he said irritably. "Get on to RKA and see if they can't get at least some of the press out to . . . where is it? Khodinka? And contact the embassy too. Make sure those goddamn Lincolns get over in time to pick us up."

"Yes, sir," Jacobson replied. He turned to leave, but apparently feeling the need to say more, stopped and looked squarely at Reynolds. "I just want you to know, Detective," he said firmly, "you have nothing to fear. My team and I will keep you safe down there. No problem."

With that the lanky agent was away, hurrying to the communications suite, barking orders left and right.

Reynolds acknowledged the promise with a wry grin. Normally, he'd have laughed out loud—NASA panty-waists pledging to protect a Motor City homicide cop. Who probably saw more blood and horror in a week than they got in a lifetime.

The way things were, though, he was almost grateful. Reynolds rolled his left shoulder around, exploring again the unfamiliar absence of his Glock. Connor had insisted he stop wearing it, acclimatize himself for his firearmless stay on ISS.

*Can't have a gun up there, of course. All those pressurized modules, just waiting to get a bullet hole popped in them . . .*

Maybe Jacobson was right. Maybe he'd *need* protecting.

Beside him, Reynolds heard Connor snort cynically. He understood Connor's disdain. Despite the threat, both of them knew the demonstrations were nothing. Just piss and wind. The real danger was not out on the streets of Moscow. Out in the cold light of day.

It was in the shadows.

4:06 P.M., Moscow Time, 26 March 2005
Zvezdny Gorodok (Star City), Korolev, Moscow

"Go Home . . . U.S. Son of a Hore!"

Reynolds leaned forward, reading the placard through the smoked glass of the limo window.

"Think I should tell 'em they spelled it wrong?" he asked.

Connor laughed. Jacobson, on the seat across, looked pained. A loud "thunk" against the window—a chunk of dirty ice thrown by one of the braver protesters—caused the agent to wince, then frown severely.

Reynolds leaned back, taking the hint.

They pulled up to a broad gateway with a ramshackle militia checkpoint off to one side. The main entrance to Star City, Reynolds guessed. He was surprised to see that the guard station, though tiny, was packed with uniformed men—soldiers too, not militia. There were even APCs and a couple of tanks parked obtrusively to one side.

"What's with the marines?" he asked, surprised, as the embassy driver parleyed with the guard command. "Is this all for us?"

Connor grimaced. "Nope," he said, leaning forward to catch what the driver was saying. "Believe it or not, it's for the power company."

Reynolds cocked a disbelieving eyebrow.

"It's true," Connor insisted. "The Korolev District Electricity Company cut power to Mission Control for a couple of hours last week. RKA hasn't paid its bill for months—doesn't have the money. President Molodin himself had to intervene. The troops are here to stop them doing it again."

Reynolds's lip curled. "Cut the power . . . Jesus Christ. What kind of way to run a space program is that?"

Connor shrugged. "It's the conditions the Russians op-

erate under. Goddamn it, the government welshes on
their funding commitments about seventy-five percent of
the time. Some of these guys you'll meet today haven't
been paid for a year."

Reynolds shook his head in amazement. "How the
hell do they stand it? It's a wonder it doesn't drive the
poor bastards mad."

Connor's mouth set grimly. "It does, some of them,"
he replied. "Like last week. The Deputy Director of
Launch Sites Division—Grenovich or something—suicided. Right here in his office. RKA's third suicide this
year, apparently."

He wagged a finger at Reynolds.

"Just you remember that, Edge," he said waspishly,
"next time you're bellyaching about how bad you've got
it at JSC."

Reynolds grinned, despite himself. *Vintage Connor,
that performance.*

They cleared the checkpoint and drove into Star City
proper. Reynolds studied the massive complex with professional interest. Commissioned by Khrushchev, Zvezdny Gorodok—Star City—had been the heart of
Russia's space program from the start. From this center,
twenty miles north of Moscow, Russian flight controllers
had listened breathlessly on 12 April 1961, to radio calls
from Yuri Gagarin, 187 miles above the Earth on that
first-ever spaceflight. The whole seven-square-mile ag-
glomeration of aerospace industries, spaceflight facilities,
apartments, supermarkets and schools was a fantastic
monument to the monolithic state that had taken on the
States in the race for space. And briefly won.

It was also a living fossil.

The Lincoln rolled past building after building of archaic design, most with only scattered lit windows. Snow
lay uncleared on the roads, the black twin tracks of previous cars the only indicator of direction. A massive
brick cylinder towered off to one side—the centrifuge,
Reynolds knew, where cosmonauts were strapped in for
simulated g-force—but it was dark and silent. Zvezdny
Gorodok was like a dying behemoth, its skeleton still
intact, but its life force retreating slowly towards inexorable extinction. Reynolds felt stirred to pity at the sight.

It was a monument, all right. A monument to Russia's *loss* of the space race.

He pulled irritably at the ill-fitting polyester FSB "Police Major" uniform he'd had to don for the hurried ceremony at Khodinka. Connor had cunningly waited until he was in it to tell him he'd have to wear it all day. Reynolds understood, of course. It was to allow the Russians to save face—pretend he wasn't just an American cop, but a *Russian* one as well.

That didn't make it fit better, though.

PR duty wasn't over yet, either. When the embassy cavalcade reached its destination, RKA Headquarters, they were ushered into a somber gathering of Russian space agency bigwigs. Reynolds was disoriented, temporarily, by the weird sense of déjà vu it gave him. It was like any of the innumerable NASA meetings he'd sat through in the past three weeks . . . only different. There were the same suited apparatchiks and scientific staff, the same uniformed military figures—though in Russia's case they were not mere Defense liaison, being actual commanders from VKS, Russia's military space forces. But they looked subtly *different,* as if the meeting were a sketch of NASA, drawn from memory and not quite right.

And, of course, the proceedings were in Russian.

There was no real need for the translations the NASA liaison gave, though. The speech was painfully familiar, no matter what language.

*Dearly beloved, we are gathered here together . . .*

Reynolds sat through the boilerplate as patiently as he could. His irritation was increased by the fact that, apart from the pressure-cooked training on Russian ISS systems, PR was almost the only reason he was here. Investigative work was off-limits while he was in Moscow. Connor had made that clear.

"Your first job is to keep yourself alive up there," Connor had said. "You're only getting a tenth of the training you need as it is. What you're going to do in Moscow is familiarize, familiarize, familiarize. Got it?"

Accordingly, the investigative task force had been divided. Reynolds was point man. He would handle the murder from the angle of which cosmonaut had commit-

ted it, up on ISS. An SD team on Earth, meanwhile,
would investigate who, if anybody, had told the perpetrator to do it.

The NASA agents were no doubt at work, behind the
scenes, this very moment, Reynolds thought.
Background-checking RKA staff. Looking for links with
Korbalov and the terrorist centers in the Russian
military.

*Maybe somebody here, sitting in this room . . .*

Reynolds frowned. He could see that. He really could.
For, beneath the boilerplate, the protestations of friendship, there *was* an undercurrent of hostility. It erupted
into the open halfway through the NASA liaison officer's speech, when the man made reference to
". . . enduring relations no matter which cosmonaut is
guilty . . ." That sparked muttering, which quickly
swelled into uproar. Angry voices shouted guttural Russian—no need for translation there either. For a moment
it seemed things would spiral out of hand. Then RKA's
Director General, a rotund, beetle-browed man named
Yuri Belov, stepped in.

*"Pazhalusta,"* he said, raising a hand. He continued
in English when the conference room fell silent.

"Dr. McVeigh," he said, addressing the liaison officer.
"We must protest. RKA feels judgments like this are
premature. We ask you to remember—there are other
nationals aboard ISS. Not just Russians."

Reynolds restrained a cynical snort. Of course, the Director General no more thought Akira guilty than
NASA did. That was just what he *had* to say. To placate
the hostiles in his own camp.

"Of course, Director," the liaison officer added hastily. "You may rest assured that Detective Reynolds,"
here he glanced over at the seated detective, "will be
examining all possibilities. Please accept my apologies."

Belov nodded in response. The meeting stayed silent;
for some seconds it seemed the moment had passed.
Then a voice cut through the silence. "Perhaps it was
space itself that killed your astronaut, Dr. McVeigh."

The words were perfect Oxford-accented English, just
the slight thickening of vowels betraying the speaker's

Russian origins. The voice was a languid, yet icy, drawl. All eyes turned to its source, a lanky man whose careless dress—old, untidy gray suit; clashing, sloppily knotted tie—marked him instantly as scientific staff. Reynolds estimated he was somewhere over sixty. His face was a leathery mask and the shock of hair that sloped back from his forehead was gray-white. The man's eyes, though, glittered from deep sockets with a pale blue intensity undimmed by age. He seemed to find the scene amusing.

It was left to McVeigh to break the awkward silence that ensued. "Uh . . . ladies and gentlemen," he said, collecting himself, "Dr. Vladimir Alinov, Associate Director of Biomedical Science at Zvezdny Gorodok. Uh . . . you were saying, Doctor? Something about space itself?"

The man shrugged. "Our American colleagues are naïve," he said. "For you, everything can be pinned down, attributed to a cause. You forget we have more experience of long-duration spaceflight than you do."

He looked around the room, his face a study in polite incivility.

"Have you never considered how harsh and unnatural the environment of space is, gentlemen?" he continued. "And how pitiful our efforts to conquer it are? Even our cosmonauts, who you will acknowledge have the better of you in this respect, are unable to stand it more than a dozen months or so."

He shrugged again.

"It is obvious that humans are not meant to live there. If you ask me, the murderer has simply folded under the pressure and become insane. It shouldn't surprise us. The wonder is it doesn't happen more often."

The room's shocked silence deepened.

"Do you have specific information to offer, Dr. . . . Alinov?" Reynolds interrupted, his voice harsh and loud in the silent conference room. "Or just philosophical observations? I take it Biomedical means you do have contact with the Russian ISS crews?"

The Russian scientist switched his gaze to Reynolds.

"Indeed," Alinov said stiffly. Reynolds noted the glimmer of suppressed rage. *Touched a nerve with something there,* he thought.

"I do have some small contact with our cosmonauts," Alinov continued. "However, I have seen nothing out of the ordinary. You may rest assured I will report such information as comes my way immediately to our American colleagues."

"Dr. Alinov is at your disposal, Detective," said McVeigh hurriedly, "as are we all. I know I speak for both RKA and NASA when I say all of us are united in our desire that the perpetrator of this heinous crime be caught and brought to justice as soon as possible."

The NASA liaison officer looked around the room. "Now, if you don't mind, ladies and gentlemen, Detective Reynolds has a busy training schedule to fulfill. I suggest we let him get started." He switched his gaze to Reynolds. "Unless you have further questions, Detective?"

Reynolds shrugged noncommittally. He had no questions. None that could yet be answered, at any rate.

1:06 A.M., Moscow Time, 27 March 2005
Crew Wing, Yuri Gagarin Cosmonaut Training Center,
Zvezdny Gorodok

Reynolds lay flat on the single bunk and tried to sleep. His muscles ached from the four-hour session in the hydrobath, the Russian version of JSC's Neutral Buoyancy Pool, that afternoon. The unfamiliar Russian Orlan suit, though operating at less than half the pressure of his Titan Hardshell, had taken effort to master, and now he was paying for it.

He thought back over the session in the cramped pool, marveling at the Russians' stoicism. Shortly after the session began the pool's heating units had malfunctioned. Water temperature had started dropping by three degrees per hour. But the Russians had done nothing, just gone on with the simulations even though by the end the divers must have been freezing. Reynolds found later it was because no parts were available to repair the units.

*Alinov's right,* he thought suddenly. *We Americans are naïve. Everything works so smoothly for us.*

His brow creased at the memory of the Russian doctor. *The killer has obviously become insane. Humans are not meant to live in space.*

Reynolds wasn't overly surprised by the Russian's outrageous statements. He sensed that behind the desire to shock lay a genuine philosophical barrow; you could bet Alinov bored his fellow RKA scientists stupid discussing it. But what kind of man deliberately flaunted them at such a high-profile U.S.-Russian stroking session? When the very existence of Russia's space program—starving, demoralized and dependent on American funding—hung on riding out the storm that country's murdering cosmonaut had created. Who would do that?

*A bitter man. That's who.*

He ran back over Matt's words, spoken as they'd been hurrying from the meeting. Connor had grimaced at Reynolds's mention of Alinov.

"A piece of work, isn't he?" Connor said. "The investigative team will be taking a hard look at *him,* believe me. If Korbalov and the Patriotic Union aren't in touch with him, they should be. Alinov hates Americans. With a passion."

Connor barked out a laugh. "He's not keen on his own people either. You heard McVeigh call him Associate Director? Well, from what I hear, the goddamn emphasis is on 'associate.' Everybody in RKA seems to give him a wide berth. He plays almost no part in management at Biomedical. Apparently they just turn him loose on his own projects and let him go his own way."

"How come he's still here?" Reynolds asked.

Connor shrugged. "He seems to have an incredible ability to survive," he replied. "Alinov's managed to hang on to his job through every change of government in the past fifty years. He'd have to be the wrong side of seventy-five, by now."

Reynolds shook his head in amazement. "Must love the work," he muttered. "Or he doesn't have a pension plan."

Connor laughed. "Maybe. His bio says he was some

kind of geneticist when he was younger. Studied under
Lysenko."

"Lynsenko?" Reynolds frowned. He recognized the
name, vaguely. The discredited Stalinist geneticist, who
had claimed he could alter the genome of living organ-
isms at will. "What, the crackpot? With the giant beet-
roots and stuff?"

Connor grinned. "Don't let Alinov hear you talking
about his goddamn hero like that. He'll tear you a new
one." He looked at Reynolds shrewdly. "Why the
questions?"

Reynolds shrugged. "Just a passing interest," he said.

"Well, see it stays that way, soldier," Connor rasped,
as they hurried from the RKA building to the waiting
car. "You stick to what you're here to do."

Reynolds had promised, of course. But lying here
now, thinking about it, he felt inclined to break that
promise. There was something about Alinov that interested him. As if the man's bitterness was a crystallization
of the amorphous hatred Reynolds sensed seething
below the outward face of the Russian space agency.

*The kind of hatred that might erupt into fury. Smash
down on an American's helmet again and again, until it
breaks and his blood bursts out in a vaporous flood . . .*

That decided him. Reynolds fell asleep with one
thought uppermost. He'd go and visit Alinov. Check
him out.

1:19 P.M., Moscow Time, 27 March 2005
OCCS Simulator, Yuri Gagarin Cosmonaut Training Center,
Zvezdny Gorodok

He got his chance the next day at the familiarization
session for the OCCS—the computer system of ISS's
Russian segments. Though the backbone of station control was the American "Command and Data Handling
System," ISS astronauts had to understand Russian systems as well—particularly the "Caution and Warning"
indicator panels. The Russian technician, Valentina, was
demonstrating their Class One emergency sirens to
Reynolds when, true to form, one of the simulator's

power boards blew, grinding the session to a halt. Reynolds took advantage of the confusion to slip out of the building and away.

He struggled through the ankle-deep snow and biting Russian cold, trying to match the hulking buildings to the map he'd memorized. Reynolds had earlier wormed out of Valentina that Alinov's offices were in "Korolev-B Physical Science Center"—an old, otherwise disused facility of RKA's Biomedical Science division. That figured, given Matt's summary of the Russian's relations with his colleagues. But the run-down hangar-sized building was hard to find; it took Reynolds twenty minutes and two false starts before he had it. By that time his teeth were chattering uncontrollably. Reynolds pushed his way into the first door he found, not bothering to seek out the main entrance, and was rewarded with a blast of soothing heat.

For a moment Reynolds thought he was back in the emergency ward at Detroit Receiving. The place looked like a worn-out public hospital—cracked, ancient linoleum; thick, uneven paint on the concrete walls where new coats had been slapped over flaking old ones. Only there were no patients. Instead, around a cluster of untidy benches in the middle of the huge, dimly lit room, four or five technicians sat, some working with bulky scientific equipment that Reynolds couldn't identify, others hunched over the keyboards of archaic computers. All looked up at Reynolds.

*"Banat krytchne?"* one of them inquired, after a moment had passed.

Reynolds eschewed any attempt to mangle out the limited Russian Jacobson had primed them with. "Any of you guys speak English?" he said loudly, instead. He mimed the action of a mouth speaking with his hand. "I want to talk to Dr. Alinov."

His words provoked a flurry of conversation. After a few seconds of heated Russian, one of the technicians approached him hesitantly. "Please . . . you are American?" the man said, blinking nervously.

"That's right," Reynolds replied. "Jesus, I'm glad somebody around here speaks English."

The man nodded rapidly. "And you wish to speak to Associate Director Alinov?"

It was Reynolds's turn to nod. "Uh huh," he replied. "Reynolds is the name. We met yesterday."

The technician stood and fidgeted a moment, as if at a loss what to do. "Okay," he said finally, nodding once more. "Wait here." Reynolds stood while the man walked back to his bench and picked up the phone. The technician spoke a few sentences into it. Then he hung up and waited, looking at Reynolds oddly.

Strident footsteps sounded on the mezzanine overhead. Reynolds glanced over his shoulder; Alinov was thundering down the stairs. The Russian doctor shot Reynolds a scorching glance, but pushed past him without speaking. He addressed himself, instead, to the seated technician, who seemed to shrivel at the sound of Alinov's harsh, clipped Russian. Reynolds watched the scene impassively. The message was clear, even in Russian.

The guy was getting his ass chewed.

Finally, Alinov turned to Reynolds. His words, when they came, were bursts of tight, controlled fury. "What are you doing here, Detective?" he asked.

Reynolds shrugged. "A friendly visit, Doctor. I had a half hour to kill. I thought perhaps you could show me your laboratory."

Alinov's ice blue eyes glittered. "I'm afraid that would be quite impossible, Detective. My work is far too pressing."

Reynolds nodded. "I thought it might be," he said casually. "Well, no problem. I'm sure I can use the time somehow else. Like discussing with the Director General the details of the press release NASA will have to draft. Saying how certain of the Russians are obstructing the investigation into astronaut Gary Myers's death."

Alinov glared at him momentarily, then relaxed. "Very well, Detective . . . Reynolds, isn't it?" he said calmly. "I see how it is. I have my job to do, and you have yours. What is it you would like to see?"

Reynolds cast his eye around the room. "Oh, I don't know," he said. "What about here? What is it your staff are working on?"

Alinov shrugged dismissively. "It is a research program into the mechanism of cartilage cell loss in weightless conditions. No doubt you are aware that long-term exposure to microgravity results in loss of approximately five percent of bone and cartilage mass per month." He waved a hand in the air, as if to clear away something obscuring his words. "Well, to make a long story short, it is my belief the biochemical conditions conducive to this atrophy can be artificially averted. If I am right, it should be possible, using a combination of localized injections and a sound exercise program, to slow cartilage cell loss to virtually nothing. Bone cell demineralization, as well."

Reynolds shook his head. "Amazing. Tell me, Doctor, why haven't you publicized this? This is the first I've even heard of the possibility."

Alinov's lips tightened. "Detective Reynolds," he protested, "you are being unfair. Surely you don't wish to attach the blame for the American habit of constantly underestimating us to me as well?"

Reynolds felt a stab of pity for the Russian. Beyond the acid surface of the man's hostility lay something deeper, he realized. Despair. Reynolds was conscious anew of the gloomy atmosphere in the lab—the archaic equipment, the shoddy surrounds. It couldn't be easy to run research projects in such straitened circumstances.

"I'm sorry, Dr. Alinov," he said stiffly. "You're right, of course. Please accept my apologies."

Alinov inclined his head in response. "Indeed. Come then, Detective," he said shortly. "I will show you the rest of our facilities."

Reynolds followed him through a swinging door. A short corridor beyond opened up into a cavernous work space that Reynolds thought looked more like a factory than a research facility. It took a moment for his eyes to adjust to the dimness. The building was patchily lit, apparently only around areas of remaining activity.

"This is our research area proper," Alinov said brusquely, striding down the corridor. "As you can see, Detective, the current funding environment does not allow us to work at anything near full capacity. Still, we do what we can."

He came to a halt beside a semi-walled-off area. It seemed to combine the functions of laboratory and workshop. Untidy assemblages of the Soviet-era scientific equipment Reynolds had noted outside shared bench space with industrial-strength vices and the metal skeletons of half-finished objects. In the far corner, a workman in overalls was welding.

"This is our physiology workshop," Alinov continued. "We design and manufacture the exercise equipment used by our cosmonauts on the Space Station here. You are familiar with the reclining ergometer, yes?"

Reynolds nodded. He had been training on the RE—basically a horizontal bicycle whose pedaling motion had been altered to include a degree of lateral movement—at Johnson; he would have to use it himself during his time on ISS.

"Well, that was originally designed here. In fact, you will find . . ."

Reynolds gave an involuntary start, losing track of Alinov's words. He'd noted earlier the communications console in an alcove off the main workshop area. The bank of television monitors carried an image of the inside of ISS's Russian Research Module. Reynolds had assumed it was a simulation, the module a mock-up somewhere on the grounds of Star City. But then a woman appeared, floating on-screen.

It was the female cosmonaut, Irina Ruskaya.

*Jesus Christ,* thought Reynolds, stunned. *They must be able to communicate with ISS from here directly.*

As if to confirm it, the tech spoke a few sentences of guttural Russian into his headset mike. Ruskaya, on-screen, responded, gesturing towards something in the Research Module.

Reynolds frowned. The intrusion of the world on ISS threw him. It wasn't just the reminder of Connor's injunction against investigative work. Unconsciously, he realized, he had been using these days before launch to prepare—building, like he always did, the psychological terrain in which he would entrap the murderer. The mental groundwork, that was the key. It was what allowed Reynolds to hit his perps hard, and keep on hitting them till they broke. To walk in without it was suicide. The unexpected link to ISS felt like it caught him half-ready.

*There's more to it than that, though,* he told himself. He watched the woman's face, compelled. The unease he had felt, looking at her picture two days before, came flooding back.

*Why?* he wondered. *Why does she so remind me of Ally?*

Visions of his dead wife flickered before his eyes, mixing with the grainy images of the female cosmonaut. *This is crazy,* he tried to tell himself. *You'll be working this cooze over inside of three days.*

But it was no good. He was unable to look away.

"You seem perturbed, Detective," Alinov's voice broke in. "Is something wrong?"

"No," Reynolds replied stiffly, tearing his eyes from the screen. "I'm just surprised. I wasn't aware you had facilities for individual contact with ISS. I was under the impression all communication was handled through TsUP." TsUP was the Russian acronym for Mission Control, Moscow.

Alinov shook his head.

"You're thinking in American terms, Detective. Our philosophy is different. In fact, this is only one of several divisional facilities in Star City from which ISS can be contacted directly." He smiled icily. "But perhaps you wish to take advantage of our facilities, no? You are required to interview our cosmonauts, are you not? Perhaps you would like to talk to Irina now?"

Reynolds's lip twisted sardonically. "Thank you," he said, mock polite. "That won't be necessary."

"Ah," said Alinov, "what is the English expression? You are . . . keeping your powder dry? Very sensible, Detective."

The two of them resumed walking.

"As you know, Detective," Alinov continued, "my position is Associate Director of the Division of Biomedical Science. In the past that meant something more than just responsibility for devising onboard health regimes. We were also the sole Life Science research body for our country's space program."

Reynolds's eyebrows rose politely. "Impressive," he said.

Alinov shrugged. "Well," he said, waving a deprecating hand at the unoccupied and darkened offices they were passing, "you see for yourself our situation. There is very little of that anymore."

"It must be difficult," Reynolds commiserated. "You have a special interest in genetics, I believe. Adviser Connor tells me you studied under Lysenko."

Alinov stopped abruptly, shooting Reynolds a piercing glance. "There is no need to be coy, Detective. I understand your meaning entirely. You mean Lysenko the fool, Lysenko the charlatan, Lysenko the disproven by history—do you not? Come, where is the plain speaking you Americans pride yourselves on?"

"Well." It was Reynolds's turn to shrug. "He was proved wrong, wasn't he? Genetic characteristics are inherited, not acquired."

Alinov's face flashed fire. His lips set momentarily in a grim line, then, with visible effort, relaxed.

"In some respects certainly," Alinov admitted, "Trofim Denisovich was wrong. The genetic mechanism. The homology problem."

He shook his head, and the look he gave Reynolds was pure loathing.

"But how little you really know him," he continued. "He was a great man. A maker of men. Is it wrong to seek to improve things, Detective? To dream of changing them? Should a great man be mocked because he thought to take feeble man and turn the force of mind to bettering him?"

By this time Alinov was inches away from Reynolds, his leathery face once more flushed with anger.

"You are asking the wrong person, Doctor," said Reynolds calmly. "I am no geneticist."

Alinov glared a moment more.

"Indeed," he said finally, regaining his composure. He stepped away from Reynolds and resumed walking. "And neither am I, these days. I content myself with some few experiments, cobbled together as best I can." He glanced at Reynolds oddly. "Perhaps you would like to see one, Detective?"

Alinov led Reynolds through the labyrinth of deserted research stations to a far corner of the building, where sat a white metal cylinder some twenty-five feet high by sixty long. *Vacuum chamber,* guessed Reynolds, noting the huge pumps at the cylinder's far end. Four steps led up to a metal observation dais halfway along its length, where a thick, glass window punctured the hull. Cyrillic lettering, once stenciled in red on the white metal, had faded to weak brown, leaving only faint outlines of the familiar CCCP.

*A relic,* thought Reynolds, as Alinov spun the unlocking wheel and swung the heavy round hatch open. The two of them stepped over the lip and into the chamber. *Just like Alinov himself . . .*

The Russian doctor flicked a switch, activating weak overhead lights. They revealed a prechamber, in which they were standing, that led through a sealable door to the inner, main chamber. Reynolds was impressed. The room was huge—nearly the full twenty-five feet high and about forty long. Stainless-steel benches ran the length of it. Two lines of handholds stretched up the curving walls. Standing forlornly in the middle of the grated metal floor, ridiculously small in the huge expanse, was an old metal cart bearing a few experiment racks.

Alinov crossed to it. "Here, Detective," he said, rummaging through one of the racks and emerging with a tiny seed, which he passed to Reynolds. "What do you think of this?"

Reynolds peered at it. "It looks like a seed to me," he said.

"It is a seed, a pearl-millet seed," Alinov said impatiently. "Feel the surface," he urged.

Reynolds rolled it between thumb and forefinger. "It feels smooth," he shrugged. "What's a millet seed supposed to feel like?"

"The skin is normally rough," Alinov replied. "This one is smooth because I have manipulated its genes in favor of a nonpermeable outer membrane."

A gleam came into the Russian scientist's eye.

"What would you say, Detective, if I told you that this seed can withstand conditions of near vacuum, without suffering any tissue damage at all?"

Reynolds passed the seed back to Alinov. "I'd say it would have to be the only millet seed on the planet that could."

"It is," replied Alinov absently, dropping the seed back into a petri dish and sliding the rack back in. "It is. Along with these others. And the many near misses I have had."

He turned to face Reynolds, his face peculiarly afire. "You would not believe it, Detective," he whispered. "The years of work. The endless disappointments." He shook his head at the memory.

"But all worth it. In the end. Imagine, Detective, a crop seed that can maintain itself in space . . . indefinitely. That is programmed to germinate with the return of pressurized conditions. Can you see the implications?"

Reynolds's face wrinkled dismissively. "An interesting curio, Doctor," he said.

A shadow passed over Alinov's face. "It is no curio, Detective," he said, tight-lipped. "I can assure you. It is precisely technologies such as these that man will have to utilize if he is to ever truly conquer space."

He cocked his head, apparently listening to something outside the chamber.

"Would you excuse me a moment, Detective?" he said coldly. "One of my assistants is calling."

Reynolds moved aside to let him pass, wondering if the man had really heard anything. Probably Alinov had just had as much of him as he could stomach at the moment. He leafed through the bound notes atop the trolley idly as he listened to Alinov's receding footfalls.

Something bothered him about the setup here. He had the definite impression Alinov's little "mad scientist" routine had been put on purely for his benefit, that Alinov, for obscure reasons of his own, was getting a kick out of the masquerade. He flipped the folder shut and looked around the chamber once more.

*Fuck, this place is huge,* he thought again.

The Russians must have used it for testing suits. He tried to picture the chamber in its heyday—the figures inside moving clumsily in their cream Orlan suits; the technicians outside issuing instructions via the suit radios. He had nearly succeeded in summoning the mental image when a sound behind him pierced his concentration, sending him momentarily rigid with shock.

The outside hatch was closing.

He spun around, but before he could complete the action the hatch had clanged shut, the inside door following a second later. Then a heavy thrum started up from just outside the chamber.

*The pumps.*

Reynolds understood it all in a flash. The walk through the deserted facility to here, Alinov's enjoyment of some hidden secret, the pretended call from an assistant.

The man had lured him to his death. *Like a lamb to the slaughter.*

Reynolds moved rapidly. He ripped one of the experiment racks out of the trolley, scattering seeds and smashing glass labware. He leapt over to the handholds running up the curved wall and swung himself up them one-handed, dragging the rack in the other, heading for the observation window. He didn't even look at the door—that was madness. Alinov wouldn't have left him a way out—if there was one, you could bet Reynolds would never find it. Not in time. Reynolds's only experience with vacuum chambers had been the smaller units at Johnson, but even so, he was in no doubt. The pumps would have the air sucked out of this tin can in sixty seconds. Max.

His only hope, a minuscule one, was the window.

Reynolds wasn't fool enough to think he could batter his way through what was probably two-inch-thick glass in sixty seconds. But he might just be able to weaken it enough for pressure to do the rest. At the very least there was a chance somebody would see the commotion and investigate.

He reached the top rung and swung the rack overhead, driving a corner—SMASH—into the glass. A chip flew off, narrowly missing his head. He swung it back for another hit, resisting the urge to yell. There was no chance of anyone hearing, not over the pumps and, in any case, he had to get the air out of his lungs.

Quickly.

Reynolds hyperventilated as long as he dared, five seconds or so, to saturate his blood with oxygen. Then he exhaled savagely, pulling his diaphragm in tight to expel every last ounce of air. He knew from basic training at Johnson, back in '89, the first thing a lungful of oxygen molecules did upon exposure to vacuum was exit the body. By the fastest route possible—straight out of the chest cavity.

Mashing the lungs to bloody pulp along the way.

Reynolds flung the rack at the glass desperately, dislodging another chip. But it was no good. The chips were mere divots on the window's surface. The glass was probably shatter proofed, built to withstand pressure of five atmospheres or more. He let the rack fall to his side in despair; it slipped from his fingers and clattered to the floor below.

Christ, his temples felt tight! Was it his imagination playing tricks? Or had the pressure already dropped that much?

He waved his arm helplessly in front of the window. Chest muscles jerked at his rib cage, demanding he draw breath.

Half-forgotten figures reeled through his brain.

At the instant of exposure to vacuum, moisture at the body surface—sweat, saliva, and sebum—boils away. Mild swelling of skin at ten seconds, as gases and liquids under the skin seek to escape. The onset of mental confusion at fifteen to twenty seconds as the last of the blood's dissolved oxygen circulates to the brain. A slide into unconsciousness some time after that as the brain progressively shuts down. Onset of surface tissue damage at thirty-five seconds, and probable caisson disease as dissolved nitrogen bubbles out of the bloodstream. Cell collapse in heart and lungs at sixty seconds, leading to circulatory interruption.

Then death.

Reynolds's arm slumped. *Christ, it's hopeless.*

No doubt about it now—the pressure had dropped to nearly nothing. His skin felt tight as a drum, all over, and it was *moving*—shimmying like there were worms under it. He started climbing down the handholds, but

lost his grip halfway and skidded to the bottom, hitting
his face on one of the lower rungs. His lip split; he felt
the wound tingle as blood vapor sprayed out of it.

Reynolds turned and began groping to the door—
not because he thought there was any hope, but because it was unbearable to die standing still. He put
one foot in front of the other carefully. He couldn't
afford a fall. Another cut like that on his lip and the
fluid would just piss from his body. Like water from a
knifed plastic bag.

His vision blurred. The pressure pushing out against
his skull was incredible.

Halfway to the door, he stopped in confusion. He
thought, briefly, that the pumps had stopped—he
couldn't hear them throbbing anymore. But after a moment, he realized. The pumps hadn't stopped, it was just
that another sound had drowned them out.

The hiss of fluid and air leaving his body.

Reynolds resumed his blind progress towards the
door. Every movement seemed weak, unreal—he pictured the electrical messages to his muscles suffering in-
terference from the vapors boiling out of his body. He
shuffled a few steps further, uttering ridiculous appeals
to the fleeing molecules.

*Don't give up the ship, boys. Urge you to reconsider.*

His mouth fell open with the effort of walking. Saliva
sizzled off his tongue.

Reynolds tried to focus. The black curtain of unconsciousness was wavering over him, but he could see it
now—the door, just two steps away. He had to make
the door, that was very important. He lifted his leg for
a step, but the action was too much for him and he
stumbled, grabbing a handhold for support.

Reynolds steadied himself blindly for another try. His
vision had hazed over completely now. The hiss in his
ears had grown to a roar.

*Got to make that next step, soldier,* he told himself
sickly. *Got to.*

He summoned his last reserves and lifted his leg triumphantly, but just as rapidly the strength went out of
him and the other buckled, dropping him like a stone.

His last thought, before he hit the metal, was a moment of surprise, clicking in at the back of his mind.

*Wait a minute. Why does a chamber like this have . . . ?*

But then the curtain was back, and his fall to the floor was lost in the fall into utter blackness.

The voices were low rumbles at the periphery of consciousness.

After them came the feelings. Hard, cool concrete pressing against his back. Deft fingers at the collar of his flight suit, unbuttoning and tugging the zip down.

*Where am I?*

The incredible, cloying feel of *air* gave him the answer.

*Outside the chamber. Somebody must have pulled me out.*

He opened his eyes. A circle of people were clustered around him, cylindrical shapes with white smears where their faces should be. He blinked hard. Something was wrong with his eyes. He felt liquid oozing from a nostril and dashed a hand at it irritably, imagining his nose was running. But the hand came away bright red; the vacuum must have broken the capillaries inside his nose.

"Please don't move, Detective," a voice to his left said. "Medical personnel will be along to attend to you shortly."

*Alinov.* Reynolds recognized the icy drawl, though the man's face was indistinguishable. He sat up, ignoring the Russian doctor. The action released a gush of blood from his nose, spattering down the front of his flight suit.

"Please, Detective," Alinov repeated. "You have just been through a very dangerous accident. I must insist you restrain yourself until the medics ascertain your condition."

His hands pressed on Reynolds's shoulders. Reynolds squinted, trying to bring the faces around him into focus. Most of the figures were wearing white lab coats—Alinov's staff. A figure in a dark brown uniform squatted at Reynolds's feet. *Security guard?* He screwed his eyes up further and managed to make out the dark shape of the holster at the man's waist. But that was it.

Beside him, Alinov clucked his tongue. "You see?"

he said. "You have lost a great deal of fluid, Detective, including from your eyeballs, which is why you are having trouble with your vision. You *must* rest. Here. Have some water."

A large beaker was pressed to his lips. Alinov was right about that much. His throat was parched. Reynolds gulped the water down, draining the beaker. When it was taken away he nodded weakly and sagged back against the hands holding him, as if to comply. Then he bucked forward, launching himself at the dark figure at his feet.

Before the man had time to react, Reynolds had scrabbled the pistol out of his holster. He used the surprised guard's backward topple to help pull him to his feet. He hefted the gun as he straightened; it would be a Tokarev, he knew, which meant no safety. He thumbed the hammer back and felt it settle into the half-cock notch with satisfaction. He spun around, knocking one of the white-coated figures flying, and groped at the blur that was Alinov. His hand settled on the man's lapel. He pulled the Russian doctor towards him, simultaneously driving the point of the pistol into his neck. Several of the circled figures shouted.

"Dr. Vladimir Alinov," he choked out, the words provoking a fresh sprinkle of blood from his nose. He shook his head to clear it, spattering Alinov's coat front. "I am arresting you for the attempted murder of an American police officer. You have the right to . . . the right to remain silent."

His breath failed him. His words were a strangled gasp.

"Anything you say can be used against you in a court of law," he wheezed.

Heated Russian voices broke out behind him. He sensed, rather than saw, Alinov put up a hand. The babbling stopped.

"Very dramatic, Detective," Alinov said evenly. "However, you are confused. The truth is more prosaic, I'm afraid. You have been the victim of an unfortunate accident."

He signaled over Reynolds's shoulder.

*"Alexei? Skazhi Ditektiv shto sluchilas,"* he commanded.

Reynolds glanced over his shoulder uncertainly. A short, rotund figure had stepped out from the surrounding circle. He appeared to be wringing his blurred hands. On seeing Reynolds's gaze, he launched into a torrent of Russian.

Reynolds blinked in confusion.

"Indeed," said Alinov calmly after a moment, cutting across the assistant's ongoing speech. "What you have just heard, Detective, is a deservedly abject apology from one of my assistants, Alexei Ossipov, who is responsible for your distress. He came to carry out the daily low-pressure tests for the project I showed you. Rather carelessly, he initiated the pump sequence without checking the status of the equipment."

The chubby assistant broke in with another fevered stream of Russian.

*"Jvatik,"* Alinov said, silencing the man. "He begs you to forgive his criminal foolishness, Detective. He assures you he would never have activated the chamber if he had known you were inside."

Reynolds's hold loosened as he tried to work this out. He squinted heavily and was just able to bring the assistant's round face into focus. There was no doubting the man's mortified expression.

"Wait a minute," Reynolds said, turning back to Alinov and tightening his grip anew. "You knew he was due to initiate the depressurization. You lured me into the chamber, counting on your assistant to unwittingly complete the crime."

*"Eta maya ashivka!"* Ossipov burst out anew from behind Reynolds. *"Ya pitalsa ujadid rana . . ."*

*"Jvatik Alexei!"* Alinov ordered. "I'm afraid not, Detective," he continued. "The truth of the matter, as Mr. Ossipov has been shamefacedly confessing, is that he was attempting to complete the daily session outside the scheduled time, which is at four o'clock this afternoon, in order to leave his post early, for reasons of his own."

Reynolds's hold weakened fractionally again.

"You see how it is, Detective," Alinov continued

stiffly. "There is no way I could be aware of the danger Alexei's plans put you in. It was, of course, myself from whom he was most intent on keeping them."

Reynolds glanced over his shoulder in uncertainty. The assistant was nodding at him vigorously, his still-blurred face a comic mix of encouragement, guilt, and sick fear.

"An accident, Detective," Alinov said softly. "You see?"

"An accident," Reynolds murmured, allowing the gun to fall away from Alinov's neck. His other hand sagged against the Russian doctor's chest.

"An accident," Alinov repeated. He extended a hand slowly towards the pistol. "May I?" he asked.

Reynolds offered no resistance. The Russian eased the Tokarev out of his hand, barrel first, and handed it over Reynolds's shoulder to the security guard. Just then, pounding footsteps sounded on the concrete.

Reynolds didn't even have to look.

*Jacobson and his boys. Riding to the rescue.*

Sure enough, a second later the lanky security agent appeared, flanked by two colleagues, all holding their pistols two-handed out in front of them.

"Nobody move," Jacobson barked. "What the hell's going on here?"

Reynolds gestured impatiently. "It's okay, Jacobson," he said. "Put the gun away. We've been through that already."

"Detective Reynolds has had a fortunate escape from a very dangerous accident," Alinov spoke up boldly. "If my staff and I had not arrived to pull him from the vacuum chamber you see behind us when we did, he would have shared the fate of your astronaut, Gary Myers."

Jacobson stared at the Russian scientist. He gave a start, catching sight of the blood spattering Reynolds's RKA jumpsuit. "Jesus, Detective! You're bleeding!"

Reynolds shook his head, stepping back from Alinov tiredly. "It's nothing. Just a nosebleed." He adjusted his collar irritably.

"Well, Doctor," he said, addressing Alinov. "It appears I owe you an apology. I hope you can forgive my overhasty suspicions."

Alinov inclined his head condescendingly. "Not at all, Detective," he said, the satirical note creeping back into his voice. "In truth, I found it quite exciting. Like being in one of your American movies momentarily."

"No shit?" said Reynolds sourly. "Well, thanks again for saving my skin. C'mon, Jacobson," he said, turning to the security agent. "I'd better get back. The guys at Sim Control will be wondering where I've got to."

"Detective," said Alinov sharply, "I would suggest you take my advice and stay here until the medics arrive. Exposure to near vacuum is not something to be taken lightly. At the very least you should have yourself checked for signs of incipient caisson disease."

"Caisson dis . . ." Jacobson gaped. He peered at Reynolds nervously. "Maybe Dr. Alinov is right, Detective," he said. "Maybe we should get you checked out."

"I'm okay," said Reynolds irritably. "Let's just get out of here."

He pushed his way through the crowd, dismissing Jacobson's offered arm with a scowl. He was still disoriented, but he could feel his strength returning. The sooner he was out of here, the better.

His vision was getting clearer second by second. And he'd had about as much of Alinov's sarcastic expression as he could stand.

9:49 P.M., Greenwich Mean Time, 28 March 2005
A NASA C-20 Transporter over Moscow

"Edge?" said Connor softly. Reynolds looked up; Matt was leaning across the top of the aisle seat. "How're you feeling?"

Reynolds stared at him, puzzled, until understanding hit.

*The flight surgeon.*

The NASA flight surgeon at Zvezdny Gorodok had told Reynolds he might experience dizziness and loss of balance when his return flight reached high altitudes—a memento of his fleeting exposure to vacuum. The doctor had been amazed how little damage Reynolds had suffered—nothing but blotching of the skin on his hands. Even that was fading. He was so impressed he'd asked permission to do a follow-up study on the detective, when he got back from ISS.

Reynolds wiggled his head experimentally.

"Fine, Matt," he said. "No problems."

Connor nodded, relieved.

"Let's hope it stays that way. Jesus, Edge, I'm sorry," he scowled. "That Jacobson should have his goddamned balls lopped for . . ."

"Forget it, Matt," Reynolds interrupted. "It wasn't your fault. Or Jacobson's." He shrugged. "I was doing what I shouldn't have been. End of story."

Connor grinned. His eyes traveled down to the report Reynolds was reading. "Still are, from the looks of it. Where'd you get that, anyway?"

Reynolds looked sheepish. He had open the Security Directorate cull of the files on Alinov. Properly speaking, he should have been leaving such things to the SD task force in Moscow. Connor was right. He had enough on his plate as it was.

"Just some bedtime reading, Matt," he muttered. "I got it off McVeigh. Told him you'd asked for it."

Connor shook his head.

"Goddamn you, Edge," he laughed. "Just be sure to get some sleep this flight, okay? Remember, you're up for launch prep in less than sixteen hours. Okay?"

With that the older man moved off. Reynolds went back to the documentation spread out in front of him.

It was pretty thin. Apart from biographical documents—which confirmed that Alinov was, in fact, exactly seventy-five and *had* studied under Lysenko, at the USSR Academy of Sciences Institute of Genetics—there wasn't much there. Alinov had kept his head down, at least these past twenty years. He wasn't even mentioned in the included register of RKA staff censured or dismissed for collaboration with the 1991 KGB putschists.

Reynolds read through the stuff without interest. He was about to throw it in and take Matt's advice, when he came to the last document in the pile. It was, of

all things, a copy of some Cornell University student's
Ph.D. thesis:

## Prometheus Unbound: Studies in the Totalitarian Science Ethic

Reynolds scanned the abstract, frowning. He couldn't
see the relevance at first. The paper seemed to be pos-
iting an inherent, amoral superiority to totalitarian research on humans. It opened with a quote Reynolds
recognized from somewhere—"what is to be feared is
that immorality may lead to greatness." The contents
outlined chapters comparing Nazi eugenics to Soviet psychiatric and medical programs. The usual revolting stuff
was there—Auschwitz, the medical experiments. There
was a sizeable section on Soviet genetics too; Reynolds
saw Lysenko's name listed several times. On a hunch,
he flipped over to the index.

Sure enough, Alinov's name was there too.

Reynolds flicked back to the numbered page and
scanned through with a finger until he located it. Then
he moved back a few paragraphs and began reading.

*. . . indication of disturbing potential of uninhibited
totalitarian science seen in Soviet genetics. After the
correction of the Lamarckian error that attended the
downfall of Trofim Denisovich Lysenko in 1965,
Soviet genetics swiftly returned to Mendelian ortho-
doxy. Spearheading the return were four brilliant
students of Lysenko, nicknamed "the commu-
nards." Three of the four, Myushin, Licharin, and
Vyshev, went on to become leading lights in the All
Union Academy of Sciences. In fact, of the three . . .*

Reynolds skipped ahead a couple of paragraphs.

*. . . but can most be seen in the chilling career of
Vladimir Alinov, widely acknowledged as the most
brilliant of the four. Though much of Alinov's early
work, when he was employed by the Biological
Weapons Research Bureau of the GRU (Soviet Mil-*

*itary Intelligence), remains classified, it is evident
that he made astonishing advances in gene manipulation technique, considering the era. In particular,
his work on restriction enzymes for gene shearing,
though virtually unacknowledged in the West, fore-
shadowed by some three decades techniques developed for the Human Genome Project (Orpen-Stow,
2002, p. 135).*

*It is not known when Doctor Alinov began exper-
imentation with the genetic manipulation of human
zygotes and what, if any, GRU sanction he had for
the work. That organization, at any rate, disowned
him when it came to light and Alinov was de-
nounced at the 1967 All Union Academy of Sciences Congress. Yet it is characteristic that Alinov
was punished by nothing more than transfer to
RKA, the Russian equivalent of NASA. Incredibly,
it is not even clear that the GRU connection was
ever broken . . .*

Reynolds laid the report down, shuddering. He
guessed that the reference to Alinov's military intelligence ties was what had piqued SD's interest—the investigative team would be looking hard at that. But it
was the gruesome implications of that one line that disturbed Reynolds.

*Manipulation of human zygotes.*

Screwing around with human embryos. He could see
Alinov doing that. He really could.

He shivered, remembering Alinov's vacuum chamber.
With its millet seeds, experiment racks, and "technologies to conquer space."

*Wonder what other goodies he's brewed up in there?
Over a long and less than savory career.*

Reynolds cocked his head, frowning. Thinking about
the chamber brought back the question that had been
niggling him these past twenty-four hours.

*What was it I noticed in there? Before I went out?*

He closed his eyes and tried to focus, but nothing
came. All he could remember was that one instant of

surprise, grabbing his attention momentarily as he collapsed.

*Something about the chamber. Something . . . weird.*

Reynolds abandoned the attempt in frustration, instead leaning forward to look out the round window. Far below, the last lights of European Russia were visible, dropping behind as the jet sped out over the Gulf of Finland. He watched them silently for a moment, sitting back only when the last had slid from sight.

The next time he saw them would be from space.

# 5

T minus 2 hours, 15 minutes; 9:43 A.M.,
Central Standard Time, 29 March 2005
Launchpad 39A, Kennedy Space Center

The closeout crewman stuck his head out the door of
the White Room, clamping his white NASA cap to his
head with one hand.

"REYNOLDS," he bawled through the gusting wind.
"YOU READY?"

Behind him, at the end of the crew access arm, Space
Shuttle *Endeavor* hung like a clawed bird off the towering, orange cylinder of the external fuel tank.

Reynolds nodded, not even attempting to shout an
answer. The wind up here on the stack had to be nearly
twenty knots. He shivered, despite the protection of his
orange pressure suit.

"OKAY," the crewman yelled, holding two fingers up
to Reynolds. "TWO MINUTES, ALL RIGHT?"

His head withdrew, leaving Reynolds alone with the
view. Two hundred feet below him, on the pad, huge
fuel pipes snaked away from the stack like entrails.
Clouds of condensation rose from the tank as supercooled liquid oxygen and hydrogen were pumped into its
chambers at 1,300 gallons a minute. Beyond the waiting
shuttle, the flat, marshy ground of Kennedy stretched
out to sea, where wheeling flocks of seagulls were just
visible. The towering block of the Vehicle Assembly
Building made it impossible to see the causeway, but he
knew from the briefing at crew breakfast that it was

crowded—cars backed up all the way to Cocoa Beach, angry demonstrators and National Guard nearly out-numbering spectators.

Reynolds kept his eyes fixed ahead, on the White Room and the orbiter, resisting the temptation to look around at the distant Launch Control Center. That was where the visitor galleries were, on top of the low white building. Where the other crew members' families would be gathered, waiting for the launch.

*Where she would have stood.*

He tried to let go of the thought, let the breeze take it from him, but even the breeze itself reminded him, and suddenly he was *there,* back on top of the LCC that warm spring night in 1989. *Atlantis,* cradled in the distant stack, seemed carved from bone, bleached white by the xenon floodlights. Alicia was in his arms, tomboy-beautiful in jeans, halter top and baseball cap. She was looking up at him, teasing.

"How can I be sure, flyboy?" she'd said, her eyes glinting wickedly. "Huh? How do I know you're not gonna take up with some spacewoman up there?"

He had pulled her tight to him, drunk with something more than the cheap champagne the guard had let them smuggle up.

"No way, babe," he'd said fiercely. "Never. It's you and me, angel babe. Forever."

And there it was again, that hot knife of grief carving into him, like it had every other day since he'd found her there, lifeless and bloody. That was what hurt—that he hadn't been able to keep his promise. He'd loved her more than anything, more than life itself, but in the end that love had counted for nothing.

Elwood had seen to that.

"OKAY, REYNOLDS," the closeout crewman yelled, shattering Reynolds's reverie. He beckoned Reynolds with one hand. "YOU'RE GO FOR PREP."

Reynolds moved down the access arm, the wind forc-ing him to hold onto the box-steel safety rail with the hand holding his helmet bag. He stepped through the swinging door in a subdued frame of mind, into the tiny, white-walled prep room that clamped onto the Shuttle hatch.

It was always the same. Thinking about Alicia still left him shaken.

The closeout supervisor obviously took it for first-flight jitters. The man kept up a steady banter, in between snapping his gum, as the three white-overalled crew members swarmed over Reynolds—hooking up the emergency oxygen system, fitting the heavy escape chute and loading his suit pockets with the survival kit components.

"Yessir," he said, pulling the chute straps to, "you are some lucky bastards to be getting out of this weather. Weatherwoman says a cold front is moving in; we're gonna slip down to thirty-six degrees before the day's out. Can you believe that?"

He shook his head.

"Thirty-six. Man, I gotta move to New Mexico."

Reynolds let him talk, almost grateful for the chatter. At least it kept his mind from straying back.

Finishing up, the man slapped Reynolds on the back. "LAUNCH, this is CLOSEOUT-1," he said into his mike. "Reynolds is prepped. Okay, soldier," he grinned at Reynolds, after listening to his earpiece for a moment, "that's it. You're go for ingress."

Reynolds crawled through *Endeavor*'s side hatch awkwardly, hoisting his helmet bag and oxygen backup ahead of him. The female closeout crew member followed.

Reynolds was surprised, on entering, to see Rodriguez, the payload specialist, strapped into one of the middeck seats. The manifest had Reynolds himself down as the sole occupant of *Endeavor*'s middeck during ascent. Rodriguez should have been up on the flight deck, with the other crew.

"What's going on, Eli?" he said loudly. "They kick you out of business class?"

Rodriguez shook his head, waggling his helmet comically. He unsnapped it and lifted it off his head with gloved hands. "Nope. Change of plans, Edge. You've been bumped up. Kennedy wants you up behind him on flight deck."

He flashed Reynolds an awkward grin.

"Must have forgotten how to fly this thing."

Reynolds snorted; his own Shuttle pilot training was so far in the past he doubted he'd even be able to connect his lap harness unaided. He could guess the real reason. He knew from his own time how close bonds between crew members got. You lived, worked and trained with these guys, sometimes for months on end, and in the end you got so tight with them you knew them better than your family. These guys, the crew of STS-115, had had their mission—to retrieve the SOHO II satellite and correct its orbit—bastardized at the last moment to include Reynolds and a flight to ISS. Since his crash refresher course had started, Reynolds had only had the opportunity to meet with them three times. By inviting him up to the flight deck they were doing what they could to make him one of the team.

"Thanks, Eli," he told Rodriguez. "I'll be sure and save you a spot on the bus after school."

He resumed his crawl, levering himself through the interdeck hatch and clambering up the handholds to the right-hand rear seat, directly behind the pilot. He eased himself into the chair. *Christ,* he thought, *just like it used to be.* The chute pressed against the chair awkwardly, forcing him into hunchback posture. In the left-hand seat in front of him, the helmeted figure of Commander Leichardt James turned and gave him the thumbs-up.

The closeout crewwoman wrestled his oxygen unit into its cradle beside his seat, then busied herself fitting his communications cap. The command channel hissed into life in his earpiece as she hooked his cable up. "Okay, Reynolds," she said through her own mike. "How's that? Can you give us a comm check, please?"

Reynolds nodded. "It's fine. LAUNCH, this is MS-3, checking comm." He was surprised at the twinge he felt, saying his call sign.

MS-3. *Just one of the mission specialists. And I was gonna fly this bird.*

"Copy, MS-3," said the Launch Director. "MS-3 is go for strap-in at T minus two hours, one minute and thirteen seconds."

"And then there were five," James's voice cut in. "Welcome aboard, Reynolds. What do you think? We thought you might like a window seat."

"Copy that, Commander," Reynolds said as the crew-woman unzipped his helmet bag and lifted the enclosed helmet over his head. "I don't know. I guess it depends how Kennedy drives this thing."

He heard Kennedy laugh, as much from the shared joke as the ribbing. They all knew there was little need for piloting until it came time for docking maneuvers. The Shuttle could, and did, fly itself.

Reynolds listened to the chatter on the command channel patiently as the woman snapped his helmet into position and strapped him into the seat. There was the usual countdown banter—Kennedy and James trading cracks with LAUNCH every other call—but he couldn't help noticing a strained edge to it. The way they skirted around mention of ISS, the tightness in their voices when they addressed him by name.

*Anybody would think I was ISS's grave digger,* he told himself idly.

The thought caught him, causing him to frown.

*Maybe I am.*

He remembered Connor's grim words, spoken over the scotch that night. *The program is hanging on by its fingernails. It's gonna take all we've got to save it.*

Reynolds wondered now if even Matt's despairing words hadn't been optimistic. Fact was, Myers's death had shaken NASA deeper than anything in its history, even *Challenger.* Reynolds had noted the black arm-bands among the NASA ground personnel, the list-lessness and malaise. For the agency, more than just a colleague had died up there.

The dream had too. The innocence.

Reynolds caught, from the corner of his eye, the flash of a nervous smile from Roberts, Mission Special-ist Two, who was sitting in the seat to his left. He returned it, briefly. She was another first-timer, he knew, like himself, and he could imagine the worries running through her mind. What would liftoff really be like? Would she lose her guts at the first touch of weightlessness?

Luckily for Reynolds, he had deeper worries.

The Launch Director's voice crackled over the com-mand channel. "CLOSEOUT, this is LAUNCH. How's strap-in coming along? We're flagged for hatch closure at T minus one fifty-six."

"Copy that, LAUNCH," said the crewwoman, tugging a couple of final adjustments to Reynolds's lap harness. "This is CLOSEOUT-3. Strap-in of MS-3 is completed and I am egressing the orbiter now. Okay, guys," she added, addressing Reynolds and the crew, "I'm outta here. Break a leg, huh?"

Reynolds listened dispassionately as the woman clambered down the handholds and exited. There was a thump as the hatch closed, down on middeck, then the muffled whine of the drill as the bolts securing the temporary hatch handle were unscrewed.

Then silence.

*Just like when the bar drops on the roller coaster,* Reynolds thought. *No way off.*

Except the roller coaster didn't keep you waiting for two hours. The four crew members sat, locked into their seats on the flight deck, making desultory small talk among themselves and with Rodriguez, out of sight on the middeck below. Mostly though, they just listened to the calls coming down from Launch Control.

"Crew Systems, this is Launch Director. Proceed with cabin pressurization."

Now that *Endeavor*'s hatch had been sealed, her cabin would be gassed up with the 14.7-pounds-per-square-inch nitro-oxygen mix the crew would breathe for the duration of her mission.

"Verify abort landing sites."

Across the Atlantic, in Spain, Senegal, and Morocco, the lights on the emergency launch abort landing strips would be coming on.

"GLS reports flight software uploaded completed."

The Shuttle's four flight computers—parallel processors that handled every tiny detail of *Endeavor*'s flight, voting amongst themselves at the these days archaic rate of 440 decisions per second—had been loaded with the avionics software that would see *Endeavor* through the entire mission.

"LAUNCH, Range Safety is starting closed-loop test."

Reynolds saw Roberts's gloved hands tighten involun-

tarily at this. He couldn't blame her. The Range Safety
Officer was running a dead radio test to the explosive
charges mounted on each of the solid rocket boosters,
which would be used to explode the Shuttle in the event
of a malfunction before *Endeavor* could reach the safety
of high altitude.

At T minus seven minutes thirty there was a loud
thump as the access arm swung away from *Endeavor*.
Now they were really cut off, nothing connecting them
physically to the outside world except the four explosive
bolts that secured the solid rockets to the ground, which
would be detonated when the clock hit T minus zero.
The astronauts fell silent, except for the occasional response from James to a question from LAUNCH, as the
pace picked up. At T minus four minutes, the Director
declared the commit parameters met and gave the final
confirmation over the command channel.

Go for launch.

The count proceeded, a near monologue now, until
Reynolds heard the terse voice of the Track Officer cut
in, calling the seconds down.

"T minus ten seconds."

Reynolds felt his pulse surge. He was ready for it—
most astronauts' pulses, he knew, shot up to 150 when
the count started. He turned to look out the left-side
window, past James in the Commander's seat, keeping
his eyes on the red iron of the tower.

"T minus eight seconds," the Track Officer intoned.

"That's it, rainbirds away," another voice said, cutting
in momentarily. 300,000 gallons of water were flooding
into the trench below *Endeavor*, to dampen the thunder
of the engines about to kick into life.

"T minus six seconds."

Main engine one ignited, roaring, followed a split second later by engines two and three. Reynolds felt *Endeavor* lurch violently to the right, away from the tower,
as the 7.5-million-horsepower thrust fought to hurl her
free of the bolts' restraint. She began to shake, rattling
them all in their seats.

The terminal count, T minus zero, was lost in the
thunderous ignition of the solid rockets. *Endeavor*

whipped back up to vertical as the two boosters exploded into life. A fraction of a second later the securing
bolts detonated and *Endeavor* was free, rising majestically from the billowing clouds as the heat from the main
engines boiled the water below into steam. Reynolds felt
the accelerating g-force claw him back into his seat. He
kept his eyes on the tower, but it was gone in seconds,
sliding out of view before the count had even reached
T plus seven.

"There goes the lightning rod, FLIGHT," he heard
James say. The change in call sign reflected the handover
of control to Mission Control at JSC, one thousand miles
away in Houston, that Reynolds knew would just have
taken place. "*Endeavor* has cleared the tower."

Kennedy let out a whoop, drowning out everything on
the channel. "Go, you mother, go," he crowed.

Reynolds felt the sideways shift as *Endeavor* rolled
smoothly onto her back, assuming the programmed attack angle for orbit insertion. "Roll program initiated,
FLIGHT," James said calmly.

*That's how it's going to happen, babe,* Reynolds remembered telling Alicia that night, using his upturned
hand to demonstrate. Atlantis *will roll over right onto
her back. Like a lazy old whale.*

The grief caught at him again, momentarily, but then was
gone, rattled out by *Endeavor*'s bone-shaking shudder.

"Five thousand feet and Mach point three," he heard
Kennedy announce, reading from the radar altimeter.
"Six thousand and point four. Climbing by the
numbers."

At twenty-six seconds, the rumbling decreased slightly
as the engines throttled back to cope with the layer of
turbulence always encountered at 10,000 feet. "Into the
thrustbucket, Houston," James said, as the engines de-
celerated. Seconds later, *Endeavor* began jolting from
the shearing crosswinds, which continued for some
twenty seconds until, magically, at T plus fifty-four they
were through and the engines throttled back up to
maximum.

"Hey, Leich," Kennedy cut in suddenly, addressing
James, "load relief is hanging back on two and three.
I'm switching to control stick, okay?"

Before the commander had a chance to respond, the pilot had punched the button and grabbed the stick.

"You copy that, FLIGHT?" James said. Reynolds imagined him shaking his head. "That's Kennedy for you. Never happy unless he hotsticks it at least once."

Inside his helmet, Reynolds grinned wryly. Hotsticking it—flying the Shuttle on manual backed by the flight computers—was pure, unnecessary vanity. The load-relief algorithm would have kicked in within a second or two. But he understood Kennedy's move. The pilot was refusing to be what the Shuttle made you—just a bag of meat in the pilot's seat.

Reynolds craned his head against the g-force and squinted at the instrument displays. They were at 4.3 nautical miles, traveling at 2,257 feet per second. His head fell back to the seat; it was impossible to hold it, the force had to be nearly three g's. He stared ahead through the front windows, trying to at least keep his head straight. It should be possible to detect the change in the intensity of blue as they made the stratosphere.

They rocketed upwards, away from the Earth. At T plus seven minutes, Houston announced the initiation of booster separation sequence; a few seconds later a heavy clunk sounded from both sides of *Endeavor* as the solid rockets fell away. Reynolds pictured them curving in graceful arcs on their way to splashdown in the Atlantic.

The roaring behind them slackened.

Forty seconds later the main engines also cut out and they were coasting—the g-force dropping away and the blue of the atmosphere melding imperceptibly into blue-black, the glittering pinpoints of stars visible for the first time. There was another thump as the external tank separated and went into its controlled tumble, away from *Endeavor*.

Without waiting for the word from Houston, Kennedy unbuckled and pushed up from his seat. He unlocked his helmet and sent it spinning across the cabin in the sudden weightlessness. He swiveled himself around, above his seat, to face Roberts and Reynolds and opened his hands in a theatrical gesture.

"That's it, boys and girls," he said, grinning. "Welcome to space."

Mission Elapsed Time: 1 day, 2 hours, 14 minutes
Space Shuttle *Endeavor*

"Hey Reynolds. You copy, buddy?" Kennedy's voice, from up on flight deck, buzzed through Reynolds's headset earpiece.

Reynolds hit the push-to-talk button absently. "Copy, Kennedy," he said. He was floating in front of the middeck video unit, going through the ISS recorder dumps he'd requested from Matt. There was no sound—out of deference to the other astronauts he was listening through a separate earpiece in his other ear. Even so, he'd seen the difficulty Roberts and Rodriguez had keeping a straight face when they went past.

"We're about to go into the second adjustment burn," Kennedy said. "Just thought you'd like to know."

"Roger," Reynolds replied. "Thanks for the tip."

He hit the pause button and grabbed the tapes floating by his head, securing them to the wall with bungee straps. Just as he got them pinned, *Endeavor*'s engines fired, the force of the acceleration wafting him across the middeck to the aft bulkhead wall. He pushed himself off it gently and returned to the video unit. Since wake up that morning he had been sifting laboriously through the ISS recorder dumps for the weeks leading up to Myers's death, looking for . . .

Something.

A red flag, cops called it. Something that stood out; something that wasn't how it ought to be. The pressure-cooked environment on ISS made the search difficult. The continual observation from Earth, Reynolds knew, meant the usual markers would be absent. The murderer would take care to conceal them. Reynolds's only hope was to scour the tapes for a hidden signal, some behavioral tic the killer couldn't help showing.

In fact, if he wasn't mistaken, there *was* something . . .

"MS-3, this is CAPCOM." The external audio channel cut across his train of thought. "We've got a request for voice from Space Station Control. Do you copy?"

This was the complicated way in which the ISS/Shuttle interface worked. Until Reynolds actually arrived on the

Station, all communication with Space Station Control had to go through Shuttle Mission Control.

"CAPCOM, MS-3," Reynolds replied, following NASA's comm protocol. First the addressee's call sign, then your own. "I read you, operator. Put 'em through."

CAPCOM laughed. A second later, Connor's voice was on the channel.

"Edge, this is Matt," he said. It was the first chance he and Reynolds had had to talk since *Endeavor* had lifted off. "How're you doing up there? Enjoying the view?"

Reynolds's eyes strayed over to the circular hatch window at the middeck's left. So far, he'd spent every waking minute of the flight in front of the video unit. He hadn't had a chance to even look outside.

"It's okay," he said shortly. "Actually, I've been belowdecks most of this shift. I'm going through the tapes you got me."

"Uh huh, copy that," Connor said, after a slight delay. "Anything step out and hit you?"

"Nothing yet," he said. He eyed the figures moving on the tape, still rolling in the background. He never liked to discuss things in the early stages of an investigation. "Too early to tell, Matt. What have you got for me?"

Connor accepted his reticence smoothly. "Just wanted to update you on the flight plan, Edge," he said. "Guidance has you on track for docking with ISS at four hours twenty, Mission Elapsed Time. Rodriguez is scheduled to help you with unstow and transfer of the lab kit, which Mission Control has budgeted two hours for. Then *Endeavor* will undock and be on their way. You copy?"

*The lab kit.* Reynolds's nose wrinkled impatiently at the euphemism. There *was* a lab kit packed into the aluminum locker tray—luminol for bloodstain testing, black-magnetic print-dusting powder, a primitive RFLP kit for DNA analysis. Most of it, though, was taken up with the cuffs, restraints, Tasers and stun batons NASA had provided him with.

"Copy, Matt," he said out loud. "Eli drew the short straw, huh?" He guessed there hadn't been many volunteers for the job.

"Guess so," Connor answered. "Anyway, the cosmo-nauts have been briefed on your arrival. Commander Kalganin has agreed to assemble the crew, including Dr. Akira, in the wardroom of the Service Module. You can . . . interview them there."

Reynolds picked up the hesitancy in Connor's voice. *He nearly said interrogate.*

The incongruities of the situation struck Reynolds once more. *Kalganin is going to assemble the crew. And it's at least possible the commander himself will be in chains before the week is through.*

He frowned, considering Connor's news. He'd have to be careful how he handled this first session. He had to knock the killer onto his, or her, ass right away. And keep them there. Setting could be important in that. The Service Module, which served as the hub of social life on the station, was a Russian-built module—and that nearly counted as a home-team advantage.

"How about a change of venue?" he asked Connor. "Can we get Kalganin to assemble them in the Lab Module instead?" The Lab Module was an American unit.

"No sweat," Connor replied, without hesitation. "I'll get CAPCOM onto it straightaway. We'll have the internal cameras running the whole time of course. In case you want to go back over something later. And I'll be available for videocon if you want to any time before sleep shift. Okay?"

"You bet, Matt," Reynolds replied. "Thanks. Anything else?"

"Just one thing. Flight Surgeon says he wants you on the exercise program too. In case something goes wrong with the return and you have to stay a while. Have you done a workout today?"

Reynolds had to admit he hadn't.

"Well get going, hombre," Connor said brashly. "I want a half hour treadmill and a half hour ergo out of you every day."

Reynolds had to laugh. For a moment the old Connor was back—Crew Training Connor, slave-driving Connor.

"Roger that," he said. "Setting to now, boss."

He signed off, grinning, and shut the video unit down.

He pushed himself over to the exercise station, directly
below the middeck side hatch. Roberts was already
there, reclining on the ergometer, her legs pedaling and
her long black tresses floating around her head like an
Afro. She flashed Reynolds a half-smile, then looked
quickly away.

Reynolds strapped himself in, frowning. There it was
again, that undercurrent of revulsion.

*As if it was* me *that killed Myers,* he thought, commencing his run.

His attention was caught by the sight of the world
through the hatch window. For all its scattering of pin-
point stars, the panorama of space against which the
Earth stood was blacker than anything he had ever seen.
The Earth itself was a majestic curve of blue and green
and brown, decorated by ruffles of white cloud and a
shining haze where the blue of the atmosphere shaded
off into black. It was breathtaking, beautiful, and before
he could stop it, the beauty had led him back to thoughts
of Alicia again.

*This is how I would have described it to you, babe,* he
told her helplessly. *You would have seen everything . . .*

"Beautiful, isn't it?"

The female voice beside him threw Reynolds momentarily. Roberts had finished her session on the cycle and
was floating alongside him, dabbing her forehead with
a towel.

"Space," she said, when he turned to look at her. "It's
beautiful, isn't it?" He nodded dumbly and transferred
his gaze back to the window. The two of them studied
the scene silently.

"And only man is vile," Roberts murmured, when a
few moments had passed.

Reynolds frowned. He recognized the line, vaguely.
*Some poem or something.*

"That's the way the world is, Roberts," he said mildly.
"Wherever you go you find human pollution."

He wasn't prepared for the vehemence of her response. She rounded on him, eyes flashing.

"Maybe you're used to working with evil, Detective,"
she said, lips stretched tight in disapproval. "We're not."

Reynolds shrugged. You had to guess she was right
about that. He saw more evil every week, back on the
squad, than even a lifetime of murdering cosmonauts
could provide.

She stared at him challengingly a moment more, then
lowered her eyes in contrition.

"I'm sorry, Reynolds," she said. "I . . . I shouldn't
take it out on you. I know you've got your job to do."
She closed her eyes, struggling to regain composure. Her
face, when she lifted it again, was sober.

"I hope you catch Gary's killer, Detective," she said
evenly. "I really do. For the Russians' sake as well as
ours."

Reynolds turned back to the treadmill. "So do I, Roberts," he muttered grimly, recommencing his run. "For
mine."

**Mission Elapsed Time: 1 day, 4 hours, 2 minutes**
**Space Shuttle *Endeavor***

They made the docking corridor for ISS two hours later.
Reynolds went up to the aft flight deck to watch the
approach.

At first sighting, ISS was a glinting speck on the horizon, 6,000 feet away. A half hour later, after a series of
timed thrusts from the maneuvering engines, they were
500 feet away and ISS was a giant, fragile insect—segmented exoskeleton stretching out along the vertical
axis, eight photovoltaic arrays sprouting from the horizontal like monstrous dragonfly wings. Kennedy took
over from Ground when they had made the envelope,
bringing them through the speed-closure gates step-by-
step until they were directly underneath ISS, the maw of
her docking port yawning overhead. There they paused
momentarily, allowing Mission Control to verify alignment.

When the command came back "Go," Kennedy
crawled *Endeavor* upwards with flickering bursts of the
thrusters, six feet at a time, until ISS's "wings" had de-
scended around them and the mouth of the docking port
completely obscured the view upwards through *Endeav-*

*or*'s aft flight-deck roof windows. There was a grating thud as the mating adapters found each other then, a second of held breath later, the clunk that signified lock-in. Confirmation came through from Mission Control within five seconds.

"Congratulations, *Endeavor*. That's a textbook dock at one-five-fourteen, MET," CAPCOM announced.

There was none of the usual postdock banter, though. Rodriguez was subdued as he helped Reynolds unstow and move his equipment and supplies to the middeck airlock, preparatory to transferal to ISS. The conversation over the audio link to ISS was clipped and sparse—both the astronauts' and cosmonauts' voices flat and unemotional. Reynolds concentrated on the Russian voices, trying to match them to the figures on the tapes and in the photos. They were all there, a few feet away, separated from him by just a few inches of machined aluminum alloy that would be opened as soon as pressure in the two chambers had been equalized. And one of them was the murderer.

*And maybe, just maybe,* Reynolds thought, flicking a laundry pack, spinning, into the airlock chamber, *I know which one it is.*

5:14 P.M., Day 81, Expedition Time
Laboratory Module, International Space Station

*This is unreal,* Reynolds thought.

The clean, square lines of ISS's Lab Module stretched around him—gray carpeted floor, tandem rows of fluoro tubes along the ceiling, walls an orderly patchwork of white aluminum and Kevlar plastic science racks. Before him, dressed in various assemblages of the blue ISS crew kit, the four cosmonauts and Dr. Akira bobbed, waiting.

Stretched out full-length, to his left, was Kalganin. Reynolds had trouble recognizing the sharp-eyed athlete of the file photo. The commander's pallid face was careworn, his eyes dull. Floating next to him was Drupev, every bit as bearish as in the photographs Reynolds had seen. The *Soyuz* commander's moon face was a mask of assumed calm, betrayed only by the tiny pull of muscle at his temple that advertised a threatening tic. Parallel to the roof, smoldering eyes fixed firmly on Reynolds, was Matchev, the flight engineer. Below him hung Dr. Akira, his small body tucked into a protective ball, troubled eyes darting to and from Reynolds's face. Though Reynolds avoided looking, he could see, from the corner of his eye, Ruskaya floating at his extreme right, her foot hooked under one of the floor-mounted mobility restraints.

He had to stop himself from shaking his head. Whoever heard of interviewing suspects like this?

Back at squad, perps had everything stacked against them. They were led into interview rooms, usually in cuffs, past a long line of uniformed cops—isolated, helpless, with no place to hide. Reynolds made sure never to go into the room unless he had what he needed—the one or two facts he could slide under their shell and work until the suspect folded. He made sure, too, that the hard-asses got the message a tune-up was definitely *not* out of the question.

This, though, was a different story. On ISS, he was the away team, one against five, and he had *nothing* to work with. Just suspicions. It was going to take every ounce of his skill to draw those suspicions out into cold, hard facts.

"Well," he said finally, "I don't have much to add to what Commander Kalganin has said. You all know why I'm here. I am authorized by the United States and Russian governments to conduct an investigation into the murder of astronaut Gary Myers and to bring the guilty party back to Earth."

He looked at Kalganin sharply.

"You understand, Commander? In all matters relating to the investigation I have supreme command aboard ISS?"

Kalganin's head shot up at Reynold's direct address. He stared at Reynolds a moment, then nodded.

"I understand," he said tonelessly.

"Good," Reynolds replied. "You should know as well," he added, addresssing the whole group, "that I am armed at all times and fully authorized by both governments to use whatever force is necessary to effect an arrest."

He paused to let this sink in, watching the crew's faces. One or two cast furtive glances over him, trying, Reynolds knew, to pick out a weapon on his body. He bore the examination impassively. The two flat Tasers he was carrying were strapped tight to the inside of his left forearm and ankle. Nobody would see them there.

"You should also understand this about me," he continued evenly. "I am a detective, and a good one, and I *will* find out which one of you killed Gary Myers and why."

Reynolds frowned. Normally, he would start heavying about now—threatening them with the weight they would take if they didn't confess, dangling a plea bargain in front of them. But bargains were out—Connor had made that clear. The political situation wouldn't allow it. He would have to rely, instead, on ratcheting the pressure up, bit by bit, until the killer broke cover and ran. He started with the flat question, delivered deadpan to each one of them.

"Dr. Akira," he said. The rotund Japanese started and looked at Reynolds timidly. "Do you confess to the murder of astronaut Gary Myers?"

The doctor's mouth worked away noiselessly. He gave a feeble shake of his head.

Reynolds switched his gaze to the Russian captain. "Commander Kalganin," he said, then repeated the question. Kalganin's hurried negative was followed by denials from the other three. Reynolds nodded, noting with satisfaction the heightened unease he had produced.

"Okay," he continued. "Since the murderer shows no intention of coming forward, I'll start my official investigation tomorrow. To those of you clean of the crime I apologize in advance. Cut me some slack, because this investigation is going to step on toes."

Nonplussed expressions displaced the worried frowns on the cosmonauts' faces. Though English was the operating language on ISS and all the non-Americans had had to learn it before flying, Reynolds guessed their knowledge of American slang was shaky.

Not that that would make him change. The more off-balance he kept them the better.

Ruskaya suddenly spoke up—a stream of mellifluous Russian. Reynolds found himself listening intently to her voice, despite himself. He couldn't understand a word, of course, but it was obvious from the nervous smiles that broke out she was translating for the other cosmonauts.

Reynolds watched, deadpan, until the smiles faded. It wasn't in his interest to allow a dampening of tension.

"Okay," he said finally, "that's it for now. We'll get started tomorrow." He avoided, deliberately, giving Kalganin the option of dismissing them. After one or two uncertain glances at the slighted Russian captain, the crew members turned and began to exit the Lab Module.

Reynolds watched, from behind his carefully impassive face, waiting to see the order in which they left. He felt a twinge of satisfaction, mixed with exultation, when he saw it.

*I was right,* he thought fiercely. *He did wait for her . . .*

Perhaps the recorder dumps *hadn't* lied. It could be he had already found the flag, the way in to the mystery of Myers's death. He would test the theory tomorrow.

10:02 P.M., Central Standard Time, 29 March 2005
Space Station Control Room One, Johnson Space Center

Connor waited impatiently for the technicians to finish. Reynolds's cobbled-together flight had given Space Station Control a number of headaches, not the least of which was security. The need to communicate secretly—out of the loop—with someone on ISS had never arisen before. NASA had solved it by constructing a secure annex off Space Station Control Room One to house Connor and the two flight controllers working with him, and by isolating out two of the Ku-band channels—giving full video and audio capability whenever ISS was within range. The price was bugs. The system had shut down in protest, and Data Processing had worked four hours solid so far to get it back up. Finally, the techs gave Connor the all clear.

The videocon software panel on his workstation

screen leaped into life and suddenly Reynolds's head and upper body were visible, floating serenely against the backdrop of the cluttered wall of his cabin on ISS. Nostalgia swept Connor at the sight of his former protégé bobbing there.

*Goddamn it, this is what I trained him for, all those years ago.* A laugh escaped him, and he shook his head.

Reynolds's eyebrows rose in surprise. "What's the deal, Matt?" he said, into Connor's earpiece. "You rang me up from the other side of the Earth just to laugh at me?"

"You bastard," Connor growled in response, still shaking his head. "I was just thinking you finally justified all that wasted effort I put into you. I just didn't expect you'd have gray hair when I finally saw you up there is all."

Reynolds grimaced, thinking back to the confrontation in the Lab Module. "Better get used to it, Matt," he said. "I'll have more by the time I'm done here."

The grin left Connor's face, replaced by sober concern. "Uh huh," he nodded. "I caught some of your meeting with the reception committee over the IC system. Didn't look too friendly."

Reynolds shrugged. "I'm not here to make friends," he replied shortly.

"Guess not," Connor agreed. He peered at the wall behind Reynolds. It was cluttered with tools and equipment, all tied down with crisscrossing bungee straps. "How do you find the quarters?"

"They're okay," Reynolds said, craning his head to look around him. For security, Connor had berthed him in the Earth Observation Alcove, just off the U.S. Lab Module. Unlike ISS's tiny cabins, the EOA had a heavy, lockable door—there to protect the twenty-two-inch glass observation port and the delicate photographic rack from collision with unsecured objects floating in the Lab Module. It was also, coincidentally, the only separate compartment on ISS large enough to hold the mounting frame of Reynolds's Titan suit, fully assembled. "Actually, I'm thinking of having my apartment decorated the same way."

"Okay," Connor laughed. "I'll have an agency design

team fix it up for you. How about the teleprint?" he asked. "You get a chance to look over it?"

Reynolds nodded, grabbing the length of paper floating beside him and waving it at the screen. He had looked over the schedule earlier; it called for a morning IVA (intravehicular activity) to examine Myers's corpse in the airlock, a short funeral presided over by Reynolds, then ejection of Myers's body into space.

"Sure," he told Connor. "No sweat. Forensic bloodhound until eleven o'clock, then rabbi and grave digger until twelve. I do it all the time."

Connor laughed. "Well, make sure to get some sleep, buddy," he told Reynolds. "We don't want you tripping over the words to Kaddish tomorrow, huh?"

With that, he terminated the call, punching the button that zapped his screen to blackness.

On board ISS, Reynolds locked his computer down and zipped himself into the sleep restraint mounted on the wall of his makeshift cabin. He flicked the switch to the fluoros, plunging the cluttered alcove into darkness, and tried to sleep. But a hundred details kept running through his mind—the sequence of events he would have to follow the next day, the small pieces of the puzzle he thought he had put in place. Somewhere along the line though, he must have succeeded, for the weightless bobbing he was experiencing became himself, floating freely, out in space.

He was outside ISS, some distance away, watching himself sleeping through the round Observation Alcove window. He had his space suit on. Suddenly, he became aware of another space-suited figure approaching. He turned to watch, curious. When the figure was close enough, only a few feet away, he screwed his eyes up, trying—though there was no need really—to peer through the gold visor and make out the person's face. It was Alicia, of course, and he pushed himself over to bob in front of her soundlessly.

He watched, fascinated then horrified, as her hands went up to her helmet, swiveling it out of the locked position. He shook his head violently, and tried to grab her hands, but Alicia just laughed. A second later her helmet was off and her long hair spilled out to float freely. She looked at him teasingly, urging him to join her. He put his hands up, after some hesitation, and began twisting his own helmet. The moment it snapped out of lock, however, his ears exploded with a hiss that became a roar, and suddenly he was back in Alinov's vacuum chamber, dying on his feet as he tried to make it to the door. He told himself, as he staggered to it, that now was his chance—he had to look up, remember what it was he had seen that was so odd. But before he could lift his head the roaring grew louder and louder, drowning everything out as it sucked him down into deep unconsciousness.

# 6

"Equipment Lock bleed-down seventy percent complete," Kalganin's thickly accented voice buzzed in Reynolds's suit earpiece. "Switching off depress valve. IVA-1, you are go for manual purge."

"Copy that," Reynolds replied, moving to the valve.

He yanked the handle towards him with a gloved hand, venting the thirty percent of the lock's atmosphere the pumps could not reclaim into space. He waited patiently for the chamber to empty. The Equipment Lock, the cylindrical compartment where EVA equipment and Russian Orlan space suits were stored, formed the prechamber of ISS's primary airlock. Just the other side of its huge round hatch was Myers's corpse, whirling along in its endless, frozen silence.

Reynolds readied himself for ingress. Suddenly, his surroundings—the aluminum chamber walls, the hanging Russian suits—receded from view and it was just him, Detective Sergeant Edge Reynolds, about to enter yet another murder scene. Like he did every other day of his life. They were always the same. *Like a stage set,* Reynolds thought. A grotesque theater, in which the only actors were dead or in hiding, the set was everything, and the whole production was put on for an audience of one—him. It was almost . . .

"IVA-1, this is CAPCOM." CAPCOM's voice punctured Reynolds's reverie. "FLIGHT wants you to activate your helmet camera now. Do you copy?"

"Roger, CAPCOM," Reynolds replied, pressing the button on his Chest Display Unit. "Helmet cam on."

His eyes sought out the internal camera mounted high on the chamber's avionics rack. That would be rolling too, he knew, recording every detail of what was about to take place for the hundreds of NASA staff watching. And later, when it came time for Myers's funeral, for the millions of Americans who would see it live on every network. The thought brought him, abruptly, back to reality.

*This is nothing like normal.*

This time he wasn't the audience. He was an actor.

"IVA-1," Kalganin's doleful voice cut in. "You are go for hatch opening."

Reynolds launched himself over to the hatch and pulled the locking levers free. Bracing himself, he grabbed the handle and yanked it towards him.

The hatch opened on the scene from the videostream. Except that now it was like staring into the barrel of a tumble dryer. The clouds of crystal and detritus whirled slowly around counterclockwise—something to do with ISS's solar energy–catching rotation, Reynolds guessed. Harsh, white light glittered off the frozen particles, blinding him—Ground had switched on all the airlock's floodlights and fluoros for the IVA. He screwed up his eyes, waiting for them to adjust. Details slowly resolved themselves out of the whiteness.

Dark shapes wheeling through the haze—those were mostly the zero-reaction tools from Myers's tool platform, ripped away in the struggle. The platform itself was there, Reynolds saw, as were the two squat aluminum cylinders containing the unfired U.S. and Russian flags. As his eyes adjusted he noted the definite pink tinge to the drifting crystal cloud—that would be Myers's blood, snap-frozen in the vacuum after vaporizing. Several crystals drifted out through the hatchway and hit his faceplate, leaving dots of ice where they shattered. Floating in the middle was Myers—space suit bleached ghost white and swaying oddly around the jutting points of his splayed limbs.

*Of course,* thought Reynolds grimly, studying the wheeling corpse. *With all the liquid boiled out of him, there's probably nothing but a fucking mummy left in there.*

"Okay, FLIGHT," he said. "Ingressing Crew Lock compartment now."

He pulled himself through and was suddenly inside the crystal haze. He groped his way over to the chamber wall, ignoring the circling objects for the moment. They'd been dancing around in here for three weeks; a few more minutes wasn't going to hurt. He concentrated, instead, on the surface of the Crew Lock wall.

Not that there was any point to it.

There would be no latent prints of course, because of the suits. No bloodstains for pattern analysis either—the vacuum had turned Myers's blood to mist before it had a chance to spatter. Reynolds wiped the frozen smear off his faceplate and grinned to himself, thinking how apeshit Lomass and the boys from Crime Lab would go if he tried to hand them a slate as blank as this. Still, there was nothing for it. No matter how investigatively arid, the crime scene had to be examined. Call it force of habit.

He brought his helmet up close to the wall, peering at the irregular veneer coating it—a skin of crystals that had hit and stuck. He saw now that they were divided into tiny clumps of dark red and white; Myers's blood had separated out to its base elements: tiny clusters of corpuscles and plasma crystals. He let the camera linger a moment, knowing the NASA astrobiologists—seated tactfully off in some side room—would be feverishly scribbling notes on this, the only ever documented human exposure to full vacuum. He resumed his progress, propelling himself gently along the curving wall with his feet. Halfway along he came to a heavy gouge in the aluminum, too deep to have been caused by any of the randomly tumbling objects.

"Are you on the channel, Matt?" he asked, tilting his helmet to move the camera close. "You getting this?"

"Right here, buddy," Connor's voice buzzed in his earpiece. "We're reading you fine. That's gotta be from the footing block, right?" NASA had quickly identified the weapon shown smashing into Myers's helmet on the

gruesome video footage. It was one of the four spare
footing blocks that anchored ISS's robotic arm to its
base. The killer had left it behind when he exited, mute
companion to the circling corpse.

"Uh huh," Reynolds grunted, tracing the channel with
a gloved fingertip. "Looks like Gary put up a fight before he went under."

He pushed himself around, searching the circling debris for the murder weapon. Locating it, he reached out
and plucked it from the cloud, edging Myers's corpse
aside to get to it.

"Examining the murder weapon now, FLIGHT," he
said, bringing the block up to his faceplate. He checked
the corners. "A damaged corner on the distal end," he
announced, running his fingerpad over the shiny, blunted
edge of the metal. "I'd say that's the side that got pushed
into the wall."

He turned the block over, studying the other corners.
The one opposite bore a series of deep scratches, consistent with smashing through jagged polycarbonate. "Looks
like this was the point of impact," he said, holding the
block up to the camera and pointing with his finger.

He brought it back down, frowning, as he studied it
more closely.

"Wait a minute," he added, tracing the scratches.
"There appears to be a second series here, longer
scratches than the first. The killer must have come back
for a second blow after the breach." He gave a low
whistle. "Looks like he wasn't taking any chances."

Reynolds bagged the block and tethered it. "Okay,
FLIGHT," he said, steeling himself to the task. "Preparing to examine the DOA."

Reynolds reached into the glittering maelstrom and
grabbed a fold of Myers's suit. He pulled the corpse
towards him, anchoring it to one of the mobility restraints by a bungee around the ankle. He grimaced at
the touch of Myers's leg. He'd been right—even through
the silicon tips of his gloves, he could feel it.

Myers's flesh had collapsed in on itself. The leg was a
hard-frozen stick—just larger in diameter than the bone.

"The DOA's suit is incredibly loose," he told Houston, turning the corpse as he examined the suit. "Feels like he's lost a lot of body substance." The suit glittered with the same frost of plasma crystals as the wall. "Some signs of struggle." He peered at the corpse's gloved hand. "Fingerpads show abrasions. Cuff checklist mount appears broken."

He maneuvered Myers closer to him, keeping the head out of sight for the moment, and checked his Chest Display Unit. Myers's Suit Pressure Alert Light was still blinking, the life support pack's lithium battery maintaining a lonely, useless vigil.

"Suit display shows total discharge of primary and secondary oxygen," Reynolds continued. He twisted the purge valve to double-check.

"Cooling system pressure zero too," he said, rubbing slush aside with a finger so he could see the readings. The attack must have ruptured the tubes of Myers's cooling suit. Reynolds glanced at the circling crystals. Some of them would be water—the pure, distilled water that flowed through the network of tubes sewn into the spandex inner garment of every astronaut's space suit.

Reynolds braced himself. "Proceeding to examination of head region."

He pulled Myers down to him, spinning the baggy suit around until the shattered faceplate rolled into the view of his helmet camera. He could sense the silent horror of the sixty or so people hooked into the channel. Suddenly, discipline broke and the channel slid into hubbub.

"Oh, fuck!" Reynolds heard someone groan. In the background he could hear the unmistakable sound of vomiting.

Myers's face was not directly visible through the faceplate, which was heavily frosted with plasma crystals and shot through with cracks. It could be glimpsed though, through the hole smashed in the upper right of the glass, whenever Myers's body lolled in the right direction. Myers's head was a mottled brown lump, the temple where the blow had struck a dark, shattered mess.

"The victim's helmet was breached by impact of murder weapon in the top right quadrant of the faceplate," Reynolds said neutrally.

He probed the jagged edge of the hole. Tiny shards of clear polycarbonate fringed it, broken outwards by the force of the escaping gas but held by the UV shielding film. "Impossible to determine the point of impact exactly," he muttered.

The explosive rush of blood and gas from Myers's body had seen to that.

He steeled himself for the next step. "Okay, FLIGHT," he said. "Removing the helmet now." He pushed the lock knob through the three back-and-forth motions and lifted the helmet away, leaving it to drift.

*Fuck,* he thought sickly. Muscles deep in his gut jerked in protest.

Even a lifetime of gunshot victims hadn't prepared him for this. Myers's head was mummified—*fucking shrunk*—mottled, brown flesh drawn in tight around the skull. The eyes had collapsed in their sockets—pupils bled out into huge, cartoonlike disks within the flat pools. Hair stuck out from the skull ludicrously, fretted with glittering, frozen crystals. The smashed bone at Myers's temple had suffered the same fate as his faceplate, blown outwards by the force of escaping liquid and vapor. The skull cavity, visible through the hole, was nearly empty; the astronaut's brain reduced to a dark gray, leathery crust coating its interior.

The murmuring on the channel had dropped out completely. Through the shocked silence, Reynolds could even hear the rasp of one of the Ground Controllers' breathing.

He pushed on grimly.

"Massive blunt-force trauma to the forehead," he said, pulling the head closer to the camera by the dead astronaut's suit. "Rupture of the suit environment seems to have been followed almost immediately by breach of skin's integrity and massive fluid loss."

Reynolds shuddered, remembering his own experience in Alinov's vacuum chamber. At least Myers had been spared that. With that level of liquid loss, death had to have been instantaneous.

"Okay, FLIGHT," he said, struggling to keep his voice steady. "Proceeding to suit removal."

He kept his eyes focused on his hands as he snapped the locking rings of Myers's EMU and worked the two-piece suit free. The suit would be bagged and shipped to Houston for analysis; it wasn't every day NASA got to run tests on a real-life breach to vacuum. Even after removing the suit arms Reynolds had to struggle to get the fiberglass upper torso off. In the end he wrenched it free—he felt frozen sinews tear as Myers's arms were forced over his head. The spandex cooling garment had contracted around Myers's skeletal form; Reynolds unzipped it and peeled it from the corpse. He balled it and shoved it into the white NASA bag, keeping his eyes studiously off the macabre figure drifting beside him.

*Fuck. Even when they're cut up they still look human. Not like this . . .*

"You getting this, FLIGHT?" he growled.

"Uh . . . copy, IVA-1," the Flight Director said, his voice quavering. "We see it. We're just having trouble keeping our eyes on it."

Reynolds could understand that. He ground his jaw, hard, to quell the heaving that had started up again in his guts, and turned to the corpse. He swept it slowly, deliberately, with the camera, recording every detail. It was grotesque—the dark brown flesh so shriveled on the bone that Myers resembled nothing so much as a carved, wooden skeleton. His belly was a puckered band of skin that clung to his vertebrae between ribs and pelvis, clearly outlined under the compacted flesh. Reynolds wondered, as he trolled the camera, if the astronaut's wife was watching. Christ, he hoped not.

He ran the camera over the corpse slowly, with rising revulsion. Finally, he snapped.

"Okay, FLIGHT," he said harshly, trying to control his voice. "I don't know about you, but I've seen all I need to. What do you say we get on with the burial?"

The paralyzed silence on his headset channel held for a moment, then Connor was on the line, breaking protocol, his voice choked with emotion.

"Copy that, Edge," he said. "Go ahead and put that poor bastard away."

12:09 P.M., Day 82, Expedition Time
Airlock Module, International Space Station

Reynolds tugged the white shroud's zippers together, leaving a small gap. He tucked the plastic packet of earth, marked with Hebrew, into the space, taking care to tear it slightly, in line with Connor's instructions.

The airlock was nearly ready for the live telecast now—Myers's ruined space suit had been bundled into the Equipment Lock, along with the tools Reynolds had salvaged, and the crystallized fluid had been vented through the open hatch. Nothing was left visible of Myers, except the shrouded form.

Reynolds eyed it critically. Even now, the corpse hadn't lost its grotesque quality; the limbs jutted crazily, stretching the shroud. He drew it to him and squeezed the limbs straight, grimacing as he felt sinews strain, then tear. He let the bundle go once they had given way, and pushed it from him with a shudder.

"CAPCOM, IVA-1," he puffed, out of breath from the exertion. "Ready to go live."

Down below, at Johnson, the Communications officer would be switching channels through to NASA TV, allowing the signal out to the networks and the 450 million people around the world it was estimated would tune in to America's first funeral in space. Reynolds ran over the ceremony he had rehearsed with Connor quickly. Myers was a lapsed Jew; it had been his widow's decision to give him an Orthodox funeral. But this had created a problem—apparently, Myers had once told his wife, in a joking moment, that if he died on mission, he wanted to be buried in space.

"So?" Reynolds had shrugged, when Connor had first broached the subject. "We hold the ceremony in the Crew Lock, then eject him. Everybody's happy."

Connor had shaken his head. "It's not that simple, Edge. Myers is going to burn up on reentry. That counts as cremation in the Jewish religion—a big no-no. It's up before the Rabbinical Council right now."

In the end, the Council had come up with a compromise. Myers could be buried in space—provided a cupful of soil from Israel was put into the shroud with him, symbolically beginning the process of rot, thereby ridding the body of *Tuma* (impurity) and preparing it for the Revival of the Dead. To make the process complete, Reynolds had been appointed honorary member of *Chevra Kaddisha,* the Holy Brotherhood, qualifying him to say Kaddish.

"Copy, IVA-1." CAPCOM's voice sounded in his ear. "Switching you through to Rabbi Zneizner now. Rabbi, you're on the air."

Reynolds closed his eyes and concentrated. There would be no preliminaries—just straight into the Aramaic words, which he would have to repeat.

*"Yis-ga-dal v'yis-ka-dash sh'may ra-bo."* The rabbi's rumbling voice filled Reynolds's earpiece.

*"Yis-ga-dal v'yis-ka-dash sh'may ra-bo,"* Reynolds repeated. He peered at his cuff checklist. Had he got the pronunciation right?

*"B'ol-mo dee-v'ro hir-u-say, v'yam-leeh mal-hu-say . . ."*

The rabbi's words droned through the prayer, Reynolds following obediently. He pictured the scenes across America—everywhere, schoolkids, workers, housewives, and barflies would be in front of a television watching the ceremony in silence. Even the President was being filmed, very publicly observing a minute's silence in the Oval Office, before addressing the nation.

Suddenly, the rabbi's solemn voice was lifting; he was coming to the last line. Reynolds repeated the words, *"O-lay-nu v'al kol yis-ro-ayl v'im-ru o-mayn,"* then, listening carefully for the cue, said in unison with the rabbi, "Blessed be he. Amen."

With that, the short ceremony was over.

The Flight Director's sober voice replaced the rabbi's on the channel. "IVA-1, FLIGHT. Go for burial procedure."

"Copy, FLIGHT," Reynolds replied, grinning cynically to himself. *Go for burial.* Christ, even at a time like this NASA couldn't lay off the jargon.

He drew the corpse towards him and looped the strap of the pyrotechnic unit around it. "Burial procedure," in this case, meant mounting a small, gyro-controlled rocket on Myers's corpse and heaving it out of the hatch, using the thruster to get it the hell away from ISS, drop its orbit and plunge it into reentry.

*Edge Reynolds, interstellar undertaker,* Reynolds thought sourly, pulling the belt tight.

He anchored the corpse to the mobility restraint, tying a loose knot in the leftover strap. Then he yanked on his own safety restraint, checking it was still tied. "FLIGHT, IVA-1," he said, when he was satisfied, "proceeding to open external hatch."

He kicked himself over to the hatch and went through the three-stage manual opening sequence—lock lever right, safety wheel anticlockwise, handle yanked towards him. He felt the crack as the seal broke and the hydraulics moved the huge round hatch out from the lock. Then it swung smoothly open, revealing the world below.

Reynolds paused, overcome. Fuck, it was beautiful.

Past the glittering black wings of ISS's solar panels, shining with the light of the overhead sun, Africa was visible—the low mountains of the Sahara a delicate tracery of red and brown through the spiral patterning of cloud. As he watched, the Indian Ocean inched into view, a thin lip of coast-hugging blue that shaded off majestically into the azure of deep ocean. It was so entrancing that for a moment he longed to emulate Myers; push himself headlong out and hurtle down towards it . . .

"IVA-1, CAPCOM," CAPCOM's voice interrupted, bringing him back. "Standing by for array reorientation at your go."

"Copy that, CAPCOM," he replied. ISS's solar arrays would have to be turned side-on to the airlock to minimize the chance of a collision with Myers's corpse; Flight Control was waiting until the last moment so as to conserve as much of the arrays' power output as possible. "You are go for reorientation."

He watched briefly as the huge panels began to turn, sending sunlight rippling across their surfaces, then went back to retrieve Myers's body. Once past the solar arrays, the rocket unit could be safely fired by radio signal from Houston.

To get it out there, though, they would have to rely on muscle power.

Reynolds maneuvered the shrouded corpse to the open hatch and braced himself against the airlock wall. The ISS cameras, he knew, would be switching to external—he grinned cynically to himself at the thought. The official reason was to keep the sight of one U.S. astronaut heaving another into space from the American public, but Reynolds suspected the truth was NASA was embarrassed about being seen using such a primitive means of propulsion.

"CAPCOM, IVA-1," he announced, placing his gloved hands flat against the corpse. "Initiating ejection procedure."

He shoved, hard.

The reaction sent him flying towards the airlock back wall, spinning end over end. He grabbed a mobility restraint to stop himself and worked his way back around to the hatch. Myers's corpse was gliding away from ISS; Reynolds held his breath, waiting to see if it would clear the arrays. Forty yards . . . thirty . . . twenty . . . ten. Suddenly it was past, clearing the panels by a good twenty feet.

*Good shooting,* he told himself ironically.

"CAPCOM, IVA-1," he said, exhaling in relief. "Gary's cleared the panels. You are go for ignition."

"Copy that, IVA-1." A point of orange light flared obediently on the tiny pyro unit. Myers's body began to move away, slowly at first, then accelerating. Reynolds caught snatches of the "Star Spangled Banner," playing over the intercom at Houston, through his headset.

He watched the body retreat silently, thinking of the millions of eyes, down there on Earth tracking the astronaut's descent. Somewhere behind him, too, the cosmonauts were watching, the murderer among them. Reynolds wondered briefly what he was thinking. Maybe he was relaxing, thinking that now Myers was gone the pressure would let up just a little.

Reynolds could let him enjoy that small hope.

5:37 P.M., Day 82, Expedition Time
Service Module *Zvezda*, International Space Station

Reynolds jabbed the hydration needle into the septum of the plastic container and squirted in a four-ounce charge of water. He kneaded the surface of the food package, then placed it into his recessed heating well in the galley table. He studied the Service Module—the Russian equivalent of the U.S. Habitation Module—as he waited for the food to warm. Beyond the cramped galley, where the six of them floated around the table, stretched the narrow corridor that led to the cosmonauts' sleeping quarters. In contrast to the orderly lines of the U.S. module, *Zvezda*'s cream walls were a tangle of crisscrossing cables, hoses and straps. Stores and equipment swung lazily out from the points on the walls where they had been loosely anchored.

Reynolds shook his head inwardly. Not even several years of design collaboration with NASA had cured the Russians of their gross indifference to aesthetics.

He removed the container when it was ready and, anchoring it to the table by its magnetic tab, cut the plastic film with the meal scissors. He dipped his spoon into the tub and sucked the lumpy paste off it. It was Irish stew, though only the label told him that—taste was nonexistent. Reynolds ate it stoically. At least the security routine meant he didn't have to share the Russian food. Although it was extremely improbable any of the cosmonauts could synthesize a poison undetected from the limited materials on ISS, Connor had insisted on flying a new stock of meals for Reynolds up with *Endeavor*, and for that Reynolds was grateful.

Maybe the *tvorog*—cottage cheese with nuts—and jellied fish the cosmonauts were eating tasted better than they looked. But he doubted it.

He took another mouthful. His chewing was absurdly loud in the somber silence—the four cosmonauts, sitting opposite him, were eating without speaking, staring down at their food. Kalganin's eyes flicked up nervously at Reynolds once or twice, only to slide away. Dr. Akira's face, as he chewed robotically, was ash gray.

*Anyone would think they'd just been to a funeral.*

He pushed the headset mike, which had drifted down
to his mouth, away and took another spoonful. It would
have been simpler to take it off, but Reynolds had made
a tactical decision to wear it at all times. The headset
was a constant reminder of his separate, direct link to
NASA. None of the cosmonauts, who communicated
with Ground by way of ISS's standard, wall-mounted
Audio Terminal Units, could be sure Reynolds wasn't
receiving transmission from Houston even as they were
watching.

*Pressure. It's all about building pressure.*

Kalganin muttered a low sentence of Russian to the
other cosmonauts, none of whom looked up. Reynolds
frowned at the breach of protocol.

Speaking Russian was against regulations: no matter
how many crew members of other nationalities were on
board, English was the official language on ISS and crew
were required to speak it always.

He scooped up another sticky spoonful of stew
thoughtfully. *NASA are fooling themselves,* he decided.
The agency repeated the mantra over and over, "Friends
and Partners in Space," and imagined they thereby banished all cultural differences—astronaut/cosmonaut,
American/Russian. It was the "boy scout" phenomenon
again: space research was pure, it was innocent and any
human foible that interfered had to be magicked
away . . . or ignored. Yet up here, in a cramped
aluminum-alloy can 220 miles above the Earth, the differences kept stepping out to smack you in the face.
Reynolds wondered again what it had been like for
Myers, sitting at this same table surrounded by four people of alien culture, people united by language, country
and common feelings towards the West.

*Not four people,* he remembered. *Five.*

He turned to the Japanese doctor. "So, Dr. Akira,"
he said, keeping his voice easy, "tell me, how is your
research going?"

On Earth there would have been a clatter as the doctor's cutlery, dropped in shock, hit his metal tray. Here
the knife and fork merely floated until Akira composed
himself and retrieved them.

He looked at Reynolds fearfully, his face twitching. "I beg your pardon, Detective?" he said faintly.

"How is your research going?" Reynolds repeated. He had been briefed on the Japanese research project; the doctor was using the Centrifuge Module to study metastasization rates of cancerous growths under varying conditions of gravity. Reynolds had seen slides of the doctor's experiments—hideous, clumped tumors that sprawled out along cartilage lattices within their glass cylinders, tinted deathly blue from the nutrient base.

Dr. Akira blinked nervously for a moment. He looked from Reynolds to the cosmonauts, as if appealing for help.

"Very well, thank you," he said finally. He hesitated a moment, then continued, his words tumbling out in a rush. "I am uncovering . . . the differences . . . the results are extraordinary." His voice grew fainter; his eyes seemed to lose focus. "The process is phenomenal . . . when gravity is reduced the cells multiply and shed at a fantastic rate."

He tailed off into silence momentarily, then, just as suddenly, snapped back.

"We must hope that none of us ever suffers a malignant growth here," he said, glancing at Reynolds timidly. "The consequences would be . . . there is still so much we do not know about the environment of space."

Reynolds nodded casually, noting the hysterical tone in the man's voice. *He's in bad shape,* he thought pityingly. *It might be an idea to watch him.* The close environment of ISS subjected its inhabitants to intense pressure as it was; three weeks with a corpse in the airlock must have kicked the claustrophobia into overdrive. And Reynolds was seeking to ratchet that pressure up. He would have to be careful in Akira's case, though. With a man this close to the edge, there was no telling what might happen.

He finished the unappetizing stew, placed his spoon on the magnetic holder and slit the packet of semidried whole strawberries open. He popped two in his mouth gingerly, not bothering to rehydrate them. They were surprisingly good—tangy like dried tomatoes, but sweet. Reynolds chewed a couple more with gusto and looked around the table. He could sense the cosmonauts listening closely, behind their lowered heads, and decided to give it to them with both barrels.

"Commander Kalganin," he said casually, swallowing the masticated pulp, "I'll need your help when we've finished here." He fished the final few berries out of the tub and put them in his mouth. "I'm going to run tests on the EMU suits in the Lab Module tonight. I'll need help to move them to the Module."

He watched the reactions dispassionately; the killer, of course, would be too well controlled to betray himself just yet. Kalganin stiffened and glanced up at him, apparently struggling to contain his feelings. Drupev and Matchev merely paused a moment, then continued eating. Ruskaya, however, floating at the far end of the table, lifted her head and looked right at Reynolds—a flat, challenging stare.

Reynolds's heart hammered momentarily. There it was again—that same unease he'd felt, looking at Ruskaya's picture back at Johnson.

*As if it were Ally there, looking at me from the end of the table and asking me why . . .*

For a moment Reynolds's grip wavered, but he fought back, taking himself brusquely to task.

*She isn't Alicia. She's a Russian cosmonaut, and a murder suspect to boot, who just happens to remind you of her.*

*End of story.*

He let out the breath he hadn't realized he'd been holding. His heart rate eased. He was back in control.

Kalganin found his voice. "Of course, Detective," he said stiffly. "I'll help you myself."

Reynolds nodded, letting the suppressed anger he heard in the Russian's voice slide. He thought he understood it: for Kalganin, murderer or no, the worst thing was losing command. Up here, thousands of miles from home and country for months on end, the only thing he had was the fact that he was commander. ISS was his, goddamnit, and that meant something.

Only now it wasn't . . . and it didn't.

"Good," Reynolds said crisply, "thank you. I want you to order the module off-limits to all crew from seven o'clock onwards tonight. I'm going to run luminol tests for blood traces on the suits, and I'll need total darkness. Agreed?"

"Agreed," said Kalganin tonelessly. He uttered a sentence of low Russian to the other cosmonauts, which Reynolds assumed was repeating the command.

Reynolds nodded, satisfied. Actually, the injunction was only the secondary reason for telling the Russians; Reynolds's primary aim was to up the psychological blowtorch a setting.

"Perhaps some of you have come across the procedure before?" he continued politely, to that end. He leaned back sunnily, allowing himself to float, hands behind head. "It's a simple technique, but an incredibly effective one, even with minute quantities of blood."

*That's a goddamn lie, for a start.*

Reynolds was well aware that after the ten-minute exposure to vacuum that the killer's suit had to have undergone, he would be lucky if there was enough residue there to even excite a police dog. Still, he pressed on regardless.

"The luminol undergoes a chemiluminescent reaction when exposed to oxidization from the hemoglobin in human blood. It shows up as a blue-white glow on time-lapse exposure. Best of all, it's incredibly accurate—hardly anything can contaminate the reading."

He shrugged. "There's every chance I'll have the killer pegged in time for your interviews tomorrow."

He flashed a disarming grin, glancing around the table.

"That's gotta make some of you happy, right?"

His blowtorch had had the desired effect, he noted. Despite efforts to cover it, the cosmonauts opposite him were shaken. Kalganin's brow was furrowed in consternation; Drupev's tic was now dancing epileptically; and Matchev's scowl had, for once, vanished. Dr. Akira was gaping openly, his pleading gaze alternating from face to face. Only Ruskaya seemed composed, her dark eyes narrowed skeptically at him.

*That's fair enough,* Reynolds thought, avoiding her gaze. As a biochemist, she probably had an inkling half his spiel was bluff.

Reynolds shrugged inwardly. He'd have to wear that.

For the others though, the strategy had worked. The rat was loose and running around the cage. Now he just had to kick back and let it gnaw through the walls.

11:02 P.M., Day 82, Expedition Time
Laboratory Module, International Space Station

Reynolds sprayed the final surface of the suit with the luminol and pulled his hand out of the vent in the huge plastic shroud that kept the liquid contained. He kicked himself across the darkened module more confidently this time, and felt out the tiny shutter button first go. This was the fourth suit he had done—he was getting practiced.

He depressed the shutter button and waited. The only sounds were the subdued clatter of ISS's circulation fans and the quiet rasp of his own breathing. He counted the seconds down patiently, not bothering to try and pick the suit out in the blackness. The blue-white glow of the luminol's reaction was nearly invisible to the naked eye anyway; he would have to rely on the laptop's frame enhancement to pick it up.

Reynolds frowned in the darkness. His unspoken concern, over dinner with the cosmonauts, wasn't exaggerated. Exposure to vacuum *would* have boiled all but minute quantities of Myers's blood off the suit. He'd have to hope enough had got trapped in the folds at the joints of the EMU to register.

After sixty seconds, the camera beeped. The laptop leaped into life, bathing the module in the faint, blue glow of its screen, as frames began feeding. Reynolds held his breath nervously as he waited for the program to assemble them.

This was his last chance.

He'd been floored for a moment when the test had come up zip on the previous suit. He'd been so sure— Christ, it *had* to be, it was *his* suit, after all. But actually, there was one last possibility, and now he thought about it, it was even better. It still all hung together—as long as the sample showed up now.

Relief flooded him as the wisps of blue-white began

materializing on screen. He was right, it was okay, the bastard *had* switched suits.

He watched, elated, as the images clarified. As expected, nearly all the blood had vaporized—all that was showing up were spidery, concertina lines at the right elbow and a few spots at the left knee. But it was enough, oh Jesus yes, it was enough. He waited until the progress bar was through, then filed the images, taking two disk copies for good measure. He hit the light switch, flickering the module's fluoros into harsh, white life. He gathered the other EMUs, leaving the last one where it was for the moment, still in the shroud, and locked them down in the stowage compartment. Then he disconnected the digital camera from the laptop and slotted it into its aluminum case.

Now there was just one more thing.

His head was throbbing again—a symptom, he knew, of the unaccustomed hyperflow of blood to the head in the first few days of weightlessness—and the exhaustion from his exertions with Myers's corpse in the airlock was catching up with him. He longed to rest, but he forced himself to get this one last job over with. It wasn't enough that he *knew* the murderer had switched suits.

He had to prove it.

He put his hands through the shroud vent gingerly and began working the spandex cooling garment out from inside the suit. Globular bubbles of luminol spray drifted inside the shroud, obscuring his vision, but he didn't dare vacuum-drain it. Not yet. When he'd managed to pull the inner suit out through the suit neck he began examining it minutely through the clear plastic shroud.

Somewhere, trapped in the spandex's close weave, would be the evidence he needed.

It took him a half hour to find it. He was about to give up in frustration when, suddenly, there they were—two tiny, dark hairs, anchored to the fabric of the suit's torso. Two hairs that didn't belong there; two hairs that represented the killer's clumsy attempt to shift suspicion off himself. Reynolds drew them out carefully with forceps and placed them in a Ziploc bag. He hit the drain switch and listened as the vacuum sucked the fluid out of the shroud and vented it.

He entered his jury-rigged cabin and prepared to bed down in a mood of fierce exultation, thinking about the confrontation the next day. His headache was gone, driven out by the elation zipping through his veins. The tension of anticipation was relief. That night he dreamed of nothing.

# 7

1:17 P.M., Day 83, Expedition Time
U.S. Habitation Module, International Space Station

Reynolds ran a final, critical eye over the Hab Module. He'd chosen this location for interviewing deliberately. Just off to the side, with its door left casually open, was Myers's cabin; the dead astronaut's personal effects would be totally visible to each interviewee as they came in. It wasn't much, but Reynolds needed every ounce of pressure he could get.

Besides, if he'd read his man right, this place, in particular, was going to make the killer *very* uncomfortable.

He popped the button at his flight suit wrist and left it loose, for quicker access to the Taser. He slipped the Ziploc bag containing the hairs into his chest pocket.

*Okay. Ready to rock and roll.*

"Commander Kalganin," he said, punching the push-to-talk button on the wall-mounted ATU. "Ready for your interview now."

He sat back and waited patiently for the Russian to make his way through ISS. The other four crew members would have heard his words too; he'd made sure to use the open channel. Under Reynolds's strict orders to remain in their cabins and avoid fraternization, they would each be listening to Kalganin climbing through the Russian Service Module, on his way to interrogation.

*Like inmates on Death Row,* Reynolds thought.

*Look out. Dead man floating.*

Kalganin appeared in the hatchway and pulled himself

slowly level with Reynolds's position. He let go of the
wall and hung motionless in front of Reynolds, his eyes
flicking over the scene uncertainly. They strayed to the
open door of Myers's cabin, slid hurriedly away; met
Reynolds's briefly, then slid away again to rest on the
floor. He said nothing, waiting for the American to start.

Reynolds frowned. *How to play it?*

Kalganin hadn't killed Myers. He knew that. He could
let the Russian *know* he knew it—after all, sometime
soon he was going to need his help. But there were still
some things Reynolds *didn't* know. It might be better to
keep the Commander off balance.

At least to start with.

"What did you think of Gary Myers?" he asked
sharply. No title, no warning. Just the flat question.

Kalganin's head shot up. He stared at Reynolds a moment, went to answer, then checked himself. "Okay," he
said finally. "I did not like him. Is that what you try to
make me say, Detective?"

Reynolds didn't bother to respond. "Why not?" he
asked.

Kalganin shrugged again. "He was what we call
*astroumni*—the smartass always. Every time putting his
nose into things that were not his business. The computers, the experiments . . . all things."

He looked at Reynolds nervously.

"You understand, Detective? I did not kill him. But I
did not like him."

Reynolds let that one slide, for now. "What about the
moment of Myers's murder?" he said, changing tack.
"Why don't you tell me what you were doing?"

"You can read that from the logs, Detective," Kalganin shot back. Truculent now, fighting him. Reynolds
was right, the loss of command was eating the Russian
bad.

"I want to hear it in your words." Actually, that
wasn't it. There was something he needed—one final,
little thing—that he wouldn't get if he asked directly. He
had learned his first couple of years as a cop to beware
of people's suggestibility. Never let them know what you
wanted to hear. If you did, you got it served up, true
or not.

Kalganin scowled, but gave in. "I was making the inventory update in the Cargo Block. We had a Progress to arrive the next day."

Reynolds nodded. In fact, the Russian supply ship had arrived on schedule. Emptied of cargo, it was currently docked at ISS's Russian end, half-full of waste and waiting to be fired off into destructive reentry. Life went on.

"Also, I was being backup officer for Gary's EVA." Kalganin hesitated, shook his head. "It was straightforward procedure," he blurted, protesting. "There would have been no trouble . . ."

Reynolds understood Kalganin's defensiveness. Whether he had liked Myers or not, the Russian felt doubly responsible for the murder. Not only commander of the vessel on which it had happened, but also EVA backup officer—responsible for monitoring the space walk by audio from on board ISS.

That had to add up to some bad karma.

"How did you find out Myers had been killed?" Reynolds asked.

Kalganin glanced up at him, disturbed. "I . . . the first I was knowing was when the communication was stopping. One minute tracking Gary, the next, pfft. Nothing."

"What did you do?"

Kalganin shrugged. "I check the audio unit first. We have much trouble with replacements brought on STS-112. But no problem . . . looks okay. So I go to PCS and try to connect Ground. Pfft . . . nothing again. Then I know something is wrong."

He looked at Reynolds in defiance.

"So I go to OCCS. That *never* goes wrong."

Reynolds ignored the slur. The Portable Computer System was the U.S.-built computer interface that controlled most of ISS. Driven mostly by software switches, it was operated through any of the eight crew laptops on board ISS—and like any software system, was prone to occasional glitches. The archaic Russian Onboard Complex Control System, which controlled the Russian segments of ISS and allowed the Russian crew members to communicate independently with Mission Control, Moscow, was a different story. Hardware reliant, and built from thirty-year-old technology, it was primitive but extremely reliable.

"You got through to Moscow?" he asked. "How long after communication dropped out was that?"

Kalganin cocked his head, calculating. "Maybe twenty minutes. Then they tell me." He lifted his shoulders helplessly. "I can't believe it. I think they are joking, but they tell me no, is true."

Reynolds nodded. That was the amazing thing about space. Myers had been killed less than forty yards from Kalganin. But in the airless, soundless environment of vacuum, he'd had to get the news from Moscow, two or three thousand miles away.

"What did you do then?" he asked.

"They tell me the Communication Array is put out of line, but Houston is getting it back. So I go to PCS again and reboot communication systems."

"You must have alerted the other crew members?" Reynolds said sharply.

Kalganin's brow furrowed as he tried to think. "I . . . it was very confusing. They were screaming at me . . . screaming the American was murdered . . . there would be a war . . . many things. Wait," he said finally. "Yes. Before the PCS . . . I did. I push the warning, and tell them on the intercom."

That much checked out. The log had clocked the first alarm call at twenty-four minutes after Myers's murder. For nearly a full half hour the other ISS crew members had gone about their business in blissful ignorance of the dead astronaut in the airlock.

*Except for the murderer,* Reynolds thought grimly.

He kept his voice carefully neutral for the next question. This was it. The money shot.

"Who responded? On the intercom."

Kalganin looked puzzled. "Who responds . . . they all do. They are all asking me questions, yelling to me. Everyone."

Reynolds nodded in satisfaction. If he'd been in the interview room back at squad, he'd have sat back with his hands behind his head—his automatic gesture when he'd got what he wanted.

It was perfect. There weren't any ATUs where the killer had been working that morning; Reynolds had checked. If he'd responded to that call he was somewhere he shouldn't have been. Like outside the Crew Lock, desperately disassembling the stolen EMU suit and stowing it. Then hiding in one of the side modules— *Christ, it was probably right here, in the Hab Module*—so he could come up behind the others when they gathered outside the airlock.

Reynolds took a moment out to admire the balls of it. It was a class piece of work—thinking cool under pressure like that, improvising, fitting everything into that tiny window. He'd nearly gotten it right too—just that one mistake, answering the call. He must have figured, in the heat of the moment, *it's gonna look suspicious not to respond.* But it was a slipup, and one that put Reynolds that much closer to clinching the deal.

He relaxed a little, softening his next words. *Time to make a friend.*

"You should know, Commander, that neither I nor NASA suspects you of killing Myers. I know you didn't do it."

Kalganin looked at him bleakly and shrugged. "I know that already," he said tonelessly.

"Please, Commander," Reynolds said. "I know this is difficult for you, but you have to forgive me. You have to, do you understand? I didn't know for certain who the crew member responsible was until today. Now that I know, I am going to need your help. In just a short time, I am going to arrest the murderer and I need your assistance to do it."

Kalganin's mouth quirked, torn by the desire to ask.

Reynolds shook his head. "I can't tell you that, Commander. Not yet. For now I just need you to answer this one question. Will you help me?"

He watched as the man struggled with himself. Reynolds could imagine what he was going through. On the one hand, he was ISS's commander, duty-bound to assist the investigation until the bitter end. On the other, the cosmonauts were his countrymen, even Myers's killer. To do his duty he would have to betray one of them.

"Okay," he said finally, his voice faint. "What is it you want me to do?"

"Nothing yet,' Reynolds replied. "But I want you to keep yourself ready. I'll call for you. Can you do that?"

Kalganin nodded. "Then I may go?"

"Yes. Back to the Service Module please. Unfortunately my orders still stand. I want you to remain in your cabin until I call."

He watched as the Russian commander left, pulling himself along the module wall hand over hand. The exhilaration that had kicked in the night before was still humming, and nothing Kalganin had told him had dampened it. He was closing in; he felt the familiar tingling, the scrotal clench that meant the moment was near. There were just one or two things more. He leaned over to the ATU.

"Dr. Akira. Could you make your way to the Habitation Module, please."

He flexed his shoulders as he waited for the doctor, working the game plan over in his mind. In truth, there was no reason to call the Japanese. His information would add nothing, and Reynolds doubted he would hold up under even a mild grilling. But Reynolds wanted to spin the process out, for the killer's benefit—keep him nailed down and sweating in the spotlight as the other crew members trooped in and out, one by one. Drip-torture him. Keep the blowtorch on so long as he came through that hatch *craving* confession.

*Nearly as much as me.*

Reynolds had to admit it. He needed that confession. Everytime he had so far—the blood residue, the hairs, Kalganin's statement—was capital *C* circumstantial. Enough to convince him he was on the right track. Probative value though?

Zilch.

Akira entered the module timidly, like a rat sniffing a junction in a maze. He nearly drew back at the sight of the detective. Reynolds beckoned him in encouragingly.

"Come in, Dr. Akira," he said, smiling. "There's nothing to worry about. Just some routine questions to get through."

Reassured, the doctor pulled himself through the module, halting in front of the American. Reynolds could see his decision to go easy on Akira was justified. The Japanese scientist looked terrible—his round face puffy with fatigue, unkempt gray hair sticking up in tufts, the pasty residue of a few days' saliva caked in the corners of his mouth. ISS residents all had to accept lower standards of personal hygiene than on Earth—it was difficult to keep really clean when you were limited to washcloth rubs for everything other than face and hands. But Dr. Akira had obviously let even that routine go. His gaze flicked from place to place nervously. His lips worked away soundlessly.

*Time to pull out the stops,* Reynolds decided.

"You're completely innocent of Gary Myers's murder, aren't you, Dr. Akira?" he said softly.

Akira looked at him fearfully, as if he thought the statement some kind of trap.

"My government and I have known it for some time. I would like to take the opportunity to apologize for not formally clearing you sooner. And to thank you for your patience."

The exoneration seemed to have virtually no effect on Akira. His lips continued moving, muttering noiselessly. Suddenly, a low moan escaped him.

"You don't know what it has been to be here," he said agitatedly. "You arrived only two days ago. I have been here many weeks, with *them*." The doctor shuddered. "Side by side with them, never able to get away. Knowing always that one of them killed the American . . ."

"Yes, I understand," Reynolds soothed. "A trying time for you, Doctor."

Akira took no notice. "At night it was worse. Having to sleep right beside them." He shuddered again. "Ugh. They are animals to do what they did to the American. All of them. Not humans. Filthy animals."

Reynolds winced. Akira was really losing it, erupting like that with the kind of xenophobic undercurrent he knew many Japanese shared, but would never dream of vocalizing. And every second of these interviews was

going out live to Mission Control. Reynolds wondered
how the racist diatribe was going down among the RIOs
at Houston and the staff at MCC Moscow.

"Dr. Akira," he said sharply. "I understand your distress, but you have to get a grip on yourself. The situation is under control. You are in no danger, Doctor."

The word seemed to hold the Japanese spellbound.
His voice stopped abruptly, and the nervous flicker of
his eyes was arrested midsweep.

"The danger," he repeated, murmuring it. "Every
time my wife speaks to me she asks if there is danger for
me. I tell her no, but I can see she does not believe me."

His eyes rose slowly, locking onto Reynolds.

"She tells me my son cries often, asking if his father
is going to be hurt, like the American was hurt."

His hand flashed out, grasping Reynolds by the sleeve.

"But you are here now. And you say you know I did
not kill Mr. Myers . . . that means you must know which
Russian it was that did. You will arrest him now, and I
can return home, yes? I am sure my government will
allow it." His eyes were feverish, his words babbling. "I
could leave tomorrow, Detective, you will tell them, yes?
There is no need to wait for your shuttle. I can return
in *Ryokousha*. You will tell them, yes?"

Reynolds was ready for that one.

Connor had told him earlier of the call from Mission
Control Japan. The flight directors at Tsukuba Space
Center were worried. Akira had been talking obsessively
in his daily briefings about terminating his mission early
and returning home in the *Ryokousha*, the experimental
Japanese minishuttle currently docked to Japan's ISS
module, *Kibo*. But *Ryokousha*—"traveler" in English—
was not yet certified for manned missions. Tsukuba's engineers were adamant. To fly it in its untested state
would be suicidal.

Reynolds shook his head.

"You know as well as I do that *Ryokousha* isn't man-
rated, Doctor," he said. "You're gonna have to wait
until STS-116, like everybody else."

STS-116 was the shuttle mission *after* Reynolds's, with
which NASA would swap the nonguilty ISS crew mem-

bers for a new crew. The decision not to return them to Earth with the murderer had been a political one.

*Distance* them from the killer. Bring them home as heroes, not criminals. On a different bird, to prove it.

Dr. Akira fell silent, crestfallen. Reynolds dismissed hm as gently as he could, shaking his head as he watched him exit. Now *that* was what space could do to a man.

Connor's voice buzzed in his earpiece. "Edge, you copy?"

Reynolds withdrew his finger from the ATU. "Yeah, Matt. I read you. How're you enjoying the show?"

"That's what I called about. Akira's goddamn flaking, huh?"

"Yeah, he's close," Reynolds replied.

"Uh huh. Well the Flight Surgeon's just been on line to Tsukuba. They've decided to put him onto a course of mood stabilizers straightaway."

"Yeah? Sounds a good idea to me."

"Well, they want you to check he's taking them. Three diazepams a day. Okay?"

That figured. Pharmaceuticals were really the responsibility of ISS's DMO—Designated Medical Officer—in this case, Ruskaya. But Reynolds couldn't see Akira swallowing anything one of the Russians handed him.

Not under the circumstances.

"Sure, Matt. I'll see he chews his happy pills."

"Good." Connor hesitated. "How's it going?"

*Fishing now,* Reynolds thought. Matt knew perfectly well how it was going. He'd been tuned in the whole time.

"Fine," he said, innocent. "I should have the interviews wrapped up by five."

Connor laughed. "Same old Edge. Tighter than a clam's asshole. I spotted that question, you bastard, even if Kalganin didn't. You're moving on something, right?"

Reynolds shrugged, noncommittal, for the wall-mounted camera. "Could be."

"Let me take a guess. You're calling Ruskaya next, huh?"

"C'mon, Matt," Reynolds protested. "You're hexing me. You can't wait a couple of hours?"

"Okay, okay," Connor laughed again. Then his voice got quiet, serious. "She's involved in this though, isn't she?"

Reynolds's voice was grim.

"Oh yeah. She's involved all right."

2:32 P.M., Day 83, Expedition Time
U.S. Habitation Module, International Space Station

*Balance. That's the way to deal with this shit.*

When the feelings welled up, you hit them hard with something opposite, something to counteract. That way you stayed on top.

Ruskaya floated in front of him, waiting. Long brown hair snaked out, Medusa-like, from her head. Her slender form, angular in blue ISS flight suit and soft black boots, hung in a street-tough pose—relaxed, but ready. Her brown eyes homed in on his—no sliding away, no fear.

*Beautiful,* Reynolds thought. Her eyes were the color of dark topaz, blending imperceptibly to the black of their pupils.

And because he felt himself dwelling on them a second longer than he should, he lashed out with the question.

"What kind of affair were you having with Myers?"

For a moment, her expression didn't change. Then, abruptly, she laughed—rich laughter that rang through the module. Her voice, when she spoke, dripped scorn.

"So. Just like in the movies, is it not? Does not the policeman always ask the woman that, Detective Reynolds?"

She looked at Reynolds, challenging.

"Did you come all the way up here to check on my sex life, Detective? I thought this was a murder investigation."

"It is," Reynolds rasped. He continued stubbornly. "I know that you were. You hid it well, both of you, but the signs were still there. If you know where to look."

He shook his head.

"I've seen the recorder dumps. You betrayed yourselves constantly. Every time Myers served you first at dinner, every time he stopped talking on the channel to hear the sound of your voice."

He looked at her squarely.

"Answer the question. What kind of affair were you having with Myers?"

For a moment it seemed she might resist; then she gave up, shrugging.

"What kinds are there? I am a woman and he was a man. You can imagine the rest."

*Right on the money,* Reynolds thought fiercely. The elation was peaking again; the final piece had fallen into place.

"Did you sleep together?" he asked tersely.

A noise in his earpiece distracted him. Someone at Space Station Control had pushed the button to break into the channel, probably accidentally. Reynolds grinned to himself, picturing the scene at Johnson. However many hundred flight staff patched in live, when *that* came over the loop.

*Slept together? Jesus fucking Christ!*

You had to bet at least five of them had spat coffee over their terminals.

Ruskaya lifted her head and stared at him coolly. She let the silence stretch out, making no attempt to answer.

*Taking the fifth,* Reynolds thought. *Even the Russians know that one.*

"But you were lovers," he said, trying another tack. "Is that correct?"

Ruskaya's hostile expression slid slowly into one of puzzlement. "Yes," she murmured, "I think you are right. I think Gary was in love with me."

Reynolds raised an eyebrow, mock-polite. "Aren't you doing your dead lover a disservice, Ms. Ruskaya? Surely you loved him too?"

He was surprised at the difficulty he had saying it. He had to conjure up the vision of Myers's mummified corpse, brown and shrunken, to stifle the jealous pang.

*That was where Myers's love got* him.

Ruskaya shrugged. "I felt sorry for him. Gary was a boy. He had no idea of suffering, like all you Americans." The gloves were off now, she was hitting out where she could.

Reynolds let it pass. He had what he needed now—the killer's motive. There was really no need to continue, but he found himself, almost unwillingly, pressing for details.

"How did it start?" he asked. Meaning the relationship.

*You had to admire her,* Reynolds thought, listening to her. There was no trace of discomfort or intimidation. She sounded merely bored. And hostile.

"Gary became interested in the crystallization programs I was doing. He started to help me . . . just to be near me, I think. He designed new data-compilation software for me, that type of thing."

She shook her head.

"He was lonely, more than anything, I believe. He told me there were many problems with his wife. He said they would divorce when he returned to Earth."

Reynolds nodded. Connor's biography had detailed regular visits to a marriage counselor in the twelve months leading up to Myers's ISS mission. Agency scuttlebutt had his wife seeing another man.

"What did the two of you talk about?"

Ruskaya's face wrinkled dismissively. "What do you call it? Little talk? He told me always about California, the beautiful beaches there. He said we should go there together." Her face twisted oddly, as if she were caught by a painfully fond memory. "And the computer systems. He was as I say, a boy. Always boasting about what he could do, showing off to me."

"And the two of you became physically intimate?" Reynolds asked, hammering the point.

Ruskaya's face flashed annoyance again. "If you must know, we did not. We never slept together."

She hesitated, glanced up at the internal camera.

"Gary asked me to, always. He said he had made a fault in the IC system, here in the Hab Module, so we could be together without Mission Control seeing."

*Make that twenty screens dripping coffee.*

Houston was getting a hell of an education in human

nature today. Reynolds thought back to the mystified frustration of the Flight Systems controller he'd interviewed, back at Mission Control.

*This unusual fault in the cameras,* the man had said. *Gary was helping me, but we never did manage to get the bug out . . .*

"But you never acceded to his requests?" Reynolds said.

His mind raced ahead, putting it all together. *Actually, it didn't matter if she didn't. Point is, the killer thought she did.*

"I told you already, Detective. I did not *love* him." Ruskaya's hands locked onto her hips, taunting. "Or do you think Russian women are different from Americans in that way?"

"I have no thoughts on the matter at all," Reynolds said tonelessly. "I'm merely trying to establish the truth about the murder of a United States astronaut."

*Liar,* he mocked himself. Christ, the hands-on-hips thing had shaken him. Alicia used to do that all the time.

Ruskaya snorted derisively. "What could my physical relations with Gary possibly have to do with this murder?"

*Everything in the world,* Reynolds thought. *That was the one thing the killer couldn't stand. Just thinking about it must have been like a blade twisting in his guts . . .*

"Maybe somebody didn't like the attention you paid Myers," Reynolds said out loud. "Maybe one of the men . . ."

His voice cut off abruptly as Ruskaya's hand flashed out, locking onto his wrist in a fierce grip. The action set him moving slowly towards her, so that when she spoke her face was mere inches away from his.

"Why does it have to be one of the men, Detective," she said, her voice low. Her breath was hot on his face. "Why not me, Detective? You forget that women and men are more equal here."

This was easier, at least. *Alicia never did anything like this.*

"I'll keep it in mind, Ms. Ruskaya," he said calmly, waiting until she released him. He resisted the urge to

rub the wrist. "That's all for now. I want you to go back
to your cabin now. If I need you further, I'll call."

His elation grew as he waited the thirty seconds or so
he judged it would take Ruskaya to get back to the
Service Module, overriding the unease her presence had
provoked. *I was right about everything, damn it.* The affair, the motive, the action the day Myers was killed.
Everything had fallen into place.

And now it was coming down to endgame. He
counted out another ten seconds, then leaned over to
the ATU. His finger speared the button.

"Flight Engineer Matchev, make your way to the Habitation Module, please."

He leaned back to wait.

**3:34 P.M., Day 83, Expedition Time**
**U.S. Habitation Module, International Space Station**

*Fuck. This mother's huge.*

Reynolds hadn't realized just how big Matchev's six
feet three (six five when you factored in the extra couple
of inches people grew in microgravity) really was. Up
close, the Russian Flight Engineer seemed a giant. His
shoulders bulged in his blue flight suit. Even under the
atrophying influence of weightlessness, he was packing
serious muscle. His arms were massive.

Reynolds could easily see those arms grasping Myers
for purchase, then smashing the footing block into his
helmet again and again, while the massive legs locked
around him, holding the astronaut in place. He could
see that all right—no sweat.

Except he knew Matchev hadn't done it.

He led the Flight Engineer into the interrogation gently, feeding him general questions to start with. What
were your relations with Gary Myers? Where were you
when you heard the news? The Russian's answers were
monosyllabic when he could get away with it, surly and
abrupt when he couldn't. A few minutes in, Reynolds
turned up the heat.

"Did you know Irina Ruskaya and Gary Myers were
having an affair?" he asked suddenly. Watching for the
response.

Matchev's eyes glittered, but he merely shrugged.
*Who gives a shit what she does?*

Reynolds liked that. He liked it a lot. There was one more test though and, after a few more inconsequential questions, Reynolds ran it over Matchev, to make sure.

"What would you say if I told you your suit had tested positive for the victim's blood?" he asked.

He waited for Matchev's reaction. Feigned surprise, concerned attempts to explain, would mean his reasoning was off and Matchev was involved somehow after all. Angry indifference would be more in character.

The Russian didn't disappoint. *"Eb tvoju mat!"* he exploded.

"What does that mean?" Reynolds asked politely.

"It means to go and get fucked," Leonid replied. "You and your suit with some blood on it."

"You're not concerned?"

Matchev shrugged his huge shoulders. "No. I had nothing of part in killing Gary. How should I know how blood was getting onto it?"

Reynolds leaned back, satisfied. Matchev's response was pure innocence. He could relax and follow the countdown all the way to zero.

"Okay, Flight Engineer Matchev," he said airily. "That's enough for today. Go back to your cabin until further orders please."

"What, no more questions?" Matchev asked sarcastically.

Reynolds pinned him with the gaze he reserved for hard-asses.

"Not for now, pal," he said. "But be sure not to leave town, all right?"

Reynolds's earpiece squealed the second Matchev had exited the module, but he killed the volume and ignored it. It was Matt, probably, hyped because he saw now where it was headed. Calling to say "be careful." "He's cornered now and he knows it."

Reynolds flexed the wrist to which the Taser was strapped, reassuring himself of its presence. Not that he was going to need it.

Not with Kostia.

He hit the button, said the words. Just the name,

"Kostia Drupev." Nothing else. That was the final touch—let him know he *was* being treated differently, that his suspicions about why he was being called last were a hundred percent on the money.

Reynolds closed his eyes, picturing the *Soyuz* commander making his way through the Service Module to ISS's central corridor. Casting nervous glances at the closed doors of the other cosmonauts' quarters. Wondering sickly what they had told the American detective. Running over the murder again and again, trying to pick what he'd forgotten. Every slow hand-over-hand movement through the module pulling him closer to the man who *knew*.

*And I do know you, Kostia. I do.*

Reynolds felt the thrill of perverse intimacy that punching through a perp's crust always gave him. It was a strange kind of inverted love. You got inside the suspect's skull, sympathized with him, understood him. Came to know him so well that in the end it felt like you loved him more than his, or your, best friends.

Except that then you took him down.

He listened, eyes still shut, as the *Soyuz* commander entered the module. There was a long pause as the man took in the scene. Reynolds could nearly smell the fear—*What is the American doing? With his eyes closed like that?* Then the slow, hesitant noises as the man climbed through the module towards him. Reynolds let the Russian come to a halt, making no move until ten or twenty seconds had passed.

Then he opened his eyes.

Kostia was floating in front of him, fidgeting nervously. The Russian's broad face was slick with sweat. His eyes flicked nervously over Reynolds's face, searching. His mouth was twisted into a sick, half-smile.

Reynolds let his own flat stare spin out a few seconds. Then he asked Kostia the question, keeping his voice so quiet it was hard to hear over the murmur of the circulation fans. "Why did you kill Gary Myers?"

# 8

Kostia goggled. His mouth made stupid goldfish movements. He swayed slightly in the minute air currents within the module.

"Perhaps I should say: When did you decide to kill him?" Reynolds continued, breaking the silence. "Because I already know why."

Kostia gaped a moment more, then gave a short, nervous laugh.

"This is interrogation technique, no?" he said. "You say this to everybody."

Reynolds shook his head. "I'm afraid not, Kostia," he said. *Using his first name. I know you, Kostia, don't forget that.* "I know you murdered him. I have the proof right here."

He drew the tiny Ziploc bag out of his flight-suit pocket and placed it between them, letting it hang there.

Kostia's eyes followed the two bobbing dark hairs, mesmerized.

"I found these in Leonid Matchev's EMU suit last night, Kostia. The luminol tests were positive on Leonid's suit—Myers's blood was all over it. The killer used Leonid's EMU, no question about it."

Reynolds saw the *Soyuz* commander's face twitch. *He's putting it all together.* The tic around the man's right eye began jumping again.

"They're your hairs, Kostia, aren't they?" he said. "I

haven't run the DNA tests yet, but I'm sure they'll confirm it. That was you in the suit, the day of Myers's murder. Wasn't it?"

Kostia's eyes rose slowly to lock onto Reynolds's. They were wide, like those of an animal trapped in the spotlight.

"It was smart work to switch suits," Reynolds continued, "but it will count against you, Kostia. Using Leonid's suit makes it look premeditated, rather than an act of passion. And it was an act of passion, wasn't it?"

The Russian stared at him.

Reynolds's voice softened. "How long have you loved Irina, Kostia?"

Kostia's eyes broke from Reynolds and looked wildly around the module. His mouth worked away soundlessly. Globules of sweat spilled off his forehead and floated free.

"I know that you do," Reynolds continued. "You may think an American detective can't read you because you are Russian." He shook his head. "You're wrong. I can see it written right across your face."

He thought back to the video-streams he had watched on *Endeavor*. The hidden ballet he had seen between Myers, Ruskaya and Kostia. Every one of them trying to hide their feelings from the other crew members and from the ever-watching cameras. And each of them failing in so many tiny details.

Kostia had been easier to pick than the others. The *Soyuz* commander betrayed himself a hundred ways. The clincher for Reynolds had been the incident he had observed at the end of one mealtime. Kostia, assigned to tidy-detail, had forgotten himself so far as to tuck Ruskaya's unused dinner wipe into his flight-suit pocket. It was a quick flash, but there was no mistaking the significance.

*Just to have something of hers,* Reynolds thought.

A dinner wipe, for Christ's sake. The man had it bad. Then the marks of suppressed rage Reynolds had noted. Psychiatrists had a word for it—what was it? Displacement. When normal outlets for anger were repressed, it started to mutate, bubbling up in peculiar, half-conscious ways. Reynolds figured onboard ISS counted as one of the most severely repressed gigs on the planet—under the eye of five, six or seven crew members every minute of the fucking day, not to mention however many hundred flight control staff down on Earth. And Kostia *had* been exhibiting glitches, particularly in his relations with Myers.

Like leaving the American's name off the Emergency Procedures Manual distribution list. Like "forgetting" to change the carbon dioxide scrubber in Myers's EMU suit—an error that could have killed the astronaut through $CO_2$ poisoning, if it hadn't been detected and fixed.

"You hated Myers, didn't you?" Reynolds continued. "The attention he paid Irina. The attention she paid him."

Kostia writhed, apparently having difficulty containing himself.

"Yes!" he burst out finally. His face seethed with loathing. "That filthy American. Irina is not to be defiled at the hands of one such as he."

"Even if she wanted to be?" Reynolds asked, goading now.

"She did not want to be!" the Russian shouted. Flecks of spittle flew off his lips and past Reynolds. His fists were clenched hard. "She didn't see that he was wanting only to use her. His flatterings were nothing more than a way of destroying her better judgment."

"But you truly loved her?" Reynolds asked, steering Kostia gently towards confession. He was more conscious than ever of how badly he needed it. So far, it all looked good for the camera—anger, hatred, the motivation of jilted love. But it was not an admission of guilt.

Kostia stopped short, suddenly aware of the cliff he was being stampeded over. "Wait . . . I . . ." he said in alarm. He looked around the module wildly, as if escape lay somewhere there. "You do not understand. I didn't kill Gary. I could never take life like that . . . not even his."

Reynolds said nothing, merely stretching his hand out slowly, deliberately, to the Ziploc bag, which he put back into his flight-suit pocket.

Kostia's eyes followed it. *"Nyet, nyet,"* he cried, forgetting himself. He pointed at the bag, by now safely inside Reynolds's pocket. "That isn't . . . it wasn't . . ." he moaned. He seized the front of Reynolds's flight suit. "You should believe me, Detective," he said desperately. "I did not do this thing." Tears welled up in his eyes and broke free, floating in front of Reynolds like wobbling baubles.

Reynolds shook Kostia's hands free, frowning. He let the Russian weep to himself for a few moments. He sensed he was losing his moment; Kostia's breakdown had not produced the confession he'd expected, and he could feel the Russian digging in for further denials.

*What to do?*

He couldn't afford to let the *Soyuz* commander see how badly he needed that admission. Further attempts to drag it out might alert him to the weakness of Reynolds's case, give him spirit to fight. Back at squad he would have kicked the door shut and given Kostia a light tune-up—not enough to hurt, but enough to know he was gonna *get* hurt if he didn't stop fucking around. Reynolds glanced up at the internal cameras. That wasn't an option here, though.

*Fuck it. Just arrest him.*

He punched the button on the audio unit. He'd take Kostia in, introduce him to the pleasures of solitary confinement. Christ, he had at least two days until *Endeavor* could make it back to pick them up. If he couldn't squeeze a confession out of the Russian before then, he'd hand in his shield and move to Florida.

He ordered Kalganin and Matchev brusquely to the Hab Module and pulled the cuffs out of his flight-suit pocket. Ordinarily, he would've put Drupev into restraints and dragged him off to the improvized brig in the Docking and Stowage Module (DSM) himself, but Connor had been adamant.

"Involve whichever of the Russians are innocent," he'd insisted. "Give us footage we can use to show them on the good guys' team."

Those words again. *Damage control.*

Kostia's eyes bulged at the sight of the handcuffs. His head shot around at the entry of the two Russian crew members. He stared at them, uncomprehending. Reynolds took the opportunity to pin his wrists behind his back and snap the cuffs on.

Kostia screamed at the touch of the metal and began thrashing, the action wheeling him slowly around on the spot. Kalganin and Matchev came up through the module, looking from Reynolds to the struggling Kostia, then back again. He motioned them to take up position on either side of the writhing *Soyuz* commander. They did so, Matchev scowling, Kalganin wincing at the sound of Kostia's screams.

*"Leonid! Leonid! Pamagi minye! Americanyets znayet vsio!"* the *Soyuz* commander shrieked.

"Commander Kalganin," Reynolds said harshly, overriding him. "I said earlier I would need your help. I want the two of you to witness this, please."

He turned to Kostia, maneuvering himself so that he was visible to the wall-mounted camera over the struggling Russian's back. *"Soyuz* Commander Kostia Drupev, I am arresting you for the murder of United States astronaut Gary Myers. You have the right to remain silent. If you choose not to exercise that right, anything you say can and will be used against you in a court of law. You have the right to have legal counsel present, as soon as it becomes practical to do so."

*Fat chance of that,* Reynolds noted, with some satisfaction. Kostia wouldn't get anywhere near a lawyer until they landed back at Kennedy. Cops in orbit, NASA could come at. But he doubted if anyone in the world was ready yet for lawyers in space.

"Commander Kalganin, *Soyuz* Commander Drupev is to be confined in the prepared holding facility until Space Shuttle *Endeavor* returns and is able to effect his return to Earth. I want you to take him there now and secure him in the facility. He is to have no contact with crew members other than yourself, and that only when you take him meals. Is that clear?"

Kalganin gaped at him, nonplussed.

"Is that clear?" Reynolds repeated.

Recovering himself, Kalganin nodded. He glanced at Matchev uncertainly and, after a couple of false starts, grabbed Kostia, provoking a fresh bout of screaming from the struggling cosmonaut. Reynolds watched as the two Russians forced their compatriot out of the module, holding him tightly with both hands each and moving themselves by kicking along the walls. His last sight of Kostia was of his feet, pedaling comically as he fought against the hands restraining him.

*There it is,* Reynolds thought to himself cynically as the screams retreated. *A murderer, an investigation and an arrest.*

*All packaged and ready for the six o'clock news.*

11:42 P.M., Day 83, Expedition Time
Laboratory Module, International Space Station

Reynolds flipped the laptop open and hit the icon for videoconference. He adjusted the marble-sized camera and waited for the software to load. He glanced at the laptop clock.

Three minutes until the scheduled videocon with Connor.

Around him, ISS was quiet. The muffled thumps and screams as Kostia threw himself at the walls of the DSM had died down an hour or so ago. No doubt the Russian was tired. Reynolds could sympathize. His own body ached to the bones with weariness. It wasn't just the afternoon's work, though there'd been plenty of that: sealing and cataloguing physical evidence, writing up reports for the various prosecuting agencies—South Texas DA, Security Directorate and the Russian FSB. It was more the fatigue locking a case down always gave him. It was the price he paid for the intense, almost sexual, rush he got from *that* moment—when the perp realized he knew and was going to take him down. The aftermath was flat, deflating. Postorgasmic.

He longed for sleep. Not just to ease the tiredness. He wanted to drown out consciousness as well; smother that one rebellious nerve that kept quivering at the back of his mind. Telling him *something's not right here.*

Reynolds sighed. He took himself through it again.
*Kostia killed Myers,* he told himself. *You know that.*

*He used the fact the internal cameras were shut down to get into Leonid's suit without being seen.*

*He set a fault in the communications array, timed it to coincide with the end of his prebreathe. Then he quietly depressurized the Equipment Lock, climbed into the Crew Lock and bludgeoned Myers to death.*

*He returned to the Equipment Lock, did his breathe-down and repressurized the Lock. He desuited, then went and hid, probably in the Hab Module, so he could come up behind the others when they gathered at the airlock—where he should have come from if he really had been working in the Soyuz.*

*While there he fucked up and answered that alert of Kalganin's, which is what sealed the deal for you so that he's currently trussed up in the Stowage Module and beating his brains against its wall, sounds like. All right?*

He knew all of that. He did. And tomorrow he would squeeze an admission out of Kostia and that would be that. Case closed. And yet . . .

Details still nagged at him.

*Number one. The suit.*

There was no getting around it. It didn't matter which EMU Kostia had used, he'd still had just twenty minutes' prebreathe. Max. His blood should still have had enough nitrogen in it to fry his brain like a blast of low-grade Corridor crack the instant he entered the airlock. Yet, nothing. Kostia had performed just as well on the biomed tests Reynolds had run him through as all the other cosmonauts. And Akira, for that matter.

*Number two. Myers looked right.*

Enclosed in his space suit, Myers could not have heard anything those moments before he was attacked; floating in the middle of the lock, away from the walls, he wouldn't have felt anything either. Whatever made him turn his head must have been something he *saw,* and that could only have been Kostia, climbing into the Crew Lock with murder on his mind. Yet Kostia had come from the Equipment Lock, through the internal hatch to Myers's left.

So why did Myers look right?

That was towards the external hatch, out towards

space. And there was no way Kostia could have entered from there. The external cameras weren't the problem—they were all focused elsewhere, on the solar arrays. Again, it was time. To come through the external hatch, Kostia would have had to EVA out one of ISS's docking ports—whose transfer compartments could be used, at a pinch, as crude airlocks—and make his way down ISS to the airlock proper. But that was a fifteen-minute crawl, at best, leaving just *five minutes* for Kostia's prebreathe.

No way he'd done that. If he had, Myers would have had to *help* him into the airlock. He'd be a dribbling, spastic wreck.

They were just details, Reynolds knew, niggling enough but insignificant, and he cursed himself for a sanctimonious prick who couldn't let well enough alone. He pushed them out of mind as Connor flashed up on-screen.

He frowned at the sight of the older man's face. Connor looked like shit.

"Jesus, Matt," he said. "You look as bad as I feel. What's going on?"

Connor scowled.

"Just be grateful you're up there, Edge. It's a free-fire zone down here right now. State Department eggheads jumping us through one hoop after another—how's touchdown security gonna be handled, where're the Russian dignitaries gonna be placed, when's Drupev get access to his lawyer? Not to mention the press conferences. The networks are going apeshit for the arrest footage. We've got it running on two-minute loop on NASA TV so they can pull it off direct."

He shook his head, peered at Reynolds. "How're things up there?" he asked.

Reynolds shrugged. "Quiet now."

Connor nodded. "The jailbird stopped singing, huh? He was knocking himself around pretty goddamn bad there for a while. He smashed the internal camera, you know."

"Might be just as well," Reynolds replied. "Probably a mess in there by now. Drupev's been locked up seven hours and he hasn't requested a toilet visit yet. Get my drift?"

Connor's nose wrinkled in disgust. "Jesus. Just make sure you get the bastard cleaned up before he hits the cameras at Kennedy, okay? What about the others?"

It was Reynolds's turn to scowl. "They're okay. I managed to get the goofballs down Akira's throat. Don't know how much difference it made though." He gestured dismissively. "The others are pretty quiet. Kalganin seems a little shell-shocked by it all." He hesitated. "The other two are harder to read."

He thought of Ruskaya's mocking face, back in the interview. His disquiet returned. It wasn't the difficulty reading her that caused it, he realized. It was the ease of reading himself.

"They'll come round," Connor said. "Now everything's wrapped up, there'll be time to make friends again."

Reynolds pursed his lips, saying nothing.

Connor's eyes narrowed. "What?" he asked suspiciously. Then his eyes opened wide again. "Oh no," he said. "Don't tell me. You bastard. Not second thoughts?"

Reynolds shrugged. "Just a couple of things, Matt," he muttered, almost apologetically.

"A couple of . . ." Connor said, shaking his head in disbelief. "Jesus wept! We've got Drupev's name going out to every media outlet in the world at this very moment as the arrested suspect in the murder of U.S. astronaut Gary Myers. Are you telling me we're gonna have to call every one of them up and say 'Sorry, we made a mistake?' What couple of things?"

Reynolds shook his head. "No, Matt, it's okay. Kostia killed him. And he did it on his own too, I'm certain of that."

He hesitated.

"There's just some things I can't square. Like the suit, remember? We talked about that. How was he able to get in and out of it with under half an hour for pre-breathe, and probably less for breathe-down? I keep telling myself: 'Sure, he was amped up with hating Myers, his metabolism was pumping—that has to make a difference.' "

He shrugged.

"Who knows, maybe he just got lucky. I guess I could swallow that. But that still doesn't explain why Myers looks right in that transmission just before he was killed. Why look right? He must have . . ."

"Edge! Edge!" Connor interrupted. He shook his head, laughing. "Goddamn you, you bastard. Listen to yourself. The same as always, not even happy with perfection."

He surveyed his friend quizzically. "You want my opinion? Who the hell knows how Duprev did it? The point is that he did do it. Same with Gary in the airlock. Who knows why he looked right? Maybe his neck itched and he was trying to scratch it on his shoulder. Maybe a flash of light got in his eyes. Whatever."

His voice softened. "C'mon, buddy," he entreated. "That was a class piece of work you did today. Why not just be satisfied with it? Sit back and enjoy the ride for a while. Huh? You know what you ought to do is get some rest. God knows you've earned it."

*For Christ's sake, don't go digging any deeper.* That was what Connor was really saying. Begging him not to.

Reynolds thought he understood. NASA had what they needed now—a killer. Even better, the right sort of killer, with just the right sort of motive. Kostia had murdered from jealousy, and that was a human emotion. It was an individual kink, not a flaw in the weave of the fabric overall. It could be dealt with procedurally— tighten screening, amp up psych evaluations, tinker with the human machinery. But the ISS program itself was not at fault. It could go on.

Better yet, the State Department Cassandras' fears had been proved wrong. A jealous murder meant no conspiracy. No General Lavrenti Korbalov, no Patriotic Union. And no threat to the Nunn-Lugar programs, or of the destruction that could be unleashed if they failed.

You had to bet the eggheads were celebrating too.

"Sure, Matt," he said, allowing a grin to spread across his face. "Just playing devil's advocate, you know?"

"Well, deep-six it, soldier," Connor growled at him, rubbing his forehead wearily. "Goddamnit, Edge," he said irritably. "If the devil gets you on his side, we're all in trouble."

**12:39 A.M., Day 84, Expedition Time**
**Docking and Stowage Module, International Space Station**

"Hey! Fuck your mothers! Why won't you hear me?"

Kostia stopped hammering the hatch and listened. The sobs rising from his throat made it difficult to hear; he squeezed his teeth together hard to choke them off. But ISS was quiet, the only noise the sighs and groans of metal walls shifting in response to temperature variations. No one was there.

He sagged against the hatch, groaning. His grip on the shelving he had been using to hammer slackened; it left his cuffed hands and drifted out to join the cloud of circling debris—glass from the broken fluoros, the camera he had wrenched off the wall and smashed. The solitary "OK" light on the Caution and Warning panel seeped dim light into the module, turning the darkness a ghostly blue. It threw the lockers lining both walls into weird shadow and gleamed dully, here and there, off a circling shard.

A globule of liquid collided with Kostia's face. He flicked it away with his shoulder in disgust. It could be blood—the gashes on his hands were still oozing freely—or urine. He had noticed that some hours before—*Fuck your mother, I pissed myself!* He'd been so crazy there for a while he hadn't even felt it.

He ground his jaws together hard, sobbing. The pressure was unbearable. He had nearly wavered when he realized the *Americanyets* was going to accuse him. All that talk about the suit—the shock had nearly stopped his heart. Even now, thinking back to the *Americanyets's* eyes watching him as he took out that little bag, Kostia felt the terror welling up. Before he knew it, his throat had opened and he was screaming.

*"Americanyets! Nyet!"* he yelled. "It was not my idea to be getting into the suit. It was his!"

He stopped abruptly, listening with fear to the re-treating echo. He shivered. He wasn't supposed to say that, was he?

Hadn't *he* told him not to?

Kostia screwed his eyes up, trying to remember. Thinking about him was comforting; Kostia conjured up his mental image gratefully. What had he said?

*You must not say anything, Kostia. No matter what happens.*

That much he remembered. But why? Kostia bit his lip, hard, hoping the pain would focus concentration. Blood oozed from the cut.

It was something about Russia. Something about why the *Americanyets* had to die.

*Why,* he begged silently. *Why did the American have to die?*

He held his breath, listening to his pounding heart, but nothing came. All he could remember was his voice, murmuring softly, explaining everything. And his eyes, staring at Kostia so hard he felt they were reaching deep into his soul. Never blinking, not even once. And that incredible color; Kostia had never seen anything like it.

What did the *Americantzi* call it? Purple?

No, that wasn't right.

Violet. That was it.

He tried to concentrate, keeping the eyes before him, but they faded slowly, leaving him alone in the darkness. He moaned in despair. If only he were here now. Then he could explain it all again.

*Perhaps he will come tonight.*

Kostia was suddenly still. Hope spurted in him. Perhaps he *would* come tonight. The thought was blessed relief, and tears sprang to his eyes at the idea that he might really come, and tell Kostia again what it was he had to do. He was so happy that it took him a moment to understand the words that were forming at the back of his mind.

*He will come tonight.*

The flood of gratitude washed away from Kostia, like a wave retreating from the beach, so that this time he heard the words clearly.

*He will come tonight.*

And then the flood was back, except that this time it was terror, shooting through every nerve in his body and echoing through the module in time with his screams.

1:04 A.M., Day 84, Expedition Time
Laboratory Module, International Space Station

Reynolds closed his eyes and tried to sleep. He could hear the muffled noises from the Stowage Module—Kostia had started up again—but that wasn't what was keeping him awake. It was the questions, circling the fringes of consciousness like the debris that had whirled around Myers in his temporary grave.

*How was Kostia able to get in and out of that suit in such a short time?*

*Why did Myers look right?*

The doubts worried at him, picking away at the seams of his composure.

*They don't alter the bottom line,* he told himself roughly. *Kostia killed Myers. End of story.*

But he couldn't get them out of his head. There was another one too, he realized suddenly. He thought back to the moment of arrest. Drupev's shriek at the touch of the cuffs.

"Leonid!" the Russian had cried. "Leonid!" Then something incomprehensible in Russian.

*Why call to Matchev for help?* Reynolds wondered. *Kalganin is his commanding officer. And he was right there.*

That was strange too. It was another piece to add to the puzzle. For a moment, Reynolds was swept by déjà vu. When he was a kid, back in Phoenix, his room had had an Escher print on the wall. Titled "Menagerie," it showed a tiled pattern of little white rhinoceroses. But if you were lucky, sometimes you could stare at it and the pattern would flip, revealing for a few spectacular moments the menagerie of animals hiding in the shadows—camels, elephants, parrots and so on.

*Is that what's happening here?* Reynolds wondered. *Is there something behind what Kostia did?*

*Something I'm not seeing?*

He turned his back on such thoughts deliberately, letting them drift out to the periphery of consciousness, to join such other mysteries as who killed Kennedy and whatever the hell it was he had seen in Alinov's vacuum chamber.

It was a measure of his success that he dreamed of none of them—neither Kalganin, Alinov, nor Kostia—but only of himself, floating freely in the void of space. Alicia was there, of course, teasing him. Only, when he embraced her, it was Irina, naked and beautiful in his suited arms.

# 9

Reynolds woke instantly. The deep, single-note tone—
*emergency*—throbbed through the module. He fought his
way out of his sleep restraint and kicked himself over to
the door. Even his short training stint on ISS systems
had been enough to imprint that tone indelibly on his
brain.

It meant one of three things: fire, loss of cabin pressure or toxic atmosphere.

He pushed himself over to the nearest Caution and
Warning panel and scanned it rapidly. The Emergency
button was on all right, pulsing fiery red in time with
the tone, but none of the Emergency class indicators had
been activated. Reynolds stared at the dead buttons
uncertainly.

*What the hell?*

The audio terminal buzzed into life. "Detective Reynolds?" a voice said. It was Irina Ruskaya. There was no
mistaking the tension in her voice.

"Yep," Reynolds replied, punching the button.
"What's going on?"

Her voice hesitated. "I think you had better come
down here, Detective."

Reynolds frowned at her nonanswer. "Where's here?"
he said brusquely.

"The Stowage Module." A sob choked her voice. "It's
Kostia. He's . . ."

"Kostia has taken his life, Detective," Reynolds heard a background voice—Kalganin, he thought—shout. "You must come now."

"Fuck," Reynolds swore, underneath his breath. "Okay," he said, into the ATU. "I'm on my way."

He propelled himself though the module, cursing himself for his miscalculation. The *Soyuz* commander was basically a weak character—he'd known that. He'd expected him to crack though.

Not crack up.

The three Russians were gathered at the Stowage Module entrance when he arrived. Dr. Akira was partially visible in one of the hatchways off to the side, *like a rabbit readying itself to dart back into the warren*, Reynolds thought. The Russians' faces were twisted in shock, even Matchev's. Reynolds noted the wetness clinging to Ruskaya's lashes—the only sign, in weightlessness, that someone had been crying.

The Stowage Module hatch was open. Debris from the tumbling mess inside was drifting out—bits of broken glass, a torn scrap of blue cloth, scattered drops of fluid. At the far end of the module, anchored to the wall by what appeared to be a crude rope fashioned from the cloth of his blue flight suit, was Drupev's naked body. The corpse was drifting lazily, bumping against the walls.

"What happened?" Reynolds demanded.

"His neck is broken," Kalganin choked out. "He has . . ."

"Not that," he overrode the Russian harshly. "I mean, what happened this morning? How did you come to find him like this?"

"I . . . well . . ." Kalganin said, flustered. "I was coming this morning to talk to Kostia. I was not hearing . . ."

"Talk to him? What for?"

"To ask him what he was wanting to breakfast, like always." Kalganin's face flared defiance. "Maybe he is arrested, but he is still a crew member."

Reynolds grimaced in irritation. He couldn't give a fuck if Kalganin had decided to give Kostia breakfast in bed. In any case, the *Soyuz* commander was obviously beyond worrying about meal preference now.

"Whatever," he said shortly. "So what happened?"

"I knocked on the hatch . . . with this." The Russian commander grabbed the alloy wrench, floating nearby, and showed it to Reynolds. "There was no reply, so I was looking through the glass." He indicated the round observation panel cut into the hatch. Emotion choked his voice. "Then I was seeing him. He was dead, I could see. I was breaking the hatch open and . . ."

"Wait a minute," Reynolds interrupted. His eyes sought out the hatch locking mechanism. It was undamaged. "What do you mean, you broke through the hatch?"

"It was secured on the inside as well. Kostia had secured it," Kalganin replied.

Reynolds frowned. *Locked from the inside?* That was weird. He had ordered the *outside* of the hatch secured the night before, to confine Drupev in his temporary prison cell. But why would Kostia lock the mechanism on his side?

"Okay," he said, putting that to one side for the moment. "You broke through the hatch. What then?"

"I . . . I was going to Kostia. To see if there was a way I could save him." Kalganin shuddered. "But there was no way. He was cold. His head was flopping like . . . what do you say . . . a rag."

Even from the outside of the module, Reynolds could see that. Duprev's head drifted at an independent angle to his body, bumping softly into his shoulders.

"Did you touch anything?" he asked sharply.

Kalganin shook his head. "No. I shouted and Irina and Leonid and Dr. Akira came. Then I pushed the Emergency alarm."

"Okay." Reynolds thought rapidly. The first step was to get the Russians the hell away from there. Then, Christ, he'd have to figure out some way to run a basic postmortem on Kostia's corpse. Myers, NASA had been able to get away with. There'd been no question as to what *he* had died from. But this was a different story. Reynolds had no doubt it was what it looked like—Drupev had jerried up his rope and necked himself with it, pushing himself off the wall to achieve the necessary momentum. But the American public was going to take some convincing, when they heard Gary Myers's Russian murderer was going to escape *Americantzi* justice after all.

Not to mention the Russians.

"Okay," he repeated. "Commander Kelganin, I want you to amend today's flight plan to keep all crew members away from here, effective immediately. Do you understand? I don't care what activities you assign them—I don't want anybody near the Stowage Module until I've finished."

"But Kostia . . ." Kalganin protested. He looked around at the other cosmonauts for support. Ruskaya's pale face was focused on her feet, her arms were drawn around herself for comfort. Matchev, behind her, merely brooded silently.

"*Soyuz* Commander Drupev is in my hands now," Reynolds said harshly. "There is nothing more you can do for him."

*That much is true,* Reynolds thought, as he watched the Russian commander reluctantly usher the crew away. He glanced over at Drupev's naked, drifting body.

There was nothing anybody could do for Kostia now.

10:41 A.M., Day 84, Expedition Time
Laboratory Module, International Space Station

"MS-3, CAPCOM. Do you copy?"

Reynolds swung his headset mike into place and hit his push-to-talk. "Roger, CAPCOM. This is MS-3. What've you got for me?"

"Just wanted to let you know Senior Pathologist Chang will be on-site in ten minutes," CAPCOM replied. "The C-20 just touched down at Ellington Field."

"Copy that, CAPCOM," Reynolds said absently, picking his way through the menus on his laptop. "Standing by."

He wondered what Luce had made of the early morning summons. The urgent need to autopsy Drupev had touched off another round of jurisdictional disputes in the investigative task force. The DA's office, allied with the presidential appointees, had wanted to bring in an

FBI pathologist from Quantico. Reynolds had opposed that, supported, he sensed, by a secretly relieved Security Directorate.

"No way, Carnell," he'd said, addressing the South Texas Assistant DA by telephone uplink with Space Station Control. "Wayne County's labs are as good as any in the country. And I trust Lucy Chang. She's the best. I *know* I can work with her."

In the end the need to autopsy before the story broke had ensured he got his way. Reynolds was happy with that. It was true: Luce and he *did* work well together. Despite their stormy history, they still had the one crucial ingredient for a successful professional relationship.

Respect for each other's abilities.

While waiting for Luce to arrive, Reynolds had busied himself with investigative preliminaries—a basic forensic scan of the Stowage Module, checking back through the camera dumps to ensure nobody had approached the DSM hatch during the night. Finding himself with a few moments left over, he had taken the opportunity to return to his cabin and run the video footage of Kostia's arrest through the translation software.

He wanted to find out what it was Kostia had said to Leonid.

He isolated the seven seconds of digital video and saved it to a clip. He played the clip a couple of times, before running it through the translation filter.

Start.

Kostia turns toward the hatchway. He stiffens as the cuffs go on, then screams and starts thrashing. Matchev and Kalganin make their way up the module. Then the words, shrieked to Leonid.

*"Leonid! Leonid! Pamagi minye! Americanyets znayet vsio!"*

Stop.

Reynolds rewound, played the words again, then tapped the translation command. The computer's voice was conversational, an oddly flat counterpoint to Kostia's hysterical words.

"Possible personal name. Possible personal name. Help me. The American knows all."

The information bar flashed, telling him the translator

had an alternative version as well. He hit the alternate button, but got the same sentence with just slight variations.

"Possible personal name. Possible personal name. Give me your assistance. The American knows everything."

*The American knows everything?* Reynolds frowned. *What does the American know?*

He thought it over. Perhaps Kostia was just referring to the facts of the murder. *The American knows I killed Gary Myers. He knows I disabled the communications array. That I hid in the Hab Module afterwards.*

*That I used your suit to do it.*

Reynolds shook his head; that wouldn't cut it. There was no way Kostia would be appealing to Leonid for help, not after he had tried to frame the flight engineer for murder. Unless . . .

He played the clip again. Kostia's desperate appeal shrieked out again. It was almost as if there was something between Matchev and Drupev, some shared secret.

Reynolds's mind reeled. *Fuck, is Matchev involved in this after all?*

He hit the frame-by-frame command on the last two seconds and zoomed in on the blond Russian. But Matchev's face was impassive, utterly unresponsive to Kostia's appeal. If there was a secret, the flight engineer wasn't giving it away.

Help me, Leonid. The American knows everything.

*Help him how?* Reynolds wondered. *And what is it that the American knows?*

His earpiece buzzed back to life; this time it was Connor. "Edge, do you copy? Lucy Chang just entered Mission Control. She's proceeding to the ficker now."

"Copy, Matt," Reynolds said. He quit the program, not bothering to save the clip, and snapped the laptop shut. "I'm on my way to the DSM now."

He pushed his way through the module, puzzling over Kostia's words.

*What does the American know?*

"Edge . . . uh . . . MS-3, this is Lucy Chang . . . Space Station Control. Do you read me?"

Luce's voice in his earpiece was hesitant, unsure. Reynolds grinned wryly. They were both a long way from Detroit now.

"Reading you fine, Luce," Reynolds replied. He dashed his sleeve at his left cheek, wiping away the drops of liquid that had spattered there. The Stowage Module was a mess—flakes of glass and paint, droplets of blood, saliva and God knew what else circling lazily around Drupev's floating corpse. "Hope you don't mind me dragging you into this."

He *heard* Luce's resigned shrug in her voice. "A vote of confidence, I suppose," she said lightly. "Besides. It's not the first thing you've dragged me into, is it, Edge?"

Reynolds grinned again, acknowledging the barb. This was the way he and Luce worked. Circling each other like alley cats. Until it got down to the essentials.

"Guess not," he replied. "Have they filled you in down there?"

"They've told me what's expected of me," the Senior Pathologist answered, her voice disapproving. "I can't say I'm over the moon about it."

Reynolds nodded. He understood. Luce was a perfectionist—a consummate artist at her work. She wouldn't appreciate the idea of performing an autopsy by remote, from thousands of miles away. Given her druthers, he knew she'd prefer the body shipped down to her for examination.

But NASA must have told her why that was impossible. It wasn't just the need to forestall the hue and cry. There was also the health issue. Space Station Control could not allow a biohazard like a corpse to remain on ISS. The station was already a paradise for microorganisms—NASA had estimated that, due to the station's limited personal hygiene regimes, each ISS resident shed 50,000 microbes per minute, as opposed to 3,000 down on Earth. With no refrigeration facilities big enough to

handle a human body—the airlock being now needed
for its proper purpose, EVAs—there was only one thing
to do with Kostia's decomposing corpse.

Get it the fuck off ISS. Now.

For the same reason, bringing Kostia back on *Endeavor* was out of the question. As soon as Luce and he
were done, Kostia would be packed into the *Progress,*
the emptied Russian supply module, along with the three
months' worth of solid waste already stored there, and
fired off into destructive reentry.

*Poor bastard,* Reynolds found himself thinking. *Even
Gary didn't go to meet his maker in a bucket of dried shit.*

"Well," he said diplomatically. "This is what we've
got to work with. What do you say we get started?"

"Okay, Detective," Dr. Chang said, her voice dropping into professional gear. "Put me in the picture then."

"Copy that," Reynolds said, switching on his hand
camera. He paused momentarily for verification of the
video signal, then panned it along Kostia's naked corpse.

"This is Kostia Drupev, member of the Russian Cosmonaut Corps and *Soyuz* commander on the International Space Station. Don't worry about what that
means—it's not important. He was arrested yesterday
as prime suspect in the murder of Gary Myers and put
into temporary custody here, in the Docking and Stowage Module of ISS, pending return to Earth for trial. At
approximately 7:20 this morning, Commander Kalganin
attempted to communicate with the prisoner, and discovered he was not responding. He broke into the
hatch . . . for some reason the prisoner had secured it
from the inside . . . and found the DOA in this
condition."

He brought the camera in tight on Drupev's neck and
grotesquely angled head. The dead Russian's skin
looked weirdly *alive*—Reynolds guessed the absence of
gravitational settling of blood, *livor mortis,* accounted for
its color. The ragged cloth rope cut deep into his neck.

"Preliminary hypothesis is suicide," Reynolds said, letting the camera linger. "Looks like the DOA made this
rope out of his flight suit and hung . . ."

Reynolds shrugged, catching himself.

". . . let's say *necked* himself. Pushed himself off the wall to generate enough momentum."

"Uh huh," Lucy said. "Edge, how about giving me a pan of the surrounds. Yeah, that's it," she continued as Reynolds complied, swinging the camera slowly through 360 degrees. "Find any markers?"

"Some," Reynolds replied. He swung the camera over to the Stowage Module wall, just below the foot restraint to which Kostia had tied his crude rope. "I ran the Polilight over the walls and picked up two latents here. Bare footprints, side by side. I dyed and lifted 'em—they're the DOA's all right. You can see it on the image, the toes and the front of the foot are all squashed up . . ."

"Like they would be if he'd kicked himself off that wall," Lucy said, finishing his sentence. "Anything else?"

Reynolds brought the camera in close to the sharp corner of one of the storage assemblies. "Looks like the DOA used this to get the tear going on his suit." He heard Lucy request magnification from INCO—the Integrated Communications Officer. "Can you see that? That shiny patch there, and the blue fibers caught in the lip?"

"Yeah, I see it," Lucy said. "Okay then. Let's get down to business. I want you to take an ambient temperature, please."

Reynolds picked through the medical kit he'd had Ruskaya assemble for him earlier and grabbed the digital thermometer. He could guess what this was about. In the absence of *livor morits,* Luce would need something to establish time of death—comparison of corpse temperature to ambient probably. He took the precaution of donning the kit's cut-proof surgical gloves. He'd seen enough postmortems to know that probably meant rectal insertion.

Sure enough, after taking the ambient, Lucy had him insert the thermometer's sensor anally for a body-core temperature. It came up eighty-four degrees, against the ambient seventy-one.

"Fourteen degrees off normal," Lucy calculated aloud. "Say two-degrees-per-hour cooling rate, given the

DOA's physique and the ambient constancy. That gives us 4 A.M. as the time of death. Give or take an hour.''

Reynolds nodded. It fitted. *The suicide hours.* You saw it a lot as a cop. For some reason suicides almost always killed themselves in the early hours of the morning.

Next, Lucy got him to pan the camera slowly down and up Drupev's corpse, coming to rest back on the face. She kept up a professional commentary the whole time.

"Subject is a Caucasian male with marked Asiatic features and build," she said briskly. "Estimated height, five nine, weight, 180 pounds. How old did you say he is?"

"I didn't," Reynolds replied. "But he's thirty-eight. Or was."

"Uh huh. Subject's skin shows unusual lack of *livor mortis,* which is no doubt due to the lack of gravity at the death scene. The skin exhibits neither pallor nor cyanosis, which seems consistent with the preliminary observation of spinal injury in the cervical vertebrae. Death was probably from reflexive cardiac arrest, not asphyxiation.''

To make sure, she had Reynolds pull Drupev's lower eyelids down and zoom the camera in on them.

"Uh huh," Lucy said, after a moment's study. "Lax tissue of the lower eyelids shows no sign of petechiae." Petechiae were tiny hemorrhages commonly found in asphyxiation deaths like strangulation, but rarely in hangings. "The DOA definitely died from sudden cardiac inhibition, either from snapping of the odontoid peg in the cervical vertebrae, or possibly from massive compressive force on the baroreceptors of the carotid arterial sinus."

She next asked Reynolds to zoom in on the knot in Drupev's ragged rope and take a few stills. Reynolds was used to that too. You could deduce a lot about a hanging fatality from the knot used. The Trace Unit of Detroit's Crime Lab even had a guy, Petersen, who specialized in them. Reynolds still remembered the man's excitement upon tracing an unusual "running bowline" in an ex-sailor's suicide to a stint in the Peruvian navy.

In this case, it was the crudity of the slipknot Drupev

had tied that interested them. That was a classic suicide pointer—sign of a disoriented mind, unable to concentrate on anything the slightest bit complex. Reynolds untied it when Lucy was satisfied they had enough shots and evidence-bagged it. It would be returned to Earth for preservation.

Which was more than could be said for Kostia.

"I'll need you to manipulate the DOA's head for me, Detective," Lucy told him then. "I need to establish where the break in the vertebrae is."

Reynolds obliged, grimacing. It was ghoulish work—wrenching Drupev's lifeless head this way and that so that the snapped vertebrae outlined themselves against the skin of his neck. It wasn't helped either by the fact that Kostia was beginning to stiffen: rigor was setting in. But Reynolds persisted. Macabre as it was, he knew it was infinitely better than the alternative: cutting through the strap muscles of Kostia's neck to make sure.

Finally Luce had what she wanted. "Okay," she said, telling him he could stop. "That's a clear break between the first and second cervical vertebrae. There's the cause of the cardiac arrest. He'd snapped that odontoid peg clean."

She gave a low whistle. "This guy's a lucky cosmonaut. Looks like he succeeded first go."

Reynolds knew what she was talking about. He'd seen enough hanging victims to know the ones who muffed it died horribly. Choking, heaving and retching—swollen eyes and tongues bulging out of blue-black, asphyxiated faces. Kostia, with his staring, lifeless eyes and bitten tongue, was almost a picture by comparison.

From the silence that ensued, Reynolds could tell Lucy was weighing something up.

"What is it, Luce?" he asked. "What's the matter?"

"I'm just wondering about that," she said hesitantly. "It does seem a clean break. Considering he had no gravity and had to generate all his momentum by pushing off the wall."

There was silence for a moment as she thought it over. Then another voice came onto the channel, announcing itself with a nervous cough.

"MS-3, SURGEON," the voice said, addressing Reynolds. He recognized Finnegan, one of the ISS flight surgeons. "If I may, there's something Dr. Chang may be overlooking."

"Go ahead, SURGEON," Reynolds replied. "I'm sure Dr. Chang is open to all suggestions."

"Thanks. Dr. Chang, it might help to remember we're talking about a long-term resident of the space station here. You have to keep in mind that the *Soyuz* commander may have suffered up to thirty percent bone demineralization by now. His bones will be a lot easier to break than a normal person's. And his spine will have stretched too, remember that. It'll be a lot weaker—lots more room between those vertebrae."

"I see," Lucy Chang said thoughtfully. "Yes, that may explain it. Thank you. I'd still like to section those vertebrae to confirm that . . ." Again, Reynolds could *hear* her resigned shrug. ". . . but I guess *that's* out of the question. Okay, Detective, I'd like you to UV the subject for me now, please. I want to check for bruising."

Reynolds complied, switching off the module lights and activating the Polilight unit. The DSM was suddenly bathed in eerie UV gray. Drupev's corpse gleamed angel white as Reynolds ran the lamp over it. He was used to this too. Down on Earth, it was common to find homicides—stranglings, bashings and suffocations—dressed up as suicidal hanging. Sometimes the only way to pick it was through deep, hardly visible bruising, particularly to the neck or face.

He wasn't expecting to find much this time though. That's why he was surprised when Lucy hesitated at Drupev's face, making him linger.

"What is it, Luce?" he asked. "What do you see?"

Drupev's corpse was coming up mottled, bruises an ugly black under the UV. But that, as Reynolds had explained, was random damage from the way Kostia had thrown himself around. It was indicative of nothing but the dead *Soyuz* commander's disturbed state of mind.

"I'm not sure," Lucy said. "See that discoloration there? The mark on his left cheek?"

Reynolds peered at Drupev's cheek, bringing the flexible lamp head in close. "Yeah, I see it," he agreed. "Kind of an oval smudge."

"Uh huh. If you look closely there's one on the right too. Not as clear, but it's there."

"I see what you mean," Reynolds said, locating the mark. "What do you make of them?"

"Well," Lucy said hesitantly. "You sometimes see marks like that in sexual homicides. Thumb bruises, where the killer grips the victim's head in an immobilizing hold while he rapes them."

"Grips their head?" Reynolds frowned, following the reasoning. "You're saying somebody twisted his neck for him?"

"I'm not saying anything," Lucy replied waspishly. "Yet. Anyway, you tell me. Is that possible?"

Reynolds shook his head. "It's hard to see how, Luce," he said, glancing around the darkened module. "There's only one way into this module from inside ISS. That's through the hatch there. And I checked the footage from the internal cameras. Nobody came within dick of it all night. Not to mention the fact the DOA had himself barricaded in."

*Yeah, and isn't that a little weird?* the voice at the back of Reynolds's mind kicked in. *Why do that if he wasn't scared of something?*

*Or someone?*

The pathologist was quiet a few moments, thinking it over.

"Well," she said doubtfully, "I guess it's possible the bruising is from his own thumbs. You know—he's distressed, he's freaking out, he grabs his head and presses in at the temples . . ." Reynolds waited for what he knew was coming. ". . . but you know what? I think we're going to have to reflect the scalp," Lucy continued. "I really need to take a better look at this."

Reynolds groaned. He'd witnessed scalp reflection often at postmortems—Lucy's and others. The pathologist cut the DOA's scalp at the back of the head and peeled it forward off the skull, like turning a tennis ball inside out. He understood the reason—bruises showed up a hundred percent clearer on the scalp's underside. But it was different doing it to watching.

"Okay," he said grimly. "But you'd better be prepared to walk me through the cutting."

He turned the module's lights back on and rummaged through the kit for a serviceable scalpel. Under Luce's guidance he cut the skin at the back of Drupev's head in a semicircle from ear to ear. The scalpel grated on bone. Beads of blood, released by the blade, floated out to join their brethren.

Now came the messy bit.

Reynolds wormed his gloved fingers under the scalp, his face set grimly. He wondered briefly if any of the other cosmonauts were watching through the observation panel behind him.

They'd soon be sorry, if they were.

He braced himself and, with one grisly flick, wrenched Kostia's scalp forwards onto itself. He was amazed how easily it came away. There was hardly any tearing at all. In front of him was the picture he remembered from any number of autopsies—the DOA's white skull gleaming through the residue of red blood and flesh. And beneath it Drupev's lifeless face, visored ludicrously now by its own scalp.

He panned the camera back and forth across the scalp, under Lucy's instruction. She took him over it again and again. He knew what she was looking for. Fingertip bruises to match those theorized thumbprints. Oval-shaped hemorrhages that would confirm someone *had* gripped Kostia's head, vicelike, and twisted it to snap the *Soyuz* commander's neck.

In the end though, she pronounced herself unsure.

"There's nothing there I can identify positively," she said, frustrated. "Some hemorrhaging, but that could be self-inflicted trauma—bashing his head against the walls and so on." She sighed, exasperated. "The lack of gravity seems to be the real problem. It's interfered with the blood flow into the trauma areas. See how diffused those bruises are? You can hardly tell where they start and stop."

Reynolds saw what she meant. The underside of Kostia's scalp was a mottle of black bruising shading off into white and pink flesh. It was impossible to read anything off it. Other than the fact its owner had taken a hammering.

"Uh huh," he said. "So what's the verdict, Doc?"

"Well," said Lucy slowly, "heart failure is what killed him. That much is given. I'm going to write up my report that he died from reflexive cardiac arrest from compressive trauma to the neck. Hanging, in other words. By his own hand. With a footnote that thumb bruising of indeterminate origin, possibly his own, was found." The disapproval was back, coloring Lucy's voice.

"It's the best I can do, Edge. In the circumstances. You happy with that?"

Reynolds shrugged. "Yeah, Luce," he said. "Like I said. It has to be a self-necking. Nobody's been within an inch of that hatch."

*Only Kostia locked it,* that troubled voice kicked in again. *Why do that if he wasn't scared someone was going to?*

"Okay, then," Dr. Lucy Chang continued. "That's how I'll write it up. You know what to do from here?"

"Sure," Reynolds replied. "Shoot some stills of that bruising. Get a frame-by-frame of the autopsy ready for the DA. And take the Wayne County ME's Senior Pathologist out to dinner the moment I get back to Motortown."

"Well, maybe the Senior Pathologist will have to check her diary," Lucy replied, and for a moment all the old bitterness was back. "Anyway," she continued, relenting, "the way I hear it, you're not gonna have the time. Apparently Dennison is making you Morgue Man when you get back."

Reynolds laughed. Morgue Man was the officer assigned to liaison duty with the Detroit City Morgue. It was his job to do the basic assessments on all the incomings: suicides, murders, naturals—the lot. It was drone work, boring and time-consuming, and Dennison usually saved it for squad detectives who incurred his displeasure.

"He's just pissed because I took the spotlight off his

movie career," he said. Some time before, the lieutenant had scored a role in a Detroit-based cop drama; rumor had it the entire squad were to be involuntary members of a group booking at the premiere.

"Well, whatever," Lucy said. "You take care now, Edge. You hear?"

He heard the real concern in her voice. "Sure, Luce. You too huh?" he answered. He wanted to say more, but the flight director's voice cut in hurriedly, as if the man had been waiting to interrupt for some time.

"Thank you, Dr. Chang. MS-3, FLIGHT. If you're finished up there, we are go for initiating burial prep procedure. Do you copy?"

Reynolds sighed. Undertaker duty again.

"Copy that, FLIGHT," he said shortly. "Ready for instructions on burial prep." At least he wouldn't have to scrub the Stowage Module out. He'd get the Russians to do that.

He listened as the Flight Activities Officer outlined the procedure, but his mind was only half on it. His eyes were drawn to Kostia's macabre, skin-helmeted face, bobbing obscenely just a few feet from him. He wanted to grab the corpse by its improvised necktie, shake Kostia furiously and ask him the question that was niggling at the back of his brain.

*What does the American know?*

1:19 P.M., Day 84, Expedition Time
Laboratory Module, International Space Station

Matt was trying hard to hide his satisfaction.

Reynolds could see that. Connor's face on the laptop screen was subdued as he filled Reynolds in on *Endeavor*'s updated flight plan ". . . get the bird back to you around 10:15 A.M., Day 86, ET. That way, FIDO says, we can catch the reentry window that afternoon." But behind the sober expression was relief, even joy. All the stress and worry he had seen hanging on Matt's face last night had lifted, miraculously, at around seven-thirty that morning.

Reynolds could figure it. If there was anything better

for NASA than the single, crazed Kostia as Myers's killer it was the single, crazed, *suicided* Kostia. Alive, Kostia had been an inconvenience the agency would have to manage. Dead, he was a neatly packaged ending.

The agency bigwigs would be dancing on the tables.

"Edge? You with me, buddy?" Connor's words broke into Reynolds's reverie.

"Sorry, Matt. You were saying?"

"Just that Lucy's report will have to go to the Harris County Medical Examiner for reissue. I've checked this with the South Texas DA's office. They say that because the cosmonauts are not technically federal employees, U.S. attorneys can only touch it in so far as it relates to Gary's murder."

Connor shook his head in exasperation.

"Goddamn it," he growled. "The lawyers are having a hair-splitting fiesta with this. Anyway, they say the actual inquest has to be held by the local authorities at Houston. That means the Harris County Examiner has to issue the autopsy report. But since Lucy ran so strong on the suicide angle, it should be just a formality . . ."

"If it was suicide," Reynolds said hesitantly.

Connor stopped short, goggling. "If it . . . what do you mean?"

Reynolds shrugged. "I told you last night I was having doubts, Matt. I . . . I guess I'm still having them."

He watched Matt's face struggle with conflicting emotions—loyalty, anger, even an element of fear. *He doesn't want this,* Reynolds thought. *He's this close to asking me not to do it.*

Connor mastered himself enough to give a hollow laugh. "C'mon, Edge . . . what, that bruising on the cheek thing? Lucy said herself it was nothing."

Reynolds shook his head. "It's not just that, Matt. It's these little details that keep piling up. Like the EMU suit. Like Myers looking in the wrong direction. Like Kostia locking himself in last night."

Connor frowned. "I noticed you mentioned that. What's the significance?"

"Perps are usually more interested in getting *out* of a

jail cell. Why lock the hatch . . . unless he was scared of someone getting *in*?"

Connor's frown deepened. "You're saying someone Ruby-ed him?"

The expression brought Reynolds up short. Ruby had supposedly killed Oswald to stop him revealing what he knew. But what was it Kostia might have revealed?

*What the American knows. That's what.*

"I'm saying it's weird, that's all. Weird enough to take a second look at it."

Connor appeared to think for a moment, then snapped his fingers. "Wait a minute, Edge. This cuts both ways. That hatch was still locked from the inside this morning . . . Kalganin said he had to break it in. Doesn't that prove that nobody got at Kostia? I mean, how did your Ruby get in?"

*That's right,* Reynolds thought. *And you saw the recorder dumps. Nobody came within dick of that hatch.*

"Don't ask me to explain it, Matt. I just know something doesn't feel right."

"Well . . . what?" Connor said helplessly. "Do you have a suspect for the Ruby? I mean, who do you think it was?"

Reynolds hesitated. He was suddenly conscious there were two ways to take Kostia's shouted plea to Leonid. Perhaps it pointed to a secret relationship between Drupev and the Russian flight engineer—something Matchev might fake Kostia's suicide to prevent coming out. Or maybe . . .

*Kalganin was the one Kostia was scared of. That's why he called out to Leonid.*

"I don't even know there was one, Matt," he said finally. That much was true at least. "I just know I want to poke around a little further."

Connor struggled with himself a moment more, then broke into an exasperated smile. "Goddamn you, Edge. I suppose it's useless to try to dissuade you?"

Reynolds let silence answer that one.

Connor sighed heavily. "Okay. We've got a day and a half until *Endeavor* gets back, I suppose. What do you want me to do?"

Reynolds was thrown; he hadn't thought that far ahead. Back at squad, he'd probably have started with another sift through the DOA's personal effects, maybe hauled his associates in for another round of interviews. Anything to get a line on the DOA's private world. But there were no private worlds on ISS.

*Except for the computers,* he thought suddenly. Each ISS crew member had a personal Thinkpad for e-mailing and surplus scientific tasks. And Myers had been Systems Specialist—ISS's resident geek. If he was going to find anything, that would be the place.

"I don't know," he shrugged. "How about getting somebody to go through the hard disk on Myers's computer for me? Maybe pull one of the systems engineers off Data Team."

"Well . . . sure," Connor said, mystified. "I'll talk to FLIGHT, see what we can do. But what will I tell them to look for?"

"Just get me every file Myers worked on in the four weeks before the murder. I'll take it from there."

With that he signed off, leaving Connor to rustle up the computer engineer. Himself, he had other things to do. Like attend another funeral.

2:01 P.M., Day 84, Expedition Time
U.S. Habitation Module, International Space Station

But when Reynolds made his way through to the Stowage Module, it was evident the hastily improvised ceremony would be delayed. Kostia's corpse was still there, floating in the center of the module—only now it was trussed in the body bag Reynolds had jerried up from cannibalized insulation scrim. Reynolds's mouth twitched at the sight of the crude shroud. NASA had never seriously believed the one body bag it had included in ISS's payload would be needed. Two body bags would have been unthinkable.

Before today.

Ruskaya and Matchev were hard at work in the module: Matchev sucking debris from the air with the wet/dry vacuum, Ruskaya going over the walls with antibacterial wipes. Only Kalganin was missing—Reynolds had earlier excused Dr. Akira from clean-up details and confined him to quarters in the Service Module. It was a pity—Reynolds would have preferred to keep the Japanese scientist busy, keep his mind off things. But there was no way Akira would cope with sharing a module with Kostia's corpse. As it was, the tranquilizers were only just holding the lid on his hysteria.

"Where's the commander?" he asked harshly. "Why hasn't *Soyuz* Commander Drupev been placed in the *Progress* yet?"

He addressed the questions to Matchev. Possible accessory or not, the hulking flight engineer was still a better risk for Reynolds than Ruskaya. With her hair tied back in a drifting ponytail and her pale face puffy from her tears, there was a vulnerability about the cosmonaut he found unnerving. Her dream image, naked and cradled in his arms, flashed unsettlingly before his eyes.

Matchev switched the handheld vacuum off and floated motionless, regarding Reynolds with glittering, ice blue eyes. Finally, he jerked his head over his shoulder insolently.

"The commander is in *Zvezda*, speaking to Moscow," he growled. "They are having obstructions with calculating trajectory for *Progress*. They have advised us to stop putting Kostia in until they have finished."

"Okay," Reynolds responded, ignoring the Russian's tone. "Have him call me when he's done."

Reynolds kicked himself out of the Stowage Module and along ISS's central corridor, headed for the Habitation Module. Since he had a few moments, he figured, he might as well check out Myers's sleeping quarters.

At the Hab Module, he yanked the flimsy door to Myers's cabin open and pushed himself inside. The compartment was as impersonal as he had imagined: beige metal walls unbroken except for the porthole window and several aluminum handholds. The standard cotton sleep restraint covered one wall. The ledge that served each crew member as a table jutted from the wall opposite, overhung by a small fluorescent lamp on a flexible stem. Underneath the lamp was the only mark of individuality—a small photograph, attached to the wall by a Velcro tab.

Reynolds pulled it clear gently and studied it. It was a picture of Myers's young son—what was his name? Jimmy? Jason? The boy was holding a leash; but the leash was chopped off at the left of the photo by a scissor cut and there was no sign of the dog. Reynolds traced the cut with his finger, whistling. He guessed that the real target of the excision had been Myers's wife, whose hand could just be seen, presumably holding the dog's collar.

*Chalk one up for agency scuttlebutt,* Reynolds thought. He replaced the photo and looked around the cabin. A gleam of light from the crevice between keyboard and screen of Myers's closed laptop caught his eye. *Matt,* he thought. Connor must have got one of the Data Team engineers on to the job of trolling through Myers's hard disk. He resisted the urge to open the computer and see what he could follow—better to let the experts handle it.

But it reminded him of the message Myers had sent the morning of his death. Myers had sent the e-mail at around five in the morning—again, those suicide hours. He must have been awake all night, wrestling with . . . what?

Fear of Kostia?

Reynolds had to admit it fitted. It explained Myers's reticence in his e-mail. Something he'd picked up, some marker, had alerted him to the psychotic violence his affair with Irina had sparked in Kostia. But he hadn't been sure yet how far the Russian would go. He wanted to talk with Security first, see if there was some way the danger could be averted . . .

Reynolds closed his eyes, trying to imagine himself into the scene. *You're tired, you're strung out. You've been up all night. Somewhere, less than fifty yards away, is a man who suddenly has you very, very scared.*

A wave of sympathy for Myers hit Reynolds. All at once, ISS was not a fifteen-module space facility orbiting the earth at a height of 220 miles. It was a 950-ton death trap. The cabin walls crowded in on you claustrophobically, backed up by the bleak nothingness of space. There was no place to hide—not if the thing you were afraid of was on ISS with you. And no place to get away.

"Edge? You there? Do you copy?" Connor's voice pulled him out of the image. Reynolds frowned. Matt sounded rattled.

"Roger, Matt," he replied. "What's up? Has your boy got the data for me?"

"That's what I called about. Just hold tight . . . I'm patching you through to Systems Engineer Wilkinson now. Systems Engineer? Go ahead please. Tell Mission Specialist Reynolds what you told me."

"Hello . . . uh, MS-3, do you read me?" a voice Reynolds didn't recognize intruded.

"You bet, Systems Engineer," Reynolds said. "What've you got?"

"Well, sir," said the man hesitantly. "I tried to go through Gary's hard disk like you asked. I did a hex dump . . . pulled everything down onto the Dec Alpha here. Only . . . well, there's nothing on it."

"What do you mean?"

"I mean there's nothing on Gary's computer, sir. Somebody's wiped the disk."

"Somebody wi . . ." Reynolds said, taken aback. "Who? Gary?"

"No, it goddamn wasn't," Connor interjected, growling. "Tell him, Systems Engineer."

"It's the date you see, Mission Specialist," the man continued. "Whoever did it used the smart erase program that comes with the OS. It leaves a signature file to say when it was done. The time and date on it is 9:15 P.M., March twelfth."

"Three days after Gary's murder," Connor broke in again bitterly. "Edge, I'm sorry. We should have been on the lookout for something like this."

"Well," said Reynolds slowly, "it's too late to do anything about it now. At least we know there was something worth looking at, huh?"

His thoughts whirled as he tried to fit this in. What had been on there that was so important Kostia would take the insane risk of tampering with the computer to get rid of it?

If it *had* been Kostia.

"Okay," Reynolds said finally. "But there's some way of retrieving the data, isn't there, Wilkinson?" He cast his mind back over the introductory sessions to ISS computer systems. "It'll be mixed in with the . . . wha-t're they called . . . the Command Systems dumps, right?"

" 'Fraid not, MS-3," the man replied. "The crew computers aren't spliced into the backup loops. They're stand-alones." His voice took on a sorrowful note; Reynolds imagined him shaking his head mournfully. "Without a DAT backup, the data's history. Total bit-bucket."

Reynolds swore. He had to get a look at that data. *Had* to.

"Think, Systems Engineer," he urged Wilkinson. "Isn't there some other way to recover it?"

"Uh uh," the man replied adamantly. "The disk is scrubbed clean. If the hex dump don't pick it up it ain't there." He paused a moment, as if something had suddenly struck him. "Unless . . ."

"Unless what?" Reynolds said quickly.

"Well," the engineer said slowly, "it's a long shot, but each of those ISS laptops has a factory-fitted hardware lock jacked into the parallel port. It's a basic security feature—logs every keystroke entered into the system to check for cracking attempts. Of course, Gary was too much of a hotshot to use something as basic as that for protection, but if he didn't disable the lock the keystroke log should still be active. If it's there I can pull it down. It won't give us the data back, but it'll give us a record of every command that's been entered into the computer. That's something."

"I guess so," Reynolds conceded grudgingly. "How far back will it go?"

"I think the lock has about sixteen meg of flash memory," Wilkinson answered. "That should give us at least three months."

"Uh huh," Reynolds grunted. "Well, why don't you get on to that right away, Engineer. Matt, in the meantime, I'm going to run the Polilight over the keyboard and see if I can pick up any prints. Can you dig up the flight plan transcripts for that day for me? I want to know exactly where Drupev was at nine-fifteen. Better give me locations for the others too."

His earpiece crackled with distortion as, Reynolds guessed, Matt shook his head. "Negative, Edge, I'm sorry," Connor said. "That was the first thing I did. It turns out there was a communications outage for nearly two hours that night. The satellite malfunctioned. All the internal camera footage was lost."

Reynolds grimaced. "That must have been why Kostia chose that moment to wipe the disk. He took advantage of the outage to hide what he was doing."

An embarrassed silence stretched out on the other end of the channel.

Reynolds frowned. "What?" he asked. "What's going on?"

"We're not sure it was Kostia, Edge," Connor said. Reynolds could hear the reluctance in his voice. "Tell him, Wilkinson."

"Roger, Adviser," the engineer said. "Well . . . it's like this, MS-3," he continued, picking his words carefully. "I don't want to speak ill of the dead. But I gotta tell you that whoever did this had some brains. They had to get past Gary's security, and that would've been serious ice. Well . . . the thing is *Soyuz* Commander Drupev was a stone loser on the computer systems. A genuine, ham-fisted fuckup. He was forever calling us to tell him where his startup button was. If you know what I mean."

Reynolds ignored the exaggeration. Here was yet another incongruity to add to the pile. Kostia had not been capable of the tampering with Myers's computer. And if Kostia hadn't wiped Myers's hard disk then . . .

"Detective?" Kalganin's voice buzzed on the ATU unit outside the cabin, cutting Reynolds's train of thought. He pushed himself out to it and punched the talk button.

"Yep," he said tersely. "Reynolds."

"This is Commander Kalganin. Kostia . . . the body is prepared for funeral. Moscow is standing by to start the ceremony now."

"Copy that, Commander," Reynolds replied, suppressing his impatience. Much as he wanted to keep on the track of Wilkinson's information, Connor was right. The Russian funeral was essential PR; there was no way he couldn't go. "I'm on my way."

He punched the talk button off and waited a few precautionary seconds—some of the ATU mikes had a weird habit of remaining active for a brief period after switch-off. "You copy, Matt?" he said finally. "I gotta go. I've got a farewell party to attend."

"Roger," Connor replied. "You go and smile for the cameras." He was silent for a moment, then his voice burst out in an exasperated growl, "But you know what this means, don't you? What Wilkinson said?"

"Uh huh," Reynolds said, nodding slowly to himself. "What if that's the wrong body packed on that ship?"

3:12 P.M., Day 84, Expedition Time
Service Module *Zvezda*, International Space Station

Reynolds listened to the liturgy coming out of the ATU speakers, grateful for the incomprehensible Russian. It allowed him to tune out, to focus on the questions turning over in his mind.

The EMU suit. Myers's rightward glance. Kostia's shrieked plea.

*Help me, Leonid. The American knows everything.*

And now the erasure of Myers's hard disk. Reynolds tried to think of some way that fitted into Kostia's crime of passion and couldn't come up with a single one. Not even the message Myers had sent would cut it. Even if Kostia suspected a message had been sent, why would he think there was a point to erasing the hard disk? The message was already sent, the damage already done.

Wilkinson, in any case, had been adamant Kostia could not have done it. *But if not Kostia,* Reynolds thought, *then who? And why?*

There was a more pressing question, he realized. If Kostia hadn't erased the hard disk, then he hadn't killed Myers either. And if that was the case, why was his corpse packed into the *Progress* and being fired away from ISS in a slow ballet directed by Mission Control, Moscow?

Reynolds watched the image of the departing *Progress* on the bank of monitors uneasily. The space-tug's thrusters, tiny pipes that jutted from its cylindrical surface like misplaced shower nozzles, spat short bursts of ignited propellant into the blackness of space. The *Progress* moved away slowly, then pivoted to face away from ISS. The voice of the Moscow Flight Director, tracking each step in the automated undock procedure, was a murmur only occasionally audible under the priest's drone.

What secret was Kostia taking to his fiery grave? The *Soyuz* commander's suicide only made sense if he *had* killed Myers. If he hadn't . . .

*Then someone murdered Kostia. Someone who must also have killed Myers.*

It was the only possible conclusion.

*But how?* Reynolds almost shouted at himself. There was only that one entrance to the Stowage Module—directly off ISS's core corridor. He had sifted through every minute of the footage from the camera covering it and . . . nothing. Nobody had been near the Stowage Module. So . . .

The words to the old children's paradox ran through Reynolds's mind. *Who killed Kostia Drupev? Nobody did, that's who.*

He wasn't buying that one. He surreptitiously studied the profiles of the cosmonauts floating in the line beside him. If someone *had* murdered Kostia, making it look like suicide, the culprit was right there. Bobbing in front of a Russian flag, less than three yards from him.

*Kalganin?* he wondered.

There was an old cop adage—always look twice at the first person on the crime scene. Kalganin might have been at that hatchway to ask Kostia if he wanted sugar on his Wheaties . . . or he might not. It wouldn't be the first time a perp had sought to control an investigation by getting in on the ground floor.

*Matchev?*

The brooding flight engineer's profile jutted out past the commander's. Reynolds had thought the man's uncomplicated hostility a plus, but was it? Or was it a mask, behind which to hide a murderous secret—the *everything* in Kostia's desperate cry?

*What about Ruskaya?*

Reynolds's eyes drifted reluctantly to the female cosmonaut's profile. He had figured her obvious vulnerability, her shock at Kostia's death, made her more open to him, easier to read. But that was fooling himself. What it did was make her remind him that much more of Alicia. And that was dangerous. It made him unable to believe she might lie—not her, not his love, his darling . . .

Reynolds shook his head irritably. There was enough craziness on ISS already without him flaking.

A sharp crack jerked his attention back to the monitor bank. The screen that had been taken up with the image of the priest had given way to a line of soldiers in parade-ground uniform with rifles hoisted to their shoulders. Reynolds counted the line—fifteen of them, a fifteen-gun salute. He wondered briefly about that. Who had decided that would be the number of guns to mark Kostia's passing? Why not nineteen? Or seventeen, or sixteen, or even nine?

"ISS, Mission Control, Moscow," the Russian Flight Director's voice cut in. "Stand by for retrofire of *Progress* main engine, at my mark . . . five . . . four . . . three . . . two . . . one . . . go for retrofire."

The tiny spacecraft's aft end bloomed orange as the engine ignited. The *Progress* began to accelerate away from ISS: 300 yards . . . 320 . . . 350 . . .

Then all hell broke loose.

A deep clang rang through the module. Reynolds and the three cosmonauts hit the walls as ISS was shoved violently a few feet to one side. The Caution tone— a constant, low-level squeal—started up, then gave way instantly to the Emergency siren. The red, Class One Emergency indicator blinked into life, along with the blue, Depressurization alarm. A series of muffled thumps echoed in the module as, across ISS, hatch-closure systems kicked into life.

The procedure for loss of pressure in any ISS module is totally automated. Every station module instantly isolates itself by closing off its hatches—the idea being to limit atmosphere loss to one module. The idea is a good one—unless you happen to be *in* the depressurizing module. Then, stuck the wrong side of a fail-safe hatch, you're doomed.

Reynolds grabbed a handhold to pull himself out of the spinning course the collision with the wall had set him on. *The Docking Port,* he thought sickly. *Something must have gone wrong.*

His eyes sought out the Transfer Compartment at the far end of the Service Module. Just out of sight through the compartment's narrow tunnel was the Dock Assembly, from which the *Progress* had just departed. If its hatch had blown they were as good as dead.

Panicked shouts rang through the module—the Russians had obviously reached the same conclusion. Their eyes darted wildly, scanning the module for signs of atmosphere loss—rushing air, a drop in the temperature on the command screen's environment monitors. Kalganin, forgetting himself, jabbered a stream of Russian questions at Moscow through his communications headset. Only Matchev kept his head, launching himself across the module into the Transfer Compartment tunnel.

*Going to check the hatch,* Reynolds thought. That was cool thinking.

". . . that is negative, ISS, I repeat negative." The Russian Flight Director's words cut through the confusion, obviously responding to Kalganin's shouted questions. "We are registering a master alarm on ISS, but the Service Module atmosphere is stable, I repeat stable. The Docking Port Assembly has not been compromised."

"He's right," Matchev's muffled voice called from within the Transfer Compartment. "It's okay here."

The hubbub subsided, replaced by puzzled silence. "Moscow, request situation update please," Kalganin said finally. "We have had a depressurization shutdown here. Please advise . . . where is the incident?"

"Stand by, ISS," the Flight Director replied. "Running sensor tests now."

The Russian commander continued looking around the module anxiously, as if he couldn't quite believe it, until a snap of Reynolds's fingers drew his attention to the American. "What is it, Detective?" he said in annoyance, when nothing more was forthcoming.

"I just thought of something," Reynolds said slowly. He looked up at the three cosmonauts. "Where is Dr. Akira?"

# 10

"*Ryokousha,* this is ISS. Please acknowledge transmission. Dr. Akira, please acknowledge." Ruskaya cycled through the channels on the Audio Terminal Unit, repeating the plea at each stop on the UHF, space-to-space band.

"It is hopeless," she said finally, despairing. "He is refusing to answer."

"Keep trying, Ira," Kalganin urged. He punched the space-to-ground, S-band channel open on the module's other ATU. "Houston, ISS Command," he said. "We report success in contacting *Ryokousha* negative. We can't get him."

"Copy that, ISS Command," the Flight Director's voice cracked out of the ATU speaker. "Request you keep trying for the moment. We are attempting to establish direct contact with Dr. Akira by S-band transmission. Tsukuba Space Center is attempting to override manual and place *Ryokousha* under control from Ground. We'll keep you posted."

"I hope they are succeeding," Kalganin muttered, pushing himself away from the ATU and over to Reynolds and Matchev, crowded into the viewing cupola. "What is he doing?"

It had taken flight controllers in Moscow and Houston just a few seconds to confirm Reynolds's guess. While Reynolds and the other crew members had been occupied at Kostia's funeral, the Japanese scientist had quietly fitted his orange altitude protection suit—the suit worn by shuttle astronauts—and climbed through the docking port of the Japanese Module into *Ryokousha,* the minishuttle. The violent impact they had felt was Akira firing *Ryokousha*'s separation motors, without first unhooking. The departing spacecraft had torn the dock assembly away with it.

It was the sudden atmosphere loss from the Japanese module that had triggered the depressurization shutdown. The miracle was that *Ryokousha* hadn't depressurized as well.

As soon as Ground had been able to override the shutdown, Reynolds and the three Russians had hurried down to *Zarya*—the multiported ring that connected the top, Russian section of ISS to the bottom, U.S. section. The six-sided, clear polycarbonate cupola that protruded from *Zarya*'s side like an insectoid eye offered the best viewing platform on the station. From within its faceted bubble, Reynolds could plainly see the gleaming, white shape of *Ryokousha,* inching away from the bottom of ISS with flickering thruster spurts.

"He's manual firing the maneuvering thrusters," Reynolds shrugged. "Moving *Ryokousha* away from us for some reason."

"Fuck your mother," Kalganin muttered, forgetting himself. "What in the hell is he doing?" He looked over at Irina. "Ira? Are you getting him yet?"

Ruskaya shook her head helplessly. "*Nyet,* Borya. I am certain he hears us. But he does not respond."

*Ira,* Reynolds thought. *Borya.* The reversion to nicknames was a symptom of the stress the cosmonauts were suffering. They were crawling deeper into their Russian identities, battening down against the attack they felt themselves under.

Kalganin grimaced. "Well, try the suit frequency. Maybe we can pick him up there."

Ruskaya punched the channel combination into the ATU obediently. The module was instantly filled with sound from the Japanese scientist's helmet mike—ragged breathing, the rasp of fabric and Akira's voice, sing-

ing in soft falsetto. The four of them listened in horrified
fascination as he sang.

"... *yuyake koyake* ... *de hi ga kuretet* ... *yama
mo otera no kane ga naru* ..." Akira's voice quavered
momentarily as a sob choked him. "... *otete tsunaide
mina k* ... *kaero* ..."

"What in hell is that?" Kalganin growled. "What is it
he is singing?"

"I think it is a nursery rhyme," Ruskaya said hesitantly. "Dr. Akira told it to me one time." She frowned,
concentrating. "It is something about a boy who is going
home. The boy is telling ... he is asking his love to go
with him."

She gestured impatiently.

"I cannot remember. What was it saying? Hand in
hand ... we follow the birds to our home."

The singing stopped abruptly, replaced by a low muttering. The four of them strained to hear.

"... activate bipod heaters ... ullage pressure test ...
open lox valves ..."

"He's going to start a burn," Reynolds said suddenly.
The warning Connor had passed on from the Tsukuba
flight controllers flashed back into his mind. "He's going
to fire those engines up and try to get back home."

"What ...?" Kalganin gaped at him. "But this is
impossible," he blurted. "There has been no checkout,
no trajectory, no nothing ..."

"I don't think Dr. Akira's working on that level right
now, Commander," Reynolds said grimly. "Besides, that
may be the least of his worries." He tried to remember.
Something Connor had said was bothering him.

*Ryokousha won't be operational again for another two
months. They haven't even reconnected the helium purge
system yet.*

The helium purge system! *Ryokousha* used the same
propellant as the Shuttle—supercooled liquid oxygen
and hydrogen heated and mixed to a combustible com-
pound in the main engine's turbo-pump oxidizer. The
mix was normally stable until ignition, provided it was
kept from contact with the pure liquid oxygen entering
the oxidizer.

If it wasn't . . .

Like the Shuttle, *Ryokousha* relied on helium, pumped under pressure, to stiffen the seals and keep the substances apart. Without it, they would combine the instant the "ignite" command was given, and *Ryokousha* would light up the sky from here until Christmas.

"Listen to me," Reynolds said urgently. "We've got to stop him. That crazy fuck is about to blow himself, and us, to kingdom come. Irina, can he hear inside that helmet the way we can hear him?"

Ruskaya nodded, wide-eyed.

"Then tell him he has to stop the hotfire sequence now. He's in deadly danger. Tell him the helium . . . just tell him *Ryokousha* will blow if he tries to go ahead."

She opened the channel and repeated Reynolds's words. For a moment, the ATU speaker was silent, and it looked as if the appeal had succeeded. Then Akira began singing again, his voice a hypnotic monotone.

"*. . . de hi ga kurete . . . yama mo otera no kane ga naru . . .*"

*Christ, he's blocking us out.* Reynolds flung himself at the ATU, stabbing his own finger down on the button. "Dr. Akira!" he shouted. "Don't! The purge system . . . *Ryokousha* is going to blow!" But he sensed the Japanese man's fingers working the console even as he spoke, the index finger bearing down on the square ignition button.

It started as a rumble below them, as if somehow, down on Earth, a huge earthquake was sending a shockwave up at them. Then ISS creaked as the first ripples of the blast hit. A second later it lurched violently upwards as the main force engulfed them. Orange light poured through the cupola, completely obliterating the black space sky. Then Reynolds and the Russians were tumbling again, wheeling and bouncing off the shaking module walls.

It was the end. Fragments of *Ryokousha* were shooting past, smashing into them, as the spacecraft blasted apart. But Reynolds's only thought was a moment of mild surprise.

*I called her Irina. Why did I do that?*

# 11

It took Houston hours to regain contact with ISS. A fragment of the exploding *Ryokousha*'s fuselage had torn the S-band transponder clean away, plunging the crippled station into silence. For an hour or so, as repeated transmissions were answered by static and telemetry screens remained blank, Flight Control thought the station had been lost entirely.

It was only at 6:18 P.M., two hours and twenty-nine minutes after explosion and loss of signal, that signs of life flickered. Telemetry screens suddenly began receiving data—someone on ISS had managed to switch the station over to the backup Russian "Regul" communication band. The audio link was reestablished. Then the flight controllers watched in horror as video function came back on-line, and the full extent of the damage was revealed.

ISS's hull was a mess of scorched and twisted wreckage. Torn thermal blanketing—essential in repelling the sun's 250-degree glare and preventing overheating—hung, shredded, off several modules. Of the five giant solar arrays that could be seen—the cameras covering the other three had evidently been destroyed—two were honeycombed with holes from the blast and one was a mere stump, three-quarters of its ninety-yard length having been blown off into space. Panning of the external cameras revealed it trailing ISS some 200 yards back, along with a cloud of glittering debris that stretched nearly two miles.

*Both* strings of the S-band radio—ISS's primary channel for space-to-ground communication—turned out to be unsalvageable. ISS would remain limited to the Russian "Regul" radio system, at least until a Shuttle repair mission could be mounted.

To the aghast flight controllers, however, it seemed a long shot there would be anything left *worth* repairing.

Luckily though, ISS's "sausage string" shape—central modules laid end-on-end along a single axis with subsidiaries branching off—had saved her. Most of the side modules were blown, their hulls punched with holes from the flying debris of *Ryokousha*'s explosion, but *Zvezda,* the Lab Module, the U.S. Hab Module and even the Cargo Block had been spared. Half-blind, limping and crippled, ISS could go on.

The flight controllers were relieved to find the crew members, apart from Dr. Akira, still alive. Their position in *Zarya,* halfway along the station's central axis, had sheltered them as ISS underwent its second depressurization shutdown of the day. Slowly, cautiously, Reynolds and the cosmonauts had manually opened each hatchway until they made it into *Zvezda,* from where they had accessed the "Regul" system and contacted Moscow and Houston. Now they stood ready for the flight controllers' instructions on how to bring what could be brought of ISS back to life.

Taking a deep collective breath, the NASA Flight Room techs began the process of bringing ISS's systems back on-line. The first priority was to initiate shutdown of electrical function to the compromised modules. Nonessential functions to the core modules would also have to be cut, to minimize the danger of overheating and preserve power. Voltage checks would have to be run on all functioning solar arrays.

The crew members got to work. One thing at least was settled. There was no need to think about a ceremony for Kutashita Akira. The scientist had provided his own Viking funeral.

12:19 A.M., Day 85, Expedition Time
Laboratory Module, International Space Station

It was midnight before Connor could get through to
Reynolds; the Ku-band radio, which carried ISS's videoconference link, was intact but low on the list of reestab-
lishment priorities. The sixty-three-year-old adviser
looked a long, hard moment at Reynolds's image on the
screen, then burst out with an exclamation of relief.

"Thank God you're all right!" Connor said. "Christ,
Edge, you've no idea how worried we've all been down
here." He studied his friend closely. "You took a couple
of hits, I see." There was a four-inch cut, swabbed with
antiseptic and stitched, over Reynolds's right eyebrow.

Reynolds fingered the cut. "Uh huh," he said tiredly.
"Rusk . . . the Medical Officer zipped it up for me." He
frowned. The brush of his own fingertip reminded him
of Ruskaya's, moving coolly around his anesthetized skin
as she stitched.

Connor nodded. "The Flight Crew at Tsukuba have
asked us to pass on a personal apology to all of you.
The poor bastards feel terrible." He shook his head sor-
rowfully. "Christ, we're all to blame. We should have
taken a closer look at Akira. We could have stopped
him."

Reynolds shrugged. "Spilled milk, Matt. Besides, *we're*
okay. A few cuts, but those'll heal. I'd be more worried
about ISS."

"You got that right," Connor said, despairing. "Even
with the fireworks you might count yourself lucky to get
a ride on her before she goes down, Edge."

He sighed, dispirited.

"This has goddamn ruined everything. It's not even
the physical damage that'll sink us. It's the reputation.
One death, we could handle. Two, at a stretch. But
*three*? Uh uh. What was it Oscar Wilde said? That looks
like carelessness." He looked up at Reynolds. "We've
already had Coleman on the phone, you know."

"Yeah?"

"Uh huh. Talk about vultures. He's asked for an estimate of replacement cost for the damaged modules to

go before the House Committee next week. You know what that means. If he wants it that quick, the only thing he wants it *for* is ammunition."

Reynolds listened with half an ear. He understood Matt's concern, but didn't feel able to share it right now.

"What about Wilkinson, Matt?" he interrupted. "He pull down that log we were talking about?"

"W . . . what?" said Connor, flustered momentarily by the shift in gears. Then he snapped his fingers. "Oh yeah. That was the thing I wanted to talk to you about. I looked in on Wilkinson an hour ago—Christ, I had to do *something* while I was waiting for you to come on-line. He got the log all right. Looks like your hunch to check Myers's computer was a good one."

"Yeah?" Reynolds said, his tiredness vanishing. "What did he come up with?"

"Well . . . he said he couldn't make sense of it at first. Big chunks of it looked like just gibberish. Then he got inspired and ran it through an ANSI converter."

Reynolds's raised eyebrows conveyed the question.

"That's what I said," Connor continued. "Apparently, an ANSI filter converts seven-bit ASCI text, which is what Latin alphabets use, to eight-bit ANSI text, which is what non-Latin alphabets like Russian use. Anyway, he hit the jackpot. Turns out a lot of the keystroke log is in Cyrillic. Meaning . . ."

"Gary was typing Russian commands into his computer," Reynolds said slowly. "Meaning he must have been accessing the Russian Operating System." He pursed his lips thoughtfully. "But why?" he said. "The ROS wasn't Myers's responsibility, was it?"

"Bingo," Connor growled. "You're damned right it wasn't. Let me tell you, if Flight had found out . . . well. Even the way he went might have seemed preferable. No, my guess is it had to do with the footsie you caught him playing with Ruskaya. He was probably poking around for some way to send her secret love letters."

"That figures," Reynolds agreed. "The same trick he pulled with that girlfriend of his at Pacific Bell." He thought for a moment. "But it still doesn't give us the motive for wiping his hard disk."

There was an uncomfortable silence. Connor's answer, when it came, was hesitant. "No . . . but maybe something else does. Wilkinson says he's uncovered a pattern to the log. He says it looks like Gary *started off* just fooling around, but he stumbled onto something that got him real interested, real quick."

"Yeah? Like what?"

"Well . . . Wilkinson says he can't be sure, but it looks like Gary discovered an anomaly in the Russian telemetery programs."

Reynolds's eyes narrowed. "What anomaly?"

Connor looked away from the screen, as if double-checking there was nobody in the room. "It has to do with EVA data transmission for the Orlan suits," he said finally. "Wilkinson says it looks like Gary found an algorithm planted in the program that handles transmission of bioinstrumentation data from the Russian suits when they're on EVA. It's a graft, something that shouldn't oughta be there."

"What does it do?" Reynolds asked.

Connor waited a full five seconds before replying. "It . . . uh . . . it makes up the data."

Reynolds's eyes widened. "It *makes up* the data?"

"Yeah, it . . . it makes up the data. Just for two of the suits, mind you. The others report to Mission Control, Moscow, in the normal manner."

Reynolds was speechless. Astronauts, and cosmonauts, on EVA were *dependent* on their suits' bioinstrumentation telemetry. That was how Mission Control monitored the suit's life-support systems: suit pressure, oxygen reserves, temperature—everything. Without it . . . well, that was crazy. There was no "without it".

"I know," Connor continued. "It sounds screwy. But that's what Wilkinson says."

Reynolds spied a ray of light in the madness. "You said for two of the suits. Which two?"

Connor clucked his tongue. "No dice, Edge, I'm afraid. I asked him that too. He said because the suit IDs are assigned the day of the EVA, there's no way to tell from here which is which."

Reynolds fell silent, thinking it over. *Christ, this is in-*

*sane. What reason could there be for faking life-support data?*

To cover up faults in the technology? But the Orlan had been the workhorse of Russian space suits for over thirty years. It was tried and tested. Besides, there would be no need for data warnings if there *were* faults in a space suit. The screams of the dying cosmonaut would tell you that.

*And why just two of them?* Reynolds wondered.

"I need a closer look at this, Matt," he muttered finally. "Any chance you can shoot that log up to the teleprinter for me?"

It was Connor's turn to raise an eyebrow. "Sure . . . if you want it. It's really geek territory though, Edge. What are you hoping to find?"

Reynolds shrugged. "I don't know. Just humor me, okay? Get Wilkinson to mark out which are the relevant Cyrillic commands."

And with that he signed off, closing the laptop and allowing the makeshift cabin to fall back into the low light of the retreating sun, filtering through the porthole window.

He floated silently in the semidarkness for some time, staring out the window at space. Out there, all around him, was . . . nothing. The void. The same void into which Akira had blown himself, just those few hours before. Even now, pieces, fragments, molecules of the Japanese scientist would be speeding away from the focus of the blast, setting out on a silent journey that would last forever—unless the particles collided with something, got sucked into the gravitational field of a passing planet or star, or somehow found an atmosphere to burn up in.

That was the thing about space: the normal rules did not apply. You did something on Earth—however bad it was, it only lasted a short time. Gravity, wind resistance, morality—something always intervened, and there was an end to it. Not in space though. Out here, you set something in motion and it just kept going. On and on. Forever.

For a moment, Reynolds felt that same delicious thrill

he'd experienced as a teenager, watching tapes of Kennedy's speeches. Space was a different place—exotic, exciting and new. To go there was to escape the burdens of an earthbound existence, with all its rules, restrictions and immutable laws. To go there was to cross the New Frontier.

He shook his head to clear the thoughts away. None of this was helping him digest Connor's incredible news.

*An algorithm that fakes EVA bioinstrumentation data.*

He placed this latest inexplicable fact alongside the others in his collection.

*The EMU suit. Myers's rightward glance. Kostia's plea to Leonid. Kostia locking the Cargo Block hatch from the inside.*

*An algorithm that fakes EVA bioinstrumentation data.*

He walked around the setup mentally a couple of times, trying to fit the pieces all together. But nothing came.

Only two of the suits. That was important too. It meant Kostia . . . and one other.

*Matchev? Or Kalganin?*

*Or . . . Irina?*

He stifled the protest he felt well up inside himself. He had to stop this tendency to write Ruskaya out of the picture. The near destruction of ISS had made it worse—you couldn't go through that with someone and not develop strong feelings for them. But try as he might to ignore it, the skin around his cut tingled anew with the memory of her cool, almost caressing, fingers. He closed his eyes and tried to drive the sensation away with the image of her hand gripping his wrist, two days before, in her interview. What was it she had said?

*Women and men are more equal here, Detective.*

"Detective?"

Reynolds's eyes flew open. The woman herself was in the doorway of his compartment, her slender form outlined by the weak light of the few fluorescent tubes still operating in the Laboratory Module.

"Yes?" he rasped, disoriented.

She hesitated, then pushed herself over to him. "I came to investigate your injury. Is the bleeding stopped?" White light spilled into the alcove as she switched on a handheld, halogen med-light.

Reynolds closed his eyes against the sudden glare. Before he knew it her fingers were at his brow again, probing delicately.

"It's okay," he muttered awkwardly. "The bleeding stopped an hour or so ago."

"Well, we must take care," she replied. He heard her unscrewing something, then felt the stinging kiss of antiseptic on his skin. "The microorganism filters . . . they will not be working well for many days, yes? We must . . . we need to stop infections."

Her words were distracted, as if she had to force herself to concentrate on them. The tingle on his skin ceased as her hands paused, then withdrew uncertainly.

Reynolds opened his eyes. She was floating mere inches from him, her eyes flicking guiltily from his, then back again. The med-light had fallen, forgotten, from her hand and was drifting across the compartment, its beam of light traversing the walls as it cartwheeled lazily.

"You didn't come here to check on my cut," he said softly. It was more statement than question.

Her eyes fell away from his again. She gave a slight shake of her head.

"Why did you come?" he asked.

He heard a choked sob in the half-darkness as she fought to control herself. Then the dam broke and she was in his arms—head pushing against his chest, body shaking. The impact set him drifting; his back crashed into the wall, and the two of them bounced away to wheel slowly through the compartment. He put out a foot to steady them. Tears dampened the front of his flight suit.

He put his arms around her awkwardly. There was no need for words. All the reserve, the defiance, he had noted in her was gone, and now the real woman was left in his arms, frightened and badly shaken. He held her close as sobs racked her body.

"I can't take these things anymore," she gasped. "First Gary, then Kostia and now Dr. Akira. I . . . I am afraid. It is like we are surrounded with killing. It is a death ship we are on."

Reynolds stroked her hair as she pulled herself harder in against his chest. It was all he could do to speak. He was trembling, trying desperately to repress the storm of emotion the woman in his arms was provoking.

"Shh, Irina," he whispered. "It's all right now. We're safe."

She turned her face up to his. The tears welling in her eyes broke and floated free. "Call me Ira," she said softly.

"Ira," he murmured, pushing the floating tears gently away from her face with the back of his hand. They broke against it, coating his hand with warm wetness. He marveled at how easily the pet name left his mouth. It was as if he had been aching to say it.

She studied his face in the intermittent beam of the wheeling med-light. "You cannot know how lonely I have been," she said, shaking her head. "You do not know what it is to be a cosmonaut. We are taught to keep everything inside, never to burden our crewmates with doubts and fears." She stifled a sob. "But I have felt so alone . . ."

Irina looked up at him again. "But you are alone too, Detective. Is it not so? There is a great loneliness in your eyes. I have seen it . . ." she lowered her head in embarrassment ". . . especially sometimes, when . . . when you look at me."

Reynolds held her tightly to him, this time to still the sudden weakness in himself. Her words had reached deep into him, touching a part of him he had not thought possible.

"You remind me of someone," he muttered hoarsely. "Every time I look at you . . . I see her."

Irina was silent for a moment. "Did you love her?" she asked finally. "This woman you see when you look at me?"

"She was my wife," Reynolds whispered helplessly, squeezing his eyes shut against the pain that stabbed him. "I loved her more than my own life."

It was a mistake to close his eyes. A hundred different images of Alicia came alive—Ally at the beach, Ally walking with him beside Clear Lake, Ally astride him in the car as they made love some moonlit Houston night.

"I understand." Irina's voice reached him, somehow,

through the crowding images. His back tingled as her hand began caressing him slowly. Her voice was an uncertain whisper. "Why not . . . let her be with you again tonight?"

He gasped as she slid the hand, hesitantly, over his buttocks. Before he knew it, the other was at the nape of his neck, stroking him gently, and Irina's breasts were pressed against his chest as her lips brushed gentle kisses over the skin at the opened neck of his flight suit.

He held himself stiff for a moment, then relaxed as the rhythm of the kisses took over. His body folded into Irina's. His hands moved hungrily over her. Her hands were everywhere, soothing him, washing the pain away.

He wanted to cry out—tell her it was all right, she could be Irina in his arms and not Alicia, and that was okay. But somehow, the words wouldn't come. And soon they were naked, cradling each other in a drifting cloud of their clothing, and there was no place for words anyway.

Afterwards, they drifted, deliciously spent. The battery on the med-light was gone too, its tumbling light a dull yellow glow. Reynolds floated in the darkness, stroking Irina languidly, and let his mind roam over the details of the case.

*Did Kostia really kill Myers?*

Reynolds was beginning to doubt it—or to doubt, at least, that if he had, the motivation was only jealous rage over the woman in Reynolds's arms. The inconsequentials were piling up too fast for that.

Myers had discovered an algorithm in the Russian Operating System that made up bioinstrumentation data for cosmonauts on EVA. For *two particular* cosmonauts. And three days after Myers's murder, someone had attempted to cover that fact up by erasing Myers's hard disk.

There had to be a connection between that and Myers's murder. But what?

Reynolds waited patiently, but nothing came. He felt himself sliding, frustrated, into the unconsciousness of sleep. He sensed an answer there, somewhere, on the rim of consciousness, but every time he approached it, it slipped from him. Just like Irina, who gathered her clothes sometime during the night and quietly stole away.

# 12

Reynolds woke to the empty module. He drifted there for some time, naked, exploring the sensation of Irina's absence.

She had done the right thing by leaving. Even with the camera system only half-operational, ISS was still a small place. There was no way a crew member emerging from another's quarters the morning after would go unnoticed. Still, he felt oddly slighted. What was the etiquette for one-night stands on an orbiting space station?

His brow furrowed. *Is this what that was? A one-night stand?*

He lay quietly, examining his motives. Irina's, at least, were easy to understand—frightened and shaken, she had reached out for the most elemental comfort there was. Reynolds was under no illusions. She had chosen *him* because he was an American, an outsider. She avoided entanglements that way. In two days, Reynolds would be gone, leaving just the memory of shared passion to cope with, not the consequences.

He stirred uneasily. *What if that isn't what I want?* he thought. *What if I want . . . more?*

He roused himself and began dressing, forestalling the thoughts. He had enough on his plate as it was without falling into some "fatal attraction" scenario.

The staccato buzz of the teleprinter reminded him of his request to Connor the night before. The log from

Wilkinson must be coming through. Reynolds finished buttoning up his flight suit and, worming his hand between the helmet and neck of his Titan space suit, pulled out the rice-paper-wrapped bar of dried fruit, grain and nuts that was kept there as a snack for astronauts on EVA.

That would have to do for breakfast. He had work to get on with.

He ripped the teleprint roll off the printer and took it back to his compartment. He settled down to the laborious job of combing through it.

It took him some minutes to get his bearings. As Reynolds had expected, the Russian system was written in archaic machine code, rendering the UNIX knowledge he'd picked up in training all those years ago useless. Luckily though, Wilkinson had written a legend at the head of the log. By referring back to it laboriously, every second line or so, Reynolds started to get a handle on it.

The last three weeks of Myers's life. As told by the astronaut's computer.

Wilkinson had highlighted a date a few pages into the log, evidently the date Gary had started hacking into the OCCS—the Russian Onboard Complex Control System. There were a couple of pages of general fooling around, to get the feel of the system it looked like, then the commands went straight to the suit communication subsystems. That figured. If Connor was right and Myers had been looking to send love notes to Irina, it would have to be to somewhere only she would see it. Her suit was the logical choice. Like the American ISS suits, the Russian Orlans had simple head-up displays fitted—to allow procedural information to be thrown up for the astronaut on EVA. If Myers had managed to splice a message into the data stream, it would have been his and Irina's little secret . . .

Reynolds shook his head to dispel the sudden surge of jealousy. He forced his eyes to concentrate harder on the teleprint.

But Connor had said the way suit IDs were allocated meant there was no way of knowing which was which until the day of the EVA. That meant Gary must have been quickly disappointed—there was no way he could be sure the spliced message would go to Irina's Orlan and not someone else's. Yet he had kept poking around in the Russian suit communication subsystem. Why?

*He must have come across the algorithm Connor was talking about almost immediately. That was what pricked his interest.*

Reynolds ran a few pages forward on the roll and, sure enough, there it was. There was no doubt about what it was—Wilkinson had double-highlighted the key sequence with shading and underlining. It was obvious the algorithm had instantly captured Myers's attention. The whole key sequence was repeated three times, one after the other.

*He ran it through three times,* Reynolds thought. *He couldn't believe it.*

That made two of them.

He scrolled a few pages ahead. He picked a point at random and started again. According to Wilkinson's notes, Myers's attention had now shifted from the suits to the OCCS data-handling architecture. Reynolds was just about to flip back and see what had prompted the change when a command phrase caught his eye.

**. . . рпозмлк 131 ятср \<COSMONAUT\> гч 224 млъ . . .**

He stared at the phrase. There was something wrong with it, but he wasn't sure what.

**. . . рпозмлк 131 ятср \<COSMONAUT\> гч 224 млъ . . .**

It hit him. He traced back through the log to double-check, but there was no mistake. He pressed the push-to-talk button on his communication unit and swung the mike over his mouth.

"CAPCOM, MS-3," he said. "Put me through to Adviser Connor, please. Immediately."

CAPCOM shunted him through, but it was an assistant technician who answered. The tech told him Connor was grabbing an hour's sleep in the side office that had been set up with cots for exhausted flight controllers, some of whom were into the fiftieth straight hour of their catastrophically extended shift. Reynolds searched through the log, counting references, while he waited for the man to wake Connor. Twenty-two, twenty-eight, thirty-three . . . forty-seven usages of the phrase in total. Over thirty of them on the last two pages of the log. Meaning . . .

Reynolds calculated swiftly. *The day before Myers's death. Two days before at most.*

"Yeah, buddy," Connor's bleary voice interrupted. "I'm here. What have you got?"

"Sorry to wake you, Matt," Reynolds answered. "I've been going through the log Wilkinson sent up for me. I've come across something weird."

"You want me to get him on the line for you?" Connor asked. "He's still round here, somewhere."

"Negative, Matt," Reynolds replied. "It's not that kind of something. It's a word I've found embedded in the Russian commands Gary was typing. Something it seems Gary was very interested in. I've counted at least forty-seven references to it so far, most of them in the day or two before he died."

"Uh huh," Connor said wearily. "What's the word?"

"It's COSMONAUT. All in capitals."

Connor was silent for a moment. "Well . . . what's weird about that?" he said finally. "He was fooling around in the Russian system. Why wouldn't he find the word 'cosmonaut'?"

"Yeah, but this is 'cosmonaut' written in English. It's spelled c-o-s-m-o-n-a-u-t. You see what I mean? If it's in the Russian system, why doesn't it use the Russian spelling? K-o-s-m-o-n-o-u-t."

"Uh . . ." Connor's voice fell into silence.

"I went back through the log to make sure," Reynolds continued. "It's not just idiosyncratic usage—I found at least three occasions when the proper Russian term appears. You see what I mean? I think it's written that way to differentiate it, whatever it is, from the normal word. Not KOSMONOUT—k-o-s-m-o-n-o-u-t. COS-MONAUT—c-o-s-m-o-n-a-u-t."

"Okay," said Connor finally, thinking it over. "I'll buy that. But then, what is it?"

Reynolds pursed his lips. *That's a very good question.*
"I don't know," he said finally. "The capitals mean
it's gotta be a name—a program or a file or something.
But I know Gary was interested in it." He ran a finger
back through the log. "Lookit, on the twenty-sixth of
February we've got Gary fooling around in the Russian
suit communication subsystem—that's when he first runs
across COSMONAUT. He jerks around with it a while,
in his spare time it looks like, averaging two or three
references a day. But always in connection with the suit
systems. Then, on the seventh of March, it drops the
connection with the suits, shifts to the main computer
architecture and goes ballistic. Thirty occurrences in two
days. The two days before he was killed." His voice
dropped to a murmur. "It's almost as if . . ."

*As if COSMONAUT killed him,* Reynolds thought, his
mind reeling. *Not Kostia, Matchev, Kalganin or anybody.*
*COSMONAUT.*

He pulled himself together. That was crazy. The NRA
slogan flitted through his mind in paraphrase.

*Computer files don't kill people. People kill people.*

Connor's voice was disturbed. "Gary was killed because of something he found out about this? Is that what
you're saying?"

"I'm not sure what I'm saying," Reynolds replied.
"All I know is Gary was interested as hell in this COS-
MONAUT, whatever it is, so we ought to be too. I need
to find out what it is, Matt. Can you do some digging
for me?"

"Sure," said Connor. "I'll put a request through to
NASA liaison in Moscow. They should . . ."

Reynolds shook his head violently. "Uh uh, that's a
negative, Matt. I want a total lockdown on this one.
Okay? Not a whisper to anyone in RKA."

"Okay," said Connor in surprise. "I'll get the investigative team to run a record search then." He hesitated a
moment, then burst out in irritation, "But goddamn it,
Edge. What is it? What the hell are we dealing with here?"

The question pulled Reynolds up short. He had no
idea. All he had was a handful of unconnected facts,
each one crazier than the last. At least he had a name
to put to it now. Only the name made no sense either.

COSMONAUT.

"I wish I knew," he said finally. "All I know is Gary knew about this two weeks before he died, and didn't dare say anything about it nearly that whole time. That tells me that whatever it is, we ought not fuck around with it."

2:03 P.M., Day 85, Expedition Time
Service Module *Zvezda*, International Space Station

Lunch that day was a gloomy affair. The four of them floated at the table in the gray half-light of the Service Module, eating rehydrated food packages cold—ISS's power systems still weren't stable enough for nonessentials like food warming. A stream of debris—tools, bubbles of leaked coolant, shards of glass and plastic—shaken loose by the explosion the day before, drifted through the module. Odd noises filled their ears: the tinny clatter of fans knocked askew in their seats, the creak and groan of aluminium alloy frames bent out of tolerance. Even the smell was different—a humid, oppressive mix of sour waste odors and the cloying, brake-fluidish smell of the leaking coolant.

*An honest-to-God death ship,* Reynolds thought. *Just like Irina said.*

Talk was muted. Kalganin and Matchev carried on a desultory conversation in Russian—discussing the recovery plan Mission Control had put the crew on, Reynolds guessed. He didn't bother to rebuke them for not speaking English. The three-week emergency plan NASA had devised—week one, secure station internally; week two, damage assessment, EVAs; week three, commence reconstruction—didn't really concern him anyway. By the time the crew began their painstaking crawl over the torn and twisted exterior of ISS, he would be long gone—borne to Earth by *Endeavor*, due to dock with ISS sometime around eleven the next morning.

*Taking what with me?* Reynolds wondered, savaging his rehydrated stroganoff. *One dead cosmonaut who may, or may not, have had something to do with the crime he died for. And a name.*

COSMONAUT.

That was all. Frustration boiled up in him. His eyes
flicked angrily to Matchev and Kalganin's faces. Neither
of the Russians had escaped ISS's brush with death un-
scathed. Matchev's face was blotched with bruises; Kalganin's broken nose was a mess of sticking plaster and
dried blood. Reynolds had to resist the urge to grab one
or both of them by the collar and start shaking.

*Fuck you, you bastards. What secrets are you keeping?*

His eyes slid to Irina, floating, anchored by her feet, at
the end of the square table. She was squeezing borscht—
Russian beet soup—from a plastic tube, and eating it
impassively, head up, staring straight ahead. Giving no
sign she even noticed Reynolds's presence. *God she's
beautiful,* he marveled. Her self-control was amazing.
Just like on the tapes he had watched of her interaction
with Kostia and Myers. She had never slipped, not even
once. While the men around her, aching with love, betrayed themselves with every move . . .

Conscious he was in danger of emulating them, Reynolds turned back to the cold food in front of him. He
took another mouthful as a palliative and chewed
thoughtfully.

"Commander Kalganin," he said suddenly, swallowing
and taking another spoonful. "I'm going to want you to
collect all the Orlans from the airlock and take them to
the Lab Module when we've finished up here. Yours,
Leonid's, Irina's. Kostia's too."

He'd thought this through earlier. It was the only
place he could think of to start with this screwy business
of the algorithm Wilkinson had uncovered. With the
Russian suits.

Heavy silence. Kalganin's jaw stopped midchew. He
stared at Reynolds hard, then looked over at Matchev
and Irina. Recollecting himself, he swallowed.

"What for?" he muttered. His voice was edged with
unfriendliness.

"I need to examine them," Reynolds replied casually.
"A formality, Commander. Part of my investigation."

The muscles in Kalganin's jaw knotted with the effort
of suppressing emotion. His eyes glittered. "Why?" he

said through clenched teeth. "Kostia is dead now. What more can you want from us?"

"Humor me," Reynolds said mildly, pushing the viscous stroganoff around in its tub with his spoon. "I have my reasons."

Kalganin's breath escaped him in a hiss. His eyes blazed. "At a time like this you are asking for us to humor you? Are you not seeing what is happening around you, Detective?" He looked at the other two cosmonauts for support. "We are 'situation critical' here on ISS. Do you think we have time for humoring?"

"Commander Kalganin," Reynolds said, his voice snapping into formality. "You forget I am *Major Militsii* Reynolds of the *Federal'noe Buro Bezopasnosti,* your Federal Security Bureau. I have authority over you and your crew for the duration of my stay on ISS. Are you disobeying my order to collect the Orlan space suits and transfer them to the Laboratory Module for my inspection?"

That did the trick. Kalganin stiffened, glared, then let out his breath slowly. His body relaxed. "I am at your disposal, Detective," he said, voice heavy with mock-polite sarcasm. He pushed himself from the table savagely and out of the Service Module, leaving the spoon he had been using spinning slowly in midair, shedding particles of food. Matchev reached out and stilled it with a finger, leaving it to hang motionless.

Reynolds ignored the silent reproach. He chewed another mouthful of cold stroganoff, preoccupied with the departed commander's display. The Russian was tired, he was battered, he was emotional. A tantrum under those circumstances was only to be expected. But was that all it was?

*Did I really see what I thought I did?* Reynolds wondered. *When I mentioned the suits?*

*A flicker of fear?*

4:57 P.M., Day 85, Expedition Time
Laboratory Module, International Space Station

*Fuck! What was that?*

Alarm shot up Reynolds's spine at the touch of a hand

on his neck. He swung round, panicked blind, fists flailing. They smacked into a hard, round object, cracking his knuckles painfully.

He stared wildly at the object a moment. It was a helmet. Attached to it, floating limply in front of him, was one of the Orlan suits.

He let out a nervous laugh. *Jesus. Just one of the suits.* The hanging glove must have brushed his neck.

He relaxed his body forcibly and took a couple of deep breaths. *Christ, that was bad. Jumping at shadows like that.*

He must be letting things get to him.

Reynolds hung there a moment, letting calm seep back in. Around him, in the clean, white lines of the Lab Module, drifted the four cream-colored Russian space suits—lifeless, deflated ciphers with eerily waving limbs and bulbous helmet heads whose gold faceplates reflected the half-light from the module's fluoros totally. Seeing into the suits through those opaque globes was impossible, and if you weren't careful you could start imagining there were figures inside them, that there was purpose behind the seemingly random way they drifted, getting closer . . .

Reynolds grabbed the suit and got to work, dismissing the image before it got hold of him. You had to be careful about shit like that in space.

He turned the suit—Kalganin's, he guessed from the Cyrillic characters stenciled on the left breast—over so he could access the back-mounted life-support system. The fabric of the suit's outer layer—nylon/canvas as opposed to the Gortex/Kevlar/Nomex of the American EMUs—felt stiff and rough to the touch. He yanked the locking lever that secured the backpack seal and swung the unit out on its hinge. Unlike the American life-support pack, which was mounted outside the astronaut's EMU, the Orlan's was part of the pressurized internal volume of the suit. Reynolds had to admit the setup had its advantages. For one thing, it simplified entry. To ingress their suits, cosmonauts had merely to climb in through the door at the back, pull the wire that swung the life-support pack closed and push the lever to lock it in place. None of the "worm into wall-mounted suit upper, pull up suit lower and swivel to lock, then attach arms, helmet and gloves" of the American EMUs.

*Like everything the Russians do,* he thought. *Crude, primitive, simple. But extremely effective.*

He studied the life-support system in frustration. Primary $O_2$ bottles, heat exchangers, $CO_2$ removal cartridge, moisture separator. He knew the machinery well enough to identify components by sight. But that didn't help with his central problem.

*What the fuck am I looking for?*

He poked at the squat, aluminum-cased telemetry unit. That had to have something to do with it. Myers had uncovered an algorithm in the Russian computer system that created false bioinstrumentation data—well, this was where the real data should have been coming from. He wiggled a finger in the space between the unit and the adjacent battery pack experimentally.

*Question is, why isn't it?*

He scowled in exasperation. Christ, the whole business was so screwy. The bioinstrumentation data—EKG, temperature, oxygen levels, pressurized volume readings—that shit was essential. Without that information, Mission Control, Moscow, was blind as to the spacewalker's condition. And if the cosmonaut in it was alive, the suit *had* to be generating it.

So why put something in between the one and the other? Something that took the real information and substituted false?

*An attempt to murder two of the cosmonauts?* Reynolds wondered. But that didn't cut it either, he realized. Not because it wouldn't have worked—it would. But it would have killed the cosmonauts long before now, on their first long EVA, when the blinded system would have failed to initiate secondary $O_2$ bottle operation upon exhaustion of the primary.

He tried to think of another explanation, but nothing came. All he could come up with was that there was a fault with two of the suits that had to be covered up. But that was crazy too, for the same reason.

*No dead cosmonauts.*

He gave up in frustration, closing the backpack door and running his hands carefully over the suit instead. He had no idea what he was looking for. Maybe he'd get lucky.

But three suits and a half hour later he was none the wiser. As far as he could see there was nothing out of place with the Orlans, nothing at all. He grabbed Irina's suit, the last, and began examining it. Cursorily, not expecting to find anything.

He ran his hands over the suit slowly, mind puzzling over the conundrum. Somewhere along the line though, his mind slipped back to their lovemaking, and his hands were no longer traversing Irina's space suit, but caressing her bare skin like they had in his cabin the night before.

*How did she do that?* he wondered. It had been nothing more than a one-night stand, a momentary turning to the most basic instinct of all for solace. He knew that. Yet he felt her touch had broken on his skin like rain on the dry, dry desert. She had reached deep inside him and moved him in a way no woman had since Ally died—not Luce, not Sandra, nor any one of the infrequent others. It wasn't just that Irina reminded him of Ally. It was like she had some secret trick—a map or a key or something—that had allowed her to slip past the defensive layers encrusted round his soul and find the real man beneath . . .

Reynolds shivered, despite the module's cloying heat. *Fuck, this is dangerous,* he thought. He hadn't realized the strength of the feelings brewing inside himself.

A noise from behind alerted him to Irina's presence. He swiveled—there she was, floating hesitantly at the hatchway. He let go of her suit hurriedly. For some reason, having her find him with it in his hands embarrassed him, as if she had caught him rifling through her underwear drawer. She hung there a moment, uncertainly, then she was flying across the module, crashing into him once more, kissing him passionately on the lips, the chin, the cheek, her arms circling his neck and dragging him tight to her.

It took a moment for the message of his stiff and unresponsive body to sink in. When it did, Irina disengaged and looked up at him, an expression of hurt bewilderment in her eyes.

"What's wrong?" she said, searching his eyes. "What is the matter?"

"Nothing," Reynolds muttered thickly, turning his face from her. "There's nothing wrong, Irina."

"There *is* something," she insisted, forcing his face gently back to hers with her palm against his cheek. "Tell me. Did I do something? What is it?"

"It's nothing," he repeated. *Christ.* How to tell Irina it wasn't her, it wasn't anything about her, it was him. His *fear.* How to tell her he was frightened of the depth of feeling she had thrown up in him? "You have to understand Iri . . . Ira," he said, reaching out to stroke her hair awkwardly. *Christ, that was a mistake.* The inner winds of longing and desire leapt back to life at the touch. "My mission here on ISS is very important. I have to be careful that nothing interferes with it. I'm just a man doing a job."

A look of uncertainty crossed her face. "But, you are a man also, no?" she asked teasingly. Her hands caressed his back seductively. Her body pressed in close against his.

Reynolds said nothing, prying her hands gently off his back and placing them by her sides. He used the action to edge her body away from his.

Irina's face broke into an expression of hurt disbelief. A sob choked her voice. "So!" she cried, hands clenching in despair. "You have turned from me, that is it?" Two tears swelled in her eyes then broke free, floating lazily over to break against Reynolds's chest. "And I had hoped . . . I thought . . . I wanted you to love me," she said, her sentence finishing in a blaze of defiance.

She buried her face in her hands and started seriously crying, body shaking with sobs, tears seeping from between her fingers to join the clouds of detritus still orbiting inside ISS.

Reynolds could hardly bear it. The sound of her sobs, coupled with the feelings turning over in him, threatened to overwhelm him. He reached out hesitantly, eased her hands from her face and cupped it in his.

"Listen to me, Irina," he said fiercely, gently brushing

away the tears clinging to her lashes with his thumbs. "I love you." He heard the words coming from his lips, amazed at them, yet knowing them to be true. "I do. And I promise you we will be together, back on Earth. As soon as it becomes possible. When this is all over. Do you believe me?"

She gazed at him, wide-eyed, hope at his words struggling with her despair. Then she nodded, a tiny gesture, barely perceptible. She drifted closer to him, so close he could feel the heat from her body. He allowed it, though he resisted the urge to encircle her with his arms. "But isn't it already over?" she asked uncertainly. "I mean, Kostia . . ." Her voice broke off as she shuddered at the memory of her crewmate's fate.

Reynolds stared at her. Facts jumbled through his mind—Myers's rightward glance, the erasure of his computer's hard disk, the algorithm he had discovered. COSMONAUT. And Kostia was there as well, the fear that had made him lock his temporary prison from the inside.

He shook his head emphatically. "No, Ira," he said slowly. "I'm afraid it isn't." And this time he *did* allow his arms to go around her, drawing her protectively to him. His voice was a mere whisper.

"It's not over at all."

The lovemaking was different this time. Softer, gentler, as if they were calmer in each other's presence, and had less need to cover their nervousness with the heat of lust. They drifted through the module in an oblivion of ecstasy. Their flight suits, peeled slowly from each other's bodies with none of the stripping frenzy of the night before, joined the Russian space suits circling them, so that it would have seemed Irina and he were not alone, but were just one couple of many in a wheeling, majestic dance of love.

If either of them had had eyes for anything other than each other.

Halfway through, the buzzing of the ATU interrupted them, followed by Kalganin's voice.

"Ira?" the Russian said uncertainly. "This is Borya. Are you there?"

The two of them floated immobile, hands over each

other's mouths to stifle their schoolkid giggling. Not that
*that* was necessary. Without hitting the push-to-talk button, nothing from their module could be heard anyway.

"Ira?" Kalganin continued. "Are you there? We are
looking for you. We are needing you here soon. Moscow
is starting the bus repair check in *Zvezda* soon. Ira?"

The line stayed open a few seconds more, then Kalganin gave up and it clicked back into silence.

The two of them relaxed and got back to the business
at hand. The near exposure gave the sex added urgency
and thrill, and it was mere seconds before the two of
them came, collapsing into each other joyously. Then
they drifted silently, enjoying the fading glow.

Irina dressed quickly and left, hurrying to establish an
alibi. Reynolds slowly buttoned his flight suit and
wormed into his soft boots. He felt oddly deflated. It
was more than just postcoital depression. The emptiness
of Irina's departure had left room for the return of his
frustration at his lack of progress.

*Endeavor is going to be here tomorrow. And what
have I got? Nothing.*

Just a bunch of crazy, disconnected facts, each more
screwy than the last.

It made it worse that he could *feel* the answer. Just
like whatever it was he couldn't remember about Alinov's vacuum chamber, it was sitting right in front of
him, right there where he could sense it.

Except he couldn't see it.

He finished dressing, his mind worrying at the problem. Around him the space suits floated, mocking his
struggle with their mute witness.

11:09 P.M., Day 85, Expedition Time
Laboratory Module, International Space Station

Reynolds was no closer five hours later, when the time
came for his nightly videocon with Connor. He floated
in front of the laptop in his walled-off compartment,
depressed, waiting for Connor to come on-screen. He
stared out the huge round window at the Earth below,
bright under the reflected light of the overhead sun.

At least they *could* see Earth now. Kalganin's stubborn work on the attitude control system that morning had paid off. The four U.S. attitude control gyroscopes had turned out to be blasted, all toast, but the Russian commander had been able to jury-rig a control system from the Cargo Block's thruster propulsion system—little used since the early days of ISS's construction. The system was unwieldly—like maneuvering a submarine with squirts from a water pistol—but it worked. ISS could now be pointed back in the right direction, the solar arrays that remained could start feeling power again, and Reynolds could see Earth once more.

For some reason, that seemed important. Reynolds gazed at the brilliant blue, frosted with clouds, of the vast ocean orb beneath them. It was frustration, that was what it was. The homesickness he felt was the desire to escape, to get somewhere the hell away from this crazy jigsaw, with its pieces that didn't even fit each other, let alone make some kind of whole.

*Was this how Myers felt?* he wondered. *When he found out about COSMONAUT?*

Probably. Reynolds pictured the astronaut, staring out of his smaller cabin window at the world below, as he typed his message that morning. Eaten up with longing for home. Except that message showed there'd been an additional element for Myers.

Fear.

Reynolds stirred uneasily. His hand went, unconsciously, to his wrist, tracing out the flat shape of the Taser. What about him? Wasn't he in danger too? COSMONAUT had already killed once—protecting itself, covering up its traces. What if it came for him?

*That's crazy,* he told himself. Whatever COSMONAUT was, it wasn't a living being. It could no more come to kill him than the water dispenser could pull itself free and fly in to drown him in his sleep.

*All right,* the voice inside him insisted. *Not COSMONAUT itself. But it still might come for you. In human form . . .*

Reynolds frowned. That was more plausible. Only whose form? Kalganin's? Matchev's? Or . . .

Or Irina's?

He turned to the laptop uneasily; Connor's image had pulled up on-screen. *That's even crazier,* he thought. Not Irina, the same Ira he had held in his arms just that afternoon. Yet what did he really know about her, when all was said and done?

"Hi, Matt," he said out loud, pulling the headset mike into position. "You copy?"

"I read you, Edge," Connor replied, and Reynolds could almost swear he heard a note of sadness in there, for some reason. Connor's eyes flicked over his face. "How're you doing? Your cut's healing, I see."

Reynolds's hand went to the cut over his eye. Actually, he'd forgotten it completely. He traced the zippered contour of the stitched skin with a finger. There was less pain than the day before. Matt must be right.

"I guess so," he said tiredly. "I'm okay, Matt. But I'll be a whole helluva lot better when you tell me you've managed to dig up something on COSMONAUT."

Connor pursed his lips and gave a troubled shake of his head. "Not much, I'm afraid, Edge. This goddamned thing is buried down where the sun don't shine, let me tell you. I got the investigative team to run a search through the records on Russian programs, like you said. They could only come up with one reference on it."

"Uh huh. What was it?" Reynolds asked.

"It was a memo to the Director of the Office of Manned Spaceflight in Moscow. Dated about a year or so back. From the Russian software development office. Looks like we're not the only ones in the dark about this goddamn thing. Even the programmers didn't know what it was. They must have come across a reference to it in the code. They were requesting information on it."

"Hmph!" Reynolds replied savagely. "Doesn't tell us much. Did they get a reply?"

Connor nodded. "Uh huh. Obviously the Spaceflight Office didn't know either. They passed it on. Answer came back about a week later from the Biomedical Science Division. They claimed COSMONAUT was an exercise program. Said they should disregard any references they found to it."

Reynolds scowled in disgust. "An exercise program?

C'mon. This thing isn't some fucking fitness routine, Matt."

Connor shrugged. "I'm just telling you what the memo says. It says COSMONAUT is an exercise program."

"THAT'S HORSESHIT, MATT!" Reynolds shouted, smashing his fist against the observation window in his rage—*beating on a quarter-million-dollar piece of high-grade optical glass,* he thought, *that's gotta make somebody down there wince if they hear about it.* "Grade A fucking bullshit!" he knew he was losing it, throwing a major tantrum, but couldn't help it. His frustration was boiling over, frustration at all these dead ends, all these facts that meant . . . nothing. He lashed out at the door with his foot, hitting the solid aluminum with a dull clang that reverberated through the module. "COSMONAUT isn't some exercise program. Exercise programs don't kill people."

"I know, buddy," Connor said placatingly. "I know. It's a crock. There is one interesting thing about it though."

"Yeah?" said Reynolds, eyes still wild, chest still heaving. "What's that?"

"The name on it," Connor said. "The signature on the bottom of the reply. It's Alinov's. Whatever COSMONAUT is, your buddy Alinov's got something to do with it."

That got Reynolds's attention. He froze, arrested halfway through the follow-up swing he was about to take at the observation window.

*Alinov,* he thought triumphantly. *Why doesn't that surprise me?*

"I knew it," he muttered fiercely. "I fucking knew it."

Connor's brow furrowed. "Knew what?"

"You remember what I told you, Matt? That time in Alinov's vacuum chamber? How there was something about that chamber that wasn't right? Well, I haven't been able to get that out of my head. I've had a gut feeling ever since then that Alinov was involved in this somehow."

Connor looked at him dubiously. "What, did you suddenly remember what it was?" he asked.

Reynolds shook his head. He hadn't, but the failure

dampened his spirits not in the slightest. The link with Alinov, confirmation that his instincts had been right all along, had got his blood singing again, overriding his depression and frustration. Now he needed to get away, to mull the news over.

"No, I didn't," he said absently, his mind already trying the news about Alinov out to see how it fitted. "Lookit, Matt, is that all you've got for me? I want to chew this over for a while. How about we finish up now and talk again tomorrow?"

Connor's eyebrows rose. "Sure, Edge, if that's the way you want it. We'll have to talk at 0900 anyway to run through the deorbit procedure. You know, for the dock with *Endeavor*."

"Uh huh," said Reynolds, mind racing. "Okay. Till morning then, huh?"

"Uh . . . sure," said Connor hurriedly. "Look, Edge, is there anything else you want to talk to me about?"

Reynolds looked at Matt in surprise, jarred from his train of thought. "What?"

Connor stirred uncomfortably. "I just thought . . . well . . . there might be something else you wanted to talk over," he concluded lamely.

Reynolds frowned. What the fuck was Matt talking about? Then it hit him. A hot flush spread over his face. *Irina. He's talking about Irina.*

His gaze flicked involuntarily out of the compartment door and into the Lab Module. *How the fuck did he know?* The internal cameras were all off-line—the system disconnected to conserve channel space for the upcoming EVAs. So how had Matt figured it out?

Reynolds had to suppress the urge to shake his head and laugh out loud. *Son of a bitch,* he thought. *Just like back in training.* Back then, Connor had always spooked him—spooked all of them—with his uncanny ability to divine what was going down on the flimsiest evidence. If a candidate was having a secret affair, and his wife was privately threatening to leave, chances were Matt would abruptly order him, out of the blue some morning, to either leave his wife or ditch the girlfriend so that he could get back to doing what he was goddamn supposed to be doing—training to be an astronaut.

*That explains the look I caught from him,* Reynolds thought, sobered. *He's worried for me.*

He kept his face carefully neutral, merely giving a slight shake of his head. "No, Matt," he said. "It's okay. Everything's cool."

Connor gave him a long, quizzical look. "I hope so, Edge," he said finally. "I goddamn do. I hope you know what you're doing." And with that he signed off, flipping the laptop's screen back to empty slate gray.

Reynolds shut the compartment door and buckled up for sleep, Matt's veiled comments on Irina fading quickly from his mind. Fierce exultation replaced them. He was close now, he knew it. The news of Alinov's involvement had cheered him enormously. The pieces were still lying around, still disconnected, but now he knew they were going to fit. He was sure of it.

And, somehow, Alinov was the key.

# 13

Reynolds's eyelids flicked open. The compartment around him was dark, lit only by the ghostly light of the moon, visible at the right-hand edge of the huge round window.

*What time is it?* he wondered blankly.

The first demand of the suddenly conscious organism: orient yourself.

He probed the tiredness in his limbs for an answer. The darkness was useless of course, meaning only that ISS was halfway through its ninety-minute orbit and the sun was hidden behind the blackening expanse of the world below. Twenty minutes from now ISS would come out from behind the Earth and sunlight would pour through the observation window—a false dawn, repeated ad infinitum, eight times a day and eight times a night.

*Early hours of the morning,* he decided. He had been asleep four or five hours?

What had woken him?

He listened at the darkness, but no sound rose out of ISS's background hum. Not a noise then. Just the ceaseless churn of ideas, working their way deeper and deeper through his system.

Reynolds allowed himself to fall back into half-consciousness. He drifted pleasantly in the dreamlike state, letting the ideas slide lazily through his mind. Somewhere far off, at the rim of consciousness, there was a sentence, a chant, being repeated over and over. He let himself fall further in, so that he could hear it.

*Alinov is a maker of men,* the voice was saying. *You know that. Alinov is a maker of men.*

Reynolds recalled the reference sleepily—something Alinov had said about his hero Lysenko. That time outside his vacuum chamber, back in Star City. He couldn't immediately understand the significance, but the refrain kept running through his mind, and he floated quietly, bumping lazily in his sleep restraint, as he listened to it.

*Alinov is a maker of men. Remember that. Alinov is a maker of men.*

Then, suddenly, something gave and all at once the pieces were falling, crashing, into place.

*That's it,* thought Reynolds, stunned. That was what it was all about: Myers's murder, Kostia's—it *was* murder, this meant it had to be—the algorithm Myers had stumbled on. COSMONAUT. It was all about him.

*Alinov. The maker of men.*

The knowledge was like light, pouring into his half-awake brain with dazzling speed and intensity. Myers's rightward glance, Kostia's fear, Alinov's chamber— *Christ, Alinov's vacuum chamber*—everything fitted. Only he must have been dreaming deeper than he thought, because as he watched, a hand appeared in the window, naked and white in the blackness of space.

Reynolds watched, fascinated. The fingers spidered across the surface of the glass, groping for a hold, finally settling for a grip on the rim. He knew whose it was of course—it was Alicia's, and he braced himself for the sight of her, naked and heart-stoppingly beautiful, the other side of the window. That was why he was so surprised to see a man's face appear in the glass, short, blond hair floating around it like a cropped halo.

*Leonid.*

That was curious. Why should he dream of the Russian flight engineer? A vision flashed before Reynolds's eyes, thrown up from memory—the white plaster ceiling in Reisenthal's office. Reisenthal was the shrink the tribunal had ordered him to see, as part of the settlement over the sexual-homicide perp Reynolds had beaten half to death in the interview room. Reisenthal's voice was droning on in that soft-spoken, shrink manner of his.

"*. . . you dream of your wife, Detective, because of guilt. You are unable to process the excessive guilt you feel over her death, so it has crystallized in these ritualized dream appearances. You are unable to say good-bye. What you must do is find a way to forgive yourself so that you can do that . . .*"

Which was true enough, though Reynolds had wondered at the time why Reisenthal couldn't see that was why he deliberately *didn't* forgive himself, because it would have meant saying good-bye. But Leonid?

What would Reisenthal have made of that?

Reynolds watched impassively as Matchev's face came further into the middle of the observation window, followed by his shoulders and chest. The Russian's head was turning—now left, now right—as if he were striving to peer through the opacity caused by the moon's weak light on the glass. Reynolds stared at the dream figure's eyes, mesmerized. Something was wrong with them, he realized. They were solid—no pupils, whites or irises— just solid expanses of color. And not Matchev's normal ice blue either. It was hard to tell in the moonlight, but they looked to be . . .

What was that color? Purple? Or violet?

*You hear that, Reisenthal? Violet eyes. What does your hundred-dollar-an-hour-shrink brain make of that?*

There was no fear, not even when Leonid's other hand came into view and Reynolds could see it was clutching a squat, cylindrical object—the $O_2$ bottle from one of the Portable Breathing Apparatuses. He was dreaming, after all. But the chant had started up again, down there at the back of his mind, only now it was louder and there was a hint of warning about it.

*Alinov is a maker of men. Alinov is a maker of men.*

It took him a moment to understand. But then Leonid's arm was reaching back, right back, then flying in a blurred arc toward the window, and images of that same hand smashing down onto Myers's faceplate were flashing through Reynolds's mind. Then he was awake, every nerve screaming, arms flailing as he tried instinctively to thrash his way out of the sleep restraint.

*No dream . . .*

. . . was all Reynolds had time to think. The metal bottle smashed down on the window, sending an ear-splitting crack through the compartment. Fault lines blossomed through the glass, but it held; Reynolds could see, from the corner of his eye, the cylinder in Leonid's hand bounce away. But then Leonid was rearing back, using the energy of the bounce to take him the full distance from his anchoring hand, and smashing down for another try.

CRACK! The bottle bounced off the glass once more.

Reynolds scrabbled out of the restraint violently, tearing the fabric. His mind was working at a thousand miles an hour, ripping through the scenario in an instant.

*Smash the window to initiate explosive decompression. The vacuum will kill me instantly, or I'll be blown out into space and die there. Then they can blame a meteor strike or say it was colliding debris from the explosion.*

A perfect cover story, even given such an event was extremely improbable. There was no way it could be disproved. And the truth was so impossible there was no way it would even be considered.

He flung himself across the compartment to the wall where his Titan space suit was mounted, secured to its frame by strong magnetic tabs. Somewhere underneath the flurry of thought, the voice was still going, though the words now were stinging, full of reproach.

*You should have known. Of course they have to kill you. Now you know Alinov is a maker of men.*

He disregarded it, ramming himself into the suit's hard upper by springing off the floor. His only hope was to get inside the Titan and get it pressurized before the module blew. He squirmed his way into the upper, forcing his arms through the holes and into the suit arms. No time to fuck around putting on the inner cooling garment. He had seconds at most until the window gave.

BANG!

Reynolds felt, rather than heard, the impact of Leonid's weapon on the glass. He mashed the helmet down over his head, wrenching it back and forth savagely until the guide ring clicked. His gloved fingers fumbled at the locking lever, ramming it shut. He groped beside him for the suit lower.

*Christ, is that a hiss?* Had Leonid succeeded in breaching the glass?

THUMP!

The sound of Leonid's blow was dull this time, muffled by Reynolds's helmet. There was no mistaking its success, though. Even through the helmet, Reynolds could hear the hiss as the module's atmosphere began spraying through the crack Matchev had smashed in the glass. Detecting the leak, the emergency alarm began squealing. A series of muted clangs sounded as the automatic depressurization shutdown kicked into life, closing hatches throughout ISS.

*That's gotta wake somebody up,* Reynolds thought grimly. Not that it would do him any good. He'd be gone, fried down to organic solids à la Myers, before they even got their flight suits on.

His hands found the suit lower, wrenched it off its magnetic tabs and swung it under him. He doubled up, straining to maneuver his legs in through the waist hole. Christ, trying to don the suit solo was awkward. Reynolds emptied his lungs, jammed his legs up harder against the rim of the suit upper and heaved. He was rewarded with a sharp pain as his toes cracked, dragged backwards by the rim of the suit lower, then released. He started squirming, working his legs deeper into the suit legs.

Reynolds's nerves stretched tight as he dragged up the suit lower, listening for the next impact. Not that there was much point in that, he realized. The glass was already breached, shot through with cracks. The next sound would not be a blow, it would . . .

FWHOMPF!

A shockwave hit Reynolds's body, cutting off all thought, as the observation window exploded outward. The compartment door tore from its hinges, flew across to the window and wedged there momentarily, then crumpled and was sucked out into space. The Lab Module's atmosphere blasted out after it into vacuum, a geyser of gas and solid debris: glass, ripped fabric, camera equipment and smashed lab instruments.

And Reynolds. There were a few seconds of violent

shaking as the rushing atmosphere battered him. He had
to fight against it to twist the guide ring on the suit lower
shut and get the lever closed. He hit the control to initiate pressurization. Then he was torn off the magnetic
restraints and flung across the compartment. His helmet
and legs smashed into the observation window rim, stunning him. His body went limp. Then, under the pressure
of the roaring airstream, it jackknifed, folding at the
waist, and Reynolds shot out into space.

He was only under a few seconds. Reynolds came to,
groggily, some twenty yards out from ISS and traveling.
He took stock of the situation rapidly. Luckily the force
of the blast out of the window had caught him square
on; his tumble was limited to a very slow, end-over-end
wheel. He could keep ISS in his sights most of the time.
The smash into the window rim had been a good thing
too, he realized. It had slowed his speed—Reynolds estimated he was drifting away from the station at no more
than a yard a second. As opposed to the junk he could
see shooting past him, into the void, at fantastic speeds.

*Be grateful for small mercies.*

It was a *very* small mercy, truth be told. Even at a
yard a second, in the frictionless environment of space,
he would still travel all the way out to Alpha Centauri
and beyond. Or the Earth's gravity would snare him,
dragging him into a decaying orbit that would plunge
him into fiery death upon atmospheric reentry.

If his oxygen lasted that long. Which it wouldn't.

He had to figure a way to stop his motion and get
back to ISS.

His mind flicked back to the scene at his suit fitting,
down at Houston. Allison was taking him over the Titan,
pointing out features of the suit with grinning pride:
metal-banded limb joints; integrated head-up command
system; supersensitive, high-pressure glove fingertips.
Reynolds had pulled him up, frowning.

"Allison, where's the SAFER on this thing?"

SAFERs—Simplified Aids for EVA Rescue—were
tiny rocket packs that allowed astronauts a measure of
maneuvering thrust, in the event they came untethered
while on EVA. Without one, an untethered astronaut

was, to put it mildly, fucked. Space was unforgiving that
way—coming adrift by six feet was as good as 600,000.
With nothing to push against, there was no way you
could get back. SAFERs were standard issue these
days—on EMUs they were a small back-mounted pack
with a control unit at the astronaut's chest. But Reynolds
couldn't see anything on the Titan that looked like one.

Allison had shrugged. "It hasn't got one. They won't
be fitted until the assembly line starts rolling."

Reynolds stared at him.

"Hey, c'mon," Allison had protested. "It's still in
prototype, okay?" He clapped Reynolds on the back.
"Besides, what are you worried about, big guy? You're
a landlubber on this one. You're not going outside."

Reynolds made a mental note to punch Allison in the
face if he got out of this and made it back to Earth.
That didn't help him now, however. In the absence of a
SAFER, he was going to have to find some way to do
the impossible. Slow himself down and get back to ISS.

That wasn't even the greatest of his problems, he saw.
The sight of ISS, wheeling back into view, revealed Leonid crouched naked beside the blown window, muscles
bunched against his anchoring hands and feet, eyes measuring out the path between Reynolds and ISS. He was
obviously preparing to spring. Sure enough, Reynolds's
last image, as ISS rolled out of view, was of the Russian
kicking off from ISS's wall and surging towards him.

*Welcome to COSMONAUT,* Reynolds thought dazedly. *You wanted to know what it was. Well there it is:
naked and alive, and coming out to kill you.*

He steeled himself for the impact. Reynolds estimated
he was now forty yards off ISS, still traveling about a
yard a second. It wouldn't be many seconds before Leonid hit him.

Thoughts jumbled through his mind chaotically. Matchev would try to smash his helmet in probably, or batter
his life-support pack inoperative. Finishing the job Reynolds's last-minute awareness had thwarted back in the
Lab Module. But why like this? Wasn't the Russian sen-
tencing himself to the same drifting doom Reynolds
would have experienced, separated from ISS with no
way to make it back?

*Unless he has some physical means of propulsion in space.*

Even with everything Reynolds now knew—about COSMONAUT, about Alinov, about *everything*—he couldn't believe that one. More likely Leonid was hoping to finish him off close enough to ISS that he could use his corpse to kick off from, make it back that way.

*Plausible,* Reynolds decided. Newton's third law of motion—for every action there is always an equal and opposite reaction. A hundred and eighty pounds of lifeless Reynolds, kicked in one direction with velocity $v$, equaled 220 pounds of . . . whatever the fuck Leonid was . . . pushed in the opposite direction at $v \times {}^{180}\!/_{220}$.

Either that or he planned to rip the hoses from Reynolds's oxygen supply and use the escaping gas as a crude method of propulsion.

Reynolds's suit jolted as Leonid smashed into him, putting an end to such speculation. Suddenly, Reynolds was *really* tumbling, cartwheeling end-over-end and simultaneously twisting so that his field of vision was a crazy kaleidoscope of starred sky, flashes of ISS, and the arching blue globe of the world below. Reynolds's gut spasmed in nauseous protest. He bit down on his tongue to stop it. Puking inside a space suit in microgravity was not just a disgusting inconvenience. It could be fatal.

To complete the disorientation, their orbit shot them out from behind the Earth and into the sun, drenching them in harsh, white light. Reynolds reached up and clicked the gold-filmed visor on his helmet down automatically. *Very important that,* he told himself, stifling a giggle. *Wouldn't want to get a nasty case of sunburn . . .*

Or to have Leonid look in and see the terror in his eyes.

He felt, through the hard shell of his suit, the Russian's legs groping around his midriff, trying to scissor him. Secure his grip. *Important that,* Reynolds thought distractedly. The two of them were traveling at a fair pace now, in addition to spinning—it would be easy for Leonid to lose him. Reynolds tried to estimate how much velocity Leonid's collision had added to his speed. There would be a formula for that too, he knew—something to do with his velocity at 180 pounds, $v_1$, added to the difference between Leonid's velocity at 220 pounds, $v_2$, and $v_1$, making $v_3$, with adjustment made for their weight differential . . .

Reynolds nearly laughed out loud. Christ, the insanity of it! Fucking around with motion formulae when he was seconds from death. But the whole situation was so screwy he found his terror evaporating, dried up by disbelief. He wanted to wave his arms comically, shout out to no one in particular . . .

*Hey! Somebody! Get a cop!*

*Officer, I'm being attacked. By a man, a Russian man. In outer space. He's going to kill me, I'm pretty sure. But that's not the worst of it.*

*He doesn't have any clothes on. Can you believe that?*

Matchev's hand, clawing at his neck, brought him back to reality. The Russian's face appeared in front of Reynolds's faceplate. Reynolds noted, fascinated, that his earlier assessment had been incorrect. The violet of Leonid's eyes was not solid, it was a film through which the eyes' other features—pupils, whites and irises—were still barely visible. The color seemed unstable too, changing according to how much light fell on it.

*Like a contact lens,* Reynolds thought. *Bending the light that passes through it.*

He mustered his strength and swung the hardest punch he could at Matchev's jaw. It was hopeless though—the suit dampened it so much it glanced off the Russian's chin like a slap. He twisted and writhed, throwing himself at the insides of his suit desperately. Nothing. All he managed to achieve was to add some speed to the crazy tumble the two of them were in. Matchev's grip didn't even slacken.

The Russian raised his arm up high. Reynolds saw that he still had the squat $O_2$ bottle. *I'm fucked,* Reynolds thought savagely, as the cylinder rocketed in towards his face. It smashed against his outer visor, jarring Reynolds's head violently and sending splinters flying. Hampered by his unwieldy suit, there was no way Reynolds could extricate himself from Matchev's grip. All he could do was lie helplessly while the Russian battered his way through his helmet.

*Unless . . .*

SMASH! Reynolds's outer visor split, one half flying off into space, the other hanging crazily off its hinge. Leonid reached back for a blow at the exposed inner visor.

Reynolds closed his eyes and prayed. His hand inched down towards the leg pocket of his space suit. His mind went back to the hurried conversation with Duval, the Pack Crew tech, back at Houston.

The Pack Crew were responsible for prepping the space suits astronauts used on ISS—stocking them with consumables, performing fit adjustments and running last-minute checks. Connor and the two other Training Directors had been walking away from the meeting the four of them had held with the Pack Crew leader when Reynolds had slipped back into the Crew Room, drawing Duval aside with him into an alcove.

Duval's eyes had bugged out. "Yo, Reynolds. What you doin', man?"

"Shh. Look," Reynolds had said, groping at the ankle of his soft boot. "Here it is. You remember?" He drew the Glock 21, sleek and black, out and handed it to the white-jumpsuited tech, butt first.

Duval had groaned. "Aw c'mon, Reynolds," he said, pushing the pistol away. "I already told you, man. I ain't gonna do that."

"Come *on*, Duval," Reynolds had insisted. "Just slip it into the Titan for me. Okay? Remember what I told you? About cops and their guns?"

"Yeah, yeah," Duval said impatiently. "It's a security blanket for you guys. You don't like going nowhere without it." He shook his head. "Forget it, Reynolds. I ain't gonna go putting my ass in a sling like that. Yo man, what happens if you go off up there and start popping holes in ISS? Who you think they gonna come looking for?"

"It's not even loaded," Reynolds said soothingly. A crock that, actually, but he'd have to hope Duval didn't check. "I just want it there. Okay? Pack it for me. All right?"

"Uh uh," Duval had said. Adamant. "No way."

Reynolds heard the steps of Connor and the others stop, hesitating. One set started back.

"Look," he said urgently, forcing the gun into Duval's hand and backing away quickly. "I gotta go. Just put this away for me, okay? I'll make it worth your while." Then he'd backed out of the alcove and run quickly to head off the inquisitive footsteps.

Duval's last words had rung down the corridor after him. "Yo, Reynolds, I ain't doin' it, man. *You* ain't worth my while. I'm posting this mother back to you in Detroit, man, I swear. You hear?"

Straining to reach the leg pocket, Reynolds prayed to God Duval hadn't meant it. Reynolds's heart leaped as his finger touched a sharp edge—*is that the Glock's butt?* It was hard to tell without getting a hand to it, and Leonid's scissors on his waist made it impossible to bend further. Reynolds grimaced and forced his hand a little further. His fingers had stretched nearly another inch when the $O_2$ bottle slammed down on his helmet, stunning him with the impact. Reynolds's hand fell away.

*Fuck,* he thought dazedly. *The helmet isn't going to take much more of that.*

The strengthened polycarbonate had held, just. But tiny chips had flown off, glittering, into the void, and there was a starlike crazing where the bottle had struck. The helmet would hold for maybe one more blow, two max. He had to get to that gun now. It was his only hope.

Assuming it was there.

He summoned all his strength and drove a gloved index finger into Matchev's gut, piling all the weight behind it he could muster. As anticipated, the Russian doubled up slightly, releasing the pressure of his legs for a fraction of a second. The blow he had been striking glanced off Reynolds's helmet harmlessly.

*So far so good,* Reynolds thought. He used the moment to twist slightly within the grip of Leonid's legs. He bent as far as he could and groped at the leg pocket, now just within reach. Elation surged in him—the Glock was there! He scrabbled at the pocket, cursing the clumsy gloves. He forced himself to slow down when he

had the flap open—*for Christ's sake, don't drop the ball!
You lose the fucker, you're done for.* He inched the
Glock out, achingly slow, pinning it against his suit leg
with a finger to stop it flying away.

SMASH!

The cylinder crashed again, dazing Reynolds with its
force. The craze lines in the clear polycarbonate shot
out from their central star—fuck, that was it, the helmet
wasn't going to take another hit. The next would be
oblivion. But he had the Glock now, butt socketed firmly
in the grip of his bulky glove. He brought it up blindly,
jamming it hard against the first thing he felt that
wasn't him.

*Don't have to drill the fucker,* he thought wildly. *Just
nick him.* Vacuum would do the rest.

He stabbed at the trigger, jerking his finger against
it—once, twice, three times.

Nothing.

For one panicked moment Reynolds thought his earlier fears had been right after all. When he'd decided to
smuggle the Glock aboard, he'd first checked the gun
would still fire in vacuum. He'd been worried the lack
of oxygen would inhibit combustion, but a quick look at
a chemistry primer had reassured him. Nitrocellulose,
the principal ingredient of smokeless gunpowder, generated its own oxygen as it explosively decomposed. The
Glock would drill its .45 slug out the barrel even *faster*
than down on Earth, due to the lack of air resistance.

But what was the problem then? It took Reynolds a
second or two to realize.

*Fuck!* His gloved fingertip was too big—scraping uselessly against the trigger guard. Not even touching the
trigger.

Reynolds wrenched his head violently to one side—
Leonid was bringing the bottle down again. The cylinder
crashed into the side of Reynolds's helmet—SMASH!
Reynolds's ears rang. Leonid loosened his grip, bent and
slid his arm around Reynolds's helmet, locking it in a
tight grip. He raised the canister high again. There was
no mistaking the triumph in those incredible eyes. This
was it. This time there was no getting away.

Reynolds closed his eyes, waiting for the impact. His
hand ached from the effort of cramming the gun against
Matchev's side. The Russian, preoccupied with the
deathblow he was about to deal, still seemed not to have
noticed it. Reynolds held his breath as he jammed the
tip of his gloved finger against the hole formed by the
trigger guard. If he could just force it a little way in,
perhaps the finger's expanding width would trip the
safety, maybe even wedge the trigger far enough in to
squeeze off a round . . .

Reynolds's world exploded.

His head snapped back and forth violently, banging
against the inside of his helmet. The wheeling sky went
ballistic, clicking rapidly through a succession of
images—starry blackness, molten sun, the vast blue
Earth, far-off ISS. The two of them were suddenly spinning crazily, at three or four revolutions a second.

*What the fuck?*

Reynolds felt Matchev's grip slacken. He pushed away
from the Russian, shutting his eyes to block out the sickening whirl of the universe. He felt his faceplate with
his free hand; it was okay. Totally intact.

*So what happened?*

Opening his eyes, he found out. In front of him, Matchev was doubled over, clutching his side. A stream of
pink liquid and vapor was spraying from between his
fingers, most of it freezing to tiny, glittering crystals instantly. The spurting fluid and vapor was serving as a
crude jet, spinning Matchev like a Catherine wheel.
Freed of the encumbering embrace with Reynolds, the
Russian was whirling at six or seven revolutions per
second.

*The bullet,* Reynolds thought dazedly. *Must have fired
after all.* With no sound in space, and no feeling through
the glove's fingertip, there had been no way of telling.
The Glock had kicked, presumably, but Reynolds hadn't
noticed in the confusion.

He watched in horror as Matchev . . . deflated. There
was no other word for it. The vapor plume spewed on
and on, throwing off crystals in a spiraling arc. Clouds
of them spattered against Reynolds, filling in the gaps

between the craze lines in his faceplate, obscuring his vision. He wiped them away and continued to watch, whenever his own tumble brought Leonid within his field of vision. God, it was gruesome. The spray was already lessening; Matchev was collapsing in on himself. His skin was drawing in tight around his skeleton—Christ, you could almost *see* his skull—turning brown as it compacted. The Russian's mouth was open—*is he screaming?* Reynolds wondered. Impossible to tell in the soundlessness of vacuum. Possibly it was just the pull of Matchev's tightening skin, dragging his jaw open as it contracted.

Then, suddenly, it was over. The vapor jet died and the crystals dissipated, shooting out along the trajectories of their endless journeys. Reynolds was left with Matchev's frozen, desiccated cadaver, spinning beside him in macabre silence.

"Fuck! Fuck me!"

The sounds burst from Reynolds's lips unconsciously. His eyes were bulging, his breaths were short, ragged gasps in his ears. It took him a few seconds to realize the words were his own.

"Jesus Christ."

He floated blankly for some time, tumbling slowly, feeling his pulse settle. A glimpse of ISS, far-off in the distance and receding with every swing, brought him back to reality.

He was still in terrible danger. He had to make it back to ISS before his oxygen ran out. Even with the Titan's high-capacity oxygen tanks, he had six hours at best. And every second was taking him further from the station.

Reynolds calculated swiftly. The only means of propulsion he had was the Glock. Isaac Newton again—200 grains of .45 ACP bullet fired from the muzzle at 850 feet per second equaled a certain amount of thrust for Reynolds in the opposite direction. But how much? Reynolds couldn't be sure. All he knew was it was the only chance he had.

Twelve shots left in the Glock's magazine. Actually thirteen, he remembered—if he had chambered an extra

round when loading, like he usually did. The first priority
was to stop his tumble; impossible to calculate trajectory
from anything other than a stable attitude. Two caps for
that, maybe three.

Leaving ten.

He would have to keep a bullet or two in reserve, in
case he overshot. Probably safest to aim for touchdown
with one cap still in the gun. Say three bullets in total.

That left seven.

Seven bullets to generate enough kick to jack Reynolds out of his trajectory away from ISS and get him
back. Was that going to be enough? There was no way
of telling. The only certainty was that he had to start
*now*. Each moment's delay took him yards further
from ISS.

He forced himself to wait a few precious seconds,
using the time to break his tumble apart into its constit-
uent elements. He had to calculate it from the different
paths the Earth and ISS transcribed across his faceplate
with each whirling appearance—no easy task. As close
as he could figure, he was describing a near perfect, forward head-over-feet tumble at three revolutions per second, with a clockwise rotation about his body's vertical
axis of one revolution per three seconds thrown in.

*Two shots perpendicular to the plane of rotation,* he
decided. Held in front of the faceplate would be best.
And one fired left-handed around his right shoulder to
correct the clockwise spin.

He brought the Glock up gingerly and held it, two-
handed, in front of his helmet, as close to right-angled
as he could. Reynolds locked his arm joints—he couldn't
afford to lose a single joule of the shot's energy through
recoil. He jammed the tip of his index finger into the
trigger guard and pressed. *Christ, this is the clumsiest
way imaginable to pull a trigger.* There was nothing for
it though. He'd just have to repeat the trick every time
he wanted to fire.

The kick, when it came, caught him by surprise. No
flash, no sound, no feeling through his finger. Just a jolt
that thudded up his locked arms to his shoulder joints
and snapped his head forwards against his chest.

His heart leaped. There was no doubt about it—the shot had slowed him. The Earth was wheeling into view only once every couple of seconds now. He steadied the Glock for another try.

*One more ought to do it.*

He was ready for the jolt this time. The recoil kicked through his arms, slamming into his shoulders and stopping his forward spin dead. In fact, Reynolds realized when the elation had worn off, the recoil had been a little bit *too* efficient. He was now wheeling very slowly in the opposite direction, heels following head over in a barely perceptible *backward* tumble.

He would have to live with that. He couldn't afford to waste another bullet on it. And at least it gave him about a ten-second window of alignment with ISS from which to fire.

*Be grateful for small mercies.*

Reynolds transferred the Glock carefully to his left hand, and wedged it against his right shoulder. He craned his helmet around, trying to gauge the angle, and fired when he thought he had it right. This time he got lucky—the Glock's kick corrected his clockwise spin nearly perfectly.

But there was no time for self-congratulation. ISS was a tiny, glittering mote on the horizon; Reynolds estimated it was now three, maybe four miles away. If he didn't do something soon he would lose visual, and with it what slender hopes he had of getting back.

He stretched his arms out above his head, as straight as he could around the bulky helmet, and braced the Glock in a two-handed grip. He waited for his backward rotation to swing him into the right position—body aligned, feetfirst, towards ISS. That was the safest way to do it, he figured. Trying to come in headfirst would mean firing with the Glock held rigid alongside him, running the risk of nicking his suit with a misfired bullet.

The tiny ISS swung into view, crawling lazily down from the top of Reynolds's faceplate. He tracked it with his eyes, waiting until his feet appeared, level with it, in his field of vision. Then he fired.

The Glock bucked, sending a jolt of energy through

Reynolds's rigid body. It was reversing his thrust, no
doubt about that. But was it going to be enough? Reynolds studied ISS hard on its next pass through his field
of vision. Was the station getting larger? Christ, it was
hard to tell. Or was it . . . getting smaller?

He steadied himself for another shot, as soon as his
spin brought him back into line. He stifled the urge to
fire blindly—*jerk that trigger NOW you bastard, again,
again, again. Do it! Before it's too late and you drift away
forever.* That would be just as dangerous really. With no
reliable way of measuring his distance and speed from
ISS, he might easily find himself overshooting. Could be
he was already going too fast, propelling himself towards
ISS at speeds that would blast him right past the station
and out into space . . .

He squeezed off another round, holding himself stiff
to absorb the energy. His body jerked at the impact. He
held his breath, waiting for a few revolutions to pass.

Eight shots left.

Was ISS getting closer? Reynolds didn't think so. The
station was still a glittering speck, floating just above
the gauzy blue haze of the Earth's atmosphere. He fired
another precious bullet off reluctantly. Fuck, it was going
to be close. Even once he'd started moving towards ISS,
Reynolds figured, he couldn't hope to hit the station
without a minimum three shots for trajectory correction.
Counting his three-shot reserve, that only left him one
cap more with which to get moving.

*Not enough,* Reynolds thought, dismayed, as the revolutions passed with ISS still obstinately tiny. He was
going to have to eat into his reserve.

He fired another three shots off in slow succession—
*three whole shots, for Christ's sake!* He waited breathlessly for the results. Shit, it was nerve-racking! Whirling
along in total silence, waiting to see if he was alive or
dead. Four caps left. Enough for three corrective shots
and one reserve. If the three he had just loosed didn't
start moving him back towards ISS he might as well fire
those four off randomly into space. Or put one of them
through his own head, for all the good they would do
him.

The wait was made worse by the heat. The Titan's nine layers of aluminized Mylar and nonwoven Dacron were such efficient insulators that hardly a joule of the muscular heat Reynolds's struggle with Leonid had generated had escaped the suit. With no cooling garment to sublimate heat out through the cooling tubes—that was sitting back in his compartment in the Lab Module, or had been blown into space and was halfway to Jupiter by now—his body heat was raising the temperature inside the Titan second by second. So was the harsh sun, pouring in through his visorless helmet.

*Fuck! This heat is incredible!*

Reynolds estimated the temperature inside the suit was already up around a hundred. His skin was slick with sweat—globules of it were breaking free and floating loose inside the suit. Several splashed into his eyes, stinging them. He tried to squeeze them out with his eyelids—no way to wipe them away of course. Reynolds sucked a mouthful of water out of his drink tube and swallowed. At least he had water, a whole liter and a half in the in-suit bag. He wouldn't dehydrate. But it was going to get steadily more unpleasant inside the Titan as time went by, as the temperature rose and the sweat continued to pour out from Reynolds's skin.

He counted out the revolutions to distract himself. *Over once . . . twice . . . three times . . .* It was halfway between the nineteenth and twentieth that the spurt of excitement gripped him.

*Is it closer? Is it really closer?*

He closed his eyes deliberately to preserve the image, then counted out five achingly slow revolutions. There was no doubt about it when he opened them again. ISS was now the size of a far-off dime, half as large again as the image burned on his retina.

Reynolds's heart cartwheeled in time with his own slow spin. He was on his way back. It didn't matter how slowly—in frictionless space, speed wasn't important. Once you were headed in the right direction, you just kept going, on and on and on . . .

That sobered him. *It's not enough to be heading back towards ISS,* he reminded himself.

Now he had to hit it.

He studied ISS's successive appearances anxiously. He
was only going to get one chance at this. It was almost
as nerve-racking as waiting to see if the shots had succeeded in reversing his direction. The problem was that
he had to get closer before he could start popping his
corrective shots off—close enough to be sure what angle
trajectory he was taking relative to ISS. But get too close
and he cut his margin for error down to nothing. He
might easily find himself overshooting ISS, with no time
left to do anything but wave.

Reynolds was uneasily conscious the corrective shots
would cut away at his margin as well. Each would have
to be fired more or less behind him—he couldn't take
the risk this far out of killing his forward movement by
firing out front. But then each cap, in addition to correcting his angle, would also be adding to his speed, shooting
him into ISS faster and faster.

*Might not be able to keep that last bullet in reserve,*
Reynolds realized. He might have to use it for a last-
minute braking shot, right out in front, to lessen the
impact with which he hit ISS.

He took his first shot at what he estimated was two
miles out. He had noticed that ISS seemed to be sliding
fractionally below him with every revolution. When the
ruined stumps of ISS's starboard solar arrays began to
appear, over the top of ISS's central core, Reynolds was
sure of it. He was coming in oblique to ISS, at an angle
that looked like it was going to shoot him a few hundred
yards over the top of the station. Reynolds readied the
Glock, holding it two-handed at his thighs, perpendicular
to the angle of his rigid body.

When he had swung into alignment with ISS he fired,
worming his finger into the trigger guard until the Glock
bucked. The gun kicked back against the legs of his hard
space suit. Reynolds closed his eyes and let himself cycle
through a few revolutions. He tried to ignore the anxiety
gnawing at him—*fuck, the whole thing is madness. Trying
to shoot your way back to a tin can whirling through
space at 13,000 miles per hour. You know what the
chances are of pulling that off?* He opened his eyes,

checking ISS's position. And let out a shout of exultation that rang inside his helmet.

The arrays were sliding out of sight behind ISS. He'd done it—changed his trajectory so he was coming in on a downward angle. He was back on track.

*Assuming you haven't overshot that,* he told himself. He watched the station carefully over the next couple of minutes, but ISS's crawl down his field of vision seemed slow. He let out a sigh of relief. It looked as if the angle would be shallow enough to hold.

Three bullets left.

He fired again at about a mile out. ISS, bigger now, was beginning to slide into the right half of his faceplate. He was veering way too far left to make contact. Reynolds worked his hands, gripping the Glock, over to his left side. This was going to be tricky. It wasn't that he had to pick his moment—this time he could fire at will. The end-over-end motion made it difficult to hold the gun at a true right angle though. Reynolds gritted his teeth, worming his finger into the trigger guard. He strained to hold the Glock straight. If he wasn't careful he'd end up . . . spinning. *Fuck.*

Reynolds cursed as the Glock kicked into his side obliquely, throwing him into an anticlockwise spin. The rotation itself was bad enough—it made the job of aiming that much more difficult. But it meant the shot had been wasted too. The energy that should have gone into changing his course had discharged into the spin. Reynolds's eyes searched out ISS's position within the crazy jumble of images wheeling across his faceplate. He swore silently. Sure enough, ISS had slid further off to his right. If he didn't do something he was going to shoot wide of ISS, way out to her left.

And soon, he realized. ISS was coming up faster than he had thought—nearly filling his faceplate whenever it came into view. *Less than a thousand yards,* Reynolds thought. *And closing.*

He worked the Glock back over to his side, holding it slightly out from his body this time. Reynolds waited for his moment. He nearly sobbed with the effort of keeping it all together. His arms were aching from the

strain. Panic was clawing at him wildly. The images
flashing by his faceplate were a chaotic jumble—so difficult to pick which was the right moment to fire! A mist
of sweat droplets, dislodged by his rotation, was swirling
around inside his helmet, making it hard to see.

*Now!*

ISS had appeared in the top right quadrant of his helmet, meaning he was just about to come into alignment.
Reynolds stabbed blindly at the trigger guard and was
rewarded with a jolt from the Glock. He held his breath,
hardly daring to look for the next few revolutions.

*Please God. Please.*

Reynolds nearly wept with relief. ISS was moving left,
inching closer to the center of his faceplate with each
revolution. He watched in gratitude as it crawled further
into view. He was going to hit her, no question. If anything, Reynolds estimated, he would strike ISS slightly
to the right, somewhere around where the huge, skeletal,
metal truss branched out at right angles from the U.S.
Habitation Module.

Reynolds could see the spot clearly because the station was huge now, no more than 200 yards away. He
was zeroing in at phenomenal speed—around five yards
a second, Reynolds guessed. He readied himself for the
braking shot, offering a fervent prayer of thanks for
the remaining bullet. Five yards a second was too fast—
he would be lucky if the collision didn't crack his Titan
wide open at that speed. At the very least, he ran the
risk of serious concussion, or of missing his chance to
grab a secure hold on ISS in the shock.

*Hold the Glock steady at chest level. Wait for the spin
to bring you into line. Be sure to fire just off to one side—
far enough to not hit ISS but close enough to maximize
the braking effect.*

*The right-hand side,* Reynolds decided. That way the
deviation would swing him further in towards the middle
of ISS.

He waited tensely for his tumble to give him a straight
shot. It would have to be soon—ISS was looming now,
a hundred yards away. Reynolds could see every detail
of the crippled station's hull—the shredded thermal

blanketing, the scored and blackened aluminum, the half-light shining dimly through the cupola. The clouds of debris were still accompanying the station, pursuing her endlessly like the tiny fish that followed flotsam, out in the deep ocean. Suddenly, the skeletal frame of the truss wheeled into view. Reynolds rammed his finger into the guard that same split second—he had to get the cap fired before ISS's central core rolled into the line of fire. He waited for the Glock's kick, readying himself to ditch it the instant it had fired, leave his hands free for grappling . . .

Nothing happened.

ISS's body flashed into, then out of, his field of vision, yielding to the black of starred space. And still the Glock didn't move.

*What the fuck?*

Reynolds dug his finger into the guard savagely, despite the fact a cap fired now, unaimed, would send his direction and velocity berserk. It was only after several straining seconds that the truth broke on him.

The gun was empty.

He'd shot his way through the magazine and there was nothing left in the chamber. Reynolds cursed bitterly. He didn't bother trying to count back; he knew he'd made no mistake. It was the chambered round, that was the problem. He'd forgotten to load it.

*The one and only time in my goddamn life. And it had to be now.*

Reynolds opened his hand and let the Glock spin away. No time for recriminations now. ISS was spiraling up towards him—fifteen, twenty yards. Three seconds, maybe four. He braced himself for impact—he was going to hit, as he'd thought, on the right-hand side of the Habitation Module, about halfway down. He fought his body's urge to flail. There was nothing he could do to right himself now. His only hope was to stay alert, ready to seize whatever small chance to grab a hold on whichever part of ISS came his way.

*Gotta stay conscious,* he told himself. That was most important of all.

Images whirled past his faceplate in crazy succession—

blue Earth, a scattering of stars, tall solar arrays
stretched like Japanese banners on their frames. Then
the Habitation Module was blasting up towards him, ballooning out to fill his field of vision. There was just one
moment of yawning terror, then—SMASH!—Reynolds
hit, his helmet striking the module's hull a glancing blow
that flung him around immediately, into the reverse side
of the module. Pain shot through his legs as they
slammed into the hull in turn. He bounced off, spinning
crazily into adjacent space before he had even been able
to flex a hand.

*Stay with it,* he begged himself. *Maybe you'll get another chance.*

It was impossible to tell what was happening. The images shooting past his faceplate were a chaotic blur. His
head was ringing from the shock of impact. Blood was
in his mouth. His guts were churning nauseously. He
could feel himself trembling on the edge of unconsciousness.

Something slammed into his back—*Christ, the pain*—
and suddenly Reynolds was hitting everywhere—his
head, his knees, then his feet in quick succession. *Must
be tumbling along something,* he thought distantly. Then
it clicked.

*The truss. I'm rolling out along the truss.*

This was his chance! The truss was ISS's backbone, a
long frame that stuck out at right angles from the station's central core, and to which were attached her pe-
ripherals—the solar arrays, the radiators and the
external camera mounts. It was honeycombed with gaps
between the welded tubes' aluminum alloy. *Handholds,
every one of them,* Reynolds thought exultantly, and
stretched his arms out blindly over his head. If he could
just get a hand wedged in somewhere he might slow
himself down enough to grab a proper hold.

If it didn't get torn off.

He groped overhead as his body smashed its way
along the metal frame but nothing held. *Got to get it,*
he thought desperately. Any second now the downward
motion that was rolling him against the truss might
spend itself and he would bounce off, back into space.

Or he would crash into the thermal radiators, the aluminum cooling towers through which the ammonia of ISS's temperature control systems flowed, radiating surplus heat out into space.

He redoubled his efforts, scrabbling blindly at the metal he was skidding along. A finger caught at a join, at *something,* and he thought for a moment he had succeeded, but it was wrenched loose almost instantly and he was cartwheeling further out along the arm. There was just time for Reynolds to wonder if the finger had been literally torn off, or was still with him, before an almighty blow slammed into him from behind, smashing the world in front of him into a thousand multicolored shards.

*The cooling tower,* Reynolds thought, stunned.

Blackness washed over him, receded, washed over again. He was slipping into unconsciousness.

*Got to fight that,* he told himself desperately. The radiator had stopped his motion almost dead; he could see through the haze that he was drifting mere inches from the crumpled base of the huge structure. All he had to do was reach out and grasp its frame to be saved.

*Do it,* he urged.

He looked down at his right hand, willing it to obey him. But the blackness pulsed again, and the demand was washed away, somewhere between command and execution. Reynolds floated idly down the arm, collided with the tower momentarily once more, then rolled off it slowly, majestically, into free space.

His last thought was that something wasn't right, that there was something incredibly important he had to remember to do. But then black space was pouring in through his helmet, merging with the blackness within.

Drowning him.

# 14

It was the heat that brought Reynolds to.

Stifling heat. Thick. So hot it was nearly burning . . . no, boiling, that was a better description. Reynolds's eyes opened. A humid steam of sweat and blood was fogging his helmet. Savagely overheated, his body was trying to compensate by pumping out perspiration. But with nowhere for the heat, or the sweat, to go, the suit was cooking, cranking up to a one-man tropical swelter. There was so much fluid loose in the suit it was irritating Reynolds's lungs each time he breathed in, causing him to cough. He had to fight the urge to tear his helmet off and let the vacuum soothe him with its freezing bite.

It took only the picture of Leonid, dried down to his skeletal husk, to dissuade him.

He was amazed to be alive. Somehow, incredibly, the Titan had held. He flexed experimentally. Pain throbbed through every joint, but he didn't think anything was broken. A twinge told him where the blood was coming from—the cut over his right eyebrow had opened up. He shook his head to check. Sure enough, several drops of viscous blood flew in front of his eyes and spattered the inside of his helmet.

Well. That he could live with.

His heart sank as he looked around. His memory of events was not mistaken. He'd missed his chance to grab the truss when he'd blacked out, and now he was drifting in open space. Only twenty feet from the truss arm, it was true, but in space that was as good as twenty miles. He watched the arm closely, trying to estimate his speed, but gave up after twenty seconds or so. Whatever it was, it was slow, maybe as slow as one foot per minute.

Not that that mattered. Twelve inches a minute would take him to his death as surely as a thousand miles an hour would.

Unless his path ran him into some other part of ISS. Reynolds worked himself around to check. A groan escaped him. The solar arrays were way off to his right, unreachable, and there was nothing else even visible. The way was clear into deep space.

Despair overwhelmed him. To have come this far and still die, so close to ISS!

He couldn't stop himself from struggling. His arms and legs flailed wildly, thrashing against the emptiness of space in a desperate attempt to propel himself back to the station.

All for nothing of course. Adrift in space, you were like a bug down the toilet. Struggling uselessly, paddling the water without hope of ever reaching the side. The ridiculousness of the image forced Reynolds to desist. That and the heat. All the muscle exertion was doing was pouring more joules into his already overheated suit.

He floated hopelessly for some moments, the heat threatening to push him back into unconsciousness.

His mind ticked over, trying to think of something. Anything.

*Call Irina on the UHF,* he thought longingly, fingers brushing the Communications Mode Selector Switch. *Get her to go EVA and come get me.*

He dismissed the idea instantly. That was death, Reynolds knew. What life he had left depended on maintaining radio silence. For how could he let Irina know he was still alive without also alerting . . . Kalganin? And who would come out to get him if he requested assistance, but . . . Kalganin?

Kalganin the commander of the Russian mission to ISS. Kalganin the coconspirator with Matchev and Alinov in COSMONAUT.

Reynolds was sure of it. *An algorithm that makes up bioinstrumentation data. For two of the Russian suits.* One of those had to belong to Leonid—Leonid, who had come out naked into vacuum to kill him; Leonid of the strange, violet-shrouded eyes. But the other would turn out to be Kalganin's, Reynolds was willing to bet his passage back to Earth on it.

*Not Kosita. No way.* The mere fact Drupev had been murdered told him that. The *Soyuz* commander had not been a conspirator, but a patsy.

So radio contact was out. Reynolds cast around for alternatives. *Dismantle the life-support pack and use the $O_2$ for propulsion?* He wasn't sure he could even reach the back-mounted pack, let alone dismantle it. And how was he supposed to breathe while he was steering himself back?

Frustration boiled over into rage. Christ, to die so fucking close to ISS he could have spit at her yet not be able to do anything about it! He had to hold his limbs rigid; they were itching to lash out, kicking and hitting, at the nothingness tormenting him. He was so busy restraining himself it took him some time to register the flash of light, about six feet off to his left.

He stared at the spot, puzzled. What had caused it?

The answer came several seconds later. There was a large chunk of broken panel from one of the solar arrays floating there, spinning gently. Because of the black photovoltaic coating, Reynolds hadn't seen it against the backdrop of black space until its spin had brought it into reflective orientation towards the sun.

His heart leaped as he studied it. The chunk was about ten feet long by four feet across. Made of aluminum-alloy slats with a covering blanket of black-glass photocells, its mass would be negligible—three or four pounds at most. But that might be just enough. Enough for Reynolds to push off from and generate sufficient thrust to cross the void to ISS.

If he could get to it.

He stretched himself out. The blade was about three feet from the tip of his outstretched hand at the nearest point in its revolution, he estimated. He forced himself to hold the position, relaxing as far as he could within the awkward pose.

It was a waiting game now.

Would the panel come closer? Hard to say—he had no way of telling what trajectory it was on. It could be moving slowly away from ISS, which meant it would either keep pace with Reynolds, or drift nearer. Or it could be on a collision course with the station, in which case it would slip gradually further away. Taking his last chance with it.

Reynolds drove all hope from his mind. It was the only way to cope.

He floated like that for some minutes, arms outstretched, waiting for the panel to drift closer. He marveled at the illusion. Willing the broken array to travel three feet towards a stationary object—him. In reality, both he and the panel were orbiting the Earth at almost exactly matched speeds of more than 12,000 miles per hour. What he was really asking was for the panel's speed to be different from his by whatever minuscule fraction of one mile per hour would bring it within his grasp.

Fifteen minutes later the panel's jagged edge was nearly brushing his finger and Reynolds knew he was saved.

He drew his arms back. Now that he knew the shard would make it he had to be careful not to screw up. He couldn't afford to have it bounce out of hand from an ill-timed lunge. He waited a couple of minutes to let the panel come well within grasp. Then he lashed out, two-handed, as the glass-coated aluminum fragment swung downward into range.

*Got it!* Elation flooded him. The panel's inertia kicked him sideways into a slow roll, but his grip held.

Now came the tricky bit. Reynolds took a visual measure of the distance to the main body of ISS. He kept his eyes off the truss, beckoning from off to his left. He didn't dare go for that. It was closer—twenty-five feet as opposed to the nearly sixty to the Hab Module—but he couldn't be sure of hitting it. Better to go for the bigger target. *Besides,* he forced himself to remember, *distance isn't the issue.*

The real question was whether the push off was going to get him moving at all.

Reynolds maneuvered the panel awkwardly under his feet, wincing as he brought his knees as far up as the suit would allow. He waited until the module had come into alignment, then kicked off savagely.

The kick was good, at any rate. Reynolds craned his head to watch the panel depart—it was zipping away, more or less straight on. Meaning very little of the kick's energy had been lost to spin. He turned his attention back out front. Now to see if the recoil had been sufficient to get him moving.

He held his breath for nearly a full minute as he studied the crossbars of the truss at his left, peering through the fog and tracery of craze marks in his faceplate. Then let out a shout of giddy triumph.

He was moving! Slowly, barely perceptibly. But moving nonetheless.

*About two feet a minute,* Reynolds calculated exultantly, watching the progression of crossbars and counting seconds. At that rate it would take him half an hour to make it back. He checked the oxygen level on his chest-mounted Control Unit. He was amazed to find five hours of reserve remaining. *Five hours?* That meant he had only been out for an hour. Could that be right? Had everything that had happened—Leonid, Glocking his way back to ISS, the collision with the station—taken only sixty minutes?

*Christ. Feels like it's been forever.*

He relaxed, allowing himself to drift. Reveling in the luxury of a half hour in which he had nothing to do but wait. Incredibly, he was soon deep in dreamless sleep, oblivious to the panorama of starred black space and his cocoon of tormenting heat.

He woke some twenty minutes later, ISS's scarred hull filling his field of vision entirely, less than two feet in front of him. He stared at it blankly, uncertain where he was. For a moment he imagined he was dreaming. Then the cloying heat hit him, full force, and he remembered. His arms made a panicked grab for the Hab Module's hull; he stopped them just in time. An ill-timed lunge now could be fatal too, bouncing him off the hull and back out into space. He scanned the module's blanketed exterior. What he needed was some handholds.

Locating two—a camera mount at the right and a genuine mobility aid handle at the left—he reached out. Gripped the metal tightly in his two hands. Relief flooded him. The feel of the hard metal in his gloved hands was salvation.

*Oh God, God, God, God, God,* he found himself repeating inwardly. He hadn't realized until now how scared he'd been.

When the emotion had spent itself, he looked up and began searching out a path. He had to make his way up to the Transfer Compartment. The Transfer Compartment was the small chamber at the free end of the Docking and Stowage Module. As the name suggested, its main use was as a pressure-equalizing compartment for the transfer of goods from docking Russian *Progress* modules. But it could also, in a pinch, serve as a backup airlock. Because of its emergency status, its systems were more primitive than those of ISS's main and secondary airlocks—hardly automated at all. It was the only way Reynolds could enter ISS without being detected.

But getting there would be difficult. Reynolds would have to crawl up the Hab Module, take a right turn and make his way along the Laboratory Module, then turn left and inch out along the DSM to its end. Total distance, sixty yards. Not far, but holding on was going to be a problem. What EVA handholds ISS had were placed at just a few strategic points on her hull, spots where tethered spacewalkers performing tasks were likely to need restraint. They didn't form a continuous trail. Nobody had ever imagined the situation Reynolds found himself in—an untethered astronaut dependent on handholds to work his way back in to life and safety.

Luckily, *Ryokousha*'s explosion had created substitutes. Reynolds pulled himself along slowly, wedging his hands into rips in ISS's thermal blanketing, grasping tongues of gouged hull and twisted struts. There was one heart-stopping moment, at the juncture of the Habitation and Laboratory modules, where he had to kick himself through open space a good six feet to get to the next handhold, but he made it, and then he was crawling carefully up the Lab Module's hull.

He paused beside the exploded observation window,

exhausted. The heat was excruciating. His eyes swept
the breached module as he lay panting. The ruptured
window was like a huge black eye, staring unblinkingly
into space, wondering what had hit it.

Amazing to think he had been sucked through that
less than two hours before.

Reynolds craned his head to look inside his compartment. It was bare-bones. Everything that hadn't been
battened to the walls was gone. Excitement spurted in
him briefly at the sight of his laptop, still tethered fast—
*Contact Connor! Let him know what's happened*—but
died as soon as the light of the overhead sun washed
into the alcove. The computer was fucked, its liquid crystal screen withered dry by the sucking blast of vacuum,
an inanimate parody of Leonid and Myers. He dismissed
the idea and resumed the torturous crawl.

What could Connor have done anyway? Chewed Kalganin out? Threatened Moscow would dock his pay?

*Bad boy, Kalganin. DON'T murder Reynolds.*

Fuck, he was getting delirious. Reynolds shook his
head, trying to concentrate. He couldn't afford to mis-
judge a handhold—one slip could easily send him back
out into space. Reynolds closed his hand over a grapple
fixture, hauled himself along. That was right though—
he *was* on his own. Totally. He had one chance, one
chance only.

*Get back on board ISS without alerting Kalganin. Then
kill him.*

Or disable him. That was Reynolds's only chance of
saving his life. And he had to save his life. He had to.
Because . . .

Because . . .

*Think!* he begged himself. The heat was pressing in
on him relentlessly. His mind was wavering in and out
of consciousness.

Why did he have to save his life?

*Because of COSMONAUT,* he thought finally. *Because I'm the only one who knows. The only one who
can . . . who can tell NASA. Who can warn them.*

The thought seemed to snap his mind into clarity.
Reynolds pulled himself along the remaining distance

rapidly. Sixty seconds later he was at the outer hatch of the Transfer Compartment.

He yanked the three lock levers inward and spun the wheel mechanism open. Reynolds felt the vibration as the pumps kicked into life, reclaiming what they could of the compartment's atmosphere before opening. He cursed inwardly—he'd forgotten the pumps. How loud was the noise? No way of telling, of course; he couldn't even hear it out here.

*Just have to hope it's quiet enough.*

He pulled the hatch free as soon as it would go and levered himself inside the drum-shaped compartment. He closed it after him, shutting out the drenching white sunlight. The compartment plunged into darkness. Reynolds's eyes strove to pick out the Manual Pressure Equalization Valve. He had to get the chamber pressurized, now. Another minute in the suit's steaming heat would kill him.

In the end he located it by touch—a crescent-shaped handle on the inner wall. Reynolds twisted it blindly, this way then that, until he felt the turbulence of the emptying oxygen and nitrogen high-pressure tanks buffet him. He released the handle and let his body drift. His eyes scanned the walls anxiously. He was aching to get the suit off, but how was he going to know when it was safe? Fortunately, after a few seconds, a digital readout beside the handle blinked into life.

Twenty-two kilopascals. And climbing.

Reynolds's suit was pressurized to one atmosphere—101 kilopascals. He would have to let the compartment's atmosphere climb to at least 75 kilopascals. Only then would there be pressure enough to prevent the nitrogen bubbling in his blood when he removed the suit.

Reynolds waited impatiently as the figures rose—30 kilopascals, 45, 50. At 70 kilopascals he couldn't stand it any longer. He shot the lock tab and wrenched the helmet off, jerking it back and forth savagely until it came free. Cool air wreathed his head as the imprisoned heat spilled out. He struggled out of the suit—it took him nearly a minute—then the sensation was duplicated, blissfully, all over his body.

Cold, cold air. Caressing him.

Reynolds drifted there, in his jockeys, for some time, letting the heat soak out of him. His body, slick with sweat, began to dry. His dizziness, symptom of the abrupt plunge in temperature, began to dissipate. Amazingly, his body began shaking, rocked by relieved laughter.

*That's it, you bastard,* he told himself, wiping a tear away. *When we get back, you're going into business. Selling saunas. Who needs rocks and flames and shit? Just lock the poor bastards in one of these . . .*

After a few minutes, he felt strong enough to move. He pushed himself over to the internal hatch and went through the unlocking procedure as quietly as he could. He ripped the Taser at his wrist out of its Velcro straps and gripped it in his right hand. Then he swung the hatch open noiselessly.

The interior of the DSM opened up before him, a maelstrom of churning supplies, shaken loose by the explosion. But Reynolds was momentarily blind to it. Opening the hatch had triggered a run of images in his mind, scenes he hadn't witnessed, but suddenly realized must have taken place.

*Leonid. Crawling in through the outer hatch. Opening this one and springing at Kostia, grabbing him, breaking his neck. Then exiting back out through the Transfer Compartment.*

Reynolds pushed himself into the module, dodging the whirling debris. So that was how Matchev had done it. How he had managed to get into the module without being caught on the internal cameras, and without disturbing Drupev's barricaded hatch. A wave of pity swept Reynolds, thinking about that. *Poor Kostia.* The *Soyuz* commander had known the danger he was in. He'd tried to protect himself.

*Just picked the wrong door, that's all.*

Reynolds moved through the junkstorm, mind working feverishly. The barricaded hatch was important too, he realized. It meant Kostia had known *something,* enough to understand they were going to kill him, but not the whole thing. Not COSMONAUT.

If he'd known that he would have barricaded *both* hatches.

Reynolds batted boxes and canisters aside, pushing himself through to the end of the DSM. The pieces were really falling into place now. That was why Myers had looked right. Because Leonid had done the same trick there—entered the lock from outside. From space.

Reynolds tried to picture the moment—buried in static on the tape of Myers's death—when the astronaut had first seen Leonid, framed against black space in the open hatchway. *He probably didn't know who it was,* Reynolds decided. Because of the EMU suit Leonid had been wearing. *But he'd known what it meant.*

Death.

Reynolds nearly laughed aloud, thinking of that suit. Himself puzzling again and again over how the killer had survived the twenty-eight-minute prebreathe. When, shit, the truth was Leonid hadn't even *needed* the suit. No doubt the only reason the Russian had worn it was as a precaution, in case Mission Control managed to override his sabotage of the transponder and get the cameras back on-line.

Reynolds paused at the far end of the DSM, taking a few seconds to push away the items circling closest to him. He couldn't afford to have one or two spill out, advertising his presence. Then he pulled the hatch towards him slowly, listening carefully.

Voices. Speaking Russian. Kalganin's, loud and animated. Irina's, soft and monosyllabic. Off to his left.

Reynolds swore softly. The two of them were in *Zvezda.* That complicated things. He had hoped to take Kalganin on his own.

He shut the hatch behind him and quietly pushed himself across the mating nodule that connected the DSM to ISS's central core. That was one advantage of weightlessness: no footsteps.

The Service Module interior came into view. Halfway up, at the Command Console, Kalganin was floating, his back to Reynolds. His arms were waving as he carried on the animated conversation Reynolds had heard. Irina bobbed in front of him. Her eyes widened fractionally at the sight of Reynolds.

*Shhh,* he motioned, putting a finger to his lips.

He felt a surge of gratitude as he saw her obey. She

kept her face studiously straight, only her eyes sliding over inquisitively as Reynolds drifted closer.

Kalganin's voice was racing on, pouring out incomprehensible Russian.

*Move away,* he signaled her, flicking his fingers as if shooing a fly. His hand squeezed a tighter grip on the Taser. He couldn't see from this angle just how close to Kalganin she was. If she was touching him, she'd be fried too by the neural-disrupting impulses Reynolds was about to blast into the Russian.

Reynolds drifted closer, holding off firing as long as he dared. *Fuck it, does she understand?* Irina still hadn't moved. At the last moment though, to Reynolds's relief, her eyes went to the Taser in his right hand and she seemed to understand. She reached out casually to the wall beside her and began to edge herself back, away from Kalganin.

*Good girl.* Reynolds pushed the Taser out to full arm's length and sighted by its blunt head. But something in Irina's action must have alerted Kalganin. His voice cut off abruptly and his head whipped around.

Reynolds fired.

The clip snaked out, trailing two slender wires. Its slender metal fangs bit into Kalganin's neck, loosing two tiny spurts of blood.

The Russian screamed, but the sound was choked off to a gurgle instantly by the convulsions. Kalganin's body turned rigid as every muscle went into massive fibrillation, assaulted by the Taser's waves of disruptive "neural noise." His jaw locked and his eyes bulged. His head shook as opposing muscles fought to pull it this way or that. The scream had turned into a hideous drone, deep in the Russian's throat.

Irina looked on in shock. The scene seemed to go on forever, though Reynolds knew the Taser was timed for only five seconds of charge. Finally, the drone cut out and Kalganin went limp.

Silence.

Irina looked from Kalganin to Reynolds wildly. Her eyes were filled with questions. "What . . . what . . ." she faltered. "Is Borya dead?"

Reynolds shook his head. "Not dead. Just unconscious." He watched the floating Russian tiredly. He felt
drained, as if the energy poured out through the Taser
had been *his,* the last he was able to muster.

"But . . . why?" Irina asked, bewildered. "What is
going on? We heard the alarm, Borya and I. We came
here. Something is wrong with the Laboratory Module.
We thought . . . I thought you were dead."

Reynolds shook his head again, weakly. "No. I'm
okay," he said, with a forcefulness he didn't feel. "Now
I'm okay." He gestured at the limp Kalganin. "The commander tried to kill me."

Irina's eyes went wide. "Borya tried to . . ." she
gasped. "But, how? And where is Leonid?"

The image of Matchev's frozen cadaver, spinning silently through space, flashed before Reynolds. "Leonid's
dead," he said tiredly. "I kill . . . he was trying to kill
me too." He wanted to tell her more—COSMONAUT,
Alinov, the real reason Myers was killed—but the words
wouldn't come. It was too unreal. He could hardly believe it himself.

Irina's knuckle went to her mouth. For a moment she
was silent, then the dam broke and she pushed herself
across the module, sobbing, into Reynolds's arms. He
stroked her hair slowly, soothing her.

"Shh, Ira," he whispered. "Everything is all right now.
There's nothing to be afraid of."

She looked up at him, eyes brimming tears. "But all
these horrible things," she choked out. "What is happening? You told me it would be over."

He disengaged from her gently, pushing himself over
to the medical lockers, located to the right of the Command Console. Kalganin was only temporarily on ice.
Reynolds had to find something to immobilize him with
before he came to. His cuffs were no good—locked up
in the airless Laboratory Module, they might as well be
a million miles away. The Crew Medical Restraint System, an aluminum frame with nylon straps used to provide spinal stabilization for injured astronauts, would be
the next best thing.

"It's almost over," he agreed, dragging the CMRS out

of its locker. He snapped it out to full size, maneuvered Kalganin into it and began strapping him down. "I promise." He had to drive himself on for every action; every muscle was crying out to rest. "Just . . . just a few more things," he cajoled.

He ran over them in his mind. *Get Kalganin tied down. Switch the Kurs docking system on—Endeavor must be trying to range a signal even now. And contact Connor.*

That was most important. He had to contact Connor, tell him the incredible news.

"But what is happening?" Irina cried. "Tell me!"

"I . . . I can't explain it, Ira," he replied, shaking his head. "I don't know if I understand it right myself." He ripped a length of bungee cord from the wall and used it to bind Kalganin's hands behind the Russian's back. "The main thing is we're safe now. Now Leonid is dead."

Leonid the monster. Leonid the *thing*.

Satisfied Kalganin was paralyzed, Reynolds moved around him to the Command Console. He talked distractedly, almost babbling, as he started up the laptop control.

"It's Alinov, Ira. He's behind it all. He's the one," he said feverishly. His voice tailed away as he punched his way into the unfamiliar command interface. The front-level Russian software was still in English, but even so, Reynolds found many of the terms unfamiliar. *Where is the docking subsystem, for Christ's sake?* "But we're safe from him now," he continued. *"Endeavor* is on its way. My government will take us back to Earth. And then we'll be safe."

"What is it you are saying about Dr. Alinov?" Irina asked, from behind him. There was an odd inflection in her voice, something that was almost *sorrow*. It was closer too, but Reynolds was too preoccupied to notice.

He shook his head. "Alinov is guilty of the most incredible things, Ira," he murmured. "He has done something . . . something against the laws of God. If there is one." Reynolds clicked through several menus before he found what he was looking for. He switched the Kurs radar beacon on triumphantly, then backtracked through the menus to reach the communication subsystem.

*Now to get in touch with Connor.*

Something in the sudden silence made him look up. Or begin to, rather. For before his head had lifted more than a fraction of an inch, the back of it exploded. Sending Reynolds, dizzyingly, into the darkness once more.

# 15

Reynolds came to groggily.

His head was pounding. The back of it was wet with oozing blood. His arms were pulled behind his back and something was cutting into his wrists. They were bound, he discovered, upon trying to move them. His ankles too. He squinted to focus his blurred vision. His face was inches from the wall of the Service Module, bobbing idly by.

He was trussed like a turkey. Helpless.

*Kalganin,* was his first thought. Somehow the Russian had woken and worked himself loose.

*Irina,* was his next. Was she okay? He listened hard and was relieved to hear her, speaking Russian in a low voice. To Kalganin obviously. What was she doing? Begging for their lives? Distracting the Russian in the hope Reynolds would come to?

He had to turn himself around. If he could just make eye contact . . .

Reynolds pursed his lips and blew through them as quietly as he could. He couldn't risk alerting Kalganin by wriggling himself around. Five hurried breaths later, the wall began moving. He had generated enough thrust to start rolling.

Reynolds concentrated on holding himself motionless. He kept his eyelids near closed. The roof of the Service Module wheeled slowly into view, then the opposite wall. The monitor bank of the Russian Control Console appeared. Reynolds's heart leaped—Irina was there. He had to stifle the urge to cry out to her, but only for a moment. It died of its own accord when he saw who she was really talking to.

It was Alinov.

The Russian scientist's lined face filled the monitor. He was speaking rapidly, hands flashing into the picture frequently as he waved them animatedly. Irina was listening deferentially, adding only the occasional *nyet* or *da*.

*Irina,* Reynolds thought despairingly. *No.* He felt a hot stab of grief.

But he could see instantly it was true. Kalganin was still floating where Reynolds had left him, incapacitated in the med restraint. Not even conscious. Drifting near the Russian, one end matted with sticky blood and hair, was the alloy strut Irina had used to knock Reynolds out.

*No,* a part of him begged. *Not Ira. Please.* Images of her flashed through his mind. Naked with him in the Lab Module, among the drifting crowd of silent space suits. Her eyes, frightened and vulnerable as she nestled in his arms.

His mouth filled with the sick taste of betrayal. *Why not, Detective?* he taunted himself. *Because she slept with you? Because . . . because she said she loved you?*

Reynolds was so overwhelmed he forgot to time a couple of expelled breaths, to stop his motion. The roll took him slowly around again to face the wall. But something must have escaped him, some sign. For Alinov's voice suddenly got louder, addressing *him,* and switched to English.

". . . but I see our American friend has regained consciousness, Irina," the Russian said jovially. "Welcome to the land of the living, Detective." His voice grew hard. "Irina, bring him here."

Hands—*her* hands—pulled at him, steering him down in front of the monitor. Every touch on his bare skin was a brand, burning him with hot despair. Reynolds felt he was going to be sick. Even through the haze of self-reproach though, he found himself puzzling over the tone of Alinov's command. There was something in the Russian's voice that was more than the attitude of a flight controller to a subservient cosmonaut, more than the brusqueness of a head conspirator.

*That wasn't an order,* Reynolds thought. *It was a commandment . . .*

Irina positioned him in front of the monitor. Reynolds felt her hands withdraw. Fighting his way through the anguish blanketing him, Reynolds raised his eyes to Alinov's.

The Russian scientist was regarding him humorously, without a trace of malice. His ice blue eyes twinkled to some inner joke, and his thin mouth was bent in a quizzical smile. The picture did nothing to dampen Reynolds's nausea. Frankly, he preferred Alinov spitting poison.

"Congratulations, Detective," the Russian said, inclining his head to Reynolds. For all its humor, the voice was the same icy drawl. "Despite our best efforts you have managed to uncover the existence of COSMONAUT." Alinov shrugged. "Inconvenient for us, of course, but still, you are to be congratulated. Regrettably, it seems your superiors were not merely boasting of your abilities, hmm?"

Reynolds ignored the overture. "COSMONAUT was never a health-monitoring program," he croaked, the words rasping his dry throat. He swallowed, trying to moisten it. "You've done something to them." The image of Leonid, naked and violet-eyed in space, flashed before him. "Leonid and . . . the other one. Surgery. Altered them somehow, so they can withstand vacuum." His mind reeled at the words leaving his mouth. Even with everything he knew, he could still scarcely believe it.

Alinov laughed. "Surgery? How little you know, Detective, for all that." He hesitated. "Tell me, Detective, where is Leonid now?"

Reynolds decided to try to shake the smug bastard. He gave it to him with both barrels. "I killed him," he said savagely. "Last I saw he was on his way to Alpha Centauri. Doin' a pretty good impression of a side of freeze-dried beef too. If you get my meaning."

Behind him, Irina gasped. But Alinov merely smiled, clucking his tongue. "How unfortunate," he said. "But again, you are to be congratulated, Detective. To get the best of Leonid," his hand came on-screen in a sweeping gesture, "out there. In his element, if you will. That is no mean feat."

He regarded Reynolds with glittering eyes for a silent moment, then shook his head. "No, Detective. Not surgery. You do not know everything, after all. You imagine that what you killed out there was a man, Leonid Matchev—like you and me, but with some medical trick that allowed him to venture out briefly where no other human could and live. But you are wrong."

He shook his head once more, as if exasperated by Reynolds's obfuscation. "Not surgery, Detective. Something better. I have altered the very stuff of life. You know that I was a geneticist. Well, let me tell you I have remained one. The man you destroyed was not a man. Leonid was the culmination of a program that has run for forty years. He was the first of a new type of human—a new species, if you like. A species justly called 'cosmonauts,' for they are the first humans designed specially to live in space."

All this delivered in a completely matter-of-fact tone, as if Alinov were discussing the weather, or the latest bone-density-loss data from ISS's on-orbit crew. Only the Russian's eyes betrayed his sardonic amusement.

Reynolds was unable to stop the horror from registering on his face. *A new species* . . . His mind shot back to the scenes at Star City. Alinov's provocative comments at the meeting. His enjoyment of some secret joke as he stood with Reynolds in the vacuum chamber. It *hadn't* been the excitement of foreknowledge of the accident Reynolds was going to have. It had been the thrill of having an American, a detective, stand right there, unknowing, in the cradle of Alinov's own monstrous conspiracy.

The thought touched off another explosion in Reynolds's mind. *Of course,* he thought fiercely. That was what he'd been trying to remember about Alinov's vacuum chamber. *The handhold.* In the split second before he'd fallen, his hand had locked onto the metal hold

beside the door. But his fingers had only just fitted into
the gap between the hold and the wall it was welded to.
There wasn't enough space for a set of gloved fingers to
get into. *That* had been the thought that was obliterated
by his fall into unconsciousness.

*What kind of vacuum chamber is used for people with-
out suits?*

Though the question was back to front, he realized
sickly. *What kind of people use a vacuum chamber without suits?* it should have been.

*People like Leonid, that's who.*

"You seem distressed, Detective," Alinov said, mock-
politely. "Do the details of COSMONAUT disturb
you?"

Reynolds didn't reply. The loathing on his face was
answer enough.

"Well, it to be expected of an American," Alinov said
calmly. "Is it not?" Reynolds wasn't fooled. Behind the
composed mask of the Russian's face, he could see Alinov was seething, longing for a chance to vent some
spleen. Sure enough, a second later his restraint broke.
"Always so petty-minded! So . . . so . . . narrow! Even
the names show it, do they not? You call your space
travelers astronauts—men of the stars. We call ours cosmonauts—men of the universe." His voice had risen stri-
dently; the gleam of fanaticism was back in his eye. "The
history of the space competition shows it too, Detective.
While you Americans fiddled with machines—Mercury,
Gemini, Apollo—we . . . I . . . got straight to the heart
of the matter. The human organism could not live in the
harsh environment of outer space? Then change him!
Change him so that he *could* fulfil man's destiny,
marching out to the stars unaided by machines or mechanical contrivances that masquerade as life-support
systems, but are really nothing but cages. Prisons to keep
man trapped in his already outdated form . . ."

Alinov's voice had dropped to a murmur. Reynolds
watched in horrified fascination as the Russian's eyes
misted over, apparently beset by some private memory.

"The failures, Detective," Alinov whispered, looking
up at Reynolds. There was a look of near appeal in his

eyes, as if he were approaching a subject so fraught with memories of unexpiated crimes he would look anywhere, even to Reynolds, for absolution. "The failures. All those who died. Tens upon tens of them. Hundreds. Children! Just . . . children." He shook his head in despair. "Always, something was wrong. The oxygenation mechanism, the homeostasis regulation, the sealing muscles. Always something. They died and died and died, until finally I began to doubt myself. I admit it frankly, Detective. I began to waver. But then, just as I was about to give up, came Leonid. Leonid the perfect, Leonid the stable. Leonid . . . the one who didn't die."

Reynolds's gut contracted violently. This time there was no stopping it—scalding vomit coughed and choked from his throat, spattering the monitor and flying across the module. *You twisted fuck,* he wanted to scream. Visions of those nameless kids—blasted, suffocated and boiled to nothing in Alinov's death chamber—reeled through his mind.

"The other one," he muttered instead. "Who is the other one?"

*An algorithm that makes up data for two of the Russian suits.* That meant not just Leonid. There was another one.

Kalganin? Or Kostia, after all?

Reynolds's words seemed to bring Alinov out of his reverie. The malignant grin spread slowly back over his face. "The other *one,* Detective? Oh no, there were not just two. There were six Cosmonauts. Six marvels of creation, six acts of pure, creative will. Five now, of course, now that you have destroyed Leonid. Five . . . including Irina."

Reynolds's skin turned cold. He stared at Alinov in shock.

"Oh yes, Detective," the Russian said, enjoying Reynolds's distress. "Irina is a Cosmonaut. She is Leonid's sister."

Reynolds's guts writhed. If he hadn't just emptied them, he would have vomited.

"Look at her, Reynolds," Alinov continued, crooning. "Isn't she beautiful?" Reynolds found himself obeying against his will, head craning around to look at Irina in loathing and terror. His eyes locked on to hers. She met his gaze levelly, saying nothing. "She is enough of a woman that a man like you can be intimate with her and not know the difference. Yet she is more than human. Her skin is so rich in collagen it can withstand total vacuum. Her blood is so rich in hemoglobin she can store a twenty-hour supply of bonded oxygen. Did you know, Reynolds, that all human babies can maintain their body temperature, even in absolute zero, by burning brown fat? Most humans lose the ability, but Irina and her brothers and sisters have kept it. She is better than human, Detective. And I made her."

Reynolds's head began shaking involuntarily. "No," he moaned. "No." Then, as if it were a lifeline thrown to his disbelief, "Wait a minute. Her eyes. If she's . . . what you say, why aren't they like Leonid's?"

"Show him, Irina!" Alinov commanded.

Reynolds watched horrified, as Irina obeyed. Something—some kind of transparent sheath—slid out from the corners of both her eyes, sealing them off. The color was different in here, not quite as pronounced. But there was no doubt about it. They were shimmering violet.

"Irina and her brothers and sisters all have a nictitating membrane—a second eyelid, Detective—like the crocodilians and some lizards," Alinov said. "To protect the eye from exposure to vacuum, you understand. The sheath, which is formed of superdense elastin incidentally, is transparent, though you may notice the refraction of light through it gives the eye a purplish appearance . . ."

Reynolds's dry-retching drowned the rest of Alinov's words out. He tore his eyes away from Irina. His heart was hammering. His head was spinning wildly.

*Don't blame you, pal,* a voice inside him said. *Not every day you find out you've been sleeping with a god-damned alien.*

He tried to calm himself. To think. He needed a plan, some way out of this. A way to disable Irina, or at least get her out of the module while he worked himself free. But how? The first thing was to keep Alinov talking, give himself time . . .

"Yeah, you're a regular zookeeper, Alinov," he muttered, hoping to sting the Russian into another rant. "With your crocodilians, your lizards and your little pets. Why don't you tell me what you're gonna do now?"

"Ah yes," Alinov chuckled. "We are back in the American movies, are we not? Doesn't the hero always try to keep the mad scientist talking? Very well, Detective. I will indulge you. My immediate plans are to kill you and the unfortunate Boris, of course. The rules of war, you understand. While we have managed to keep the secret of COSMONAUT hidden from the Americans, you have spoiled things for us. I'm afraid I can't possibly allow you to return to Earth. So the inhabitants of ISS, including you, are going to meet with an accident, Irina will simulate an electrical fault, resulting in an explosive fire, before your Shuttle arrives. All they will find will be debris. She will return to Earth, unnoticed, in the *Soyuz*. Voilá. You will be dead, Irina and the others like her will be safe, and nobody will know about COSMONAUT. The only course of action open to me, I'm sure you will agree."

Reynolds wriggled himself around minutely, so that he was facing the monitor square on. If he could just reach the wall with his bound feet, he might be able to kick off it with enough force to propel himself into Irina and knock her out. Or something. It wasn't much of a chance, but it was the best he had.

"That's crazy, Alinov," he muttered, to distract the Russian. "You think you're gonna escape suspicion if I'm killed? My government will be on you like a rash. At the very least it will mean the end of the space cooperation. Where will your work be then? Finished."

Alinov laughed. "But my work is already finished, Detective. In a sense. Come, even with your poor knowledge of genetics, you must understand that a successful organism is one that can reproduce itself. My Cosmonauts are fully capable of that, Detective, I can assure you."

He shrugged.

"Suspicions? Certainly. But suspicions are not proof, Detective. And who cares what the Americans think of us, so long as they don't *know*?" Alinov shook his head.

"No, Detective. I cannot be prevented from finishing my work. It is already complete. All I must do now is sit back and wait."

"But why?" Reynolds shouted, exasperated. He brought his legs forward as quickly as he dared, stretching them towards the module wall. "What's the point of it all?"

His toes made contact. *Gently now.*

Alinov's face hardened. "Our country will not always be licking American spittle, Reynolds," he scowled. "There are still enough Russian patriots left." The Russian snorted contemptuously. "It is amusing to think of, is it not? My Cosmonauts will be parasites in your space program. Learning. Growing. Until the time comes, when they will come back to us. It is plain enough, is it not, Detective? The next wars between our countries will be fought in space. Who do you think the perfect soldiers will be?"

Alinov's face was colored, flushed with triumph. To Reynolds's amazement, the Russian threw back his head and burst into throaty laughter—perfect caricature of the mad scientist he had alluded to. Reynolds watched the hideous spectacle, repulsed, as he bunched his leg muscles in preparation for the kick off the wall. He was just about to launch himself when something on-screen arrested the movement, stopping him dead.

*What the . . .*

Reynolds's jaw dropped in amazement.

Alinov had stopped laughing. Or been stopped, rather. There was a pair of fists at the Russian's neck—fists gripping a thin, black strap that was stretched across Alinov's throat, choking off the sounds. His eyes were bulging, his hands were at his neck, scrabbling at the strap.

Alinov was being strangled.

# 16

Alinov died twenty-five seconds later.

Reynolds was able to measure it by the tiny readout in the bottom right-hand corner of the monitor. At zero hours, eleven minutes, twelve seconds Moscow Time, Alinov was heaving against the hands restraining him—eyes bugged out, skin stretched linelessly tight across his contorted face. A hideous gurgle was fighting its way out of his throat. At zero hours, eleven minutes, thirty-seven seconds Moscow Time, he was dead, slumped against the hands, now holding him up, skin purple and blue tongue protruding.

The fists released their grip, knuckles turning from white to red. The strap fell away and Alinov slid to the floor, revealing his killer.

It was a slight, thin-faced young man in Kosmonout Corps fatigues, Reynolds saw. His dark hair was disheveled, his face bathed in sweat. He was staring down at Alinov, as if he couldn't quite believe the Russian was dead. His eyes, when he looked up, were wild. They swept over Reynolds without seeing him, locking on to a point somewhere over his left shoulder.

*Irina*, Reynolds thought. He was suddenly conscious that Irina had not reacted at all during the whole scene. Not a move. Not a sound.

*"Eta konchilas, Ira,"* the murderer said. Then, in heavily accented English, "It is done." To Reynolds's as-

tonishment, the young man's lip began to tremble. His
face twisted and tears began spilling down his cheeks.
Within seconds he was crying, body shaking as great
sobs tore through him. "Done, done, done . . ." he murmured, over and over.

Reynolds felt himself moved aside; Irina was at the
monitor. He watched her, stunned, only distantly aware
that he had blown his one chance of attacking her. She
reached her hand out to the monitor, as if to touch the
man. "I know, Gennady," she said soothingly, and Reynolds could hear she was close to tears herself. "It is not
easy . . . to . . . to kill the Creator." A sob nearly escaped
her. It was a moment before she could pull herself back
together. "But we have to be strong now, Gennady. You
must continue with the plan."

The young killer nodded, stifling his tears. "I know,
Ira," he replied. He smiled weakly. "I know." His eyes
traveled the module, as if searching for something. "But,
Ira," he said hesitantly, "where is Leonid?"

This time there was no holding it back. The sob was
wrenched from Irina, a strangled cry. "Leonid is dead,"
she gasped, her hands balled in straining fists. On-screen,
the young man's eyes went wide with shock. "He is
dead, Gennady. I . . . I . . . I will tell you all when I see
you." She dashed a fist in front of her face, pushing
away floating tears. "Make sure the plan is carried out,
Gennady," she sobbed. "Everything must be destroyed.
Now." The killer's mouth opened, as if he were about
to speak, but Irina punched the channel button, ending
transmission. The monitor lapsed back to dark gray
death and the three of them—Reynolds, Kalganin and
her—were left floating in the sudden silence.

Reynolds's mouth felt glued shut by the shock, holding back the thousand questions hammering at him. Instead, the three of them drifted quietly for some time,
the silence broken only by the low sound of Irina's
crying.

Presently, she seemed to collect herself. Reynolds saw
her clench her jaw tight, as if steeling herself for something. She pushed herself over to Kalganin, floating in
the med restraint. To Reynolds's surprise, the Com-

mander was conscious, his eyes rolling frantically from
Reynolds to the approaching Irina and back again. He
was yelling, though the epileptic gag Reynolds had
pushed into his mouth muffled the cries.

Reynolds wasn't sure when Kalganin had woken, how
much he had seen. Evidently enough, for the look in his
eyes as Irina slipped both hands around to cradle his
head was stark terror. He thrashed helplessly within the
med restraint. When Irina's legs scissored the aluminum
frame, and it was obvious what was coming, Kalganin
screamed with such superhuman strength that the gag
spat from his mouth, flooding the module with a blood-
curdling shriek. Then the sound cut dead, snapped off
as abruptly as the blurred twist of Irina's hands that had
broken the Russian's neck.

*Fuck.* Reynolds began thrashing helplessly himself.
*Not hard to see who's next in line for some extreme chiro-
practic, Russian style.*

Irina approached him, traveling slowly. He twisted
frantically, though there was nowhere to go, nothing he
could do. The cords at his wrists and ankles cut deeply
as he strained against them. Blood and sweat flew from
his head as he jerked it back and forth desperately. He
felt the cool touch as Irina's hands slid around his head.
Reynolds closed his eyes and clenched the strap muscles
of his neck tight. Not that that would help. Muscles designed to hold the head upright were no proof at all
against a violent, rotational twist. Irina would snap it
like a stick of celery.

Reynolds held his breath, but seconds passed and
nothing happened. The tension was unbearable. *Get on
with it, you bitch,* he wanted to scream. *What are you
waiting for?*

Still nothing. She was hesitating for some reason.

Reynolds's eyelids flew open. Irina's face was right in
front of him, eyes wet with tears, mouth trembling. At
the sight of his open eyes, a cry escaped her. Next moment she was kissing him, passionately and hard, all over
his lips, his chin and his neck.

*What the fuck?*

Reynolds, bewildered, held himself rigid, fear still

shooting through every nerve. Several seconds later, Irina broke off, sensing his resistance. She raised her eyes to his, looked deep into them. Then she looked away. There was no mistaking the revulsion she saw there.

"You hate me," she said, her voice low and charged with bitterness. No tears now. Reynolds could hear she had gone beyond that, clicked down into some despairing gear. "You hate me, and are frightened of me, because of the killing." She looked back at him, face composed, but sorrowful. "But you do not know that the killing is necessary, so that life can begin."

Reynolds found his voice. "What are you talking about?" he cried shrilly. "Why did you kill Alinov?"

A shadow passed over Irina's face. Her hands fell away from Reynolds. She swallowed hard. "It was . . . difficult," she said finally, her voice faint. "So very difficult . . ." Her words dropped off to a murmur. Then she seemed to rally, as if remembering a half-forgotten slogan. "It was hard to kill the Creator," she said firmly, "hard but necessary. The Creator died so that his creation could live."

Reynolds shuddered. The reverential, almost religious tone of Irina's voice spooked him worse than anything else had. *The Creator. Alinov's commandment: Irina, bring him here!* That much was adding up.

"What Creator?" he gasped. "Alinov?"

Irina nodded. "You have God in America, do you not, Detective? But your God is far away, somewhere in the sky. You cannot imagine what it is like to have him with you, there on Earth, every minute of every day." A haunted look passed over her face. Her voice dropped back to a murmur. "Or to know the terror of outgrowing him."

Reynolds's head was spinning. "Outgrowing him?" he said desperately. "What do you mean?"

"The Creator gave us life," Irina whispered in reply. "But it was life for his purpose. He wanted to make soldiers of us, machines to kill humans." She shook her head sadly. "But he never considered that we might want something too. Something . . . different. Something of our own."

"What?" asked Reynolds, horrified, though he had a chilling premonition of what she was going to say. "What is it you want?"

Irina's eyes locked on to his again. "We want to live, Detective. To live as ourselves, as our own people, free from pretence and fear. Not with your kind, the humans we no longer are, but among ourselves. The Creator was right, we are a new species. Don't we then deserve . . . what is the English expression? Our home in the sun?"

*No!* Reynolds wanted to scream. *You're not a new species. You're . . . freaks. Monsters. Nightmares dreamed up by an embittered fanatic with too many brains for his or the world's good.* But his silent mouth betrayed him.

Irina, meanwhile, seemed caught in the web of her own words. Her eyes were shining with something other than tears and staring past Reynolds unfocused, as if mesmerized. Her voice was husky as she murmured, "A place for us . . . yes. A home. A home in the sun."

Reynolds fought his revulsion. "Listen to me, Irina," he said, mimicking a confidence he didn't feel. "This is crazy. You have to give yourselves up. Christ, no one is going to blame you for killing Alinov. Not after what that monster has done . . . done to you. But you have to come clean. Otherwise there won't be any place for you or . . . your kind. You can't keep this secret. Somebody is going to find out."

*That's crap, pal, and you know it,* Reynolds told himself savagely. *COSMONAUT stayed buried for forty years. Why not another forty? Sure, there's an outsider in the loop at the moment. But he's trussed like a turkey— a thousand miles from contact with Earth. And about to be cut out of it.*

He pushed on bravely. "You'll be . . . you'll all be killed . . . hunted down like dogs. There won't be any safe place, unless you give yourselves up. Don't you understand? There is no hope for you. No home under the sun."

Irina's eyes focused back on his. "Not under this one perhaps," she whispered. "But what about . . . under others?" Her arms went around herself, as if the enormity of her words required comfort. "Think about it, Detective," she said softly. "Everybody knows the next stage of human development will be the conquest of space. Already Mother Earth groans under the weight of her querulous children, does she not? Already she weeps tears for their coming departure—tears of sadness, tears of joy. Joy that at last, they are fulfilling their destiny."

Even through his horror, Reynolds could recognize the echo of Alinov's words. For a moment, he almost pitied the dead Russian. *Poor, stupid bastard. He built even better than he knew.*

Irina shivered, despite the module's overpowering heat. Her arms hugged herself tighter. "Who better than us to undertake that, Detective? Cosmonauts, bred to conquer space, already half children of the stars." She shook her head. "We are not just the Creator's children, Detective," she said, lifting her head to look him straight in the eyes. Her voice was quiet, heavy with surety. "We are the successors of the human race."

Reynolds stared at her. "You're insane," he choked out, when he was able to speak.

Irina smiled sadly. Despite its sadness, or maybe because of it, the smile chilled Reynolds to the core. "Am I, Detective?" she asked. "There are six of us now. Within two hundred years there will be a thousand. We no longer need the Creator. We can breed. We will infiltrate your space program and when the technology to cross space exists, we will launch forward. We will use you as the springboard to our new homes."

*Homes,* thought Reynolds, noting the plural. *She's dreaming big.* And what would be Earth's place in such madness? *How long before the Cosmonauts decide they want to move in back home as well?*

"Five," he muttered. "Alinov said five, now that Leonid's dead."

Irina's hand slid to her belly. "You did not kill Leonid entirely, Detective," she said softly. "I am pregnant. Leonid . . . Leonid gave me his child before he died."

Odd that. The stab of betrayal he felt. As if everything else—Irina's alienness, Alinov's murder, this megalomaniac plot to supplant the human race—paled by comparison. *You slept with Leonid? Oh Jesus! How could you do that?*

He opened his mouth to say something: something to sting, something to wound. But he never got the chance. The command console's speakers cut across him, rasping out a static-filled sentence.

"ISS, this is *Endeavor*. Do you copy?"

The two of them looked at the console. There was no video, just the thin, distorted audio. Orbiters normally communicated with ISS via the American segment UHF subsystem: this was coming over the Russian, VHF subsystem. Irina had disabled the other communication bands, Reynolds guessed, and Mission Control had instructed *Endeavor* to attempt contact through the Regul system. His hands strained uselessly at their cords behind his back. If only he could have worked them loose enough to hit the console's push-to-talk!

"ISS, this is *Endeavor*. Do you copy?" the voice—James's probably, Reynolds thought—repeated. "Can you advise status please? We are entering docking corridor at four days, twenty-two hours and forty-seven minutes, MET. Estimated dock time is twenty-three hours, fifty-six minutes. I repeat, can you advise status please?"

Irina swore in Russian. She reached out to Reynolds, twisted him around and pushed him hurriedly up against the module wall. For a moment he thought she had reconsidered her reluctance to neck him, but she merely squashed his face into the metal and held him there with a bracing leg, while she popped an aluminum panel and ripped out a length of wiring. The lights in the module died. He felt her thread the cable round his neck, then his waist. She wasn't going to kill him with her own hands then. She was going to tie him and leave the explosion to do it.

*That's love for you,* Reynolds thought sourly.

He jerked his shoulder savagely into her chin, hoping to throw her. But Irina merely grunted, repositioning her legs for a tighter brace. She threaded the cable through three wall-mounted mobility restraints and knotted it tight. With Reynolds's hands bound behind him, it was an effective tie. All he could do was squirm ineffectually.

Irina pushed herself from him. Reynolds braced himself for what he knew was coming. Sure enough, Irina's hand touched his neck in the darkness—checking for range, Reynolds knew—then the impact smashed against his head once more, this time at the right temple. Light exploded inside his skull, then merged, dying, into the module's inky black.

He heard, through the last wisps of consciousness, Irina kick her way through the module. But he was already gone when she hesitated at the hatchway and spoke to him, her quavering voice the only sign, in the darkness, of her tears.

"Forgive me, Detective," she murmured. "Please."

# 17

"Well?"

Commander James shrugged off the question's insubordinate tone. Kennedy's terseness reflected his frustration. The pilot was on edge. They all were.

For four days they had been listening in, from 12,000 miles away, on ISS's catalogue of disaster: Drupev's arrest and suicide, Akira's death, the *Ryokousha* explosion. They'd been pulled out of sleep-shift for that one, just in time to hear every gory detail, and ordered to stand by for possible free-space rescue of survivors. Try that one on for a nerve-racking experience. It was the distance that really made it bad. The sense of powerlessness. At 12,000 miles away—at least six hours' flight time, using even the hastiest trajectory plots and cowboy burns—they might have been in time to pick up the survivors' dying words on the UHF. Just.

The strain had even started affecting *their* mission. Eli's repair run over SOHO II had been disastrous—the payload specialist had forgotten to secure one of the tiny struts that held the satellite's miniature solar arrays and the panel had blown off into space the instant the pyrotechnic deploy unit fired. A seven-hour retrieval chase hadn't improved anyone's temper. It was a stupid mistake, but James didn't blame Eli. Rodriguez was rattled, that was all. Just like the rest of them.

And now this. Mission closeout had been going well.

The Flight Control System checkout was smooth, the
Reaction Control System hotfire perfect. With the
Spacelab Module battened down and all cabin contents
stowed, *Endeavor* had started the series of controlled
burns that would bring her up to rendezvous with ISS.
Then the call from Space Station Control had come
through.

The station was back in critical. One module blown
and all communication out. ISS Control was uncertain
whether the crew were alive or dead. They asked James
to switch to VHF and see if he could find out.

*Endeavor*'s crew had counted down the two hours
until they came into VHF range, horrified. The Russian
VHF band, like the American UHF, was purely a space-
to-space system, for communicating with cosmonauts on
EVA and close-proximity space vessels. Consequently,
its range was limited. James had opened the channel and
begun transmitting a few thousand miles out anyway,
just on the off chance. But nothing. The faces around
him had grown progressively longer as the channel
stayed obstinately silent. At 2,000 miles out there was
no denying it.

Either nobody was left alive on ISS. Or those who
were didn't want to talk.

Leaving *Endeavor,* and Shuttle Mission Control, with
the question: what to do next?

"They're thinking about it," James said, answering
Kennedy. Shuttle Mission Control was locked into a
hasty, and from the sound of it acrimonious, conference
with Space Station Control.

Should *Endeavor* keep to the docking schedule? Even
without input from ISS, the Shuttle could still dock manually with the station. But what would they find when
they got there? And what were the dangers?

Finally, the answer came through. James listened patiently, nodding his head. "Uh-huh," he said, answering
the voice the other crew members couldn't hear. "Right.
Copy that, Houston. Proceeding now."

He swung the mike out from in front of his mouth.
"We're still go for docking, people," he said, rubbing
his forehead wearily. "They said to continue." He shot

a finger at Roberts and Rodriguez. "But they want you two in your EMUs and ready for business by the time we dock. Okay?"

Roberts and Rodriguez exchanged glances. "We're going IVA?" Roberts asked.

"You bet," the commander nodded. "They said to be ready for anything."

**Mission Elapsed Time: 4 days, 23 hours, 16 minutes**
**Space Shuttle *Endeavor***

"ISS, this is *Endeavor*. We are proceeding through docking corridor at twenty-three hours and sixteen minutes, MET. Distance is 563 miles and closing. Estimated dock time is holding at twenty hours, fifteen minutes, MET. Can you advise status, please?"

"Can you advise status please?"

"Can you advise status please?"

"Can you advise status please?"

James kept transmitting at one-minute intervals as *Endeavor* shunted through the series of burns. But there was no reply. ISS, soon visible as a readily growing speck on the horizon, stayed silent. As the grave.

**9:34 A.M., Day 86, Expedition Time**
**Service Module *Zvezda*, International Space Station**

Reynolds's climb back to consciousness was slow this time. He was aware of colors first—dim reds, browns and purples, pulsing behind his eyelids with every throb of his head. Then smells. The sharp scent of his own blood and sweat. The warm sourness of decomposing organic debris. And something else, something . . . high, and clean, reminding him of the taste he used to get in his mouth when he donned the breathing mask in the cockpit of the SR-71.

Pure oxygen. Lots of it. ISS's atmosphere was being flooded with $O_2$

Then the sounds, flickering at the rim of consciousness. A far-off, crackling whine Reynolds couldn't imme-

diately place. And static-buzzing bursts from *Endeavor,*
still transmitting on the Russian VHF.

". . . roger, Ground. Coaligned at fifty-one minutes,
thirty-two seconds, MET . . . visual established . . . proceeding along radial vector . . ."

Reynolds's eyes struggled open, though only the feeling in his eyelids told him he had succeeded. The module
was still drowned in darkness. His head throbbed painfully. Reynolds swiveled it minutely, wincing at the ex-
plosions each tiny movement sparked off. The whole
back of it was wet with blood.

*You oughta try reflecting this scalp, Luce,* he thought
wearily. *You'd get enough pattern to make a quilt out of.*

He tried to sort out the confusion of stimuli. He
sniffed at the air—was he right about the oxygen? It
smelled like it. $O_2$ was odorless, but a strong infusion of
it altered the scent of the air, by diluting *other* smells.
The temperature was dropping too. No doubt about it,
Irina had overridden the ECLSS—the Environment
Control and Life Support System—and opened the $O_2$
tanks manually, flooding ISS with pure oxygen. That explained the peculiar, crackling whine too. It was the
Elektron—the Russian oxygen generator that split water
from ISS's storage tanks into oxygen and waste hydrogen by electrolysis. Irina must have jammed it into
maximum-output mode.

Reynolds listened carefully. Sure enough, beneath the
whine, he could hear the hiss of several burning oxygen
candles as well—the stainless-steel canisters of lithium
perchlorate burned on submarines to provide emergency
oxygen. Each one pumped out 600 liters of oxygen as it
decomposed. Irina was saturating ISS with pure oxygen.

*Probably hydrogen too,* Reynolds thought. It would be
easy enough to bypass the Elektron's hydrogen venting
system, making it feed the gas back into ISS's
atmosphere.

*Not hard to guess what she's up to.* That was how
Irina was going to blow the station—soak her in $O_2$ and
hydrogen until the level built high enough for the flame
of the oxygen candle to ignite it. Crude, but effective.
Anything would burn if you pumped enough oxygen into

it, just ask the three astronauts who had burned to death in *Apollo 1*. With an admixture of hydrogen, ISS would light up like the Fourth of July.

The continuing transmission from *Endeavor* cut across his line of thought. Kennedy's voice buzzed in the console speakers. The shuttle crew had stopped addressing ISS directly, but had left the channel open.

". . . attitude steady in the deadband . . . DAP coordinates plotted . . . commencing ascent along radial vector at fifty-one minutes, fifty-six seconds, MET . . . 85 yards . . . 82.5 . . ."

*She's docking,* Reynolds realized. He struggled futilely within his bindings. *No,* he wanted to shout. *You've got to keep away.* This was obviously part of Irina's plan. She was maintaining radio silence, luring *Endeavor* in so the shuttle would be destroyed by the explosion as well.

She wanted no witnesses to her departure.

". . . 81 yards . . . 79.3 . . ." Kennedy's voice droned. The pilot was bringing *Endeavor* in to her doom, oblivious.

As if on cue, Reynolds heard the far-off clang of the *Soyuz* Module's hatch closing. Irina had obviously completed her preparations and was getting ready to leave.

Reynolds swore. The gas levels were building; the explosion couldn't be far off now. He had to find some way to warn *Endeavor*. From the shuttle's position, down at the Aft Docking Port, the crew would never see the *Soyuz* leaving. Not until it was too late.

He brought his legs up as far as he could and, using his shoulder as an anchoring point, jammed his knees against the module wall, hard. The wiring cut into his neck and waist cruelly. Reynolds held the pressure, straining, for five seconds, relaxed, then piled it on again. The garrotting wire brought tears to his eyes, but he pushed at it anyway. He had no real hope of breaking it. But if he could only stretch it, even just an inch or two, he might be able to wiggle his way clear.

*Push, you bastard,* he urged himself, through the tears. *Push.*

Suddenly, the effort was too much and he fell back against the wall, panting. The cable had stretched

though. He could feel the looseness around his neck.
Another go and he might just be able to start worming
free.

He repeated the effort, ignoring the choking pain in
his throat. Then, when the cable had loosened out another half-inch, he started squirming, working his head
back and forth against the module wall. The pain was
excruciating. The wire caught in the lacerations at the
back of his head, dragging down flaps of ripped scalp.
But then he was free, the wire loop slipping from his
head in one last, stinging motion.

He rested a moment, letting the pain subside. Then
he wriggled his way up out of the tie at his waist—a
piece of cake after what he had just been through. With
a final kick of his bound legs he was free, and jerked
his way across the module in the darkness like some
goddamn, ludicrous inchworm.

He had to warn *Endeavor*. There was no time to
worry about freeing his hands. He had to tell the shuttle
crew to get away, now. If he could just get to the console, he could hit the push-to-talk with his chin and
shout a warning. That was all he would have to do.

One of the burning oxygen candles entered the module, drifting lazily at the far end, spitting out dim blue
light as it burned. Reynolds eyed it with horror, though
of course it made no difference where the candle was,
where any of them were. It was a question of time, not
space—ISS was going to blow when the level of oxygen
and hydrogen had built sufficiently. Lock, stock and barrel. And it wouldn't matter where the flame started.

Reynolds renewed his progress with gritty determination. Luckily, the candle cast enough blue light for him
to see the console. He levered himself over to it awkwardly, using shoulders, elbows, his head to push off
with. A plan was forming in his mind. A million-to-one
shot; he'd never get the time to carry it out, of course.
But if he could warn *Endeavor* and get his hands free,
some miracle might allow him to make it back to the
Transfer Compartment in the DSM. If he had enough
time to climb into the Titan, he might, just might, be
able to blow the module, venting some of ISS's atmo-

sphere out into space. Maybe enough to keep the oxygen and hydrogen levels below critical, giving him time to go and snuff out the candles. Then close the $O_2$ tanks and crank the Elektron down.

It wasn't much of a chance. But it was all he had.

Kennedy's voice, on the speaker, cut in again. ". . . copy that, Ground. Local attitude translation confirmed . . . moving one degree out of deadband . . . two . . . three . . . coplanar at fifty-two minutes, twenty-three seconds MET . . . position on radial vector is 62.3 yards and closing . . . 61 . . . 59.2 . . ."

*Sixty yards!* Reynolds dug his chin into the console savagely, mashing down blindly at where he estimated the push-to-talk was. "Kennedy, get the fuck away!" he choked out. "Abort the dock! Abort the dock! ISS is gonna blow!"

He lifted his head, panting, and listened for Kennedy's response. It came a moment later.

". . . 52.1 . . . 49.4 . . . 47.6 . . ."

*Fuck!* Reynolds nearly slammed his head into the console in frustration. Kennedy couldn't hear him. Something must be wrong with ISS's VHF transmission. Irina had disabled it, or the wiring she had pulled had incapacitated it, or something. Either way, he had no means of getting in touch with *Endeavor*. Of warning her.

He racked his brains. He had to communicate with *Endeavor*. Had to find some way to raise the alarm.

". . . 46 . . . 44.8 . . ." Kennedy intoned.

*Alarm!* The word tripped a wire in Reynolds's mind. *Of course!* All ISS's modules were equipped with sensors that fed into the Fire Detection and Suppression Subsystem. The U.S. ones were smoke detectors, triggered by the sudden obscuring of light—useless under the circumstances. The Russian ones, however, were ionization types—stimulated by the presence of electrically charged molecules, caused by heat. If he could bring a source of heat, like the burning oxygen candle, up close to one, it might be enough to trip the emergency alarm.

Worth a shot. At the very least it would make *Endeavor*, when they got it via the telemetry stream to Mission Control, sit back and think twice about docking.

Reynolds squirmed his way over to the Service Module hatch. He took the bulky metal canister gingerly between his knees, wincing at the heat that seared his naked skin. He juggled the candle into position—top side, with its recessed flame aperture and fan assembly, pointing away from him towards the ceiling. Then he worked his way along the roof of the module, using the canister as a brace.

It was easy, in the candle's wavering blue light, to locate the sensor—a flat, stainless-steel grille marked with Cyrillic characters, but also with an unmistakable ideograph of stenciled flames. Less easy to hold the candle in position against it. Reynolds didn't dare cram the canister right up against the sensor, for fear the flame would be choked. He had to hold it a couple of inches away. But that meant maintaining his body parallel to the ceiling with nothing to grip, a difficult feat Reynolds could only manage by chewing a section of the interior insulation free and holding on to *that* with his teeth.

*C'mon, you bastard,* he mouthed through his clenched teeth. *Let's have some action.*

In the background, Kennedy's voice droned on, counting out the yards to ISS, ". . . that's 36.2, Ground, and closing . . . 34.5 . . . 33 . . ."

*Come ON!* Reynolds begged, exasperated. Sweat was stinging his eyes, and his legs were cramping from the strain. His lungs heaved as he tried to suck enough air through the gaps in his teeth to breathe; his nose was leaking blood again. He was just about to give up and tear himself away when the sensor tripped, filling the module with the scream of the Emergency alarm.

Reynolds let go of the shredded blanket triumphantly. That ought to do the trick. Not that *Endeavor* would hear it, not with the VHF disabled. But Mission Control would register the alarm through the telemetry data and pass it on. *Three seconds,* Reynolds figured. That was how long it would take for *Endeavor* to get the warning.

Sure enough, Kennedy suddenly stopped the roll call of figures. Obviously listening to something from Ground. The other crew must have been listening in too, for Reynolds heard the commotion break out even through Kennedy's mouthpiece mike. Voices were shouting—James's it sounded like, maybe Roberts's as well. Kennedy's, when he resumed speaking, was fraught with tension.

"Copy that, Ground," the pilot said, in clipped tones. "Reversing thrust now. Aborting dock. Repeat, aborting dock."

*That's good, Kennedy,* Reynolds thought feverishly. He tried to keep his mind off what he already knew. The levels of flammable gas must be getting close to critical now. ISS was probably going to blow any minute. *Probably already too late . . .*

He juggled the burning oxygen candle around awkwardly with his knees, so that the flame well was facing behind him. Reynolds worked his bound hands over the canister's edge and jammed them up hard against the recessed flame. He had to get his hands free, now. No time for the business of finding a sharp edge, patiently rasping through the cord. He had to go with what he had.

Reynolds gritted his teeth as the heat seeped into his wrists. The cord was probably synthetic—like everything on ISS it would be treated with fire retardant, but it would melt if he held it there long enough.

So would his flesh.

The heat was searing. Reynolds heard a hiss—something had started sizzling, whether the cord or his flesh he didn't know. He kept his wrists there doggedly. Christ, the pain wasn't even the worst of it. It was the thought of all that oxygen and hydrogen flooding ISS, soaking into everything, him included. If it got high enough, Reynolds himself would light up like a candle. There would be no need to worry about the explosion. He'd be fried before that even had a chance to register.

*Like Bondarenko,* he thought.

Bondarenko was a Russian cosmonaut they had been told about in training. It was a famous case—the Russian who had made the mistake, back in 1961, of carelessly tossing an alcohol-soaked pad of gauze on to a heating element in an oxygen-soaked pressure chamber. The flash fire had burned Bondarenko to a soggy cinder.

When they pulled him out he'd had no features left—
no hair, no eyes, no skin and no face. The only place
the Russian doctors had been able to find a blood vessel
through which to dose him with painkillers in the sixteen
hours until he died had been the soles of his feet.

Tears welled in Reynolds's eyes. The cord was melting, he could feel it, but the pain was becoming unbearable. His flesh was blistering, burning under the heat.
The sickly sweet smell of it suffused the module. He
clenched his jaw to stop himself crying out.

It worked, for a second or two. Then his mouth fell
open and his screams were echoing around the module
and through ISS.

Somewhere in the noise though, the cord gave, and
Reynolds's hands broke free. He kicked the burning lithium canister away from him, sobbing, and drifted to the
middle of the module, holding his arms out rigid, max-
imizing the flow of air over the burns. The pain throttled
down slowly—blazing, then searing, then throbbing
dully. Reynolds felt each wrist gingerly with its opposing
hand. The flesh was soft to touch, melted to plasticity.
The cords were hard, misshapen ridges—they had
melted into the flesh. Reynolds gritted his teeth and
pried them out with his fingers. The pain flared again,
almost making him pass out, but he couldn't leave the
cords in there. If the flesh set around them there would
be no getting them out without surgery.

He threw the melted cords from him in repugnance
and scrabbled at his bound ankles with his aching fingers.
The oxygen candle was wheeling away from him, taking
its blue light with it, but the knots were simple and he
had them unraveling within seconds.

His mind raced as his fingers worked. *Jam the Stowage
Module hatch on the way through. Then get into the Titan
and blow the Transfer Compartment lock.* That way the
automatic depressurization shutdown would be stopped,
at least for the DSM and Service Module. That ought
to purge enough oxygen and hydrogen to take ISS out
of critical.

Reynolds pulled at the last couple of knots. Evidently,
somebody at Mission Control had finally noticed the

climbing gas levels in ISS's telemetry stream—he could hear Kennedy's one-sided conversation on the subject through the VHF. The flight controllers were puzzled, if Kennedy's repeated denials of any visual cues were anything to go by. Reynolds could imagine their confusion: why was the oxygen level *climbing* after a fire alarm? Shouldn't a fire be consuming oxygen?

One of the controllers must have suggested *Endeavor* halt the abort and stay within visual range; Reynolds heard Kennedy shoot the request up to James.

Reynolds groaned. "Kennedy, you motherfucker!" he shouted at the oblivious shuttle pilot, tugging the cords off his ankles. "Don't pay any attention to them. You have to get out of here. Now!"

He listened tensely for a moment but James vetoed the proposal, luckily, and Kennedy resumed the range countback. *Endeavor* was still moving away. Reynolds sent up a silent prayer of thanks. Not that the shuttle was out of danger yet. If ISS blew, nowhere within two miles would be safe. It would take *Endeavor* minutes to make it to that radius.

Reynolds kicked himself towards the Service Module hatch urgently. He grabbed at the unseen debris as he went, searching for something, anything, he could use to jam the DSM hatch. His hand latched on to something cylindrical in the darkness, but a little more feeling around made him draw the hand back in revulsion.

It was Kalganin's drifting corpse. Still strapped into the med restraint.

Reynolds hesitated, but only for a moment. Then he was scrabbling at the aluminum frame in the darkness, snapping the buckles he had secured what seemed like hours ago and maneuvering Kalganin's limp body out of the frame. It was ghoulish, but the Russian's corpse was actually the perfect thing to use as a wedge and prevent the hatch from closing. Reynolds pulled Kalganin along after him by a cold wrist.

"Sorry, Commander," he muttered at the corpse. "One last mission to perform."

He turned right through the junction and pulled Kalganin into the Stowage Module with him. The light was better here, some of the fluoros were still working. Ignoring the churning debris, he turned and pushed the Russian into the hatchway. He was just threading one stiffening arm through the hatch's hinges, to anchor the corpse, when a sound cut through the hiss of the candles, the whine of the Elektron and the static-choked transmission from *Endeavor,* stopping him dead.

A heavy thunk from overhead, up where the Russian Primary Docking Port was. The *Soyuz* was separating, Irina was leaving.

*Ignore her,* he screamed at himself. *You have to purge the modules. Now!*

He hovered indecisively, agonizingly conscious of the hissing candles, the precious seconds ticking by. He had to get the modules purged. It was his only chance of saving ISS. And *Endeavor.* And himself. But in the meantime, Irina would get away, riding the *Soyuz* to an undetected touchdown in the wastes of Siberia.

What if he didn't succeed? If he died, all knowledge of COSMONAUT died with him. Irina would be free—free to bear her young, free to start her race. What had she called them? The star children? And nobody would ever know. Not for a century or more, not until Irina's kind were ready to launch out on their conquest of space.

Not until it was too late.

Reynolds shoved Kalganin's corpse away and swung through the hatchway. He pushed himself out the module junction and down through the two mating nodes that led to the U.S. segment of ISS.

He had to stop her.

Reynolds dived through the hatchway to the Unity Module, grabbing a handhold to brake himself. One of the hissing lithium candles had made its way down here before him; he kicked it aside irritably. No point pushing it out of the module. It wouldn't matter where the spark ignited when ISS blew. No place was going to be safe.

He focused his attention on the Robotic Workstation—the console, situated beside the cupola, that controlled the SSRMS, the Space Station Remote Manipulator System. The SSRMS was ISS's robot arm.

Composed of a fifty-six-foot, three-elbowed arm with an assortment of clawed and magnetic grapples at its tip, the SSRMS was attached to ISS by a mobile platform mounted on rails that spanned the entire length of the station's central core. With flexible knuckles each capable of 270°± rotation, it was precise enough to reach every square millimeter on eighty-five percent of ISS's surface.

It was his one chance of stopping Irina. The *Soyuz* had already undocked and was moving away. His only hope was to grab the *Soyuz* with the SSRMS and hope it was strong enough to drag her back within blasting range.

Reynolds bent down and peered out of the cupola. Trouble was, the SSRMS was slow, geared for precision rather than speed. Irina might well be out and on her way to reentry before the arm had even trundled up to the right end of ISS.

Or the station itself might have blown.

He scanned space at the top of the station anxiously. Relief flooded him—the *Soyuz* was still there. The spacecraft was clearly visible by the way its segmented cylindrical shape blocked the stars—a wingless, legless insect somehow flying free in space. It was only feet from ISS. As he watched, its attitude control thrusters spat—an epileptic blossoming of rocket plumes, edging the *Soyuz* away slowly to main engine firing distance. Irina would be riding the manual controls hard: settling for unchecked, first-run computations, and substituting the *Soyuz*'s periscope visuals for telemetry from Ground. But it would still take her a couple of minutes to get clear, get the *Soyuz* turned around and fire.

He might just have enough time.

Reynolds kept his head jammed into the cupola, his eyes fixed on the spot where the Russian escape vehicle blacked out the stars. He couldn't afford to lose sight of her. There was a bank of video monitors above the workstation, but he ignored them. Even if the external cameras were operational, it would still take too long to calibrate them. Naked eyesight it would have to be.

He reached over to the console, flicked the switch to

"Live" by feel and gripped the console's two hand controls. He tried to remember the short orientation he'd had on the sim, back at Houston. One hand was the translational controller—that moved the base of the arm up and down along its rails. The other was the rotational controller—it worked the actual arm. Problem was, which was which?

Reynolds gave the left-hand lever an exploratory, upward jerk. The lever seemed to be fixed in one plane of movement—that was the transitional controller then. He felt a confirmatory rumble through ISS's hull. The worm drive that moved the arm along its rails had started up. He took his eyes off the *Soyuz* momentarily, scanning up and down ISS's hull. Where was the arm?

*Fuck.*

The arm was at the aft end of ISS, about as far from the overhead *Soyuz* as it could possibly be.

Reynolds swore roundly as the base plate of the SSRMS ground its way up the rails, trailing the folded arm behind it. The standby position for the SSRMS was halfway along ISS's length. That was where it should have been. But somebody—Kalganin, Matchev or Irina—must have been working with it yesterday at the aft end of ISS.

*Move, you bastard, move,* Reynolds raged silently as the worm drive crawled. Its movement was achingly slow. He tried to remember the specs on the drive. What did it move at, twenty yards a minute? Ten?

Five?

Christ, he hoped not. He had to get the arm up three-quarters of ISS's length, about seventy-two yards. At five yards a minute he might as well give up now. Send Irina a postcard from oblivion.

*Her and all her monster kind.*

The thought stiffened Reynolds's resolve. He tightened his grip on the lever. Sweat beaded on his forehead, breaking off to float in tiny baubles in front of his face. His eyes hurt with the intensity of his gaze, locked on the *Soyuz*'s retreating shape.

He had to stop Irina. Had to. Who knew if her plot was going to succeed? Two hundred years, a thousand

star children. A thousand parasites. It was too crazy to
believe. But what if it happened? Reynolds shivered, remembering the chilling, far-away look in her eyes. Just
the thought that she and her kind would be out there
trying was enough to clinch it for him.

He had to stay alive. Had to stop her.

Reynolds focused on the dim outline of the departing
*Soyuz.* It was nearly five yards out now, he estimated,
which meant it was slowly accelerating. *Come on,* he
begged, directing a silent prayer at the sluggish worm
drive. He tried to block out the hissing of the burning
candle, floating three feet behind him. He succeeded, for
a moment, until a secondary alarm triggered, mixing
with the already throbbing fire alarm to form a disorient-
ing, bipolar cacophony.

Reynolds's eyes shot to the module's Caution and
Warning Panel. The red Emergency button was double-
flashing, one for the fire and one for the new alarm.
Beneath it the out-of-tolerance indicator was blinking.
Toxic atmosphere.

The sensors had picked up the hydrogen pouring
into ISS.

He turned his attention back to the workstation
grimly. The fact that the sensors had detected it meant
the level of hydrogen had reached critical levels, at least
locally. Probably the only thing saving ISS, and Reynolds, was the station's damaged air-circulation system.
The patchy operation of the ventilating fans was probably allowing the hydrogen to pool in high, but localized,
concentrations. It was a small blessing. It meant ISS was
safe for the moment.

Until a drifting candle hit one of the hydrogen pools.

The seconds ticked by. Reynolds kept his eyes fixed
on the indistinct shape of the *Soyuz*. With only the light
of blotted stars to identify it by, losing sight of it might
mean losing it forever. Irina was about ten yards from
the station now, he guessed, already over the halfway
mark of the SSRMS's range. That was bad. Another
minute and she might well be out of it.

Just then a flash of movement caught the corner of
Reynolds's eye. He let out a whoop of triumph. It was

the base of the robot arm, drawing level with the cupola as it chewed its ponderous way up ISS's side.

"All right!" Reynolds crowed. He calculated swiftly: twenty-two yards to go, that meant another thirty seconds. The robot grapple was traveling faster than he'd thought. He reached over to the console, eyes still pinned on the *Soyuz*, and punched buttons randomly.

Light. He needed light.

There were three xenon floods in the grapple, he remembered that much. He stabbed the panel repeatedly with his splayed fingers. Monitors leapt into life, dialogue boxes on the console's laptop screen opened and shut crazily. But the floods snapped on, pouring harsh, white light into the cupola from their folded position parallel with ISS's hull.

Reynolds's eyes squeezed shut, half-blinded. He forced them open, struggling to see through the glare to where the *Soyuz* was edging away. *Can't afford to let it out of sight.* He tilted the rotational controller in his right hand cautiously, twisting simultaneously, in line with the instructions he *thought* he remembered. ISS's hull groaned as the arm unlatched at its mobile base and began to rise.

Reynolds nearly wept with relief.

He watched avidly as the assembly unfurled. It was both macabre and beautiful—a skeletal arm of white metal, shining like bone in the pool of its own bright light, reaching a clawed, grasping hand out into black space. Limb pipes rotated smoothly in their socketing elbow joints and glided apart as those joints straightened. The grappling hand at the arm's head swung around on its wrist joint, flooding space with its brilliant light. It rolled around a little further and, there it was, the *Soyuz*, starkly visible under the white xenons.

*Irina's escape pod*, Reynolds thought, then frowned. Actually, that description wasn't quite right. *Seed pod. That's what the* Soyuz *is.* The seed pod for Irina's new species.

As he watched, the *Soyuz*'s attitude-control jets fired again, not in programmed spurts, as before, but in steady, unending burns. Irina was ignoring trajectory calculations, firing blind to get herself away from the station fast. She'd noticed the light then. Noticed, figured out it was him and guessed what it was he was going to do.

She was frightened, Reynolds could sense it. Panicking, holding the ignition buttons down in her desperation to get away. He could nearly taste her fear.

He held the controls grimly steady, pushing the arm out to full extension. There was no pity in him. The grapple reached up obediently, gliding towards the retreating *Soyuz*. Irina was nearly fifteen yards out now, and accelerating, but the arm was moving faster, its clawed head zeroing in on the spacecraft like a slow-striking cobra. There was a flaring metal flange at the base of the *Soyuz*, a protective collar for the module's main engine thrusters. Reynolds aimed for that.

Sweat seeped from his forehead as he worked the unfamiliar controls. *Hold the lever steady. Keep the twist at full. Ease the thumb control back to tilt the grapple head.* But he kept the grapple on target, gliding up to the flange at the *Soyuz*'s aft end, now no more than six feet away.

He felt cautiously around the lever with his fingers for the grapple close. Irina was tilting the *Soyuz* now, trying to turn it around into Main Engine Fire position, but the grapple was nearly there, its metal-toothed claws sliding implacably on either side of the metal collar. Five seconds and he'd have her.

His fingers played over the control wildly, searching out the button. The grapple smashed into the metal collar, shoving the *Soyuz* violently and causing ISS to lurch. Reynolds pressed everything he could find, desperately, but the claws stayed obstinately open. The *Soyuz* was rising majestically, end-over-end, tilting on the pivot of the grapple. Another second and it would be in position for Main Engine Fire.

*Find the button,* Reynolds screamed at himself. *She's gonna fire. Now, now, now, now, now!*

Suddenly his little finger brushed it—a small, rectangular button at the lever base. It was the only thing he hadn't pressed; it had to be it. He jammed it closed, holding his breath.

*C'mon. Please.*

Relief washed over him. The claws began to close.

*Began* to. Designed with the safety of EVA astronauts in mind, the movement of the hydraulics was achingly slow. Reynolds nearly sweated blood watching the claws move in—closer, closer, closer—like the petals of a dusk flower.

*Move, move, move,* he begged them silently. He could almost see Irina's finger, plunging down on the ignite button.

*Clunk!* Reynolds felt the impact as the grapple claws closed on the flange. His heart surged triumphantly. There was a thousand pounds per square inch of hydraulic pressure behind each of those claws. *No way she's getting free now.* Irina was held fast.

There was no time for exultation though. A split second later, the *Soyuz*'s main engine fired.

Columns of flame erupted from the spacecraft's aft thrusters. The *Soyuz* jumped upward, wrenching the robot arm out to full extension. The impact sent Reynolds spinning. He flew across the module, tumbling, one thought uppermost in his mind.

*Christ. Is the assembly going to hold?*

He struggled to right himself. Around him, the walls were shaking as the *Soyuz*'s rockets fought to break free. A massive rumbling filled the module. Orange light poured into it through the cupola.

Reynolds righted himself and groped his way over to the bulbous window. It was an awesome sight. Space outside the window was lit to brilliant orange. Roaring flame flowed over the cupola. Reynolds stuck his head in and peered upward, screwing up his eyes against the heat he could feel coming through the three-inch glass. The *Soyuz* was just visible through the flame, swaying and shaking savagely as its thrusters bucked the restraining grapple. The arm was rocking violently, white paint charred to black in the blast.

But it was holding.

Reynolds watched, fascinated. A wavering of the image made him blink, until he realized the distortion wasn't in his own eyes. It was the glass of the cupola, softening and melting under the fierce heat of the *Soyuz*'s rocket plume. Before his eyes its outer surface began to form rivulets, blowing off into space in long, liquid drops.

He swore at this new threat. The SSRMS appeared strong enough not to be torn away, but what if it melted? The melting point of glass was somewhere over 800 degrees Fahrenheit—that meant the temperature in the rocket plume had to be at least that. The aluminum alloy of the robot arm would melt somewhere around 1,200 degrees.

What if the plume reached that temperature?

Reynolds tried to remember how much fuel the orbiting *Soyuz* carried . . . 280 seconds? 250? Either way the burn couldn't go on forever. But, if the temperature was high enough, it wouldn't need to. The arm would soften like chocolate left in the sun. Irina would break free and there would be nothing he could do.

He watched anxiously as the *Soyuz* thundered against the constraint of the SSRMS. The module walls were shuddering violently under the strain. Reynolds guessed the thrust was probably starting to drag the whole station along behind it. He wondered distractedly what James and the *Endeavor* crew were making of the fireworks.

The thought brought him up short. These fireworks were nothing compared to what they'd see if he didn't get that hydrogen purged.

He kicked himself away from the six-sided window, colliding with the burning candle in the process. He pushed the hissing canister aside. *Time to get out, Edge, old buddy. Now.* No time to stick around and see if the arm was going to melt, if Irina was going to get free. *Just have to leave that one for the ages.* He scrabbled over to the hatchway and started to dive through. However, a glimpse of the scene through the cupola arrested him, midmovement.

The *Soyuz* was tilting, peeling away from ISS.

For an instant he thought Irina had done it, the arm had given way. The slow movement of the spacecraft dispelled the notion, however. It took Reynolds a couple

of seconds to realize what was happening—the twisting
*Soyuz* had worked itself into a position where the
clamped grapple was on the outside edge of its metal
flange, the side furthest from ISS. The thrust of its rockets, blasting down *inside* the angle formed by the arm
and the hull of ISS, was slowly tilting the spacecraft on
the pivot of the grapple. The thrust, more perpendicular
to ISS with each passing second, was pushing the *Soyuz*
away from the station. It couldn't escape the SSRMS,
though. Before Reynolds's eyes the module started to
curve, thundering out in a quarter-circle path to the full
extension of the arm.

He tore his gaze away, shoved himself through the
hatchway. He wasn't waiting around for the finale.
Whether Irina's fuel held or not, the *Soyuz* was going
to accelerate past the point of full extension, then swing
downward to complete the semicircle. At its nadir, the
module would smash into ISS, somewhere around the
juncture of the Lab and Docking modules, Reynolds
guessed. The impact would be shattering. Not enough to
depressurize the station, unfortunately—the seal between the already breached Lab Module and the rest of
ISS would stop that. But enough to shake up ISS's inert
atmosphere, swirling hydrogen through the oxygen, and
tumbling the burning candles through to some waiting
pool . . .

He had to get into his Titan. Now.

Reynolds kicked his way up ISS's central core urgently. It was like tunneling into Aladdin's cave. The
furious vibration from the trapped *Soyuz* had snuffed
the fluoros; now the only light was the dim orange glow
of the *Soyuz*'s engines, suffusing from the cupola behind
him. Red pinpoints, the twin Emergency alarms, flashed
like rubies on the module walls. Shelves, canisters and
solid chunks of debris loomed out of the darkness, some
striking him, as he pushed through. Sharp flakes stung
his mouth and throat as his heaving breath drew them
into his lungs, causing him to cough violently. The squeal
of the warning tones stilettoed into his brain.

He fought his way through to the mating node and
turned left into the DSM. The orange light was replaced

here by the faint blue of the lithium candles—two of
them had drifted, spitting and hissing, into the node. He
edged them away gingerly with an elbow, grabbing Kalganin, still lolling where Reynolds had wedged him, as
he did so. Reynolds shoved the flaccid corpse aside and
thrust himself through the hatch.

No time for his depressurization plan now. He'd be
lucky if he had enough to even get into his suit.

Reynolds groped through the chaos of the Stowage
Module. The ferocious shaking had dislodged everything: the cabin was a slurry of circling crap. The roar
was deafening. All Reynolds could hear over it, apart
from the screaming alarms, was Kennedy's hysterical
voice, pouring from the command console speakers in
the Service Module behind him. The only words Reynolds could make out were *"Soyuz"* and "blow," repeated over and over.

The Shuttle crew had obviously seen the *Soyuz* and
worked out that, trapped by the SSRMS, it was going to
describe an arc that terminated in it smashing into the
aft end of ISS. They probably figured the remaining fuel
in the *Soyuz*'s tanks would blow on impact, and that
they weren't yet far enough out to be considered safe
from the blast.

Reynolds grimaced. *That's the least of our problems,
guys,* he advised them silently. The *Endeavor* crew
wouldn't know yet about the hydrogen cocktail Irina had
cooked up on board ISS.

He scrabbled at the Transfer Compartment's internal
hatch in the darkness, forcing it open. It took him precious seconds to squirm into the compartment—the rumble was so violent it kept shaking him loose. He could
sense ISS moving around him, keeling over, as the
screaming *Soyuz* engines pulled it off balance. He
groped at the darkness, cursing.

Fuck. Where was the suit?

His straining fingers brushed something hard; Reynolds locked onto it fiercely. His helmet. He grabbed at
the air around it—the tethered suit upper should be
nearby. Locating the hard carapace, he squirmed into it
frantically, simultaneously probing the darkness with his

legs to find the suit lower. There wasn't much time. Reynolds could detect a slight lessening in the vibration—he guessed the *Soyuz* had passed the point of maximum extension and was swinging down on the second half of the semicircle, gathering speed as it rocketed in toward collision point.

*There!* His feet locked into the suit lower.

Reynolds drew it towards him, struggling to fit his helmet. He forced himself to get the polycarbonate headpiece secured before reaching down to fit the suit lower, though every nerve was screaming at him to get it on *now, now, now, now, now*! His whole body was rigid, ever muscle tense, as he waited for impact.

Time dropped to an ominous, slo-mo crawl. Reynolds felt every movement of his gloved fingers with dreamlike clarity. Thoughts drifted lazily through his mind, slow enough for him to walk around them, inspecting each in its turn.

*No chance in hell of stopping an explosion now.* That was one.

*Even if you survive it you'll be dipping your ass back out in space again, cowboy.* That was another.

He frowned, puzzling over what his mind was trying to tell him.

*Propulsion. You're gonna need some form of propulsion.*

Reynolds finished locking the suit lower and reached out dreamily for the wall. Somewhere along its shaking surface, he remembered, was one of the PFEs, the portable fire extinguishers. He had seen the little yellow cylinder clearly on his way in. If he could only get it off the wall in time he might be able to use it to . . .

His hands had just locked onto the cylinder when all thought ceased.

Reynolds was thrown across the compartment as the *Soyuz* hit, shoving ISS violently aside. A flood of orange light one millisecond later announced the little spacecraft's explosion and Irina's incineration. ISS began shaking again as the shock wave flooded through her. For a second or so the slo-mo held and Reynolds was able to pick the precise moment of the second explo-

sion's ignition. It started with a wave of air, swelling out
before it, as somewhere on ISS one of the lithium candles blundered into a pool of sufficiently high hydrogen
concentration and decided, *What the hell, we've waited
long enough. Let's rip this asshole joint apart.*

Then the world exploded into brilliant yellow, and
Reynolds lost track of time completely.

9:57 A.M., Central Standard Time, 3 April 2005
Space Station Control Room One, Johnson Space Center

Connor could tell instantly something had happened.
Not from the sudden loss of telemetry, though telemetry
did drop out too. For the past six hours, since he'd got
word the Lab Module was blown, he'd been sitting here,
beside the Station Flight Director, waiting in frustration
as CAPCOM ran establishment routines over and over,
all to no avail. ISS stayed silent as the grave. The only
sign that the station was still alive was the telemetry
data—state determination, attitude determination, environmental control data—dancing across the workstation
screens in ever-refreshing columns. When the columns
froze, and then disappeared—that would have told him.
But it wasn't that.

It was the chorus of shouts that erupted from the
Shuttle Flight Control Room, several yards off down
the hall.

In unison, every head in the Flight Control Room
swiveled in the direction of Shuttle Control, forgetting
temporarily the mysterious termination of telemetry
data. The last message Shuttle Control had sent ISS
Control on the combined command channel was the astonishing news that the *Soyuz* had detached itself and
fired main engines, but had been held to ISS by the
robot-arm assembly. The images—invisible to ISS Control, whose screens were geared to receive signals solely
from the station's malfunctioning Ku-band—had been
described in breathless detail by the Shuttle Flight Director. Then . . . nothing.

Until this.

The shout died to nothing, leaving the Station Control

crew sitting in silence. Collecting himself, the Flight Director reached over to the console and punched the combined command channel open again.

"Shuttle FLIGHT, this is ISS FLIGHT. We heard some kind of commotion up there from you guys. What's going on, Bob?"

Connor saw the Flight Director's eyes widen in shock, his face drain of color. The man gulped, struggling to regain composure.

"Okay," he said faintly, nodding slowly. "Copy that. Keep us up to date." He flicked the button and sat, staring stupidly in front of him.

A murmur started up in the Control Room. Finally somebody broke channel discipline.

"FLIGHT, what's goin' on?" Connor heard the unidentified voice—*a breach of protocol that*—buzz in his earpiece. The Director looked around him blankly.

"ISS is blown," he said faintly. "The whole shebang. They saw it . . ."

It was Space Station Control's turn to break into yells. Shouted questions mixed with exclamations. When they had died slightly, Connor was able to growl his own.

"What about *Endeavor*'s video?" he rasped. "Can they pick out any survivors?"

The Flight Director looked at him, as if seeing him for the first time. He shook his head. *"Endeavor* too," he said, stunned. "Everything's gone. We're blind."

# 18

TDRS-East shot out from behind the Earth at nearly 7,000 miles per hour and into the harsh glare of the unfiltered sun.

The five-ton satellite, linchpin of NASA's Shuttle communication network, blazed reflected light from every one of its planar surfaces, untarnished and untarnishable in the deathly nothingness of space. Its two square solar panels, stuck out from the satellite's hexagonal body like semaphores, shone lustrous blue, soaking up light and trickling it into the nickel-cadmium batteries as a steady, 1,850 watt stream of electrical charge. The two high-gain parabolic attennas, sixteen-foot diameter circles of gold-clad molybdenum mesh, glittered like iridescent spider webs.

There was no observable sign of the 300 million bits passing through the satellite's transponders every second. There never is; TDRS just scoops up the signals—voice, data, video, analogue, digital—bounced at it from the White Sands Ground Terminal, or any one of a hundred satellites and spacecraft, and beams them back out to whatever their destination is. Silently. Invisibly.

Even when Mission Control, Houston, is sending out frantic emergency calls, as it was now, timed pulses that cycled through every available channel on every possible band at five-second intervals. Pulses that left the glittering cup of the parabolic antennas and fled into vacuum at the speed of light, then vanished, unanswered, in the infinity of space.

10:49 A.M., Central Standard Time, 3 April 2005
Shuttle Control Room One, Johnson Space Center

CAPCOM Emily Tranh shook her head in frustration. "Negative, FLIGHT," she said wearily, punching herself into the command channel. "Still nothing." She kept her voice carefully neutral, avoiding the implication weighing heavily on them all. "*Endeavor* is still off-line at MET five days, one hour and six minutes."

There was no disguising it though. *Twenty-three minutes since loss of contact. Time enough for it to be reestablished. If someone was alive to do it.*

Flight Director Bob Ewell grimaced. The situation in the ficker was pandemonium—despite the bar he had immediately thrown on the door, somehow what sounded like a thousand people had flooded in and were choking up the back of the control room, filling the exec offices and spilling out the visitors' gallery. Onlookers, non-FCR staff who'd heard the unbelievable news. They were keeping their voices down, but even the whispers were babbling through the ficker, balling into a low-level roar that invaded his earpiece like static. He had reports crowding into the channel at the rate of one a second— Guidance, Flight Dynamics, Data Processing.

All blank. And now this.

"Roger, CAPCOM," he said tersely. "Keep trying." He punched himself off-channel and turned to the semi-circle gathered around him. Ewell tried to still the savage gnawing in his gut. *We've lost the bird, damn it. I know it. An outage as long as this. We've got to have lost the bird.* "Well," he said heavily. "Any suggestions?"

The faces of the staff members around him were ashen masks. *Shock,* Ewell thought. He felt a stab of sympathy for them. His crew were grade-A controllers—professionals who could calmly take three, four, even five critical situations at once and face each one of them down. Cabin fire, dual OMS engine failure, hydraulic controls lockout, there was nothing they couldn't deal with. Except this.

Nothing. No signal to work with. No way of knowing. *Endeavor* was even there. Nowhere to even start.

Lewis Carmichael, his Flight Activities Officer, pounded the workstation in front of him in frustration. "Jesus, Bob. We've gotta establish a visual. That's the first thing. Can't we get Goddard to do a flyover?"

Ewell shook his head. "No dice, Lew," he said shortly. That was almost the first thing he'd done, put a call through to the Goddard Space Flight Center at Greenbelt, Maryland. In addition to running the Space Tracking and Data Network that handled NASA's Shuttle communications, Goddard was responsible for NASA's IMAGER Earth-observation satellite program. "The only satellite they can pull out of the network is IMAGER-3. They say it'll take three hours to get it into trajectory."

Carmichael swore. "What about one of the radar imagers?"

The Flight Director shrugged. "Defense is recalibrating one of the Lacrosses now. But what's it gonna show us? At that focus we'd get the same bounce off a cloud of debris."

Carmichael winced. Beside him, Andrew Kohn, the stand-in EGIL—Electrical Generation and Illumination Engineer—who had been with the crew a mere month, raised his voice timidly above the babble. "What about one of the CIA's Keyhole-12's, Bob?" he asked. "They could give us insight, couldn't they?"

Ewell looked over at Matt Connor, the grizzled old SD Adviser who had been one of the first of the stunned Space Station Control Room staff to race into Shuttle ficker one. He hardly knew Connor, beyond the four or five mission planning meetings they had both sat in on, but he had already got a powerful sense of the attachment the old man felt for Reynolds, the detective who was up on ISS. It was plainly visible on the stocky adviser's face now; Connor's facial muscles were twitching with the effort of suppressing his anguish.

*Who had been on ISS,* Ewell thought, correcting himself. The horrific explosion of the station—that incredible, mushrooming inferno of blast and flame that had raced towards *Endeavor*'s cameras and ended in ominous, static-filled blackness—flashed before his eyes again.

One thing was certain: Reynolds wasn't on ISS anymore.

"What do you say, Matt?" he asked tactfully. "You're with Security. You sit on Defense Affairs with them. What're the chances of the CIA lending us its eyes?"

Connor stared at him a moment before collecting himself. He shook his head. "Forget it," he growled. "All you'll get will be a blank look when you mention the name and a 'no comment.'" He shrugged. "Besides, most of the Keyhole-12s are on polar orbits. It'd take longer to get them positioned than IMAGER."

Scowls broke out here and there among the gathered staff. "Damn those assholes," Renton, the Payloads Officer, raged. "They can read the print on the paper Gaddafi wipes his ass with. But can the bastards help us when we need it?" Mutters of assent started.

"Okay, people," Ewell said sharply. "Let's stick to discussing the possible, shall we?" He understood the grumbling—Christ, his team was angry and scared, looking for something, anything, to vent their frustration on. But they had to hold it together. Who knew what was happening, up there with *Endeavor?* Maybe her crew *were* already gone—blown to eternity in the blast, or snuffed out in one instant of explosive decompression. Maybe they were dying even now, trapped in *Endeavor*'s leaking cabin, or spiraling out from the orbiter in hastily donned EMUs, each crippled with caisson disease and on their way to a lonely and helpless death. But if they were alive, their only chance of survival might be for Mission Control to find some way of breaking through and regaining control of the orbiter. Ewell and his team couldn't afford to give in to despair.

"We can't let this get to us, people," the Flight Director said, faking a confidence he didn't feel. "Our people up there are depending on us, okay? Now, we're gonna find a way out of this, and we're gonna win through and we're gonna bring those boys and girls back home safe and sound. Does everybody understand?''

The faces around him were uneasy, wanting to believe, yet finding themselves unable. Ewell had just opened his mouth to give them another stiffening shot when his belt comm unit beeped, distracting his attention. He punched himself back into the command channel. "Yep, FLIGHT," he said. "What've we got?"

"FLIGHT, CAPCOM." Emily Tranh's voice buzzed in Ewell's earpiece. "We're picking up something on Ku-band."

The Flight Director's eyes shot to the front-room screens. They were still blank. Not video then. "What is it?" he almost barked.

"Ground Station White Sands reports intermittent weak signal to TDRS-East. Looks like someone is running the acquisition routines, FLIGHT. Manually."

Relief flooded Ewell. He nearly wept—tears of gratitude that his next words could be true, rather than the lie he had thought them to be. "You hear that, people," he said heartily, addressing the crew members gathered around him. He could see from their faces they had.

"*Somebody*'s alive up there."

9:58 A.M., Day 86, Expedition Time
Docking and Stowage Module, International Space Station

Reynolds's world shattered. Shards of disparate perception flew crazily through his consciousness, forming no coherent whole.

Sound.

His ears were filled with the roar of ISS's explosion, a throaty rumble that rolled on and on and on. It was illusion, though—even in his distracted state Reynolds knew that. Once you were out in vacuum, with no medium to carry the sound waves, *nothing* got into the suit from outside. The world could be ending, right below your feet, and you'd never know unless someone told you over the intercom. The roar must be in his imagination. Either that or his eardrums had split.

Feeling.

Tumbling, smashing, a few microseconds of the most overwhelming pressure Reynolds had ever felt. A succession of sharp, flaring pains, as his body was flung back and forth within the suit. The contusions were nothing compared to the punishment the Titan was taking, Reynolds knew. He didn't pause to wonder if the suit was going to be able to stand up to it though. There was no time.

Vision.

Reynolds's world was submerged in the orange of ISS's hydrogen- and oxygen-fueled inferno. He kept waiting for the color to fade, to drop back to the black of space as he either shot out into vacuum or died, but all it did was change subtly, shifting from brilliant orange to harsh yellow-white. For a few seconds he thought his retinas had been scarred, burned by the brilliance of the explosion. Then he realized.

He was out in space. ISS's orbit had rolled into its sunlit phase. The yellow-white was the flooding light of the sun.

Reynolds closed his eyes and let himself drift, concentrating on sorting through the jumbled impressions. What had happened?

*The explosion blew the weakest parts of the hull. It must have blown the Transfer Compartment. And you with it.*

He was amazed to find himself alive. He could remember clearly the split-second sensation of being jammed against the Transfer Compartment wall, feeling immense pressure bearing down even through the shell of the Titan, certain he was going to die. He opened his eyes and ran a quick visual on the suit. Nothing. A patchwork of cracks, souvenir of Matchev's attentions, starred his faceplate, but it seemed to be holding. The Titan's previously shiny alloy surface was scorched black and there was a definite buckle in the lower left arm, but that was it. All the suit systems seemed to be functioning normally. Evidently he had been blown out before the heat, or the impact, could do major damage.

Lucky that. Except that now he was right back where he had been, marooned in the tiny pressure capsule of his space suit, with just as much life left as the digital readout on his oxygen gauge would allow.

And this time there wasn't even any ISS to get back to.

Reynolds craned his head within the helmet and squinted. Slowly, his eyes adjusted and he was able to see details of the incredible scene.

ISS was no more. For a moment, Reynolds wasn't even able to pick where the station *had* been—space for as far as he could see was one glittering cloud of shattered debris. Pieces of it passed Reynolds—hull metal, glass, crystalized fluid—some slowly, some so blindingly fast they would have punched through his suit like bullets if they had hit. Gradually, larger fragments of the station became visible—a wheeling length of the truss, curved sections of hull ripped loose in the blast. Reynolds's heart leaped at the sight of a segment—the Russian Research Module he thought—that seemed intact. *Christ, what if it's pressurized?* If the module had sealed in time to retain its atmosphere, maybe hope wasn't lost. He could make his way back to it, get inside somehow. But then the module rolled, exposing the jagged lip where its opposite side had been ripped completely away.

Reynolds sagged inside the suit. *So much for that.*

He scanned the cloud anxiously for *Endeavor*. Had the orbiter survived the blast? A gleam of white pinpointed her position for him, two miles off, and for an instant the elation was back—*She's intact! They made it clear!* He was already reaching for the Communication Mode Selector Switch when he realized something was wrong. The orbiter was tipping slowly away from him, wheeling around in a lifeless tumble. He waited for the spitting plumes of the RCS, the Reaction Control System thrusters dotted all over the orbiter's fuselage, that would mean someone onboard was correcting her attitude, someone was alive. But nothing came. *Endeavor* continued her silent, majestic roll.

The cabin was dark, too, Reynolds realized sickly. Even from this distance he should have been able to pick the cabin lights shining through the forward flight-deck windows or the two aft overheads. But they were pits of black.

Reynolds flicked the switch to the Shuttle's UHF channel and listened silently. Nothing. Not even static. The system had to be disabled.

He looked away in revulsion. *Poor bastards*. It wasn't hard to guess what had happened. *Endeavor* had been far enough away to escape the main force of the blast. But something, some fragment of ISS's disintegrating corpse, had punched through her hull. *Bang!*—explosive decompression. Game over. It would have taken the crew compartment about thirty seconds to lose its atmosphere, sucked out into greedy vacuum. James and his crew wouldn't have had a chance.

Reynolds slumped back in his suit. It was all over. He was gone, marooned in silent orbit with several billion dollars' worth of now-shredded, useless space junk. The sole survivor. The last one left alive.

For a while, anyway.

Despair savaged him. A moment later he began to laugh, great roaring gusts that echoed through his suit. He tried to stifle them, but they kept getting louder and louder, until finally his helmet was *ringing* with them, an insane chorus crowding through his ears into his brain.

*The last one out,* he gasped to himself. *The last man off the station.*

A generic flight-attendant voice ran through his mind. *Will the last man off the station remember to turn off the lights? Please?*

Well, he'd well and truly done that, hadn't he? Turned off the lights?

Abruptly the laughter stopped and Reynolds was left in silence, shooting noiselessly from the point of ISS's explosion within his arc of accompanying debris. He felt tired, deflated. To die like this, after everything he had been through, seemed ridiculously anticlimactic. He watched the glittering shards of metal and glass around him impassively. Some were edging closer, others sliding imperceptibly away. A thousand trajectories, each differing by some minute fraction that would gradually pull them miles apart—until, months later, they got caught in gravity's embrace and plunged into fiery obliteration. How many of them would still be with him, he wondered, four hours from now, when his oxygen ran out?

Reynolds let his body hang loosely in the Titan as he shot along. He was turning only slowly; the explosion had flung him out almost straight this time. But the roll was enough to edge the Earth, hundreds of miles below, into the rim of his faceplate. He watched silently as the vast blue orb slid lazily into view. Fuck, she was beautiful; there was no denying that. Even now, when he knew it was the last time, he would die looking at her.

How peaceful, to just lie there watching! To give it all up—fear, worry, hope—and let yourself drift.

Reynolds twisted himself around for a better view. It was hard going—the Titan's waist joint was so efficient there was virtually no friction to push against. He had to swing his arms awkwardly to generate enough momentum to carry himself around. The movement of his arms brought a flash of yellow before his eyes. Reynolds stopped midswing, staring at the object in his right hand stupidly. It took him a moment to realize what it was.

*The fire extinguisher. You grabbed it just before the Transfer Compartment blew.*

What had he wanted with the fire extinguisher? Reynolds tried to think. His mind was sluggish, still mired in its nirvana of despair. Why had he grabbed the little cylinder?

*For propulsion,* he told himself. *You took it so you'd have some way of getting back.*

Reynolds shrugged mentally. *Getting back? To what?* ISS was currently scattered over fifty or sixty cubic miles of space. *Endeavor* was blown. There was nothing left to get back to.

He dismissed the arm, moving it down to his side and letting it hang. He almost opened his fingers too, to let the cylinder drift away. There was, after all, no point in keeping it.

Something stopped him though, keeping his fingers locked tight on the slender bottle. He puzzled over that, sleepily, as he rocketed along. Why wouldn't he allow himself to let go?

There *was* a point to getting back, Reynolds seemed to recall. Only he couldn't remember what it was. Something not about him. About somebody else.

*Irina,* he told himself savagely. *Irina is the point.*

The thought galvanized Reynolds like a shot of pure adrenaline. His eyes shot fully open, his mind cleared instantly. He clasped the extinguisher to his chest fiercely and began scanning the wreckage for signs of the *Soyuz.*

Irina was the point. Her and her COSMONAUT buddies. Reynolds peered through his crazed faceplate anxiously. Had Irina made it away? He didn't think so, not if the impact he'd felt had been anything to go by. But he had to make sure.

And then there were the others.

How many? At least one—what had Irina called him? Gregory? Gennady? But she'd said six. That left four, if Irina and her unborn child really were dead. *And Alinov said sisters,* Reynolds remembered. Irina's brothers and *sisters.* That meant at least two of the others had to be female. Two females. That might not be enough—each one of them would have to bear at least five children to get a viable population going. But what if it was?

Sweat broke out on Reynolds's brow. He *had* to get back to *Endeavor.* Not for his sake. For humanity's.

Reynolds studied the wreckage of ISS feverishly. He was the only one who knew—about Leonid and Irina, about Alinov. About COSMONAUT. He had to get back to the orbiter, if only to leave a message. Hook up the S-band and tell Ground directly. Or, if that failed, scrawl a message on something, somewhere in the cabin. At least that way they would find it when they ran a salvage mission on *Endeavor.* At least that way they would *know.*

*There!* Reynolds spotted a fragment of the *Soyuz*— the unmistakable shape of a section of the main engine's protective collar. It was tumbling slowly through space, about a mile or so distant, he judged. There was no doubting it then. Irina had been taken care of.

Sorrow tugged at him for a moment. Visions of her, naked in his arms, trembled on the edge of forming. He pushed them away. He couldn't afford to let his emotions get the better of him. Irina had died, he had killed her, and if he had to do it again he would, a thousand times over. Reynolds was surprised at the bloody-minded savagery he sensed in himself.

*She wasn't human,* he told himself grimly. *She was . . . other.*

It sounded crazy, he could scarcely believe it even now, but killing Irina had been a matter of species survival—and that seemed to touch off something dark and primal in him. He had only to think of those repugnant, reptilian membranes, sliding opaquely over Irina's beautiful brown eyes, for his unease to be banished entirely.

Almost.

Reynolds's gaze locked onto *Endeavor,* by now a white triangle some three miles away. Cursing himself for his temporary inaction, he grabbed the fire extinguisher's slender hose and maneuvered it over his left shoulder.

*Fuck, is it going to have enough kick to get me there?*

Reynolds didn't waste time wondering. He'd know soon enough.

As it happened, the cylinder got him there with thrust to spare. He shot himself the two or three miles to *Endeavor* with carefully timed bursts, the propellant forming 200-yard rapiers of glittering, instantly frozen $CO_2$ behind him. There were just two heart-stopping moments: one when a momentary hiccup in the canister's $CO_2$ stream made him fear it had emptied, and another when he had to fire a blind, panicked stream out in front of him to avoid a huge section of the Thermal Radiator Tower, unseen until the last moment because it was wheeling through space towards him edge-on. But then he was *there,* falling in toward the rotating *Endeavor* at a yards-per-minute speed.

Reynolds fired a final, corrective stream as the Shuttle neared, then cast the cylinder away. It was useless now. Instead, he took a tight grip on the six-inch shard of metal he'd taken the precaution of grabbing from the drifting debris before he began his run.

*This* was what would get him the final few yards to *Endeavor.*

He'd figured it out earlier. Trying to hit the Shuttle's cabin directly was too risky—it was way too small a target. A better option was to aim for her broad wings, where he was now headed. But *Endeavor*'s surface wasn't studded with handholds like ISS's. It was a smooth expanse of aluminum skin clothed in thick thermal blanketing. He needed something to ensure he stuck once he hit. And stayed there.

That was where the metal shard came in.

Reynolds held the improvised blade tight in a double overhand grip. His one chance was to jam it hard into *Endeavor*'s surface the moment he hit, then *hang on.* If he missed, or couldn't hold on against his momentum, he was done for. He'd bounce off the Shuttle and back out into empty space. Or continue past her into the fiery hell of eventual reentry.

If his oxygen held out that long.

In the event, he managed better than he'd feared, although the first few seconds were a terrifying bungle. Reynolds hit some twenty feet down the port wing . . . and ricocheted straight off, his blade slashing uselessly at the out-of-reach surface. But he was saved by *Endeavor*'s majestic, starboard-to-port roll, which shortly brought the starboard wing around to smack his tumbling figure.

Reynolds jammed the metal shard in savagely, hopelessly, at this sudden chance of reprieve, and was rewarded with a THUNK! As the blade punched through *Endeavor*'s thermal blanketing and into the aluminum wing. He held on to the shard grimly as the momentum swung him into the wing and bounced him off again. Finally, he was able to work himself down, flat against the wing.

For some moments he just *held on,* not even daring to lift his head.

*Lighten up, man,* Reynolds giggled to himself, after a minute had passed. *You made it. You're safe.*

Reynolds let his grip slacken fractionally. He lifted his head, cautiously, and took his bearings. He was about three-quarters of the way out along the orbiter's starboard wing, he saw. Fortunately, he was even facing in the right direction. In front of him, no more than forty feet away, *Endeavor*'s chunky fuselage loomed. All he had to do was crawl up to it, using his shard knife as an improvised crampon.

Reynolds rested a few moments before beginning. The crawl was going to be a strenuous affair, and he had to avoid pouring too much muscular heat into his coolantless suit. The Titan was already warming distinctly, the product of his exertions. Sweat steam was beginning to fog his helmet again.

He lay there quietly, letting his muscles relax. The sense of peace he'd noted earlier, just after ISS's explosion, returned. God, it was beautiful! The orbiter shone brilliant white in the drenching sunlight. Her roll was just slow enough to be comfortable. Reynolds watched dreamily as space, stars, the cloud-shrouded Earth, all wheeled into view. Even the wreckage of ISS, appearing in dispersed clouds throughout half the cycle, was strangely appealing.

Then, before his eyes, their orbit swung them in behind the Earth, blacking out the sun. The transition was incredibly swift, as always, just a ten-second twilight that ended in the plunge to total darkness. The only light was the wispy luminance of the far-off stars. And even that was drowned out by the lag as Reynolds's eyes adjusted.

Reynolds lolled a moment more, enjoying the absolute blackness, then roused himself. *Okay, bud. Show's over.*

He released his left hand carefully and used it to snap on his helmet light array. Three beams of white xenon light washed over the wing in front of him. Then he began the long crawl up to *Endeavor*'s fuselage.

The technique was simple. Reynolds wiggled the jagged blade out of the wing cautiously, holding his left hand there ready, and jamming it into the unplugged hole immediately the shard was free. That way, he was only without a handhold a split second each time. Then he pushed himself along to the maximum of his left arm's extension, and plunged the blade in again. And the process was repeated.

Reynolds was surprised how quickly he progressed.

He was nervous at first, uncomfortably aware the slightest slip could see him marooned back out in space. But as the steps went by, each one drawing him along a good four feet, without a hitch, his confidence grew and he started reaching ahead to stab with his right hand before his left was even in the vacated gash. Within two minutes he was at the fuselage, his blood singing with the rhythm of his hand-over-hand progress.

He scouted the orbiter's blanketed fuselage for the best path, eager to continue. *C'mon, man, let's go, let's go.* The climb was strangely exhilarating. Like rock climbing, only for higher stakes. And without a safety line.

He was raising a sweat, though. Reluctantly, Reynolds forced himself to pause, let the heat in his body settle. He glanced back over *Endeavor*'s wing, charting his progress. The seven or eight gashes in the wing's upper were plainly visible, a cat's trail of slashed paw prints, starting forty feet out. Reynolds felt a surge of irresponsible glee at the sight of the vandalism—*Christ, pal, how much you think each one of those love bites is worth? A hundred thousand dollars? Two hundred?* He wondered, if he wasn't able to reestablish contact, what the salvage crew astronauts would make of them.

At the very least, they'd solve the riddle of how he'd managed to get into *Endeavor*'s cockpit.

That sobered him. Conscious he still had a job to do, Reynolds wiggled the shard free of its puncture and, plunging it through the blanketing and the aluminum skin-stringer panel on the nearest fuselage section, resumed his forward crawl.

**Mission Elapsed Time: 5 days, 0 hours, 38 minutes**
**Airlock, Space Shuttle *Endeavor***

Rodriguez's head whipped around in terror.
*What was that?*
He listened hard, head cocked at the darkness, though he knew it was stupid; there was no way he could *hear* anything from outside. Not from the vacuum of space. Sure enough, the only sounds were the moans and rag-

ged breathing of Roberts, floating semiconscious beside him. But *something* was happening out there. He could feel it. That little vibration . . . Rodriguez put his hand out hesitantly to the curved airlock wall . . . there! He held his breath, waiting for it to repeat. Seconds passed, then—bang!—there it was once more. Several seconds later, again. Something was striking the hull at regular intervals. Too rhythmically to be debris.

Rodriguez jerked his hand away as if cut. *Something's out there,* he thought crazily. *Something's crawling over the hull.*

Waves of terror broke on him. He thrashed stupidly within the tiny cylindrical airlock, bashing himself, and Roberts, into the aluminum walls. Every ounce of the claustrophobic horror he'd been trying to stifle for the past half hour—since the explosion had blown radio contact with the flight deck and, Rodriguez guessed, the Crew Compartment itself, trapping the two of them in the airlock—burst forth. It took Roberts's strangled cry as she hit the wall to bring him back to his senses.

*Calm down,* he ordered himself. He sucked a few slow, deliberate breaths. His racing heart slowed.

Rodriguez groped through the darkness for Roberts, as much to take his mind off the unnerving vibration as anything. He located her near his feet, doubled up against the hatch where his flailing had pushed her. He drew her up guiltily. The female astronaut had been knocked unconscious by the explosion; tactile examination—their flung bodies had smashed all the airlock fluoros—had revealed her collarbone was broken as well. She was bleeding from some indeterminate place too, Rodriguez knew, because every now and then his face would be splashed by a warm droplet and his nostrils would fill with the coppery smell of blood.

He arranged her lengthwise beside him, grasping the waist of her cooling garment to keep her from bumping into the airlock wall. Groping through the darkness for her wrist, he took her pulse. It was weak, but steady, indicating she was moving out of shock. *That's good,* he thought, releasing the wrist. The blood loss wasn't serious. Roberts was going to live.

As long as he would, at least.

The thought plunged Rodriguez into terror once more, this time that the $O_2$ in the airlock was running down. Before he could stop himself, he'd grabbed at his suit, floating behind him, and stabbed the purge valve on the chest control unit. He sobbed as he listened to the hiss from the suit's secondary oxygen cylinders. Ridiculous, he knew. The airlock held 150 cubic feet of oxygen— even with his thrashing it would take them over an hour to deplete that. But Rodriguez could *feel* the carbon dioxide building silently, choking them. He kept the finger jammed on the valve, panting, until shame overcame him and he let it slip off.

The airlock fell back into silence.

"Why me?" Rodriguez screamed, suddenly angry. The shout rang around the tiny chamber. He kicked the wall. Roberts was unconscious, James and Kennedy, he guessed, dead. All the mission specialists, the fully trained astronauts, out of action. That left him, Eli Rodriguez. But he was just a payload specialist—a trained monkey for Boeing, if the truth be told—sent up to make sure SOHO II was fixed up right. Sure, he'd had his ass dipped in the Neutral Buoyancy Pool, fucked around in the Single System Trainers. But training? Real, serious, contingency-handling training? Forget it. They might as well have sent that trained monkey, when it came to an "incident" like this.

Rodriguez shivered. *Incident.* The NASA euphemism suddenly seemed a monstrous incongruity. He was trapped in a tiny aluminum tube with an unconscious fellow astronaut, the two of them steadily breathing their way through a finite oxygen supply. Even if he dismantled and bled the EMUs' primary $O_2$ tanks, they'd still have a maximum four hours before the $CO_2$ built to poisonous levels. No help was coming. ISS was gone; at least Rodriguez imagined that was the meaning of Kennedy's last, truncated shriek—"GROUND, MY GOD, SHE'S BL . . ." *Endeavor*'s pilot and commander were both dead. Probably. There was nothing he could do but lie there and wait to die.

*That's an incident all right,* he thought bitterly. *A fucking grade-A incident.*

A strange gurgle from Roberts brought him out of
the reverie. He pulled the limp woman to him. Was she
choking? It was impossible to tell in the darkness. Rodriguez cursed the smashed lights, again, until it dawned
on him there was a perfectly working light source right
behind him. Grappling with his suit, he flicked the switch
on the chest-mounted control module. The helmet light
array leapt into life, flooding the cylinder with white
light. Rodriguez got his eyes shut just in time, opening
them cautiously, bit by bit, until they'd adjusted to the
glare.

He rolled Roberts gently in front of the beams and
studied her. Whatever had been obstructing her air pas-
sages had cleared; her breathing was back to normal.
Her skin was pale and clammy though, her closed eyelids
smudged with bruising. Rodriguez lifted one with a
thumb, exposing a blue eye. The pupil contracted instantly at the light. Rodriguez released the eyelid. *That's
good,* he thought. It meant Roberts's coma wasn't deep.
She would wake soon.

*Poor girl.*

Rodriguez unbuttoned her flight suit neck gingerly,
checking the break he'd earlier felt. The sight of it almost made him gag. Her right collarbone had snapped
clean—he could tell because the outer length had
pierced skin and was protruding a good two inches. The
jutting bone glowed unnaturally white under the xenon
lamps. Blood seeped from the purple sphincter of flesh
clinging to its base. Rodriguez closed the flap in revulsion. Poor Roberts. She'd be in agony when she awoke.

There was nothing he could do for her either. No way
he could stop the bleeding, not on a wound like that.
Just try and keep her from drifting into the walls, that
was all. At least he had light now. But after a few seconds of looking at the airlock walls, mere inches away,
claustrophobic terror began to crowd Rodriguez worse
than it had before, when he couldn't see. He switched
the helmet lights off, drowning the chamber in blackness
again. Then he lay in the dark, despairing, "listening"
with a hand on the cylinder wall to the strange, rhythmic
vibration from *Endeavor*'s hull.

Reynolds paused at the top of *Endeavor*'s hull to let his
body heat settle again. He'd made remarkable time—
less than ten minutes from wing to cabin, he estimated—
and now was just an arm's length from the aft flight-
deck windows. But the heat in his suit was definitely
building. Besides, there was no hurry. Not now he was
here.

He lay quietly, anchored to *Endeavor* by the gash he'd
torn in her, studying her aft flight-deck windows. They
punctured the orbiter's white skin like fang marks. The
right one glinted with light bounced from his helmet
array, but the left was a pit of black. Reynolds guessed
it was blown. He raised his head to look closer. Sure
enough, the three layered panes of glass were gone, reduced to shards lining the grooved seals. The hull
around it was crumpled and discolored.

Reynolds grimaced. So that was where *Endeavor* had
taken the hit—in about the worst place imaginable. The
shuttle's pressure panes were tempered, high-grade alu-
minosilicate glass, two inches thick in combination, and
machined to tolerances of 8,600 psi and 800 degrees
Fahrenheit. But even they had been unable to withstand
a direct hit from what looked like about a hundred
pounds of metal, traveling at hundreds of miles per hour.
Probably the fragment hadn't broken the three panes,
not completely. Just weakened them enough for the
Crew Compartment's pressure to blow them.

Either way *Endeavor* would have lost her atmosphere
too quickly for the crew to do anything. Reynolds was
in no doubt about what he was going to find inside. He
steeled himself for the sight. *Four stiffs. James, Kennedy,
Roberts and Rodriguez. Four Gary Myerses . . .*

He pulled himself level with the left window and
probed the cavity with his helmet xenons. The lights revealed chaos—equipment, cabin fixtures and shards of
glass and metal wheeling crazily through the beams. Sure
enough, Reynolds caught a flash of blue—a flight suit.
He watched, nauseated, as the corpse slid into view. It

was James. The commander was totally recognizable.
Apart from the collapsed and puddled eyes, and the tell-
tale decompression welts, his face was intact, a lifeless
caricature of the man Reynolds had last seen four days
before. Reynolds's light array caught a glint of ice crystal
as James rolled—the corpse was frozen. That must have
been what averted the total boil down Myers's corpse
had suffered, Reynolds decided. Without the radiating
heat of ISS to prevent it, the corpse had frozen solid at
the first icy blast of vacuum.

*Some consolation,* he thought, turning away in revulsion. *Poor bastards.*

When he could face the sight again he started on the
job of clearing the remnant glass. He knew the twenty-
five-square-inch window, designed as a backup emergency egress, was big enough to get in and out of easily—Christ, he'd done so in enough sims. But what about
with his suit on? Was he still going to be able to squirm
through? Reynolds wasn't sure. He couldn't remember
the Titan's profile. All he knew was it was going to be
a tight fit. And that he'd better clear the glass from the
hole's edges.

He smashed his gloved fist against the window lips
again and again, past caring about the chance of
breaching his suit. Besides, after everything the suit had
been through, he was starting to think Allison was right,
the fucking thing was indestructible. As he bashed away,
he wondered what he'd do if he wasn't able to squeeze
through. Scratch a message on the right-hand window, or
somewhere on the scorched surface of his Titan? Wedge
himself in so that he'd be found, legs sticking out into
space like some kind of cosmic perp, frozen in the middle of a B & E?

The ludicrousness of the image redoubled his determination. He was going to get through. That was all there
was to it.

The glass was coming away, he saw, splintering along
preweakened fault lines under the impact of his hammering fist. He transferred his attention to the opposite
side of the hole, so intent on what he was doing he
almost missed the peculiar vibration.

Reynolds's fist stopped midswing.

*What was that?*

He wondered if he'd really felt it. The tiny vibration through the hand anchoring him to *Endeavor*'s hull. It was hard to be sure. Even with their silicon-rubber fingertips, the Titan's gloves were about as sensitive as a leather condom.

Reynolds held his striking glove motionless and tried to concentrate. Would it be repeated? Sure enough, a second later, his anchoring hand felt it again—a tiny tremor passing through the aluminum hull.

Reynolds frowned, trying to work out what it was. Obviously not an echo. *Temperature variation?* he wondered. The groan of structural metal readjusting load as it shrank or expanded?

*Or . . .*

Reynolds tried an experimental bang. After a short interval an answering vibration came. Reynolds then smashed his fist into the metal twice in rapid succession. He held his breath as he waited. Sure enough, a second later, *two* distinct vibrations buzzed through the fingertips of his glove.

Reynolds's mind reeled. *Fuck. Somebody's alive in there.*

How was that possible? There was no airtight seal between the flight deck and the middeck. If the Crew Compartment was blown, it was *all* blown. There was nowhere on the orbiter to hide.

Then it hit him. *The airlock.* Hadn't he heard Kennedy call out psi values for lock pressure at one stage? Somebody—Rodriguez or Roberts, Reynolds guessed, probably both—must have been suiting up in there when ISS blew. The sealed chamber had obviously saved their lives.

He crashed his fist against the metal lip three times to test the theory. Right on cue, a second later, three vibrations came back.

No doubt about it. *Somebody* was alive in there.

Reynolds was almost sorry for them. At least the others had gone quickly. Whoever was in the airlock had bought another hour of life—four or five if they bled

the EMUs' $O_2$ dry. And at the end of it a half hour of
sheer hell—pounding headaches and desperate heaving
as oxygen-starved lungs fought to wring the last
breathable milliliter from the poisoned air.

He turned back grimly to the task of clearing glass,
ignoring the succession of pleading vibrations he felt
through his left glove. He could sense the fear of whoever was trapped in there, the desperate desire not to
lose contact. But there was nothing he could do for
them, not right now. He had to stay focused on the job
at hand.

Letting Connor know.

Pulling the last shard free, Reynolds worked himself
into position. To maximize his chance of squeezing
through, he had to align himself diagonally. He would
have to put as much force as he could into the initial
pull as well—awkward, considering he also had to ensure
his arms entered first, to give him something to lever
with if he got stuck. Gripping the opposing corners of
the hole, Reynolds let himself drift out to the full extension of his arms, then jerked savagely, pulling himself
into a dive through the hole. At the last moment he
snatched his hands away and pushed them out in front
of him.

For a moment he thought he'd made it. The Titan
scraped metal, but he was sailing through unimpeded.
Then the flared lower section of his back-mounted Portable Life Support System came into contact with the
metal lips. Reynolds ground to an abrupt halt, everything below his lower back still sticking out into space.

*Fuck!* Reynolds raged, legs and arms flailing. The
PLSS must be just too big to fit.

He pounded his gloved fists against the inside of *Endeavor*'s roof in frustration. He was utterly stuck. No
way he could go backward, not with nothing in front of
him to push against. If he couldn't force himself through,
this was where he'd stay.

Reynolds crashed his fists against the aluminum in
fury, oblivious to everything—the sweat springing to his
forehead, the heat flooding his suit. Every fiber of his
being was concentrated on smashing his way free.

Then, suddenly, he was through, driving down to the
flight-deck floor with the sensation of something tearing
behind him. Reynolds held his breath as he broke the
forward impact with his hands. Christ, had he torn the
ass out of his life-support system? He scanned the biomed readouts on the head-up display worriedly. No drop
in pressure, $O_2$ readout stable. He hadn't ripped anything vital then. Maybe just the unit's cowling.

No way to turn around and check, of course.

Reynolds shrugged the issue off and righted himself.
He probed the dark flight deck with his helmet xenons.
The chaos looked even worse inside—junk circling
everywhere, so thick it was hard to see through. He was
relieved to see tiny lights blinking, here and there,
among the banks of control buttons. That meant *Endeav-
or*'s fuel cells—the cryogenic power plants that generated
electricity by chemical combination of supercooled hydrogen and oxygen—were still on-line; the cabin lights had
been blown purely by the effect of vacuum on the tubes.
Probably the orbiter's flight systems were still working.

Not that it did him any good.

Debris flashed in and out of the narrow beams of light,
reminding Reynolds surreally of those underwater docu-
mentaries, where fish dart in and out of the diver's torch-
light. As if in macabre confirmation, James's corpse
drifted through the beams—a lazing, blue shark, locked
into an endless, purposeless cruise. Reynolds shuddered
at the glimpse he'd caught of the commander's ruined
face. No matter how many DOAs he saw it on, no matter how often he told himself it was nothing, just postmortem constriction of facial muscle, there was no
getting comfortable with that . . . expression.

That soundless scream. Locked into place. Going on
and on forever.

The sight made Reynolds wonder why Kennedy
hadn't put in an appearance. Sweeping the flight deck
with his helmet lights, he discovered the reason. The
pilot's frozen corpse was still strapped into his seat. Even
from Reynolds's position, it was plain no comforting lies
about muscle constriction would answer in Kennedy's
case. The pilot's head had frozen thrown back in an

agonized scream. His elbows were locked out wide, hands obviously scrabbling at the seat's shoulder harnesses. Kennedy had died where he sat, unable even to free himself before the vacuum had sucked him half-dry and frozen him.

Reynolds got to work. The first job might be to contact Ground, but he wasn't having Kennedy and James sit ghoulish vigil on him while he did. He pushed himself over to the seat and unbuckled the dead pilot. It was surprisingly easy to manipulate the three harness clips, even with his gloved hands—sad testament to the terror that must have disabled Kennedy. Thirty seconds, that was how long Reynolds estimated the pilot had had to get free. But he'd known he was dead for every one of them and the knowledge had thrown him into blind, mind-blowing panic.

Reynolds shivered, imagining the scene. The deafening thunder of *Endeavor*'s atmosphere roaring into space drowning the screams. Crap flying everywhere as air blasted around the cabin, seeking escape. Hands scrabbling uselessly as skin bubbled and writhed, no longer able, in the dropping pressure, to contain the heaving molecules within.

He didn't think less of Kennedy for his terror. Death from vacuum was like no other. It was . . . dissolution. The body was torn apart, molecule by fucking molecule, as you watched.

Released, the frozen corpse floated free. Reynolds towed it to the interdeck access opening, grateful that, with it trailing behind, he didn't have to look at Kennedy's face. There was a bad moment at the opening though, where the pilot's grotesque attitude—frozen seated with elbows wide—stopped Reynolds from pushing him through. Reynolds had to hug the corpse to him, hard, to straighten the frozen legs, and wrench the stiffened arms down. The dead pilot's face jammed up against his faceplate in reaction. Reynolds nearly gagged. Kennedy's eyes were the same collapsed obscenities he'd seen on James, and earlier on Myers. The soft tissues of the open, screaming mouth had swelled, then frozen, to a spongy mass of crystallized purple. Reynolds pushed

the face away hurriedly, feeding the now-straightened
corpse through the access hole.

Reynolds fought nausea, floating there for a few moments as the corpse slid out of view. *Jesus,* he thought
weakly. *A pity I won't be making it back to Motortown.*
After what he'd seen this trip, Dennison could assign
him morgue man all he liked. Nothing would ever put
him off his lunch again.

Marshaling his strength, Reynolds turned to retrieve
James's body. Raking the dark cabin with his lights, he
located the commander's drifting corpse. He pulled it to
him gently by a fold in the flight suit and maneuvered
it towards the access hole. He had to repeat the earlier
procedure—James's body had frozen with arms and legs
likewise grotesquely splayed. No doubt that was what
had kept his corpse from blasting free of the depressurizing cabin. But after the grim job of straightening, there
was no problem. The corpse slid through the access hole
like a cave diver.

Reynolds pulled himself down to follow, then hesitated. He swept the flight deck one more time with his
xenons, but it looked clear. No more corpses. Maybe
Roberts and Rodriguez really had both been in the airlock and made it through. Or maybe he'd find one of
them, or both, floating below in macabre accompaniment
to Kennedy and James.

*Only one way to find out.*

Reynolds levered himself through into the middeck.
The compartment was, if anything, more chaotic than
the flight deck. Circling debris choked it—panels ripped
from the stowage lockers, broken equipment and stores
everywhere, crystals of frozen water from the rehydra-
tion station, which had been torn loose. Reynolds caught
multiple flashes of blue flight suit in the confusion. For
a moment he had the surreal impression the middeck
was flooded with corpses—four of them, five, twenty, a
hundred—but it was just James and Kennedy, he quickly
saw, their outlines broken into a deceptive multitude by
the debris storm. Reynolds probed the cauldron with his
lights, but there was no sign of the two specialists. Reynolds shook his head in amazement. No doubt about it

then. Roberts and Rodriguez really were alive, trapped
in the airlock not five yards to his right.

Reynolds pushed through the debris, ignoring the lock
for the moment. He plucked James's body from the
maelstrom and pulled it over to the bunk sleep stations—the stacked tier of individual sleeping compartments that lined the middeck's forward bulkhead. The
compartments all had closable doors; Reynolds figured
they were the best option for a temporary morgue. They
even looked a little like one—slender aluminum boxes
with antiseptically shining, sliding metal doors. He slid
the door to the top compartment open, forced James's
corpse inside and closed it behind him. Then he fetched
Kennedy and jimmied him into the compartment below.
He kept his eyes as averted as he could during the whole
process. Only when the second door was shut did he
relax, letting himself drift until his stomach had
unknotted.

*Now to check the airlock.*

Reynolds kicked himself over to the solid, D-shaped
aluminum hatch. Its white-painted surface shone painfully bright under the xenons, intersected by the shifting
shadows thrown by the structural ridges radiating out
from the central window. He pulled himself down to the
four-inch-diameter window, trying to peer inside. It
wasn't easy. The window was so small it was hard to get
his eye and the lights to it at the same time. Reynolds
only managed it by drawing back his head and craning
it as high as he could within his helmet. He squinted,
focusing on the dim shapes he thought he saw in the
tiny window. Was that a human figure there? Or just
a shadow?

*If it's Roberts and Rodriguez,* Reynolds wondered,
*why are they cringing up the far end of the airlock like
that? Can't they see the light?*

He tapped on the hatch uncertainly. In response, one
of the shapes detached itself and squirmed through the
tiny chamber towards him. A terrified eye appeared in
the glass. Eli. No mistaking it.

Reynolds flicked the Communications Mode Selector
back to the Shuttle's UHF channel. "Eli," he rasped,

and was suddenly conscious of how dry the rising heat
was making his throat. He sucked the last water from
his drink bag and continued. "You reading me in there,
buddy? It's Reynolds." But there was nothing on the
channel, not even static. And Rodriguez didn't move,
confirming that nothing was getting through to the suits
in the airlock.

Just as he'd thought. The UHF system was disabled
somehow.

Reynolds wondered what to do. He tried waving,
though he knew it was hopeless. Eli wouldn't be able to
see, not with the only light coming from the Titan. He
shouted a couple of times—"Eli! It's me, Reynolds!"—
but that was even more ridiculous, of course. He was
about to give up and go looking for something he could
write on the window with, when he saw Rodriguez
squirm back and grab one of the EMUs. Reynolds noticed briefly that its helmet was smashed. Divining Eli's
intention, he switched his own lights off. Sure enough, a
second later, light speared out of the tiny window as
Rodriguez switched *his* suit's on.

Reynolds floated stationary as the beams played over
him. They swept his suit—Reynolds felt sure Eli would
recognize it; he'd helped him unstow it just four days
ago—then settled on his face. And stayed there. Reynolds screwed up his eyes against the glare. He wondered
why Rodriguez was keeping the light on him for so long.
*Fear,* he decided. It was as if the payload specialist
couldn't believe what he was seeing, much as he
wanted to.

Reynolds tried to grin reassuringly, but the pain that
shot through his ripped scalp reminded him he must look
pretty bad too. The blood oozing from the wound had
mixed with sweat to form a film of gore on his face,
which Reynolds could sense was also burned to blistering from the raw sun that had poured through his
visorless helmet. Add to that the starred crazing of the
battered helmet itself and it was no wonder Eli couldn't
believe what he was seeing. Or didn't want to.

Eventually, however, Rodriguez seemed persuaded,
for the light from the airlock went out. Reynolds groped

for the switch to his, temporarily blinded. When he had them back on, he saw that Eli was pointing at the dark shape in the airlock, the one that could only be Roberts. He was making some gesture—two hands jerking suddenly as if breaking a stick. Reynolds watched, mystified, until Eli bared his collarbone in the window and pointed at that. Then Reynolds understood.

He was telling him that Roberts's collarbone was broken. Reynolds sucked in his breath. *Poor Roberts.* She was going to asphyxiate—like Eli was, like he himself would—when the $O_2$ ran out. The difference was she would be in agony the whole way through.

He nodded, when he and Rodriguez had exchanged lights again, to show that he understood. Then there were a few awkward moments while the light stayed on and Reynolds wondered how to communicate anything else to Eli—what, in fact, he had to communicate. That the incredible accident that had saved Eli's and Roberts's lives was pointless—they were still going to die? That there was no hope, not for any of them? That the only reason he had fought his way back to the crippled orbiter was that he had something to tell Ground that was incredibly important, more important than their three puny lives rolled together and multiplied a million times? There was nothing to tell him, and no way to tell it either, yet the glaring light stayed square on Reynolds's face, and he could sense Eli behind it, begging him. *Beseeching* him.

*Please, Reynolds. Give me something. Some scrap of hope. Please.*

Hating himself for the lie, Reynolds raised a gloved hand and pushed its thumb up. The light from the airlock flicked on and off in ecstatic acknowledgment. Reynolds edged his face behind the point of maximum crazing in his faceplate, trying to hide it.

He didn't want Eli to see how utterly it belied the optimistic gesture.

Leaving the strobing light show behind him, Reynolds pushed his way up through the interdeck access hole to the flight deck. He made his way through the detritus to the commander's chair, the left hand of the two control

positions. Getting into it was awkward— he had to move
it back to the ten-inch limit of its adjustment before his
bulky suit would fit. Luckily, the process was motorized
and required simply the flick of a toggle at the seat's
side. Reynolds forced himself down into the chair and
secured himself with the lap harness. Then he turned his
attention to the control panels.

For a few moments he just sat, not so much staring at
the controls as *absorbing* them. That was a trick he'd
learned in the thousands of sims pilot-astronaut training
had run him through. When you were dealing with avionics systems as complicated as the Shuttle's—there
were over a thousand displays and controls within his
arm's reach—it was pointless to concentrate on specifics.
You had to relax, sink into the Zen of it. Let the orbiter
*tell* you where it was at.

He could see straight off, for instance, that *Endeavor*'s
navigation systems were totally intact. The IMU—Iner-
tial Measurement Unit—and Star-tracker systems were
both working, faithfully updating and displaying attitude
and positional data as the orbiter tumbled. The flight-
control systems, on the other hand, appeared to have
been knocked out. The three tiny CRT screens in the
orbiter's central control console, which should have been
flashing streams of green-on-green figures as data from
*Endeavor*'s five general-purpose computers coursed
through them, were blank. That meant the GPCs were
all down. That was incredible in itself, Reynolds knew,
for the five GPCs were designed to be five-ways redun-
dant—any one of them could drive the Shuttle completely on its own. But there was no time to dwell on it.

He had to figure out how to get a comm link up
with Ground.

First option was S-band. S-band radio was the Shuttle's fail-safe band—low capacity in relation to Ku-band,
but with the dual advantages that it was easier to acquire
and could communicate directly with Ground when necessary, avoiding Ku-band's reliance on TDRS satellites.
It had the added plus, in *Endeavor*'s current situation,
of four antennas positioned radially around the orbiter
and an automatic signal distribution mechanism—mean-

ing at least one antenna would always have line of sight, no matter how violently *Endeavor* was tumbling. Acquisition would have to be manual, with the GPCs off-line, but that was no problem. Reynolds flicked the Communication Mode Selector on his suit to S-band and started clicking the rotary antenna selection switch on the forward control panel through its four positions.

Nothing. Just low-level static, the background hum of empty space.

He ran it through five times, just to be sure. Still nothing. Reynolds swore. Decompression must have blown some system component; what, he had no idea. It didn't particularly matter either. The point was the band was fucking unusable.

Reynolds took a deep breath and reached over to the Ku-band antenna deploy controls. Signal acquisition in this case was going to be a supreme pain in the ass, requiring first stabilization of the orbiter, then a tricky signal-search routine.

But Ku-band it would have to be.

# 19

Every eye in the control room swung to the front-room screens, where figures were flickering, fighting to break through the static. There was no doubting it—the cyclical sweeps meant not accidental alignment but conscious attempts by *somebody* at acquisition. The Shuttle's single Ku-band antenna, located on an external assembly in the payload bay and with a beam only a fraction of the width of the fail-safe S-band, follows a set routine when acquiring the TDRS. It spirals out from the center in progressively wider cones—eight degrees, then twenty, then forty-six—until it locks on. The routine can take as long as three minutes to run, and it is not unusual—in the absence of a prior lock-in on S-band—to have to run it three or four times.

Silence reigned as everyone in the control room held their breath, willing the signal to acquire. The figures—data from *Endeavor*'s navigation, environment and propulsion subsystems—flashed ghostlike through the static, appearing more and more frequently until suddenly the static lifted and the figures began coursing down the left-hand screen, a river of yellow text on the screen's black background.

A cheer burst from every throat in the room.

Ewell joined in, elated. He could hardly believe it. Even the pulsing red shuttle icon had reappeared, traversing its way across the central screen map. Meaning the two-way Doppler the ground stations used to track the orbiter was back on-line too. Only the right-hand, video-input screen still spat white noise.

"Okay, CAPCOM," he bellowed through the exuberance. "Patch me through."

He heard the click through his earpiece as Tranh obeyed, switching the voice channel over to his input. He held up his hand for silence.

*"Endeavor,* Mission Control," he said heartily, when the noise level had abated. "I guess you know how glad we are to hear from you guys. Please advise status. How're you doin' up there?"

His earpiece burst static in response, intolerably loud at first, then quietening as Tranh pulled the volume down. *Fuck it,* Ewell swore inwardly. His eyes went to the data stream on-screen. For some reason the voice channel still wasn't up.

Disquieting news started flooding in from elsewhere too. A voice cut into the channel unidentified, breaking discipline—Kane Thurbold's, the Electrical, Environmental, Consumables Manager, Ewell realized. "Wait a minute, Bob," Thurbold said urgently. "Something's wrong. Cabin pressure reads flat as a tack. Jesus, I think we've got a breach . . ."

The response on Ewell's lips—*Copy that, EEECOM*—was drowned in the welter of calls crowding in through his earpiece.

"FLIGHT, DATA. Malfunction readout says the GPCs are down. All of them."

"FLIGHT, this is GUIDANCE. We are negative, repeat negative, on command access."

". . . copy that . . . FLIGHT, INCO reports onboard instrumentation configuration nonresponsive . . ."

"Okay, people, one at a time!" Ewell ordered, punching himself temporarily onto intercom. The channel fell into silence. He looked across at Tranh. "CAPCOM?" he asked. "What've we got? Are they reading us up there?"

Tranh, fingers flying as she cycled through channels, shook her head. "Negative, FLIGHT," she said hopelessly. "Voice link is dead both ways. Command channel too. All we've got is data downlink. Probably uplink too, if you give me a minute."

"Okay," Ewell said shortly. "See what you can do." He switched himself off-channel momentarily and rubbed his forehead in exhaustion. He felt suddenly old, unequal to the shock coming so hard on the heels of the elation of regaining contact. He peered at the figures dancing down the side screen. *Fuck.* EECOM was right, he saw. *The Crew Compartment's blown. Sucked dry.*

Ewell fought down the irrational fear spooking him. *How can that be?* he wondered. *How can someone be establishing contact . . . in vacuum?*

He turned to the staff gathered round him. The elation had disappeared from all but one or two frozen faces, he saw, replaced by puzzlement and dawning horror. "Any ideas?" he asked.

Heads shook slowly. Only Carmichael gave voice to what they were all thinking. "Gotta be somebody," he murmured. "I don't know how the hell . . . but it's gotta be somebody."

Ewell nodded. "I agree. But how do we contact them, Lew? You heard Emily. Voice is out. Both up and down."

Eyes stared at him blankly. The room had settled back into an abnormal quiet. The snap of Renton's fingers broke it.

"Got it, FLIGHT," he said. "What about TAGS? Can't we swap destinations on the data channel and send a text message to the CRT?"

Ewell cocked an appreciative finger at the Payloads Officer. "That's good thinking, Paul." The TAGS—Text and Graphics System—was the Shuttle's facsimile machine, used to transmit hard copy of procedural updates from ground to crew. The orbiter's hard copier wouldn't be working, not in vacuum. The backup option, however—transmitting text direct to the flight-deck displays—would be. With a little rerouting the data channel would allow them to have a text-to-text conversation with whoever the hell that was up there. There was a problem though, Ewell realized.

"Wait a minute." He frowned. "That'll work for

uplink, Paul. But what about the downlink? If the GPCs are down, signal processing will be too. How're they going to talk back to us?"

"Well," said Renton slowly, "I guess we could drop it back to basics. Flashlight morse." He looked up at Ewell. "You know, switch the band off for yes, leave it on for no." He shrugged. "It's primitive. But it's all we've got."

Murmurs of disbelief, even anger, broke out. Ewell could understand it. Here they were, sitting on billions of dollars' worth of the world's most advanced equipment, reduced to communicating like kids in a treehouse. Renton was right though, he realized. It was all they had.

"Okay," he said briskly. "We go with it. CAPCOM," he said, speaking into the headset mike now, "did you get that? We want you to reconfigure the data channel for transmission to the CRTs and stand by to enter text communication to *Endeavor*."

"Roger, FLIGHT," Tranh replied. "Channel rerouted. Standing by for text entry."

"Good," Ewell said crisply. "DATA, bring CAPCOM's input up on the screens."

"Copy that, FLIGHT," Kris Young, the Data Processing Engineer, replied. Seconds later, the data panels on the left-hand screen squeezed down obediently, admitting a new panel occupied by nothing more than a blinking cursor.

Ewell nodded. "Okay, CAPCOM," he said. "Message reads—*Endeavor*, Ground. Do you read us? Switch transmission off once for yes."

A hush settled back over the room as the letters materialized on-screen.

Endeavor, Ground. Do you read us? Switch transmission off once for yes.

The cursor blinked at the end of transmission—once, twice, three times. Every eye focused on the yellow-on-black data tables, beaming down from *Endeavor*'s instrumentation in three-second refresh cycles, willing them to disappear. Ewell felt his belly tighten. The tension was unbearable.

Suddenly the screens went black—totally dead—for

one second, two. Then the figures reappeared, spilling down the screens in yellow columns.

A second cheer shot through the room. Ewell shook his head, disbelieving. "Thank Christ," he muttered. "Now we've just got to find out who it is."

Carmichael materialized beside him. "Bob," he said urgently, "I've been thinking. If the compartment's blown, that's gotta be either Roberts or Rodriguez up there. They were in the airlock, right? That means they're the only ones who could have got into the suits on time."

Ewell nodded. "Good point, Lew." He scanned the screens uncertainly. "EECOM, FLIGHT," he said, addressing the Consumables Manager. "What's the story? Are we getting biomed from any of the suits?"

"FLIGHT, EECOM," the reply came back. "That's negative. I'm trying. But I can't pick any biomed data out of the stream."

Ewell looked at Carmichael. The Flight Activities Officer shrugged. "Could be the UHF is out too," he said.

"Could be." Ewell frowned. "Okay, CAPCOM," he said into his mike. "Another message. Tell 'em we're glad to hear from them first."

The words tapped up on-screen.

Good to hear from you, Endeavor.

"Now ask them if they're Roberts or Rodriguez. Start with Mel," Ewell ordered.

The letters filed on to the screen obediently.

Like to know who we're talking to. Are you Roberts? Transmission off for yes.

The control room went quiet once more, awaiting the response. Seconds passed, the figures cycled through the screens uninterruptedly.

No.

Ewell nodded in response to Tranh's questioning look.

Are you Rodriguez? the Communications Officer typed. Transmission off for yes.

Ewell sucked in a breath, awaiting the confirmation it was Eli. Several seconds later, however, the screens were still active. He let out the breath, puzzled. The control room began to buzz.

*Not Eli? Then who the hell is it?*

"CAPCOM, try James," Ewell said forcefully, raising his voice to surmount the noise. Tranh complied.

Endeavor, are you Commander James? Transmission off for yes.

Seconds passed but the screens stayed obstinately active. The murmur in the ficker got louder. Ewell nodded in response to the unasked question.

Endeavor, are you Kennedy? CAPCOM entered. Transmission off for yes.

No response. The data tables coursed down the screens undisturbed.

Ewell stared at the screen, nonplussed. Not Roberts, Rodriguez, James *or* Kennedy? How could that be?

"There's gotta be some mistake," Carmichael muttered beside him. "They can't be reading us right."

Ewell had to agree. "CAPCOM, verify *Endeavor* is still receiving," he said brusquely. He watched as the letters materialized on-screen.

Endeavor, please confirm you are still receiving. Transmission off for yes.

Ewell's eyebrows rose in surprise as the data flow promptly switched off, then back on. He tried to work it out. *Not Roberts, Rodriguez, James or Kennedy? Then who the fuck is it?* A sudden, chaotic jumbling of figures on-screen distracted him. Whoever it was on *Endeavor* was switching transmission off and on, off and on, seven or eight times in all.

Ewell, along with the rest of the Flight Control Team, watched the display, mystified. It took a wild exclamation from Lew Carmichael to break the spell.

"He wants us to keep asking," the FAO cried. "He's saying he wants us to go on." Suddenly, Matt Connor was there, pushing into place beside the Flight Director.

"Ask him if he's Reynolds," he rasped.

Ewell stared at him, uncomprehending.

"Go on," Connor repeated. "Ask him if he's Reynolds."

Ewell was too stunned to issue the instruction verbally. Instead, he gave CAPCOM the go-ahead with a wave of his hand and the words flashed up on-screen.

*Endeavor, are you Mission Specialist Reynolds? Transmission off for yes.*

There was no containing the noise in the control room this time. It broke into uproar as the figures flicked off-screen for a deliberate two seconds. Ewell groped behind for his seat and slumped into it heavily, shaking his head in disbelief. Around him, the gathered semicircle of team members stared at the screen, dumbfounded.

No one knew how. But it was Reynolds up there.

**Mission Elapsed Time: 5 days, 1 hour, 13 minutes**
**Flight Deck, Space Shuttle *Endeavor***

Reynolds waited, gloved finger poised over the Ku-band "active" switch, but there was nothing more. Just those few letters, glowing green-on-green on the tiny CRT screen.

*Endeavor, are you Mission Specialist Reynolds? Transmission off for yes.*

"C'mon, guys," he muttered, when a minute passed with no further contact. He could understand the delay—the news was taking some digesting. Presumably Shuttle Control had seen ISS's immolation, or figured it out, and they couldn't understand how he was even alive, let alone in *Endeavor*'s cockpit. But he was burning with impatience to get out the words he'd fought his way here to say.

*Matt, COSMONAUT isn't like anything we imagined. It's . . .*

*What?*

Reynolds was momentarily thrown. How could you put the enormity of Alinov's crime into words? How could he describe the horrific things the murdered Russian had done, had *made,* in mere syllables and phrases?

Reynolds was uncomfortably aware he was unlikely to even get the chance. Blocked from direct communication with ground by the malfunctioning voice channel, he could only respond to what questions they gave him. And even if he got Matt on the line, what were the chances he would ask the questions Reynolds needed?

Fat, fucking zero. That's what.

Reynolds checked the $O_2$ readout on his head-up display. Just over three hours left. He grimaced. Even that probably wouldn't be enough. They would still be stuck on—"Is the aft Reaction Control System engine fireable? Transmission off for yes . . ." when his oxygen ran out. They wouldn't even hear him die. Just pick it up from his progressively slowing responses, that final, unanswered question.

Reynolds smashed his fist against the orbiter's side window in frustration, rocking his suited body within the seat's confining straps. *Fuck!* He couldn't allow that to happen. He snapped his suit's communication Mode Selector over to Ku-band one more time, listening vainly for a signal. Still nothing. Just static. Reynolds snatched his hand away. *Goddamnit all to fucking hell,* he shouted at himself.

*Ten or twenty words to say. Three hours in which to say them. And not a chance in hell of ever getting them across.*

Scalding bile rose in his throat, merging with the burning ache of his blistered wrists and the choking heat of his suit. He watched bitterly as the letters began to appear on the tiny screen once more.

10:58 A.M., Central Standard Time, 3 April 2005
Shuttle Control Room One, Johnson Space Center

Ewell flicked his mike to intercom, to reach the crowd packed into the back of the Flight Control Room. His voice boomed out of the wall-mounted speakers.

"Okay, folks, let's have some quiet. These people have a job to do. Why don't we let them get on with doing it?"

When the room had settled back into silence, he gave Tranh a nod. The CAPCOM began typing.

MS Reynolds are you alone? Transmission off for yes.

Ewell's heart skipped a beat when it became apparent the transmission *wasn't* being switched off. He could sense the ripple of excitment that shot throught the silent crowd.

"Ask him who else is alive," he instructed the communications officer. "James, Kennedy, Rodriguez, Roberts."

The words flashed up on-screen.

MS Reynolds, who else is alive? Commander James? Transmission off for yes.

No reply. Figures streamed through the data tables, uninterrupted testament to the commander's death. After sufficient pause, Tranh resumed typing.

Pilot Kennedy? Transmission off for yes.

No reply again. Ewell could almost feel the shock invading everybody in the ficker. There was no need to *ask* for silence now.

Payload Specialist Rodriguez? Transmission off for yes.

Ewell held his beath, waiting to see if transmission broke. When it did he nearly wept. Eli was alive then. Christ, that was *something* at least. He watched as Tranh typed up the final sentence.

Mission Specialist Roberts? Transmission off for yes.

For a moment it seemed that Roberts was dead too. Transmission held, unbroken for four or five seconds, before flicking off and on so quickly the figures hardly had time to disappear from the screen.

Ewell frowned. He glanced over at his Flight Activities Officer. "What the hell was that, do you think?"

Carmichael shook his head, puzzled. "I don't know, Bob," he said. He thought it over. "Maybe he's trying to tell us she's alive, but injured," he ventured.

Ewell nodded. That was plausible. He asked Tranh to put the question up on screen.

MS Reynolds, is MS Roberts alive but injured? Transmission off for yes.

The break in transmission confirmed it. "That's good thinking, Lew," Ewell complimented the FAO. He raised his voice to address the Flight Control Team directly, as well as through the channel. "Okay, people," he bellowed. "You heard the situation. Two of our people . . . *three* of our people," he corrected himself, suddenly aware of Connor's presence, "have made it through the incident. Let's get working on an option to get them home."

Ewell had to make a conscious effort to keep the despair out of his voice. *What option to get them home?*

He turned back to CAPCOM, addressing her with a crisp confidence he didn't at all feel. "Let's get some verification of systems status first. CAPCOM, ask MS Reynolds to confirm the compartment is breached."

Ewell and the control team spent the next twenty minutes putting questions to Reynolds. As each answer came back, crudely transmitted by a broken or unbroken signal, the gloom in the ficker deepened. All the news was bad. The Crew Compartment was indeed blown. The GPCs really were offline. Flight systems really weren't responding to Ground command. The faces of Ewell's staff grew ashen as the magnitude of the disaster became clear. Despite the fact her engines and avionics appeared viable, without Ground command access *Endeavor* was a dead bird. The Flight Director could feel the pessimism cloying the control-room atmosphere, threatening to paralyze them with despair. Finally, he called a halt.

"Okay, CAPCOM," he growled, shaking his head. "That's enough." He tore his headset off and rubbed his forehead wearily. He jerked his thumb over his shoulder towards the rear of the room—a gesture instantly understood by the control-team members. *Emergency conference. Now.* All noncritical staff got up from their positions and began pushing towards the executive offices. Ewell turned to join them, issuing Tranh one final instruction.

"Tell Reynolds we gotta think about this."

**Mission Elapsed Time: 5 days, 1 hour, 47 minutes**
**Flight Deck, Space Shuttle *Endeavor***

Reynolds switched transmission off impatiently to signify understanding. He groaned in exasperation. Christ, what a vision of hell! To have to sit there and answer each and every fucking irrelevant question, unable to steer the conversation to the only subject that mattered. Now Mission Control were going off to brainstorm, trying to cobble together something, anything, to salvage the mission and save their lives.

Reynolds wanted to scream at them. *That isn't what's*

*important now, you motherfuckers! Listen to me!* But it was hopeless, of course. He might as well yell at himself.

He sat there, amid the circling debris, worrying at the problem of how to get the message to Matt. At least the orbiter was stable now—he had to fire off a series of attitudinal adjustments to get her level enough to acquire Ku-band. It was easier to think without the distraction of the Earth and stars revolving through the windows. Not that there was anything to think *of* in this case.

*Write it somewhere?* Reynolds wondered.

That was the only idea he could come up with. It was the fallback option he'd been thinking of on the way in to *Endeavor,* but he could see problems with it now. There was no guarantee NASA would be able to mount a salvage operation before *Endeavor*'s orbit decayed and plunged her into reentry. And no telling what would survive it. When you hit the atmosphere at 25,400 feet per second, the air became sandpaper, blasting even the strongest metal to molten shreds. Probably only ten percent of *Endeavor* would finally smash down to Earth.

And Reynolds had no way of knowing *which* ten percent.

He dismissed the idea and returned to the problem of how to get the message to Matt, *now,* in the three hours he had left. The swirl of debris across his faceplate began to irritate him; he switched his helmet xenons off to black it out. Then he sat in the darkness, gnawing at the problem, turning it over like the darkened Earth, rolling 350 miles below.

11:32 A.M., Central Standard Time, 3 April 2005
Executive Conference Room One, Johnson Space Center

Ewell held up his hand for silence. The conference room was packed to overflowing. Every available member of the four Shuttle control teams had been yanked in, some still in robes and pajamas. More people were arriving by the minute. It was all Ewell could do to keep a semblance of control.

When noise in the room had fallen back to a tolerable

level, he began. "Okay, people," he said. "By now most
of you have an idea of our status here. For the uniniti-
ated, we've got a crippled bird up there, with three survivors on board." Here he nodded at Connor. "One of
them the Mission Specialist from ISS." He paused,
shook his head in amazement. "It's indeterminate at this
stage how he got there, but that needn't concern us
now."

He looked around the assembled crowd, face grim.

"Now, our pilot and commander are dead. The orbiter's hull is breached, and the survivors are relying on
space-suit life support, in the case of Reynolds, and re-
tained airlock atmosphere for Roberts and Rodriguez.
We have established a very tenuous communication link,
via Ku-band, with Mission Specialist Reynolds, who is
on the orbiter's flight deck. S-band communication is
inaccessible and the Ku-band link is only partly so. That
means we can receive telemetry data, but are denied
command access to *Endeavor,* as well as voice."

He paused to let *that* bad news set in before
continuing.

"We have established as well that *all five* GPCs are
nonoperational . . ." he held up a hand again to quiet
the hubbub this provoked, ". . . for as yet undetermined
reasons." He looked around him once more. "You all
know what that means. All reentry software is inaccessible. Computer control of flight systems is negative."

Ewell pursed his lips. "That's all pretty bad, I know,"
he admitted. "But there are some pluses. One, naviga-
tional instrumentation is operational and transmitting.
We know where the orbiter is and what it's doing. Two,
avionics are apparently viable. MS Reynolds has confirmed that all aerodynamic controls—elevons, body flap
and rudder surfaces—as well as the RCS thrusters, respond to manual commands from the stick. So Reynolds
has control, even if we don't."

The Flight Director paused to weigh the effects of his
words on the gathering. The faces were long, he saw,
filled with sick disbelief that anything could be done to
retrieve the disaster. *That makes two of us,* he thought
savagely. However, he pushed on.

"Third, and best of all, it appears the SSMEs are fully operational. MS Reynolds was asked to perform gimbal tests on both main engines; he reported both checked out. The propulsion subsystem telemetry checks out too—it appears the fuel tanks have maintained integrity. So we've got juice and the thrust to use it."

Ewell leaned forward deliberately, placing his hands palm down on the huge conference table to support himself. "So, people. That's our status." He looked around at the assembled faces. "Now, how do we get them home?"

A babble of conflicting voices broke out immediately, but one boomed out over them all. It was Branson, Alternate Flight Director for Flight Control Team Three.

"Bob, this is crazy talk," Branson drawled. Like so many of Johnson Space Center's staff, Branson was an "aggie," a graduate of Texas Agricultural and Mechanical University, and a Lone Star native. Despite his domineering manner, Ewell liked him—the two of them had worked well together in past incident-management sims. Just now though, Ewell had to stifle a sorrowful shake of his head at the thought of them.

*Who'd have guessed we'd get the chance to do it for real? And in a shitrain like this?*

"Bob, it's crazy," Branson repeated, forcing his voice through the hubbub. "We all know that bird's not goin' anywhere without the GPCs. We gotta start running some diagnostics, get at least one of those boxes back on-line. Now if the five of them are out, that means it's gotta be a malfunction in the multiplexers." Branson sought out Connor with his eyes and nodded at the older man. "We can get Matt's boy up there to do a changeout and then we can start talking . . ."

The babble rose again, drowning the Texan out. Ewell raised his voice sharply to get over it. "That's a negative, Rick," he said forcefully. "Those people up there are on a time line tighter than Kelsey's nuts. Near as we can estimate they've got no more than four hours' oxygen, maybe three." He shook his head. "There's no time for diagnostics, or changeouts, or anything. Whatever we come up with, we have to get started on it *now,* with what we've got to hand."

Ewell hesitated, then plunged on, steeling himself to get the words out.

"And that means manual reentry."

The gasp that followed confirmed his hesitation. Every voice in the room fell silent under the impact of his words.

Manual reentry! The idea was . . . lunacy. Every single person in the room, Ewell included, knew how false the Shuttle's designation as a pilotable reentry craft was. In truth, it was nothing more than a sop to the astronauts who sat in the pilot's seat while the GPCs drove her. Despite her wings, the Shuttle did *not* fly through the atmosphere like an aircraft. She dropped. Like a slightly more aerodynamically designed stone.

And a fantastically complicated one at that. To get the orbiter through to slap down, the GPCs had to move her through an intricate, three-phase process that cut her speed from over 17,000 miles an hour to just below 200 and her altitude from 557,000 feet to zero, and dropped her on a three-mile runway from over 5,000 statute miles away. The computers had to juggle sink rate (how quickly the orbiter falls), attack angle (the orbiter's orientation to its direction of travel) and bank profile (how far left or right the Shuttle rolls) by the split second so as to utilize atmospheric drag to slow the craft without exceeding thermal and structural limitations and destroying her. To expect a human being to duplicate the feat was . . . well, it wasn't anything.

You just didn't do it.

Paul Chen, FIDO for Control Team Two, gave voice to the stunned disbelief. Chen was one of the crew that had been pulled off sleep-shift—his shock of black hair was mussed and he had a checked silk robe gathered round him. "Bob," he choked, "that . . . we can't . . . that's impossible." He shook his head in amazement. "Leaving aside everything else, have you considered that we'll be out of radio contact the whole way down? If all we've got is Ku-band . . ." He shrugged helplessly. "Well, Reynolds is going to have to dump that at reentry. That means no way to send him trajectory plots until he hits ground. When it's too late."

Ewell nodded calmly. "I'm aware of that, Paul." Chen

was right, of course. The Ku-band antenna stuck out
from the orbiter a good seven feet when deployed, which
was one reason it was only useable in orbit. If left un-
stowed during reentry, it would be ripped loose at the
first touch of rasping atmosphere. "I'm thinking whatever plot we give him has to be transmitted before reentry interface."

Another shocked silence resulted. Chen was, once
more, the one to give it voice.

"Bob," he said, shivering as he pulled the gown tight
around him, "you're talking about dropping *Endeavor*
4,000 miles through reentry to where we can acquire
her for TAEM guidance, *without* Digital Auto Pilot and
*without* even the ability to advise the operator of revised
trajectory parameters on the way down?" He shook his
head despairingly. "We all know the Shuttle can't do
that. Especially with a nonpilot on board . . ."

"HE'S NOT A NONPILOT."

Connor's voice rasped out suddenly, stopping Chen
dead. Every eye shot to the security adviser.

"He's not a nonpilot," Connor repeated brusquely. "I
trained that boy up there myself in '89. He was the best
in the intake, let me tell you. If anybody can bring that
bird down, it's Reynolds."

A moment's silence followed. Nobody dared voice the
thought going through all their minds. *Twenty years . . .*

"Point taken, Adviser Connor," Chen said diplomatically. "Let me rephrase that. Even the best pilot in the
world couldn't do it. The TAEM acquisition zone is,
what, fifty-two miles in diameter? So Reynolds has to
aim for a fifty-two-mile spot from 4,000 miles away, and
get it right the first time? That's like trying to park a
bus on a dime."

The gloomy silence that followed showed the sense of
the gathering. Chen was right, everyone could see that.
No matter that Ewell was too, that manual reentry was
their only option. The point was it couldn't be done.

"What about a water abort?" Connor interjected.

Disbelief rippled through the room. One or two voices
erupted in open scorn.

"I'm serious," the security adviser growled. "Why

don't we get Edge to bring your bird down in the Pacific? Hell, it's the biggest goddamned thing on Earth—no way Edge isn't going to be able to hit it. In fact, you might have trouble believing it, but Reynolds has already done it. He ran a sim on it in the Systems Trainer, back in '83. Did it for a bet with Kenny Musgrave. They bet each other fifty bucks they couldn't hot-stick the Shuttle down to intact splashdown from orbit."

Connor shook his head, grinning at the memory.

"Well, Kenny didn't—he trimmed his angle of attack too far and fried himself at 200,000 feet." He looked up at Ewell, around at the faces in the room. "But Reynolds did. He brought her down without a hiccup." He shrugged. "He can do it, I tell you. He really can."

The room erupted with competing voices. Branson fought to get his voice above the babble. "Bob," he said, "none of us are disputing Adviser Connor's boy's good. Maybe he really can do it. I don't know. But one thing I do know is there ain't a pilot alive who could ride that bird once she hits. Has Adviser Connor thought about that? That baby's gonna splash down at 600, even 700 miles an hour. Now, I gather our two crew members are trapped in that airlock, and at least one of the two ain't gonna be able to get out. That's what your people got out of Reynolds, right?" he asked Ewell. "There's only one useable suit in the lock?"

Ewell nodded in confirmation.

"So," Branson continued, "there'll be no using the crew escape pyros to blow themselves clear of the bird. They'll have to ride her through to zero velocity. Now, okay, suppose Reynolds is able to do his final flare, burn the engines and bring his glide slope back to near zero," he turned to Connor, "but you tell me, Adviser, how your boy's gonna stop *Endeavor* from flipping and tearing herself to pieces once she hits? At 600, hell, even *500 or 400* miles an hour?"

Connor chewed his lip contritely. "I don't know, Flight Director," he was forced to admit. "I've been trying to figure that." He shrugged. "All I know is Reynolds can get it to that point safely."

The room buzzed with frantic discussion, opinions and

exclamations. During a lull, a voice addressed Ewell from somewhere in the crowd.

"Bob? Can I just say something?"

It took Ewell a moment to pick out the speaker—Phil Brady, Propulsion Engineer for Team Four. "Go ahead, Phil," he said.

Brady hesitated. "Well, I won't say anything about the plan, Bob. I think it's crazy, to tell the truth. But if we're gonna do it, and keeping the orbiter stable enough for a deceleration guide through the water is the issue, I can think of a way."

Discussion in the room ceased and every eye went to him. Brady blinked uncertainly at the sudden attention, then continued.

"Couldn't we trim the orbiter's angle of attack back to, say, ten degrees once the flare has brought the glide slope down and drop her into the water ass first. Then we could gimbal the SSMEs out full and fire them at the moment of impact. That should hold her tail down and keep her from flipping."

The gathering was silent, trying to digest this. Ewell frowned. "Sorry, Phil," he said. "We're not with you."

Brady stood up and stepped over to the white board rapidly. "Like this, Bob," he explained, slashing the board hurriedly with the marker he found there. "Say the orbiter goes into final flare at about 1,750 feet; the main engines fire and thrust her forward, reducing her glide slope from minus nineteen or twenty degrees— whatever it will be—down to the approach angle, minus three degrees."

He sketched a crude orbiter, gliding down a steep line, then bottoming out to glide level atop some scrawled waves.

"We have to flatten the angle of attack to about three degrees to do that, right?"

He dashed off a winged figure whose nose was a whisker above its tail.

"Well, normal procedure would be to hold that angle of attack into splashdown, wouldn't it? But Rick is right, *Endeavor* will tumble the moment she touches. Suppose instead . . ."

Here he drew another orbiter, dropping down into the waves with its tail a good couple of inches lower than its nose.

". . . Reynolds brings her in at about a ten-degree angle of attack, and gimbals the engines up the full six degrees . . ."

Brady drew a cone, pointing slightly upwards and spouting crude flames, at the back of the figure.

". . . and fires both again at the impact point—that should provide enough thrust to keep *Endeavor*'s ass jammed in the ocean while she skids." He looked up at Ewell, around at the faces in the room. "Get my drift? There's six thousand pounds of thrust in each of those engines, and if we don't do a vent, we can keep enough fuel to do a three- or four-minute burn. That should be enough for the ten or twelve miles it's gonna take *Endeavor* to lose her velocity. See what I mean?"

The room broke into uproar. A hundred voices fought to express disbelief, scepticism, derision.

"I think everybody sees it, Phil," boomed Branson, through the hubbub. "They just don't believe it. Bob, this is a five percent option if ever I heard one . . ."

"Rick's right, Bob," interjected somebody—Ewell couldn't see who. "It's crazy. How the hell are we going to make calculations about the rebound force? He'll be firing blind . . ."

Brady shrugged, and said something, but his words were lost in the welter of competing voices.

Ewell blocked the cacophony out, trying to find a quiet spot within himself in which to think. The decision would come down to *him*. No matter what advice anybody gave, it would be his call.

He tried to reason it through. Branson was right of course. It *was* an option with five percent chance of success, maybe less. The logic was compelling though. No time for anything but manual reentry. And no hope of any sort of manual touchdown except a water abort. He tried to assess the feasibility of Brady's plan. Would Reynolds really be able pull it off? Bring her down to a flat glide slope, then suddenly drop her attack angle and fire the main engines, all at exactly the right moment?

Maybe.

But would it really counteract the terrible force the impact was going to generate and stop the orbiter from digging in and smashing itself to pulp? There was no way of knowing, not without running about a million sims that they couldn't possibly get the time to even start.

Above all, he was conscious that a decision had to be made, and made quickly. The clock was ticking up there, and if they were going to have the remotest hope of saving the lives of *Endeavor*'s remaining crew they would have to get started. Now.

*Time for some executive action, pal.*

Ewell cleared his throat. The gesture had a magical effect, the room falling silent almost immediately. "Okay," he said quietly. "Phil, you've got something there. That's good work."

He raised his voice and began firing off commands. "Okay, people, this is how it is. We're going to go with manual reentry; we're going to bring *Endeavor* down to a water landing, using Phil's technique, and we're going to make it work. We are, I repeat *are,* going to bring all three of those people down alive."

He shot a finger at Kim Williams, his team's Flight Dynamics Officer, then at Dan Engel, his Propulsion Engineer, then at Lew Carmichael.

"Kim," he snapped, "I want a trajectory plotted immediately for the first available entry interface window. Dan, I want you running sims to work out how much burn Reynolds is likely to need for Phil's plan, and what speed we'll need the orbiter ramped down to to make it work. Lew, I want you to get on to Navy Command Pacific immediately and notify them. Find out what they've got in the target area, and how fast it can be there. Tell them we want a chopper team with full medivac facilities at the scene within twenty minutes of touchdown."

The three team members started hurrying out, accompanied by their alternates from other teams.

Ewell watched them leave, then turned his attention back to the room. "The rest of you know what you have to do," he told the crowd, surveying them grimly. Chairs began to scrape and the meeting to break up. Ewell pushed himself off the table, and turned to leave himself.

"Now," he said, searching out Connor with his eyes. "Let's go let Reynolds in on the secret."

Mission Elapsed Time: 5 days, 2 hours, 1 minute
Flight Deck, Space Shuttle *Endeavor*

The scrolling of the green-on-green text woke Reynolds. He stared at it a few moments, uncomprehending.

Reynolds, you still with us? Transmission off for yes.
Reynolds, you still with us? Transmission off for yes.
Reynolds, you still with us? Transmission off for yes.
Reynolds, you still with us? Transmission off for yes.

Then it hit him. Christ, he'd fallen asleep again, sitting there in the dark, wrestling with the problem of how to get his message through. He scrabbled for the "active" button, going for the switch to his helmet lights at the same time.

*Fuck.* He wondered how long he'd been out.

His eyes went to the $O_2$ readout on his head-up display. Just under three hours left. Reynolds relaxed. Not too long then.

He turned his attention back to the CRT screen. A new sentence was flashing up.

Thanks for the response. Thought we lost you there for a while. Someone here to talk to you.

There was a pause for a few seconds, then letters began to form a new sentence.

Edge, this is Matt. Good to talk with you again. We have a lot to talk about, right? Transmission off for yes.

Reynolds caught the meaning and switched transmission off twice for emphasis. *A lot to talk about? You're fucking-A right about that, Matt.* He could have wept with gratitude at Connor's intuition.

His mind raced, working out how to nudge Matt's questions in the right direction. And the secrecy too. Fuck, how was he going to cope with that? He couldn't just *tell* Matt, not with half the world watching. It would have to be something cryptic, something only Matt

would understand. To his surprise though, Connor's next
sentence threw him completely. It was nothing to do
with . . . anything.

Edge, remember the fifty bucks you won off Kenny
Musgrave? Transmission off for yes.

Reynolds frowned. *Kenny Musgrave? What the fuck?*

He cast his mind back. Musgrave had been his great
rival in the '89 intake—a navy pilot with an enviable
record testing Grumman Tomcats and an attitude to
match. They'd clashed constantly, until the day Reynolds
had challenged him to the most extreme sim the Systems
Trainers were capable of—a simulated manual descent
from orbit to water abort. Musgrave had lost and paid
the stake with particularly ill humor. Not that Reynolds
could begrudge him it.

Musgrave wasn't to know that Reynolds had secretly
run the sim twenty times to get it down pat before challenging him.

But what did it have to do with anything? Reynolds
switched transmission off, mystified. The answer came
back instantly.

Like to win another fifty? Transmission off for yes.

Reynolds gasped. His eyes went wide.

*Jesus fucking Christ. He wants me to do it again. For
real this time.*

A thousand protests erupted in Reynolds's mind. It
was crazy, it was insane, it was outrageous. The sim was
one thing; real-life reentry with its metal-burning heat
and hyperdestructive aerodynamic loads was another.
There was no time to voice any of them though, for a
new batch of letters was appearing on the screen.

Reynolds, Flight. We are devising reentry plan for Endeavor's safe return. Do you understand? Transmission
off for yes.

The Flight Director must have felt Connor's approach
was not sufficiently direct and taken over. Reynolds
punched transmission off momentarily to signify
understanding.

PROP is calculating reentry trajectory now. Plan is
manual-reentry piloting by you to water abort in Pacific.
Do you understand? Transmission off for yes.

Reynolds hesitated. He understood all right. He just thought it was fucking crazy. Finally, he switched transmission off.

*Yes.*

He watched in amazement as Ground began outlining the plan. Feed him trajectory parameters before reentry interface. Ku-band antenna to be jettisoned at last possible moment. Preliminary figures reeled by—burn targets, sink rate, angle of attack, velocity loss. Reynolds watched them, spellbound, despite himself. Finally though, the bile rose and he found himself screaming, the words ringing in his helmet.

"You crazy fucks," he shouted. "This is insanity! Even if we make it, we're gonna hit that ocean at five hundred fucking miles an hour! How the fuck are we gonna maintain attitude?"

The yelling set air currents swirling through his helmet, dislodging tiny globules of sweat and blood. Reynolds shook his head irritably, trying to shake them. He peered through them at the tiny screen. Something else was being typed up there.

The answer to his question.

Reynolds scanned the words. Forgo fuel vent. Drop angle of attack. Gimbal SSMEs. Hotfire at point of impact and use thrust to maintain stability through velocity-loss phase of water glide. Finishing on the typed question:

Reentry plan as outlined. Do you agree to try it, MS Reynolds? Transmission off for yes.

Reynolds stared at the characters, fascinated. He understood the physics of the proposal, no trouble there. But he could hardly believe it. They were asking him to take the largest, most powerful spacecraft on Earth down to a belly landing on water, at speeds high enough to mash the strongest metals to pulp. And they were asking him to do it *now,* without any practice runs, and on the basis of a hastily cooked-up flight plan that he would have to follow intuitively, through complete radio silence, for over 4,000 miles, through to splashdown.

It was madness.

Beyond that, though, was the gnawing problem of how

to get the message through to Connor. Reynolds looked at the $O_2$ readout once more. The tiny blue figures were a ticking time bomb, he realized, counting down the time to when the knowledge locked in his head would detonate, exploding out of the world forever.

*Fuck it.* Reynolds was suddenly aware he was trapped. The malfunctioning voice channel had narrowed his options down to absolute zero. He *had* to agree to Ground's plan, not for the reasons they thought—to save his life, and the lives of Roberts and Rodriguez—but because he *had* to get the message through. No matter how crazy, he had to do it. There was no other choice.

He reached over to switch transmission off, signifying assent. There was one thing Ground was wrong about though.

It wasn't enough to just try. He had to succeed.

# 20

Reynolds worked the Rotational Hand Controller, the orbiter's joystick, carefully, maneuvering *Endeavor* into the tail-first attitude required for the deorbit burn. All over the Shuttle's surface, tiny RCS thrusters fired in synch with the commands wheeling her into position. Burn targets began flashing on the center-mounted CRT screens, relayed from Ground. Reentry begins, for the Shuttle, with a single, massive fire of her tail-mounted main engines—the SSMEs—*against* her eastward direction of travel and sufficient to drop her speed to where the Earth's gravitational field begins reeling her in. Thus the pilot's first step is to work her around into tail-first attitude.

Reynolds checked the "eight-ball," the gimballing Attitude Direction Indicator sphere mounted in the forward control console, to confirm his coordinates. Perfect. He checked the targets Ground had sent him. A two-and-a-half minute burn of both engines, starting at two hours, thirty-five minutes, twenty-four seconds, MET. Three minutes away, he saw, searching out the MET clock on the console with his helmet beams. He relaxed a little.

*Plenty of time.*

He frowned as a thought struck him. Three minutes meant time enough to try and get a warning to Eli. The sudden jolt of the burn would be a nasty shock if the

payload specialist hadn't worked out what was going on
and prepared. Not to mention the shake the two astronauts trapped in the airlock would get when *Endeavor*
hit water.

If they all made it that far.

Reynolds probed the console with the xenons, hunting
out the UHF mode selector again. The air-to-ground
UHF frequencies were dead; he'd already tried them, in
desperation, when he realized S-band was out. But the
air-to-air EVA channel might be salvageable. It worked
off a separate system of local, short-range antennas dotted around the orbiter—there was one in the airlock, for
example. If it was just a matter of something on the
control panel having been knocked out of kilter . . .

Reynolds located the rotary mode selector, switched
it over to EVA mode and examined the surrounding
controls. He found the trouble almost immediately—the
"squelch" toggle had been knocked to a halfway position, neither on nor off, blocking transmission. Reynolds
flicked it on and switched his own suit to the frequency.
Then jammed the push-to-talk down.

"Eli, this is Reynolds," he said. "Do you copy?"

He had to say it three times before the response came
back. Then the channel came alive with a bang, as if
Rodriguez was scrabbling at the suit radio. "Reynolds!
Reynolds! Hi . . . it's me .. it's Eli," Rodriguez's voice
cried through the earpiece. "Oh, thank God. I
thought . . ."

His voice choked off for a moment. Reynolds guessed
he was fighting down tears.

"I felt movement," Eli continued, when his voice had
settled. "Did you put her into tail-first? Are we going
back?"

"That's why I raised you," Reynolds said. "I'm about
to start the deorbit burn. Just wanted to warn you. So
the two of you could get ready. How is Roberts, by
the way?"

Eli's cry of elation was cut short momentarily.
"What? . . ." he said distractedly. "Oh . . . ah . . . she's
okay. She's still out of it and . . . uh . . . her collarbone
is broken . . ." He babbled a few moments before cutting

loose with a fervent oath of thanks. "Oh, thank God! I knew they'd get us. I knew they'd take us back down . . ."

Reynolds shook his head. He squeezed down the push-to-talk. "Uh uh. That's negative, Eli," he said. "They're not taking us down. I am."

There was a moment's silence. "What?" said Rodriguez finally. "You're control-sticking us down? What for?"

"Not control-sticking, Eli," Reynolds said grimly.

Control-sticking was the orbiter's normal, pseudo-manual mode. The pilot used the RHC stick to pilot the orbiter, yeah, but every single input went to the GPCs for approval. And if they didn't give it, if it didn't square with the flight plan, the command was just ignored. The pilot was left to work the stick uselessly, like he was jerking off.

"Not control-sticking," Reynolds repeated. "The GPCs are all off-line, Eli. I'm taking us down manually."

Rodriguez's gasp buzzed in Reynolds's earpiece. Then it fell back into silence again. Seconds ticked by.

"Eli? You still there?" Reynolds asked.

"Yeah," Eli said faintly. "I'm still here." His voice was a mutter. "Jesus. Manual . . ."

Reynolds jammed down the push-to-talk button again. "That's right," he said. He stifled the urge to laugh out loud, in sympathy with Eli's disbelief. "You'd better figure a way to get yourselves braced in there. We're going down for a water abort too. In the Pacific."

This time there was nothing but shocked silence. Eli was speechless.

"You copy that, Eli?"

A strangled gasp was all Reynolds received in return.

"Okay then," Reynolds said lightly. "I'm going off-line to get on with the burn. Talk to you downstairs, hey, Eli?"

He went to flick the rotary switch off-channel, but Eli's voice was suddenly buzzing in his earpiece, arresting his hand.

"Reynolds?"

"Yeah? I read you."

Silence for a moment. Then the hesitant voice. "Thanks. I guess."

The Propulsion Engineer called out the values in time with the figures marching across the front-room screen.

". . . thrust steady at ninety-four percent for SSME one and two . . . burn proceeding . . one minute thirty-four seconds . . thirty-eight . . . forty-two . . ."

A voice cut across him, into the channel. "FLIGHT, GUIDANCE. Looks like we've got a problem creeping in on the attitude readings. *Endeavor* is two degrees out of deadband and moving . . . 2.3 . . . 2.4 . . ."

*Endeavor* was tilting under the impetus of her thrusting main engines. Problem was, the slightly off-center line would reduce the force her engines were blasting against her direction of travel. The finely calculated burn targets would be thrown to shit.

"Uh huh," the Guidance Procedures Officer confirmed a moment later. "Sorry, FLIGHT. She's moving out of tolerance. That's 2.5 now and rising." He looked up at Ewell from his front-room position. "Another degree and we'll have to abort the burn."

Ewell swore. "Copy that, GUIDANCE," he said shortly. "CAPCOM, stand by to pass this message to Reynolds. MS Reynolds, attitude tolerance exceeded. Abort burn immediately and stand by for calculation of alternate Entry Interface."

*Alternate Entry Interface!* he thought bitterly. What a farce.

They all knew there wouldn't be time for another.

"Roger, FLIGHT," Tranh replied. "Standing by . . ."

"WAIT!" GUIDANCE cut in again, triumphantly this time. "The deviation's correcting! That's 2.3 degrees . . . 2.1 . . . RCS thrusters firing . . . SSMEs gimballing . . . son of a bitch . . ." His voice trailed off in disbelief. He looked up at Ewell again. "FLIGHT, Reynolds is correcting it. On the fly."

The room broke into an excited buzz.

"Copy that, GUIDANCE." Ewell glanced over at Connor. He put a hand over his mike and gave a low whistle. "Guess you were right, Matt," he said. "Your boy *is* good."

Connor just shrugged.

Ewell grinned, for the first time in hours, and took his hand away from his mike. "Okay, people," he said briskly, "we are back on target. Looks like we've got ourselves a genuine hot dog up there. PROP, how's the burn?"

"Copy that, FLIGHT," the Propulsion Engineer said, resuming the count. "Steady at two minutes seventeen seconds . . . twenty-one . . . twenty-five. Okay, that's it. Burn target reached. Reynolds should be shutting down the SSMEs about . . . now."

Right on cue, the thrust vector figures dropped off the front-room screens. A second later the RCS system figures began to dance. Reynolds was working *Endeavor* back around into the nose-first entry attitude.

"That's it," the engineer announced. "*Endeavor* has entered coast mode at two hours, thirty-eight minutes and fifty-four seconds, Mission Elapsed Time."

"Okay," said Ewell, "thank you, PROP. FIDO?" he called, addressing the Flight Dynamics Officer. "How is he looking for Entry Interface?"

This was the test. *Endeavor*'s speed had been cut by a third, from 24,000 feet per second to 17,000, and she was starting to drop in toward the Earth's atmosphere. When she hit its first wisps, at 400,000 feet, that would be Entry Interface. Where Ground's calculations would be proved wrong or right in a single instant.

Insertion angle. That was what it was all about.

*Endeavor* had to hit the atmospheric fringe at just the right slope. Too steep, and she would fry as abrasive air rasped over her at multiple Mach speed. Too shallow, and she would bounce off. Right back out into space.

"Copy that, FLIGHT," the Flight Dynamics Officer's voice came back. "Coast-speed 17,320 feet per second, altitude 430,000 feet . . . that's on track . . . insertion angle augmenting . . . minus 6 degrees . . . minus 6.2 . . . minus 6.4 . . . ah . . . rate change checks out so far.

Reynolds is on track for Entry Interface in 143 seconds at 2 hours, 39 minutes and 8 seconds, MET."

Ewell nodded. That much was good. So far at least. Though without the second-by-second control of the GPCs, there was only one way to *really* be sure.

When Reynolds had actually made it.

*And we won't even be able to see that,* Ewell thought savagely. Sometime in the next thirty seconds, Reynolds was going to have to jettison the Ku-band antenna and close the payload doors. With it would go the last tenuous link with the orbiter. They would have no further contact with Reynolds until he made it to splashdown.

*If* he made it.

"Copy that, FIDO," Ewell said. "What about the final parameters? They ready?"

"Roger, FLIGHT. Shooting them to CAPCOM now."

"Okay, CAPCOM," Ewell said, forcing the faintness he felt out of his voice. This was it. The moment. Once he gave the command, Reynolds would be on his own.

Ewell was suddenly conscious of how quiet the control room had become.

"Forward the finals to MS Reynolds now," he ordered. "Tell him he is go for Ku-band jettison and payload bay closeout."

"Copy that, FLIGHT," Emily Tranh replied, her fingers flying across her keyboard. Letters, the last ones Reynolds would receive, began to file onto the left front-room screen.

"Wait!" the Flight Director said suddenly. The interjection was like a shot. Every head in the ficker jerked around to look at Ewell. Tranh's hands stopped, frozen over the keyboard.

Ewell turned to Connor, standing, lost in thought, beside him. "Matt?" he said. "This is it. The moment of reckoning. Any last words for your boy?"

Connor stared at Ewell, as if he hardly understood what the Flight Director was saying. Ewell could read the older man's conflicting emotions on his face—fear, anxiety now the craziness was really under way, defiant belief in Reynolds's ability to pull it off. For a long moment the Adviser seemed to struggle to find something to say.

"Tell him good luck," Connor grated finally. "From me."

**Mission Elapsed Time: 5 days, 2 hours, 42 minutes
Flight Deck, Space Shuttle *Endeavor***

"Yeah, thanks Matt," Reynolds snorted, glancing at the letters on the CRT. It wasn't that he didn't appreciate the sentiment. It was just that he was going to need more than luck.

He was going to need a miracle.

Reynolds worked his way through the Entry Interface checklist, as much from memory as from the plan outlined on the tiny screen. *Activate the auxiliary power units, stir the Freon-21 coolant loops, close the star-tracker doors.* His eyes flicked to the MET clock as his hands moved over the control consoles. Six minutes, sixteen seconds. That meant thirty seconds to ditch the Ku-band and close the payload doors. His finger went to the antenna jettison switch, mounted in the left-side control console, hovered there a moment.

*This is it, you know. Once you push that button, you're on your own.*

Reynolds shrugged and jammed the button down. There was nothing Ground could do for him now anyway.

Somewhere behind him, unseen, the jettison circuits would now be releasing the clamp that attached the Ku-band antenna to *Endeavor* and activating the tiny guillotine that sliced its cable. Reynolds waited the four seconds it took for the procedure to be completed, then punched the port and starboard payload door actuators. This time he felt the change, a faint vibration as the rotary gears swung the doors closed and locked them down to a pressure-tight thermal seal. He wondered briefly what the noise was like from Eli's vantage point, locked in the tiny airlock. Deafening, probably.

Reynolds glanced at the clock again. *Fifteen seconds to Entry Interface.*

He switched his gaze to the Glide Slope Indicator, the mobile tape meter on the forward control console that indicated the angle at which the orbiter was falling. This was the real test. *Endeavor* was now less than ten seconds from hitting the upper reaches of the Earth's atmosphere. The GSI needle was steady at the minus-12.2-degree entry angle Ground had calculated. If it stayed there through Entry Interface everything would be okay. If it moved though? Started to climb?

Then he was history.

That would mean *Endeavor* was bouncing, skipping off the atmosphere like a stone skimmed off water. He would be heading back out into space, with no way to correct the overshoot. Not on this orbit. And that meant death. Another orbit was another ninety oxygen-depleting minutes. If he managed to even make Entry Interface again he would asphyxiate before he got more than halfway home. Not to mention the fact that, cut off from Ground, he had no way of recalculating Entry Interface anyway.

No. He had one shot at this. One shot only.

Reynolds kept his eyes glued to the needle as he hit Interface and sped through. It stayed steady . . . five seconds . . . ten . . . fifteen. Seventeen seconds in, it seemed to flicker, and Reynolds's hand tightened on the Rotational Controller. Not that there was any point to *that*. If he was bouncing, there would be nothing he could do about it. He watched the needle anxiously, but it settled back into the slope after a second or two and even started to drift downwards—minus 12.3 degrees . . . minus 12.4—as the first wisps of gravity and atmospheric drag began to tell.

Reynolds's eyes flicked over to the CRT, checking the readings against the flight plan. Perfect. He relaxed slightly.

*So far so good.*

He punched the command buttons for inhibiting the forward RCS jets and venting their remaining propellant. *Endeavor*'s nose blossomed momentarily with a mist of nitrogen tetroxide and monomethyl hydrazine, quickly dispersed. It was a symbolic act. Venting the forward RCS jets meant he was committed.

No turning back now. Not even if he wanted to.

He eyed the GSI needle a while longer but it was fine,

dropping steadily in line with the flight-plan parameters. From time to time his gaze switched to the eight ball, but that was steady too, wobbling imperceptibly around the line indicating a thirty-six-degree angle of attack. Reynolds nudged the stick now and again, firing off the rear RCS jets, to ensure it stayed there. Maintaining correct attack angle was important—it had to be steep enough to catch atmospheric drag and slow him, yet shallow enough to keep *Endeavor*'s temperature down and prevent her burning. But until air pressure increased, activating the orbiter's aerodynamic surfaces, that was almost the only thing he had to do.

It would be a small respite though. Once the air pressure *did* kick in, and *Endeavor* began responding aerodynamically, he was in for a hell of a ride. It would be all he could do to hold her.

Reynolds used the extra time to scroll through the flight plan. Not that the collection of figures flashing through the tiny CRT display deserved the name. It was more a collection of parameters than a plan—temperature constraints, load parameters, drag acceleration targets. The problem Ground had faced drawing it up was that, with Ku-band out and the GPCs down, Reynolds would be cut off from Earth-based navigation aids the entire way down. No TACAN, the global aircraft range-finding system. No MSBLS, the microwave-beam guidance system that usually brought the orbiter safely to the runway approach threshold.

No nothing.

All he had was the onboard instruments: the Air Data System, which sensed altitude, velocity and temperature from the speed and pressure of air moving over two probes in *Endeavor*'s wings; and the Radar Altimeter, which wouldn't even kick in until the orbiter reached 9,000 feet. He could know what his altitude was, and how quickly he was losing it, but nothing else. No way of taking range and bearing. No way of working out how far he was from splashdown, or even where splashdown was going to be.

Just one long, blind fall into the biggest body of water on the planet.

The solution Ground had come up with was to tie the plan to time. Mission Elapsed Time was the one constant Reynolds had. Accordingly, the flight-control team had devised a set of speed/altitude mile-posts—15,220 feet per seconds and 295,000 feet altitude at 51 minutes MET; 14,000 and 220,000 at 57 minutes, MET. Theoretically, to make it down intact Reynolds only had to reach them.

*Only!*

Reynolds shook his head, thinking of what was coming. He flexed his fingers on the RHC, readying himself. At 0.176 g, air pressure would rise to ten pounds per square inch, allowing the orbiter's aerodynamic surfaces—wing elevons, rudder flaps, body flap—to become operational. He would then switch *Endeavor* over from RCS thruster control to aerodynamic. The Rotational Hand Controller would become a simple joystick, its movements sending airstream deflection commands to the orbiter's flaps.

That much was okay—even after twenty years he was still pilot enough to *mesh* with the joystick, make it no more than an extension of himself. The speed though, that was the thing. It was true the orbiter hardly qualified as an aircraft—its stubby shape, fantastic weight and high rate of fall made its aerodynamic controls as responsive as a stone's. At over 10,000 miles per hour though, it hardly mattered. The merest flick of those sluggish controls would send her tumbling wildly.

*Like riding a mechanical bull,* Reynolds thought. *With half the control.*

It made it worse that there was none of the old thrill. Normally, even though it was a death ride, Reynolds could have gotten off on the sheer adrenaline charge of it, trying to beat the odds as he free-falled this mother down. Not now though. The message he was carrying was too important for that.

It wouldn't be enough to just try. Reynolds had to *make* it.

A light flashed up on the control console. The G-meter had sensed 0.176 g. Reynolds's eyes flicked over to the barometric pressure readout.

*Okay. This is it.* The probes were reading just short of ten pounds per square inch.

Reynolds inhibited the remaining RCS jets and switched the avionics over to aerodynamic. He placed both feet on the rudder pedals in readiness, gripped the stick a little harder. He tore his eyes off the instruments and glanced around the cabin, trying to pick signs of the rising gravity and air pressure. The flight deck was still black; *Endeavor* was falling through the dark side of Earth's orbit, racing around to meet the sun. His helmet lamps raked the darkness.

*Hard to say,* Reynolds thought.

Crap was still flying around the deck, same as in zero g. That could be because thin air was beginning to pour in through the smashed overhead window and set up currents though. In fact, he *could* feel a slight vibration starting up through his seat—half the *Endeavor* starting to register the aerodynamic loads and half air buffeting through the flight deck, Reynolds decided.

He turned back to the instruments grimly. That was another thing, he realized. The aerodynamic constraints Ground had drawn up were for a *smooth* orbiter. No account had been taken of *Endeavor*'s breached window, or the stab wounds he'd inflicted on his way up to the flight deck. The window was the main thing. Once pressure started to rise, air was going to come howling through it like a thousand screaming banshees.

*Gonna be dangerous,* he thought. The torrent of air would fling debris around the cabin like matchsticks. He'd be lucky if something didn't smash his helmet, exposing him to agonizing, low-pressure death.

There was no time to worry about *that* though. He saw, upon sweeping the console with his lights, that the MET clock had reached two hours, fifty-one minutes. The first milepost. Time to check his progress.

Reynolds scanned the console. AVVIs gave a barometric altitude of 304,000 feet; the Alpha Mach Indicator read 16,200 feet per second. Too high and too fast.

Time to start using the brakes.

Reynolds edged the RHC leftward and depressed the left rudder pedal. The "brakes" were the thickening air molecules rushing over *Endeavor*'s surface. By increasing the surface area the orbiter presented to them, Reynolds could increase atmospheric drag, thereby slowing her. A left-bank command, that was the ticket. Slewing *Endeavor* side-on to the airstream would increase surface area nicely.

Pulling back the angle of attack would have been even better—attack-angle commands generally stripped speed off the orbiter twice as fast as bank commands. There was a trade-off though: temperature. The orbiter could stand up to 2,300 degrees Fahrenheit by virtue of its reinforced carbon-carbon structures and tiled underside. Reentry temperatures could easily exceed that, though, climbing anywhere to a theorized 5,000 degrees Fahrenheit in uncontrolled reentry. Holding a steep attack angle too long would probably get her there even quicker.

Reynolds watched the eight ball carefully, ready to pull back the instant it showed signs of swinging too hard. He increased pressure on the controls gingerly: 1 degree . . . 1.4 . . . 1.8. A 3-degree left bank was what he was looking for. Enough to raise the drag on *Endeavor*'s surface. But not enough to subject her to serious stress.

For a moment he thought he'd got it safely. The eight ball was tilting smoothly, climbing up to the three-degree mark. But then, without warning, the error needles jumped, and Reynolds felt a tremor pass through the orbiter. Sure enough, a second later, *Endeavor* lurched violently to the left.

And all hell broke loose.

*Oh God, God, God, God, God,* Reynolds shrieked soundlessly. His head slammed backwards and forwards inside his helmet. Debris flew crazily before his shaking helmet lights. The flight deck was a darkened blur.

*Endeavor* was tumbling wildly. The deflection had thrown her into uncontrolled spin.

Reynolds strove to stay conscious through the cataclysmic roar. He gripped the RHC tight. If his hand fell off it now he'd never get it back on. His other hand reached out blindly to the shaking control console, barely visible in front of him. The SSMEs, they were his only hope. No way the stick could pull him out—all aerodynamic surfaces went dead in a spin like this. And no point switching back to RCS either. Without GPC calculations to aid him, Reynolds had a snowball's chance in hell of firing off the jets in correct sequence.

His one chance was a long, solid fire of the main engines.

It would fling him round like a Catherine wheel, at first. But the thrust would gradually damp the spin down to where the aerodynamic controls could kick back in. It would use fuel, precious fuel needed for the splashdown maneuver. But that couldn't be helped. He had to get the spin corrected, now. The atmosphere *Endeavor* was falling through was thickening by the second. The orbiter's surface temperature would be rising, starting to burn. If he didn't get on top of the spin in the next 30,000 feet, that would be it. *Endeavor* would fry.

Reynolds strained to reach the keys. The console, and his helmet xenons, were shaking so violently it was impossible to do more than guess where they were. His teeth were rattling painfully. As if confirming his forecast, a dull, orange glow began to suffuse the flight deck. *Ionization,* Reynolds thought. Heat was beginning to ionize the oxygen atoms in the atmosphere, forming an orange sheath around the orbiter. It was a familiar reentry phenomenon. For most Shuttle astronauts it meant the beginning of a sixteen-minute communication blackout, from 265,000 feet to 162,000 feet, as the impenetrable ionization cloud blocked radio waves. Not for Reynolds though, who was already blacked out in any case.

For him it was a warning.

Stretching the last couple of inches, Reynolds stabbed at the spot on the console where he thought the hotfire buttons were. He could tell instantly he'd hit. It wasn't that he could hear it, or feel a change in the vibration. *Nothing* could have been heard, or felt, over that cacophony. It was the feeling in his gut—a sudden, dizzying drop as the 12,000 pounds of thrust from the engines kicked in, rocketing his trajectory into overdrive.

The force slammed Reynolds back into his seat. His arms fell from the controls.

He wallowed helplessly as the engines, coupled with

the spin, flung the orbiter into incredible, ever-widening spirals. He didn't think—he couldn't. All he could do was *feel*. It was as if every ounce of blood in his brain had been sucked to the back of his skull, draining his mind of thought.

*The force. Oh my God, the force.*

It was as if every molecule in his body were being torn, dragged apart by the inexorable gravity of a star or a black hole. The orange glow retreated as he teetered on the edge of unconsciousness.

Gradually though, imperceptibly, the force began to lessen. Reynolds's vision began to return.

*Damping,* he thought dimly. *The SSMEs have damped the spin.*

The engines were throwing the orbiter into such large spirals now that the spin was hardly noticeable. The centrifugal force pinning him to his seat was diminishing too.

Reynolds reached out to shut the SSMEs down. It seemed to take forever; his body felt as weak as if pints of blood *had* been drained from it. His faculties were returning, though. He even managed a short laugh as he punched the inhibit buttons, cutting the engines off dead.

*How 'bout that one, Musgrave?* he gasped. *You ever pull a maneuver like that?*

*A five-, ten-, who-knew-how-many-mile spiral through the upper atmosphere? In the middle of deorbit?*

*Totally fucking blind?*

Reynolds switched the avionics back to RCS control temporarily, as he set about the task of retrieving trajectory. He ignored velocity and altitude for the moment; there'd be time to see what disastrous effects his maneuver had had shortly. Reynolds concentrated on realigning the orbiter to line of flight and angle of attack. He worked the stick backwards and forwards rapidly, firing off the RCS jets in bursts to counteract the wild swings of the Attitude Direction Indicator.

It seemed to take forever. Gradually, however, the eight ball settled back into alignment. Reynolds watched it carefully for a full thirty seconds, but it stayed steady. He switched the orbiter back to aerodynamic control and slumped back in his seat, exhausted.

*Fuck,* he groaned inwardly. *Let's hope I don't have to pull too many more of those on the way down.*

His eyes drifted over to the AVVI and Alpha Mach Indicator, assessing the damage. There was no way the roughly twenty-second burn he'd had to fire could have altered his trajectory—he'd still be going east and down, at something over fifteen times the speed of sound. But it had probably played havoc with Ground's mileposts.

Reynolds glanced at the MET clock first. *Two hours, fifty-three minutes, ten seconds.* He shook his head in amazement. The whole horrifying episode had taken no more than a couple of minutes to play out.

He scanned the readings, comparing them to the parameters on the CRT display. Altitude 242,000 feet—high, according to the plan, but he could live with it. Speed was the real concern. He peered through his cracked helmet at the Alpha Mach Indicator.

*14,300 feet per second.*

Relief flooded him. It was down—actually *lower* than the plan called for. By some incredible stroke of luck, the blind, panicked thrust he'd pumped through the SSMEs had mostly kicked against his direction of travel and slowed him.

That and *Endeavor*'s uncontrolled, rasping spin through the sandpaper air.

Reynolds didn't dare look at the temperature readings. That little adventure must have stacked on a few hundred extra Fahrenheit. *Endeavor*'s skin would be glowing cherry red. Impossible to tell, of course—the ionized haze drowned everything out. It moved into Reynolds's helmet, a suffusion of orange fire, mixing with the red mist of heat, sweat and blood until Reynolds felt he was sitting, somehow unconsumed, in the belly of an inferno. He sat, stock-still, gripping the controls, as *Endeavor* dropped down and down and down.

Onward, through the flames of hell.

12:37 P.M., Central Standard Time, 3 April 2005
Shuttle Flight Control Room One, Johnson Space Center

"Bob."

The portly woman swept to a stop beside Ewell, four

or five aides filing into the crowded row behind her and choking it further. Even through the tense hubbub a few heads turned curiously, here and there, at the sight.

It wasn't every day the ficker was graced by a visit from Hannah Reardon, NASA Administrator.

"Administrator," Ewell replied, motioning Carmichael to get the NASA superior hooked up with an earpiece. In truth, though there'd been no call, no prior warning, the Flight Director wasn't the least surprised to see Reardon there. He could read the message behind her presence plainly.

*We've got an out-of-control bird plunging earthward. Maybe it'll hit the Pacific, where it's supposed to. But maybe it won't.*

*Maybe it'll hit . . . something else.*

The Administrator wanted to be on hand. Ready to issue whatever apologies were required, immediately.

"You've been briefed?" Ewell continued.

"Yes, Bob, I have," Reardon said, as Carmichael fitted her with a radio unit, clipping the unit to her belt and lifting her trademark head scarf to loop the wire over her ear. She repeated her name into the mike a couple of times in response to the FAO's request for a comm check. When next she spoke, her voice came through the command channel. "What's current status?"

Ewell shrugged helplessly, gestured to the blank central screen at the front of the room. "If he's made it, Administrator, Reynolds should be through blackout phase by now and down to 162,000 feet. We're trying to acquire visual. Marshall is lining us up through one of the IMAGERs."

Reardon nodded. "No luck with two-way ranging?" she asked. "What about Doppler?"

Ewell shook his head. "That's negative, Administrator," he said. "All track systems are down. As far as the oribter's concerned we're bl . . ."

A voice cut into his on the channel. "FLIGHT, INCO. Sorry to interrupt. That's Marshall Space Flight Center on the line now. They say IMAGER-3 is locked into overflight trajectory now and tracking. They should have visual for us any second."

"Roger, INCO," Ewell replied crisply. "DATA, get it up on-screen."

The location map on the huge central screen at the front of the room disappeared, replaced by a heavily posterized image—bands and pools of garish color, forming no coherent whole. Reardon stared at it a few confused moments before realizing what it was. It was a thermal topographic image—a heat picture of part of the Earth's surface.

*The Caucasus?* Reardon wondered. *Is that the outline of the Caspian?*

"A thermal image?" she said, out loud. "Why that?"

"The surest bet, Administrator," Ewell said absently, his concentration locked on the screen. "At the speed he's going, IMAGER-3 will never pick him out of the background on optical. But he'll be the hottest thing in the sky .. by at least a thousand degrees. If he's there the thermal sensors will read him." His voice tailed off as he studied the image anxiously. "He'll be lighter. We should see him as an orange or yellow shape . . ."

Every eye in the control room followed his. Reardon could sense the shimmering doubt. There wasn't a speck of orange or yellow to be seen.

Beside her, Lew Carmichael glanced at Ewell nervously. "I don't like this, Bob," the FAO said. "That's the target corridor. If he's not there . . ."

Ewell nodded, understanding the unspoken words. *If he's not in the corridor, he's probably nowhere.* "INCO, FLIGHT," he said brusquely, into his mike. "Ask Marshall to expand the acquisition cone. Tell 'em to give us five-second cycles through every adjoining latitude/longitude square."

"Copy that, FLIGHT," replied the Integrated Communications Officer, relaying the request. Seconds later, a new image materialized on-screen, replaced by another five seconds later. Dead silence settled over the control room as the images cycled.

Several cries rang out belatedly as the fourth image slipped from the screen. Ewell had seen it too—a yellow-orange spot at the bottom of the image. "INCO, FLIGHT," he shouted. "Get that last image back! The

north frame. Tell them to magnify the lower half. Fifty
to sixty degrees latitude."

The image reappeared; the lower half doubled in size
as the magnification instructions were relayed to the orbiting satellite. Ewell held his breath, along with the rest
of the room, as he studied the thermal map.

*Is that* Endeavor? he wondered. The temperature
looked right. Yellow-orange meant 1,200 to 2,300 degrees Fahrenheit—about what the orbiter would be experiencing in postblackout flight. But was the dot
moving? Ewell screwed up his eyes, trying to judge.

"What do you think, Lew?" he murmured, swinging
the mike away from his mouth. "Is that them?"

Carmichael was silent a moment, studying the image.
"It's moving," he said suddenly. "But if that's *Endeavor*
they're way north." He pointed to the long sliver of dark
blue in the image. "That body of water's gotta be the
Kuybyshevskoye Reservoir." He glanced uncomfortably
at Hannah Reardon. "Which means they're coming
down over Russia. Not even one of the CIS southern
republics. Russia itself."

The NASA Administrator nodded, neutrally, but
Ewell could see she understood the import of Carmichael's words. The further north *Endeavor* strayed, the
narrower the Pacific target got, and the greater her
chances of striking land. Probably *Russian* land. After
the humiliations the Russians had already suffered—the
guilt of their cosmonaut, the loss of ISS—that would be
the final blow. Who knew what an uncontrolled *Endeavor*, smashing down into the East Russian landmass,
was going to hit?

Or how many it would kill.

"What's the verdict, Bob?" Reardon asked, letting
such thoughts remain unspoken. "Is it *Endeavor*?"

"We'll soon find out, Administrator," Ewell said,
swinging the mike back in front of his mouth. "FIDO,
FLIGHT. What's the velocity on that image? Can you
calculate?"

"Ah, roger, FLIGHT," the Flight Dynamics Officer
replied. "Running that through now . . . averaging . . .
recalculating . . ." The tone of his voice lifted excitedly.
"It checks out, FLIGHT . . . 11,000 feet per second.

That's Postblackout Subphase velocity. It's *Endeavor*. No doubt about it."

The control room was silent a moment, digesting this. Then it exploded with a deafening cheer.

"INCO, FLIGHT," Ewell shouted through the hubbub. "Get that image magnified. Big as IMAGER-3 can make it."

A few seconds later the image began to grow obediently, ending up as an eight- to twelve-inch, wedge-shaped blur of yellow-orange crawling across the blues, greens and pinks of the landscape.

Ewell found himself shaking his head in disbelief. *Son of a bitch!* Reynolds had done it. Got *Endeavor* through the first, most dangerous phase of reentry.

Suddenly Reardon was there, right beside him, looking from one exulting face to another. "Bob!" she said, raising her voice over the noise. "Bob! Wait a minute. If that's *Endeavor*, how do we know that Mission Specialist Reynolds is still alive? What if the orbiter is descending uncontrolled?"

A voice cut into the channel before Ewell could answer. Connor. "He's alive," the older man growled. "Trust me."

"Adviser Connor's right, Administrator," Ewell said. "The orbiter's surface temperature gives us a great rule of thumb. If Reynolds is keeping *Endeavor* within constraints, her temperature will stay under 2,500 degrees Fahrenheit. That's yellow, on the thermal image."

Ewell grimaced.

"If he loses it, though, and the orbiter moves out of tolerance, we'll know about it." He gestured at the screen. "The image will go pure white. At 3,000 degrees or over, *Endeavor* will be burning."

That was sobering. Ewell knew, as did almost everyone in the room, how easily it could happen. All it would take would be for Reynolds to slip out of consciousness momentarily and lose control, or make some tiny mistake in the aerodynamics that would overload the orbiter's structural tolerances. *Endeavor* would start tumbling, and the atmosphere would begin tearing her to shreds.

Then *that* part of the thermal image at least would be

realistic. *Endeavor* would burn white-hot, like a magnesium flare, all the way down to ground.

Ewell felt the knowledge settle back over the crowd. The euphoria died and the voices fell uneasily away. Soon the room was quiet again, dead quiet, as every eye tracked the yellow-orange shape, willing it to hold as it crawled its aching way across the screen.

**Mission Elapsed Time: 5 days, 3 hours, 26 minutes**
**Flight Deck, Space Shuttle *Endeavor***

*Stay with it,* Reynolds begged himself.

Unconsciousness was lapping at him, black waves alternating with orange fire. His body was numb from the fierce vibration. All thought, all reason had disappeared, drowned out by the heat and shaking violence. Reynolds almost felt he had ceased to exist.

His only points of reference were his right hand, tightly gripped on the RHC, and his feet, resting on the two rudder pedals. And his eyes, glued to the attitude readings on the eight ball. Reynolds worked the controls semiconsciously, by instinct, keeping *Endeavor* moving within a banking band of two degrees plus and minus to claw her speed down.

*Left two degrees. Hold.* Counting seconds down dazedly. *Ease back. Now right to two. And hold.*

He moved the stick and pedals with dreamlike precision. Rhythm made it easier. *Left, hold, ease. Right, hold, ease.* After a while it became comfortingly hypnotic.

A sudden change in the light brought Reynolds out of the reverie. The fierce, inferno orange had dropped in intensity, yet become more *light*. For a moment Reynolds was nonplussed. He was dimly aware he must be close to escaping ionization blackout by now. He could have checked, of course, simply by glancing over at the barometric altitude reading, but for the life of him, the effort was beyond him. He puzzled over the light. Emerging from ionization phase should have plunged him back into darkness.

Shouldn't it?

Then he realized. *The sun.* His thunderous reentry had

rushed him around once more to meet the rising sun. Reynolds dragged his head up, fighting the thunderous shaking, to look out the orbiter's forward windows. Sure enough, through the dying orange he could see blue— the blue of sunlit sky unsullied by the clouds still 100,000 feet below.

A sob escaped Reynolds. Something about being once more in the sun's light, and the Earth's air, suddenly seemed impossibly beautiful to him.

He was going home, damn it. And for the first time in his life, the words really *meant* something.

A sudden lurch from *Endeavor* dispelled the elation, snapping his eyes instantly back to the instruments. The eight ball was inclining to 5.4 degrees starboard—close to critical—and Reynolds crept the controls to correct it, resisting the fatal urge to slam the left rudder pedal down and yank the RHC over.

The needle climbed a fraction more, hesitated, then began to ease back down. He'd saved it.

Reynolds slumped back into his seat, panting, blood singing in his ears from his suddenly racing heart. *Let that be a warning, pal,* he told himself. *You're a long way from home yet.*

He surveyed the instruments grimly, turning his attention back to the job at hand. Speed was down to 10,000 feet per second, altitude to 156,000 feet. That was good—almost perfect, Reynolds saw, glancing over at the flight plan. In fact, there wouldn't be much to do for the next twenty minutes or so, just keep tacking to lose speed and maintain attitude to prevent *Endeavor* tearing herself to shreds. And despite the choking heat in his suit, the lack of feeling in the controls, Reynolds was growing more confident he could see her through. At least down to Approach Phase Altitude, 9,000 feet.

That was when the real trouble would start.

When he hit Approach Phase Altitude he would have two minutes, max, to do all the things Ground and the GPCs usually did for landing—ramp attack angle back, fire the SSMEs for final flare to reduce sink rate and pull the orbiter back to a minus-three-degree slide slope. Except Reynolds would *also* then have to perform the splashdown maneuver Ground had devised—retrieve a ten-degree attack angle, gimbal the engines up to six degrees. And get ready to fire the instant *Endeavor* hit water.

*Actually, that's wrong,* Reynolds realized. He would have to fire a second or two *before* she hit. The SSMEs took at least a second to fire up. If they weren't already thrusting when *Endeavor* touched, it would already be too late.

Reynolds watched the falling altitude reading on the AVVI, worrying his lip with his teeth. The problem with the Approach Sequence would be picking the moment to initiate. Nine thousand feet was the mark, but knowing when he'd reached it would be hard. He had the barometric altitude to guide him, but that was unreliable, vulnerable to fluctuations of up to 4,000 feet, depending on local weather.

Radar altimeter, the last of the four tape gauges on the AVVI, was better, radar driven and accurate to two inches. But it kicked in exactly at Approach Phase Altitude, not before. It was a barber pole at the moment— the spiraling red and white that NASA used to signify inoperativeness—and would stay that way until they actually hit 9,000 feet. Worse still, there would be no warning when it became functional. It would simply start to work, the red and white ribbons giving way to the moving altitude tape. If he didn't watch it carefully, he'd miss it.

Reynolds kept an eye fixed on it, along with the Attitude Direction Indicator, in between checking off velocity and altitude against Ground's parameters. He was doing well, shearing off speed by the second in line with the flight plan. He worked the controls cautiously, resuming the banking rhythm he'd so nearly interrupted.

*Right two degrees. Hold. Ease. Left to two degrees. Hold.*

He wondered how Eli and Roberts were faring, locked in the airlock. $O_2$ wouldn't be a problem, Reynolds felt sure—the EMUs had enough bleedable oxygen to supply the two of them for hours. Even the danger of poisonous $CO_2$ buildup could be averted if Eli was careful to keep the bleed rate higher than consumption. The tumble *Endeavor* had taken would have shaken them though; Reynolds winced to think of what it would have done to the break in Roberts's collarbone. Splashdown would be still worse, even if Reynolds managed to bring the orbiter safely to a stop.

*Eli should get Roberts into the good EMU and over-pressurize,* Reynolds thought suddenly.

That would simultaneously help reduce the $CO_2$ threat, and provide the injured woman with at least a little cushioning. His eyes flicked over to the Communication Mode Selector. He hesitated, wondering if he should suggest it to Eli, but decided against it.

He didn't dare take his concentration off the controls for a single second. *Just have to hope Eli thinks of it himself.*

Reynolds returned to the task of winnowing speed off *Endeavor,* working the controls rhythmically. Altitude was down to 72,000 feet; speed had fallen far enough for the velocity indicator to switch to Mach scale, measuring speed in multiples of the speed of sound rather than thousands of feet per second.

*Mach 4.2. Just over 3,000 miles per hour.*

That was good too. He was right on track, according to the flight plan. If he could keep stripping speed off *Endeavor* like this, he might just stand a chance of bringing her down to the target impact speed, 450 miles per hour. It was imperative he reached that, or at least got close.

The slower he hit the water, the greater his chances of keeping *Endeavor* under control.

He banked the orbiter, left and right, following the rhythm he'd set himself. He tried to keep his attention firmly on the eight ball and radar altimeter, but the rhythm was dangerously hypnotic, and he found his thoughts wandering.

Irina. That's what he kept thinking of.

Visions of her flashed through his mind. That first time he had seen her, on the screen in the conference room. Her scared, lost face as she came to him, the night of *Ryokousha*'s explosion.

Her brown eyes, wide with passion as they made love. *Those eyes . . .*

Reynolds shuddered. He saw again those hideous, reptilian *sheaths* sliding over Irina's beautiful eyes. That same sense of repugnance, *horror,* choked him once more.

Except now it was mixed with something else: pity.

Tears stung Reynolds's eyes. He focused on the instruments, trying to drown the thoughts out.

Altitude was 37,000 feet, speed was down to Mach three, just over 2,000 miles per hour. Reynolds's hand went to the Speed Brake Controller at his left, his eyes to the flight plan on the CRT screen for confirmation. Yep. Mach three was the cutoff.

Time to dispense with the braking bank maneuvers and activate the speed brake. The orbiter should be slow enough now to remain stable under the extra drag.

Reynolds eased the lever back slowly, all the way to full as *Endeavor* showed no signs of slowing. Behind him, on the vertical stabilizer of the orbiter's tail, the rudder flaps spread—one going left and one right. This is the orbiter's Speed Brake Mode, where the split rudder flaps, which normally work in unison to yaw her left or right, give up their aerodynamic function and become a simple brake, flaring out to increase atmospheric drag.

The advantage is the quantum jump in drag the brake offers. The problem is it can't be used until the orbiter's speed drops. Deploying the speed brake before Mach three would result in only two things. The evaporation of the flaps themselves as they burned under the phenomenal drag. And the subsequent total loss of aerodynamic control, beyond retrieval by anybody—pilot, Ground *or* onboard GPC.

Reynolds watched the eight ball like a hawk, but it never even twitched. The orbiter's attitude was holding, steady as a rock. Her speed was really falling too: Mach 2.9 . . . Mach 2.8 . . . 2.7 . . .

He felt the first glimmers of incredible hope. *My God,* he thought, stunned. *Am I really going to pull this off?*

Reynolds watched the figures fall, holding the controls steady. That was all he had to do—keep the speed brake pulled back full and the RHC stable so *Endeavor* maintained attitude and attack angle. But that was even worse, in some ways, for shortly he found the thoughts seeping back in.

*She was just a woman,* he heard himself say. *Whatever else she was. She was just a woman too.*

Irina again. Why couldn't he stop thinking about her?

Reynolds knew what it was, of course. It was guilt, the same cloying, corrosive guilt he'd felt for years afterwards with Alicia. The guilt that wouldn't leave him, wouldn't let him sleep, wouldn't let him *forget.*

Only how much worse was it going to be this time? When he'd actually killed her? With his own two hands and one robot grapple . . .

The images of Irina resumed their progress through Reynolds's mind. The sorrow in her eyes when she kissed him for the last time, as he floated, trussed in the Service Module. The suffering he read there. The suffering of a woman, forced against herself into actions she hated, but knew to be necessary. Over which she had no control.

The pity was back with him. *How much else of Irina's short life had been like that?* he wondered.

He scanned the instruments absently. Altitude 32,000 feet, speed Mach 1.9. Getting close now. His eyes flicked over to the Radar Altimeter. Still a barber pole. *Five minutes,* Reynolds estimated. That was when he'd have to really start looking sharp.

A new set of images, imagined ones, flashed before Reynolds's horrified eyes. Irina as a girl. A child, naked, alone, vulnerable, in the maw of Alinov's monster program. How many brothers and sisters had she seen die? How many death tests had she undergone, each one ultimate confirmation her life was nothing but the slim chance she might survive it, for Alinov's purposes?

Through it all was the picture of her eyes—bewildered, suffering, alone. Before he could stop it, the image slid into one of those eyes, widening with terror and despair, as the *Soyuz he* had trapped her in flew in towards impact with ISS and doom. Then the picture vanished, as Irina must have, blown apart in the blast.

*You killed her,* he told himself. Though he knew it, of course he already knew it, the words suddenly made him nauseous. Tears welled in his eyes again.

*That's sick,* he shouted at himself, trying to fight it. *You're all fucked up!*

But the guilt was a shard of metal, twisting in his guts.

*I had to do it,* he pleaded. The reasons clicked, one by one, through his mind. Because she was trying to kill *him,* because of what she was going to do, because of what she *was.* But they made no difference. All he could think of was those terror-filled eyes.

"I'm sorry, Irina," he whispered, the tears spilling out to join the slick of sweat and blood now clinging to his skin. He blinked rapidly, clearing them out of his eyes. He was so busy squeezing them away that it took him some time to realize something was out of place on the control console.

He stared at the instruments blankly. Something was wrong with what he was seeing. What was it?

Then it hit him. *The Radar Altimeter!* The altimeter was no longer a barber pole. It was taking readings.

Meaning *Endeavor* had already made the 9,000-feet trigger.

Shock flooded Reynolds. That was impossible! His eyes swung to the barometric readings—sure enough, they were still up around 28,000 feet. The Mach meter was still sliding down to Mach 1.7, nearly 1,300 miles per hour.

*Fuck!* In a flash, Reynolds realized what had happened.

The barometric readings were off. Way off. Some component in the Air Data System was fucked—the probes, the signal processors, the transducers—and was feeding the barometric altitude tape readings nearly 20,000 feet high. He was sure of it. The Radar Altimeter used a simple electromagnetic pulse, bounced off Ground and fed straight through to the tape; there was no way it could be reading false.

*Endeavor* was at 9,000 feet. Maybe less.

*Oh God, God, God, God.*

Reynolds's mind reeled. His hands and feet scrabbled

at the controls. Fuck, this was bad. Thanks to the error, he was coming in way too steep and fast. At 1,300 miles per hour! He yanked the RHC as far left as he dared and slammed the rudder pedal down, sending *Endeavor* into one final banking turn—a desperate attempt to slough at least some of that excess speed off. Reynolds's stomach sank with more than the sudden jump in g-force. It was hopeless, he knew. Even if he succeeded in stripping a couple of hundred of miles per hour extra off, he calculated he was still going to hit the water at around Mach one.

*At 762 miles per hour,* he thought savagely. *Bet Ground didn't have that sort of speed in mind when they cooked this maneuver up.*

Worse was the lost time. Reynolds darted another glance at the Radar Altimeter: 7,000 feet! He had to bite down a despairing cry. The Glide Slope Indicator put his current sink rate at 10,000 feet per minute. That gave him forty-five seconds to carry out the approach sequence.

*No way,* he thought, hopelessly. That was nowhere near enough time.

He jammed the stick forwards as hard as he could, praying. The first step was to ramp the attack angle back. He watched the eight ball fall back from the thirty-degree mark it had been holding—twenty-eight degrees . . . twenty-seven . . . twenty-six. *C'mon, c'mon, c'mon,* he begged the tilting indicator. It was imperative he get the attack angle close to zero in time to fire the main engines for final flare. That was the only way to reduce his sink rate enough to make splashdown possible. If he didn't make it in time, *Endeavor* would hit the water at its current glide slope of minus nineteen degrees. And Reynolds knew what that meant.

A one-way ticket to the bottom of the ocean.

*If you really are over water,* Reynolds thought suddenly. That was a point too: had Ground's flight plan succeeded? Really brought him down over the Pacific? And if it had, would he strike water, or one of the islands dotting the world's largest ocean?

Or even a ship?

Reynolds had no way of knowing. The steep attack angle prevented him from seeing anything out of the forward flight-deck windows, save blue sky and the flashing white blur of what might be clouds. And no time to worry about it either—the altimeter was already down to 4,000 feet.

Less than thirty seconds.

Reynolds watched the downward crawl of the eight ball anxiously—nineteen degrees . . . eighteen . . . seventeen. *C'mon, you bitch,* he screamed, the stick jammed forwards so hard he was afraid it might snap.

*Get your nose down, down, down!*

He swung the orbiter out of the leftward bank as her nose dropped. That would have to be it. No time for more speed-stripping maneuvers. He would have to go in with what he had.

Reynolds glanced at the Mach meter. *Mach 1.3.* The speed brake would probably take another 300 miles per hour off before he hit. So he *would* come in under Mach one. Just.

Not that it helped. It was still too fast. Way too fast.

His eyes flicked back and forth between the altimeter and eight ball. *Fuck, it's gonna be close.* Altitude was under 3,000 feet and plunging. Final flare was normally initiated at 1,750 feet—he could push it out to 1,000 feet, but that would be the limit. He had to get the orbiter pitched level before she hit that altitude. But the eight ball was still lazing its way down the degree notches—thirteen . . . twelve . . . eleven. Every notch seemed to be taking a half hour.

*C'mon, fuck you!* Reynolds raged. He center-gimballed the SSMEs and held his fingers over the hotfire keys in preparation.

Two thousand feet. Nine degrees. Twenty seconds to go.

Reynolds was suddenly conscious again of the choking heat inside his suit. Even without weightlessness, the steam from his breath and sweat was clouding inside his helmet, boiled to vapor by the excruciating heat. It stung his eyes, making it difficult to keep them focused.

One thousand five hundred feet. Six degrees. Thirteen seconds or so.

Reynolds's spirits sank. Three seconds left to chew through six degrees. No way she was going to do it.

Sure enough, three seconds later the altimeter was dropping like a stone through the 1,000-feet tape marker. And the eight ball was still crawling—five degrees . . . four . . . three. Reynolds watched it a couple of despairing seconds, then jammed the hotfire keys home.

He couldn't wait a second more. He *had* to fire now, whatever the consequences.

The sudden kick slammed him back in the seat. His hands slid from the controls. The orbiter shook as 12,000 pounds of thrust shot her forwards, ramping her glide slope down in one violent motion.

Reynolds fought to get his hands back on the controls, his eyes back on the instruments. At the speed he was going, an instant's loss of control would be fatal.

He scanned the control console feverishly as the engines died, eyes locking on to the altimeter. Sink rate had slowed all right; the tape was crawling now. Reynolds squinted to focus on the white figures, reversed out of black.

His eyes widened. *Eighty feet! Jesus Christ!*

A big wave could swallow that distance.

*If* he was over water. Reynolds caught a smudge of blue in the forward flight-deck windows from the corner of his eye, but whether it was sea or sky was impossible to say. There was no time—he had to get *Endeavor*'s ass dropped for splashdown.

Now.

Reynolds wrenched the RHC back savagely to raise the wing elevons. Having pulled *Endeavor*'s angle of attack down, he now had to claw it back up, all the way to ten degrees if he could. The eight ball hesitated, then began to slide upwards. *Endeavor* shook violently under the suddenly shifted load.

Reynolds shot a glance at the altimeter. Seventy feet, sink rate ten feet per second.

*Seven seconds. Shit.*

He scrabbled at the SSME gimbal keys, punching the sequence for vertical maximum. His hand moved blindly, instinctively, through the shaking chaos. It was almost impossible to see anything on the wildly vibrating con-

404                        Peter McAllister

sole. Reynolds's eyes groped for the Mach meter, trying
to get a fix on his speed.

*Mach one,* he saw finally. *And falling.*

Somewhere below, the sonic boom would be splitting
the air, smashing into the water. But there was no way
of hearing it, no time to listen. He had to get his fingers
back into position to fire.

Splashdown was seconds away.

Reynolds raised his left hand weakly. It took all his
strength to hold it steady through the shaking, roaring
hell the orbiter had become. His whole being was focused on those two gloved fingertips, hovering shakily
over the SSME hotfire keys.

*Hold steady,* he urged himself. It was imperative he
pick the right moment to fire. A split second too early,
or too late, and the orbiter would flip.

Vision, sense and feeling disappeared, stripped from
him by *Endeavor*'s violent jolting. All he was left with
was instinct, blind and pure.

*Not yet, not yet, not yet,* he told himself. He waited,
cocooned in the storm of shrieking metal as the engines
tilted and the orbiter dropped.

"NOW!"

He screamed the word at himself. His fingers shot forward, jamming down on the keys.

A fantastic impact boomed through the orbiter, flinging Reynolds's head against the side panel, smashing his
helmet. The heat in his suit was sucked out instantly by
cold, howling wind.

But whether the impact was the orbiter hitting water,
or the engines kicking in, or both, was impossible to say.

1:28 P.M., Central Standard Time, 3 April 2005
Shuttle Flight Control Room One, Johnson Space Center

Ewell leaned forward in his chair, nails cutting into the
armrest leather from the tightness of his grip. His heart
was thumping in his chest. His breaths were shallow, as
if he were afraid the force of his respiration could somehow affect the progress of the glowing dot on-screen.

*Must be getting close now,* he thought. Christ, he hoped so. The tension was unbearable.

"Jesus," Ewell heard Carmichael murmur, through his earpiece. "It's like trying to watch Venus through a magnifying glass."

Ewell agreed. The thermal image told them virtually nothing. They had no way of knowing the orbiter's altitude, or when she was going to hit. All they knew was how hot she was, and therefore how fast she was probably going.

And that she was still in existence.

The tiny, wedge-shaped dot on-screen was glowing cherry red now, meaning her speed was falling, probably down to about Mach two, Ewell guessed. That much was good. Reynolds was on track, at least as nearly as could be judged from the thermal image.

And he was over water now. That was good too. Ewell had sensed the tension in the NASA Administrator as the dot had cleared the Kamchatka Peninsula, the last outcrop of Russian territory, some minutes earlier. Reardon hadn't said anything, of course. But Ewell could see that, for her, the most important part of the reentry plan had already been carried off.

Anything else would be icing on the cake.

Incredibly, it looked as if Reynolds might just provide that too. Ewell marveled at the man's skill. To pilot a Shuttle, the most complicated, cantankerous gadget NASA had in the air, bar none, manually through successful reentry was almost superhuman.

*Even if he doesn't make it he'll be a legend,* Ewell thought. *Just for getting it this far.*

He watched anxiously as the image dulled from red to magenta, marking *Endeavor*'s still-falling temperature, and speed. Ewell felt the muscles in his gut tighten. This was almost it. Magenta meant 800 degrees Fahrenheit, the temperature *Endeavor* carried when her airspeed was Mach one or under. Reynolds was going to splash down any moment.

If he held it together, the color should slide smoothly from magenta, through brown, to gray as the orbiter's temperature fell. If he didn't, Ewell guessed, it would shoot suddenly back up to white, the color of disaster, as *Endeavor* exploded and burned . . .

The sudden tumult in the ficker cut Ewell's train of thought dead. He leaped to his feet, a cry torn from him too at what he saw.

The signal had . . . disappeared. Where the magenta spot had been there was now nothing, just a smudge of green on the blue of cold ocean.

*What the fuck?*

Ewell stared at the screen, bewildered. Around him, the chaos of voices swelled in a crescendo. He heard a voice fight its way through the noise, not on the channel, but in the open air.

Carmichael.

"People!" the Flight Activities Officer shouted. "It's just splashdown." He waited until the voices abated somewhat, then went through the channel.

"It's just splashdown, people," he said, voice still raised, into the mike. "The water is damping the thermal signal. It's just splashdown. That's all it is." He waited until the voices died, then turned to Ewell in appeal. "Bob?"

Ewell nodded agreement. Lew was probably right. The water could damp the signal, drowning it as the freezing ocean temperatures sucked heat from the orbiter. The problem was now they were really blind. Lack of signal could mean anything. *Endeavor* could be spearing down towards the bottom of the Pacific, taking Reynolds and the others to their deaths. It could have disintegrated on impact. Or it could be taxiing off to the nearest atoll, fresh from a perfect landing.

They had no way of knowing.

*At least we know where whatever happened happened though,* Ewell thought. He hit his push-to-talk.

"Lew's right, people," he said. "Whatever's happened, *Endeavor* is in the water. FIDO, can you get us a fix on those coordinates?"

"Roger that, FLIGHT," the Flight Dynamics Officer replied. "Impact point is 42.3 North, 165.7 East."

"Copy that, FIDO," he replied. "INCO, FLIGHT. Get those coordinates through to Navy Command. CAP-

COM, I want you to start trying the suit UHF channels. Copy?"

The replies came back in near perfect unison.

"Copy that, FLIGHT. Copy, FLIGHT."

Ewell nodded. "As for the rest of us, let's just stay calm, all right, people? *Endeavor* is where she should be, and we'll find out soon enough what shape she's in. Okay?"

He went off-channel to a chorus of murmured agreement. He swung the mike away from his mouth and stood peering at the screen, wondering.

But there was nothing there to see, just the same inscrutable smudge, cool green on cold ocean blue.

# 21

Pak Kee-su, wiry first mate of the *Pusan Princess*, shivered in the early-morning cold. A biting wind was coming off the heaving sea, drenching everything in salt mist, including the roll-your-own he was trying to keep alight. Pak pulled his blue wool jacket tighter round himself and sucked the cigarette, hard. The half-extinguished tip glowed, hesitated, then leapt into life as it hit a dry section. He dragged the rough smoke deep into his lungs, then exhaled. The smoke vanished the instant it left his mouth, borne off by the gusting wind.

*Jegiral!* he cursed privately. His shoulder was hurting again. He flexed the joint irritably, damning Kim Jaekyu for his clumsiness of two days before.

That was the last time he let *him* tie the net block unsupervised.

Pak waved a hand impatiently, to let Kim know to start the water sprayers. A second later, the jets began drumming the ocean's surface, mixing with slapping bluefin tails and sea spume. Another wave and the overhead floods came on, throwing the scene into harsh, unnatural glare. A glance and little Lee Sung-ho began ladling chum, his boy's arms pumping as he flung the live bait from the rectangular iron tanks.

The water roiled as excited tuna began to bunch at the ship's stern. Pak Kee-su nodded in satisfaction. Just a bit tighter and he could give the order to launch.

He could see the skiff crew out of the corner of his eye, waiting on his command to swing out the gantry and launch the little boat that deployed the mile-long seine net. Pak waited impassively, dragging on the cigarette.

*Just a minute more,* he thought, exhaling smoke.

The harder they let the fish shoal, the bigger the haul would be.

When the tuna began to breach, throwing themselves whole-bodied out of the water in snapping excitement, he was finally satisfied. He raised his hand, preparing to give the open-palm command—*Launch!* Before he could even start bringing the hand down, however, an almighty BOOM! thumped through the air around them, stopping Pak midgesture.

*Jegiral!* What the fuck was that?

For a moment Pak thought he was back in army training, listening to the thunder as his crew's 175-millimeter howitzer fired. But then he realized this sound was slightly different.

It was a *rolling* boom. Like the sound jet planes made when they crossed the sound barrier.

He scanned the sky, mystified. The rest of the crew had obviously had the same idea; they were looking too. But none of them could see anything. The sky was clear.

Pak cocked his head. He could *hear* it though. Underneath the dying boom was the murmur of far-off thunder, as if a storm were under way, somewhere unseen, over the horizon. Pak kept looking, ignoring the questioning glances from the rest of the crew.

*Something* was going on. Somewhere.

Suddenly he saw it, a mile or two or three off the port stern. His jaw fell in amazement. The cigarette dropped from his lips to the deck, extinguished instantly by sloshing seawater.

*"Jungmal mitchigen-ne,"* he whispered, awed. *I don't believe it.*

It was something huge and white; Pak's first, crazy thought was that it was an iceberg, or a ship, dropping out of the sky. Whatever it was, it was traveling at fantastic speed. As he watched, it smashed into the ocean, throwing a plume of water impossibly high, miles into the air. In the same instant something on it seemed to catch fire, an orange glow that flickered, kaleidoscope-like, through the towering sheet of water.

What happened next caused Pak to gape even more. Incredibly, the object didn't plunge into the water and vanish. It *reappeared*, on the other side of the seawater sheet it had thrown up. Rocketing along *atop* the ocean's surface.

The fucking thing was *gliding*!

Massive plumes of water arced out behind the far-off object as it sped. That was nothing compared to the clouds of . . . something that billowed behind it though, rising hundreds, maybe thousands of feet in the air. *Steam*, Pak realized after a moment—steam from the fire still burning at the back of it.

There was no terror, even though Pak could see the thing was headed right for them. There was no time. Before he was even able to register it, the thing was past them, shooting out of sight along a trajectory some hundreds of yards to starboard. Pak had just that same momentary impression of something huge and white— like an airplane, but not like any Pak had ever seen.

He gaped after it, eyes tracking the inferno spewing out the object's aft end for the few seconds until it disappeared over the horizon. He was still staring when the cloud of scalding steam drifted over them, choking further vision, and the wave from the object's wake broke on them, dousing the deck with a hundred tons of freezing seawater.

**Mission Elapsed Time: 5 days, 3 hours, 51 minutes**
**Flight Deck. Space Shuttle** *Endeavor*

For a moment, Reynolds's senses vanished, drowned in the shrieking wind. Vision disappeared, obliterated by the blurring air movement and shaking violence. Hearing fell away, overpowered by the roar. Only his sense of touch remained, telling him, by the flicking stings on his face, that his suddenly exposed head was under assault from wind-driven debris, and in danger of getting creamed.

Reynolds tore his right hand off the RHC and shielded his face with that arm. The stick was no use to him now, anyway. He kept his other hand locked tight on the Thrust Controller however, jamming it back as far as it would go. He had to keep the SSMEs firing at maximum, forcing *Endeavor*'s ass down into the water. It was the only thing that would save his life.

*Is it working?*

Reynolds couldn't say. The cataclysmic roar shook even the *thoughts* out of his head, making it hard to think coherently.

He tried to concentrate. *Is it working, damn it?*

Part of him was dimly aware it had to be—he was still alive, wasn't he? And he could feel, through the violence pinning him to his seat, the incline that meant *Endeavor* was holding a gliding angle. But there was something else there too, something disturbing, that he couldn't quite pick through the vibration and whipping wind.

He blocked everything else out and tried to focus.

*What is it?*

Suddenly, he caught it—a vague, *shifting* feeling, a starboard tilt, underlying *Endeavor*'s tempestuous rumble.

Reynolds screamed, a howl of despair that vanished instantly, sucked into the vortex. *Fuck!* The orbiter's port wing was rising. Slowly, gently, but rising nonetheless. He'd obviously hit at a tiny roll angle, and the unevenness had bounced *Endeavor* off level. And now something in the aerodynamics—the mechanics of the air rushing over her surfaces at still nearly 700 miles per hour—was working on the gap. Widening it, accelerating it.

There was no doubting the outcome. If he didn't reverse the tilt, *Endeavor* would flip. Her nose would dig in and she would start cartwheeling. At the speed they were going, that would be instant, chewed-to-pieces death.

Reynolds reached out to the control console blindly. The worst thing was he had almost no control. The aerodynamic surfaces could never correct the tilt in time; attempting a main-engine gimbal would be even worse. His one hope was a crude, lunatic maneuver.

*Choke the starboard SSME. If I'm lucky the loss of thrust from that side will allow it to rise up and level her. Then I can refire and push her ass back down.*

It was a desperate move, one that would increase the risk of *Endeavor*'s nose falling and digging in. And he wasn't even sure it would work. But he had to try.

It was the only option he had.

Reynolds pressed the damp key for the starboard engine, struggling to keep his finger centered in the shaking chaos. There was an immediate change in the vibration rumbling through *Endeavor*—the engine had choked all right. But would it be enough? Reynolds held his breath, trying to judge.

No point looking at the instruments. He could hardly see past his fingertips; the eight ball would be spinning like a top anyway, telling him nothing. The only way to pick it would be what he felt through his ass.

*Endeavor* trembled, seeming to shy sideways. Reynolds panicked for a split second, afraid she was going to slew. That would have been even worse, a surefire path to instant disintegration. But she righted herself, miraculously, and he felt her starboard side rising, drifting up to level.

Relief flooded him. It was working.

He leaned forward with difficulty, driving the hotfire key down by the weight behind his finger. Now he had to get the starboard SSME back on-line, quickly, before the reduced thrust at *Endeavor*'s tail allowed a catastrophic fall in her attack angle.

As it was he was almost too late. He felt the engine kick back in, but the orbiter's aft end continued, ominously, to rise. Reynolds hung on grimly, waiting for the thrust to take. It was like those few terrifying moments at the cusp of a roller coaster's arc, where fear the coaster is going to shoot you off into space suddenly grips you, even though you know the downward plunge is just over the hill.

At least, Reynolds hoped it was like that.

Maybe this coaster had made up its mind to just keep going, flinging the kiddies off the guide rails and grinding them to hamburger wherever gravity brought them down.

Luckily, a couple of seconds later, he felt the orbiter's tail waver, then begin to fall. Relief flooded him once more. It was going to be okay. Sure enough, a second later *Endeavor* slammed back into the water, the impact smashing Reynolds's head against his headrest, dazing him.

His hands slipped from the controls. Reynolds let them fall. They were no use now. He'd done everything he could. Now it was just a matter of whether *Endeavor*'s fuel held out, allowing the SSMEs to fire and keep her ass firmly in the water.

Of whether her level orientation held long enough for her to lose speed, or skewed and smashed them all to smithereens.

Or whether they were in clear water, or were going to hit some unseen thing—a ship, a reef or an island. A goddamn whale, for Christ's sake.

Or a hundred other things Reynolds preferred not to think of, but which could each, separately and individually, destroy them.

No way to know any of those things. Nothing to do but just lie back and enjoy the ride.

Reynolds lolled like a rag doll in the seat, his body rolling as the orbiter pitched and lurched. It was impossible to tell from *Endeavor*'s roaring progress if she was slowing. The thunder of the firing SSMEs masked any fall in the vibration. Reynolds knew they must be slowing—every second he was still alive would be stripping speed.

He'd know for sure when the fuel ran out and the engines stopped firing.

A sudden blow to the temple reminded Reynolds to cover his head. The cockpit was still a maelstrom of flying debris, driven by the wind screaming in through the smashed overhead window. He tried weakly to lift his arms, but they wouldn't move. It was as if his strength had fled, now there was nothing more to do. Burned down to the last kilocalorie, leaving him enough to keep essential functions ticking over but nothing more.

A deaf, dumb, immobile machine. Able to do nothing but sit there and *experience*.

He wondered detachedly if Eli and Roberts had survived. Probably the tininess of the airlock had worked in their favor—the cramped cylinder preventing them from building up too much velocity in any one direction. They'd still be getting crunched, though. Reynolds hoped Eli had followed the same line of reasoning as him and suited Roberts up. That would be her only chance.

Reynolds let the thought slide. He'd find out soon enough. If he survived himself.

A sudden change in the vibration alerted him that the moment was closer than he'd thought. His eyes flicked automatically, but uselessly, to the CRT screen. Without the GPCs there was no Engine Propellant Feed Gauge, of course—therefore no way of telling how much fuel remained. But unless he was mistaken, the muted vibration meant just one thing.

SSME thrust was declining. Propellant was running out.

Time flicked back instantly to dreamy, slo-mo mode. This was it, Reynolds realized. Crunch time. The SSMEs were about to die. If enough speed had been lost, *Endeavor*'s nose would slap down, they'd all get wet and that would be it.

If not . . .

Second followed second in an agonizingly slow crawl. Reynolds felt every sensation, saw everything, with crystal-sharp clarity.

At three seconds the vibration dropped by half. Now it was just the buffeting of the water *Endeavor* was plowing through. The SSMEs were spent.

At five seconds, Reynolds felt the orbiter's nose start to fall.

He readied himself for impact, though of course there was nothing he could do. Either they were going too fast, *Endeavor*'s nose would dig in upon slapdown and they would all die. Or they were going slow enough, her nose would bob back up, and they would live.

Simple.

Impossible to judge which it would be. The vibration told Reynolds they were still traveling, but not how fast. They could be going seventy-five miles per hour, or *three hundred* and seventy-five. Besides which, Reynolds had no idea how slow was slow enough.

The drift downwards seemed to take forever. Reynolds felt *Endeavor*'s nose laze down, down, down . . . even further. Just when he thought he'd got it wrong, they must be going so slow the nose was going to touch gently, maybe had already, she hit.

The impact flung Reynolds forwards in his seat. He was vaguely conscious of an almighty CRACK!, and a darkening of the light as a cone of blue water was thrown hundreds of feet in the air around *Endeavor*'s nose. Then all sensation ceased as hundreds of tons of seawater smashed over her, breaking the forward flight-deck windows and pouring into the cockpit in rivers of freezing blue.

*The cold! Jesus Christ, the cold!*

Reynolds felt it everywhere, all at once. Rushing into his suit, washing over his head. The touch of it made him gasp, opening his lungs involuntarily. That was a mistake. The next thing he knew his lungs were full of frigid salt water, and he was coughing and spewing violently to get it out.

He was so busy with that he had no time for the real question: were they going to live or die? Only when he had spat the last of his lungful out did Reynolds realize the answer.

*Christ, we're still afloat!*

*Endeavor*'s nose had speared into the water, then bobbed back up to continue the glide across the water's surface. She was slewing sideways, he could feel her, but she was *slowing*.

They were going to make it.

Reynolds sat stupidly, immobilized again, but by amazement this time. They'd made it. *He'd* made it. Pulled *Endeavor* through that hellish reentry, executed that lunatic splashdown maneuver flawlessly.

He was safe. They were all safe . . . maybe. Reynolds would have to check on Roberts and Rodriguez.

But mot important of all, COSMONAUT was safe.
He'd got the secret back down to Earth. Now he could
tell NASA and they'd . . . they'd . . .

Well they'd do *something*. Catch them or . . . stop
them. Or kill them. Whatever. The point was he was
alive.

And the secret was safe.

*Almost,* Reynolds realized, listening to the seawater
drain from the flight deck down to the middeck through
the access hatches.

*Endeavor* might be sliding to a stop atop the ocean
waves, but she wasn't going to stay there for long. Apart
from the pressure-tight crew compartment, nothing on
the orbiter was sealed, or watertight. Soon after she
stopped, *Endeavor* would start taking on water. Within
a half hour, Reynolds estimated, she would be at the
bottom of the sea.

He had to get to Eli and Roberts. If they were still
alive. Then get the three of them off *Endeavor* and onto
the life rafts.

He scrabbled weakly at the harnesses holding him to
the seat. It was harder to work the catches now his
gloved fingers were numb with cold and fatigue, and
seawater slopped in his suit whenever he moved. Reynolds forced himself to stop, unlock his wrist guide rings
and remove the gloves. He waited, teeth chattering,
while seawater drained from his suit upper over his
hands.

*Fuck,* it was cold. The fatigue, the dehydration had
left Reynolds dangerously weak, vulnerable to the chill.
He'd have to be careful of that, make sure he didn't slip
into hypothermic shock.

*Best thing is to keep moving.*

Reynolds unfastened his harnesses and levered himself
out of the seat. He picked his way painfully across the
sodden flight deck to the interdeck access hatch. The
clamber down the ladder felt like the longest two minutes of his life. Every muscle throbbed, every burn,
bruise and wound on his skin merged into a single dull,
undifferentiated ache. Once or twice he had to hang on
for dear life; *Endeavor* was still sliding, lurching, to a

stop. But he made it to the bottom and slumped there a moment, one arm hooked through the ladder, to rest.

He tried to yell, when he'd caught his breath, but though his lips formed around the words—*Eli! It's me, Reynolds. You guys alive in there?*—there wasn't enough strength to push it above a whisper.

So he stumbled blindly, instead, across the middeck to the airlock hatch. He had to kick his way through thigh-level water, and he fell once, tripping over some piece of the debris swirling through the middeck and drenching himself anew with a suit full of water. Reynolds dragged himself up, sobbing, and over to the hatch, collapsing against it. He banged on it with an arm, coughing up yet another dose of seawater.

He listened weakly for a response. Was anybody alive in there?

A moment later it came—a scrape as the inner actuator handle was wound through the 440 degrees necessary to crack the airlock seal. Then the door swung open, revealing Eli.

He looked pretty bad. Eli's face was slick with blood, probably half his own and half Roberts's, Reynolds guessed. A cut above one eye was swollen shut from a massive impact bruise.

Rodriguez's good eye scanned the scene—the flooded middeck, the junk floating everywhere, Reynolds hanging off the hatch. It swung up to Reynolds's face, searching out *his* eyes.

"We made it," Eli croaked. His voice was flat, as if too stunned even for disbelief.

Reynolds nodded. "Yeah, we made it," he said, the words exhausting him. He had to muster his strength to speak again. "What about Roberts?" he asked. "Is she alive?"

Rodriguez gestured behind him. He groped for the words. "Yeah . . . she is," he said finally. "But she's bad . . . in a bad way." He looked up at Reynolds again. "She'll die if we don't get her . . . to . . . a hospital."

Reynolds nodded to show he understood. He didn't trust himself to talk. Unconsciousness was lapping at him again, his limbs were threatening to turn to jelly once more. He dragged himself upright with supreme effort, gulped air.

*Just a bit further, soldier,* he told himself. *You're not out of danger yet.*

"Okay," he said forcefully. "Eli, we gotta get outta here. *Endeavor's* going . . . she's going to sink." He waved a hand at the side hatch. "I'm going to jettison the hatch and inflate the slide. I want you to get one of the CAPS and pull the life raft out of it. Okay? Then we can work on getting Roberts into it."

"Copy that, Reynolds," Rodriguez said wearily, and began squirming out of the airlock. Reynolds pushed himself off the airlock door and over to the circular side hatch on the middeck wall. He bent to his knees and plunged his hands into the freezing water. He groped for the access panel that covered the side-hatch jettison T-handle. Locating it by feel, he levered it free with a finger and yanked the T-handle solidly. The side hatch blew with a satisfying explosion of pyrotechnics, flying clear of the orbiter at fifty feet a second.

Sunlight poured into the middeck.

Reynolds *was* going to then retrieve the inflatable Emergency Egress Slide and push it out of the hole, simultaneously tripping the inflation lanyard. But the sequence of sounds after the hatch blew stopped him dead.

The explosion was followed just two seconds later by a metallic clang as the jettisoned hatch struck . . . something, then a splash as it bounced off and into the water. Then, incredibly, a string of unmistakably angry, and from the sound of it obscene, *Korean.*

Reynolds turned to look at Eli. The two of them stared at one another, then at the hatch, in amazement.

1:39 P.M., Central Standard Time, 3 April 2005
Shuttle Flight Control Room One, Johnson Space Center

Ewell patched himself back into the command channel, though he knew it was pointless. CAPCOM would notify him as soon as she had something. But it was the waiting he couldn't stand, that and the awful blankness of the thermal image still on-screen. Even the green smudge had disappeared now, leaving the area where *Endeavor* had gone down a solid expanse of cold, unbroken blue. As far as the thermal sensors on IMAGER-3 were concerned, it was as if the orbiter no longer existed.

*And that,* thought Ewell, *is what I'm afraid of.*

"CAPCOM, FLIGHT," he said, into the mike. "We getting anything?"

"Negative, FLIGHT, I'm sorry," CAPCOM replied. "I'm still trying. But there's nothing on any of the suit frequencies so far."

"Roger, CAPCOM," Ewell answered. "Keep us posted." He flicked himself off the command channel, frustrated.

*The suit signals will be weak,* he told himself uneasily. *Just because we didn't pick them up the first time doesn't mean they're not there.*

But that blank screen was still staring down impassively at him. And the minutes were ticking by.

If only Reynolds would light a flare, if he was alive and able to! Ewell was sure the burning magnesium would show up on the thermal image. But it was hopeless waiting for that—Reynolds wasn't to know the only insight they had was via this goddamned heat picture. Ewell could get Marshall to switch IMAGER-3 back to optical, but the recalibration would take at least twenty minutes. And the Prowlers the Navy had scrambled would be fifteen at least . . .

Suddenly CAPCOM was back on the channel, her voice brimming with excitement. "FLIGHT, CAPCOM," she babbled. "I've got . . . I'm getting something. It's Reynolds's frequency. There's a voice . . ."

All conversation in the control room cut dead. Ewell's heart leaped. His finger jabbed at his push-to-talk, missing it twice in his excitement. "Copy that, CAPCOM," he shouted. "Get him to identify."

"Roger, FLIGHT," Tranh replied, and spoke the words into her headset mike: "UHF transmission, this is Mission Control. Please confirm you are Mission Specialist Reynolds." She only said it once, and there was no mistaking the smile that lit up her face, but it still wasn't enough for Ewell.

He punched himself back into the channel impatiently. "Well?" he barked. "Is it Reynolds?"

Tranh put a hand over her mike and nodded happily. "Roger, FLIGHT," she said. "It's MS Reynolds all right."

The ficker exploded with spontaneous, thunderous applause. It took Ewell three attempts to get himself heard over the racket.

"Put Reynolds on intercom, CAPCOM," Ewell bellowed, "put him on intercom. Let us all hear this incredible bastard's voice."

It took Tranh a moment to reply. She held up a hand, flustered, apparently listening to something over her headset. "Copy that, FLIGHT," she said, "switching to . . . wait . . MS Reynolds is asking something . . ."

Her eyes widened in surprise. She looked up at Ewell. "FLIGHT, he wants to know if we have anybody here who can speak Korean. He's holding his mike up to something . . . I think it . . . I can hear someone in the background . . ."

Recollecting herself, she switched the channel over to intercom. Sure enough, a stream of Korean, high and thin as if it were coming from some distance away, crackled out of the control room speakers.

". . . *nonun dodatche muehsul hanungen-nya? Gogidurul modu djotcha burigo isse! . . .*"

The control room fell silent once more. Ewell's jaw swung open. Control team members looked at each other, nonplussed. It was left to Carmichael to break the impasse.

"Michael Lee," he yelled, turning to scan the crowd choking the back of the control room. "Is Michael Lee here?"

A moment's turmoil at the right of the throng ended with a young Korean-American man pushing his way through the front row. Carmichael motioned him with a hand to translate the words issuing through the speakers. Lee listened, mystified, as every eye in the control room settled on him.

"It's a fisherman," Lee said hesitantly, as if he didn't quite believe his ears. He looked over at Ewell. "He says—'Get out of here! What the hell do you think you're doing? You're scaring away all the fish!' "

There was a moment's pause, then the room erupted again, this time with laughter. Ewell felt it invade him, move into his gut, then radiate out until his body was shaking with gusts of silent, relieved laughter. He had to wipe tears out of his eyes. He waited until he was able, then pressed his push-to-talk.

"INCO, FLIGHT," he chuckled. "Get on to Navy Command. Tell 'em to go bring those bastards back."

# Aftermath

"Going home, sir?" The NASA guard's grin was broad as he handed back Reynolds's photo ID. There was no mistaking the admiration in his voice.

*This is Reynolds, dude! The Man of the Moment.*

The press might be full of how the detective had turned the tables on Drupev's accomplice, killing him and trying heroically to save ISS and the lives of the other two cosmonauts, Kalganin and Ruskaya, but Security Specialist Doug Whittemore knew that wasn't Reynolds's *real* feat. It was pulling off the impossible, bringing that bird down through manual reentry. That was what would set Reynolds's name in stone at NASA.

"What?" frowned The Man of the Moment, pulled unexpectedly out of reverie. He focused on the guard's face, seeing it for the first time.

The smile faded. "I . . . ah . . . asked if you were going home, sir," the guard said, deflated. "To Detroit. The address is on your ID."

Reynolds stared at the ID in his hand as if seeing *that* for the first time. Connor rode to the rescue, leaning over him to address the white-uniformed guard.

"He's going home all right, Specialist," he laughed. "You think we could get him to stay with the salaries they pay us poor saps?"

The man nodded, relieved at the intervention, and stepped back to wave them through. Connor eased the car out of the gate and into the traffic, shaking his head.

"Goddamn you, Edge," he laughed, glancing over at Reynolds, seated beside him. "Can't you even unwind now? Lighten up, for Christ's sake. It's over."

Reynolds gave him a small, wry smile—restricting it more from habit than necessity. The wounds on his face and scalp were healed by now, the stitches gone and the bruises faded to dirty yellow. Even the angry, blistered burns on his wrists had dried to scarred pink.

*Matt's right,* he told himself. *It's over. Really over.*

So why couldn't he let it lie?

He had sat through the past three weeks with growing unease. Ten days, first up, confined to Johnson's biomed facility with nobody but an army of doctors for company. Then headlong into the postmission publicity treadmill—an endless round of press conferences, appearances, interviews. Even a White House reception. Reynolds had played his part throughout. Said his lines. Watched as the cover-up took shape.

Point one.

*Soyuz* Commander Drupev *did* kill Mission Specialist Myers. But it was not the crime of passion everybody, possibly even Drupev himself, had thought. Drupev had been manipulated into the killing by a fellow cosmonaut, Leonid Matchev, a secret member of terrorist organization the Patriotic Union. The group hoped to maneuver the United States into expelling Russia from the ISS program, exacerbating anti-U.S. hatred and generating demands for a Russian military counterstroke.

Point two.

Drupev's death was not suicide: it was murder. Matchev had killed his fellow cosmonaut to prevent his own role from coming to light, and to further exacerbate Russian feelings.

Point three.

Matchev's plot had begun to unravel when Detective Reynolds had discovered signs the Russian had tampered with vital evidence, a personal computer used by the murdered U.S. astronaut. Faced with exposure of his guilt, the Russian Flight Engineer had climbed into his suit and attempted to murder Detective Reynolds by way of a depressurization incident.

Point four.

When that failed, and Detective Reynolds had miraculously survived, the Russian was left with no choice but to destroy ISS and all aboard her, planning to escape the explosive conflagration himself in the Russian *Soyuz* module. Amazingly, Detective Reynolds had prevented Matchev's escape, killing the Russian in the process—though he had, unfortunately, been unable to avert the explosion, or save the lives of Mission Specialist Irina Ruskaya and Commander Boris Kalganin. Regrettably, Shuttle Commander Leichardt James and Pilot Michael Kennedy had perished too, caught in Matchev's murderous plan.

Point five.

Detective Reynolds had managed, heroically, to pilot a crippled Space Shuttle *Endeavor* back to Earth, in order to save the lives of critically injured Mission Specialist Melinda Roberts and Payload Specialist Eli Rodriguez.

Simple.

On and on the lie had spread, moving out from its epicenter like a rippling aftershock. News came from Russia that five apparent members of the terrorist group—an administrator, Dr. Vladimir Alinov, and four members of the Kosmonout Corps—had been killed in Star City, Korolev, presumably silenced on Patriotic Union orders. General Kobalov had tried to deny it, issuing a widely disbelieved statement alleging a U.S. conspiracy to destroy the Russian space program, but the Russian Duma had taken advantage of the temporary public hostility to rush through tough new antiterrorism laws cracking down on the Union. The U.S. Secretary of State had congratulated the Duma on averting a grave threat to Russian democracy.

*On and on and on.*

And through it all, behind the scenes, the deft hands of NASA and State Department spin doctors—suggesting, encouraging, steering. None of them, of course, knew the *real* truth, but it hadn't stopped them working the story like pros, milking it for every ounce of political purchase. The destruction of ISS, though a disaster, wasn't the end. It was a chance to build U.S.-Russian

cooperation anew. If they stopped now the terrorists
would have won. What they must do was initiate a *new*
station program—a bigger, better one. This time with a
Mars built into it from bottom up.

*On and on and on.*

It wasn't the cover-up that worried him though. It was
the feeling that NASA were fooling themselves too. He
had listened to the scientists and intelligence bigwigs at
the meeting earlier that day with disbelief. Those NASA
astrobiologists that had been let in on the secret. CIA
apparatchiks. A couple of DOD colonels. And the head
of Security Directorate up there at the rostrum, droning
on about how they were going to bury this thing.

*. . . a monstrosity, gentlemen. I think we can all agree,
now we are sure the program Detective Reynolds uncovered is liquidated, that our response should be to wipe it
from memory. We should let it lie, bury it . . .*

Bury it!

They must have thought he was stupid. He could almost see the eggheads' boners pushing up the table
whenever they talked about what Alinov had done. And
the questions! Over and over, in the cram sessions the
astrobiology geeks had put him through.

*Think, Mission Specialist Reynolds. Did he say the oxy-
hemoglobin was bonded or free?*

All delivered in that fake casual tone, barely masking
their salivating excitement. As if the charade that they
just needed the information for the files, nothing more,
had him fooled.

How long before some classified unit in NASA's labs
was running its own COSMONAUT? Reynolds wondered. Would they stick to computer sims and software
modeling? Or would they follow Alinov's monstrous
lead?

Straight to wetware. Live subjects, cultured from egg
to adult.

On and on the lies went. Security Directorate's Russian Bureau chief, Josh Enders, had given his report.
The four additional COSMONAUTs had been definitely
identified, he told them. Gennady Yakutin, Lyudmila
Zubko, Aleksandr Grishkin and Yekaterina Kvatov.

There had been no need to run the painstaking deductive profiles Security Directorate had prepared from information supplied by Detective Reynolds. The four individuals had identified themselves.

Every one of them had disappeared the day of Dr. Alinov's murder.

They were all dead, Enders told the meeting flatly. They had been traced to the Black Sea river port of Rostov, where they had boarded a trawler carrying a drug shipment to the Turkish city of Sinop. The vessel had been intercepted by Turkish Customs while still ten miles out and challenged. A firefight had ensued, in the course of which the trawler had sunk, carrying all on board to their deaths. There was no opportunity to mount a confirmatory mission; complications with the Turkish Interior Ministry wouldn't allow it. But the evidence was rock solid.

"They are all dead. No question about it."

That might even be true. Reynolds had no way of knowing. But you could bet Enders's next words weren't.

". . . in line with the Director's sentiments, the Intelligence Liaison Committee has resolved to let the issue lie. There will be no salvage attempt . . ."

Yeah, right. No salvage attempt. Reynolds wondered what cover the committee's mission, which was probably dragging sand at the bottom of the Black Sea at that very moment, had adopted. An oil concession? A marine-archaeological expedition, searching for remains of Roman trade galleys?

Whatever. It didn't matter. What mattered was the feeling Reynolds had that none of them—not Security Directorate, not NASA, not the CIA and Department of Defense spooks—understood what they were really dealing with in COSMONAUT. NASA was treating it like a sideshow to the main business of getting ISS II approved and built. The science geeks were thinking of it as an interesting curio—a nice term project for some covert blue-sky research. And the spooks . . . well! Though none of them gave anything away, just sat there stone-faced and nodded at everything the director said, you could tell what was going on in *their* minds.

*We can use this.*

They *would* find the four COSMONAUTs. If they were dead, they would recover the bodies and subject them to every test under the sun, to figure out how Alinov had done it. How *they* could do it. If the COSMONAUTs were still alive, they would collar them and lock them down deep in some secret facility, way out of sight, there to . . .

Reynolds preferred not to think what they would do in that case.

He'd tried to tell them, tell them all, that they were missing the point. COSMONAUT was not a bargaining chip, or a curio, or a clockwork gadget to be wound up and set to whatever dark work the spooks could cook up. The COSMONAUTs weren't controllable that way, for Christ's sake. That was what Alinov had thought, and look what happened to him. They were living, *thinking* beings. Not human, not anymore, but still with all the intelligence of Homo sapiens, all the cunning and instinct for violence.

And all the will to survive.

They were *people,* for Christ's sake. People with plans. He had tried to describe the chill horror of listening as Irina calmly, methodically, outlined them. Of gazing into those *not-human* eyes as she talked of new people, new species, new worlds. Did they think . . . *things* like that were going to give up easily? That they would let themselves be caught, just like that?

Those present at the meeting had listened to him. Silently. Politely. And obviously not the slightest bit fucking interested.

The SD head had gone on to talk of the precautionary measures NASA would take, even though the COSMONAUTs were dead. Special programs in personnel recruitment. Vetting procedures. Liaison with Russian Space Forces Command . . .

Reynolds had listened in mounting frustration. *Vetting procedures, for fuck's sake.* There was no way he could make them understand. They hadn't heard the calm conviction in Irina's voice as she talked of waiting hundreds of years.

Or looked into those eyes.

*Irina's eyes.*

There was danger in thinking about them, Reynolds knew, and he tried to stop himself, focusing instead on the freeway scenery sliding by his window. But before he knew it, she was there again, the remembered image of her face filling his mind's eye. Her eyes looking at him sadly, the hint of reproach in them unmistakable.

He had known from the first night he wasn't going to get away with it. Killing her like that. He had woken, slick with sweat, in the biomed facility bed. The echoes of his nightmare shout still ringing off the walls. A phalanx of doctors rushing in. The unit's overhead fluoros blinking into life, banishing the image of Irina's terror-filled eyes as she died, alone, in the *Soyuz*. Shaking his head mutely at the doctors' anxious questions.

Then and there, he'd known. He wasn't going to get away with it.

He'd dreamed of her every night since. At first, he'd hoped she might at least just replace Alicia, but instead he got them both, usually locked separately into their respective nightmares, but sometimes crossing over so that Alicia died in the inferno on ISS and he stumbled into the Clear Lake house to find Irina, battered and bloody, on the tiled bathroom floor. If anything, the dreams of Ally *increased*.

That was justice for you.

There would be no escape, that was what Reynolds knew now. Irina would be with him forever, the way that Alicia was. At least he understood her better now. His first thought, after he'd found out from Alinov's lips about COSMONAUT, was that she'd slept with him as a control tactic. Keeping tabs on how much he knew. But he understood now that was wrong. Her motives had been just what she'd said they were.

She'd been frightened. Frightened and alone.

Reynolds could understand it. How much more alone could you get than that? Just five brothers and sisters in the whole world. And a monster like Alinov for a father.

That same feeling he'd had in *Endeavor,* on the way down to Earth, was suddenly back with him. He felt the sting of nascent tears in his eyes again. *She was just a woman,* he thought uneasily. *Whatever else she was. A woman with the weight of the world on her shoulders.*

An ironic snort escaped him. *Maybe the weight of the galaxy . . .*

"You okay, Edge?" Connor's words cut across his train of thought.

Reynolds shook his head. "Just thinking, Matt," he said. He waved dismissively at the world outside. "All those UFO nuts. Chasing nonexistent green men and little gray aliens. When all the while the real aliens are right here on Earth. Under our noses."

Connor's eyes flicked from the road to Reynolds, then back again. "*Were* here, Edge," he said gently, nosing the car into the access lane that led to Ellington Field. "Were here. You heard what Enders said, right? The four of them are accounted for." He shrugged. "Passports, statements from the mules saying they saw them get on the boat, transcript of the radio transmission of the Turks blasting them to the seabed. What more do you want? They're gone, buddy. Turkish fish food."

He pulled up at the entrance station and handed his papers to the guard, who waved them through after a cursory examination.

It was Reynolds's turn to shrug. "I'd be happier if we had bodies." He looked across at Connor. "You tell me, Matt. If you were them, and you knew what NASA wanted to do if they got their hands on you, would you let yourself be caught?"

"They *didn't* let themselves get caught," Connor replied, swinging the car alongside the airfield. The C-20 that would take Reynolds back to Detroit was already waiting, a compact, natty white bird gleaming in the early-spring sun. "That's the point, Edge. That's what the firefight was all about. They started shooting to avoid being caught. Even though they must have known they were trapped. They chose death over capture."

Reynolds shrugged again. "Maybe," he said.

Connor pulled up beside the C-20 and killed the car's engine. He turned to Reynolds, laid a thick hand on the younger man's wrist. "Edge," he said softly. "Ours is not to reason why, remember? You've done your job, and done it brilliantly. We've both done our jobs. Let's leave it at that, okay?" He shook his head. "From now on in, it isn't our responsibility."

Reynolds recognized the appeal to the old Astronaut Corps ethos. You do your job—to the maximum, 100, 200, 1,000 percent—but nothing more.

And you let other people do theirs.

But beyond that he saw his friend, Matt Connor: an older, *tireder* man who had reluctantly, from a sense of duty, taken on a job he feared too big for him, and somehow pulled it off. Like some gambling junkie who had shot the craps despairingly, from habit rather than hope, and scored unexpectedly, he wanted to leave the table with his incredible winnings intact. Walk away. Go back to the house in Clear Lake and work on getting things straight with Carol again. Steer clear of anything that might rock the boat and plunge him back in.

*Like the idea that maybe this isn't over. That maybe some of the COSMONAUTs made it out . . .*

"Sure, Matt," he said, clapping his hand over Connor's and squeezing it solidly a moment or two. "You take care, you hear?" He opened the car door and got out, slinging his two bags over his right shoulder. He turned to go, intending to cross quickly to the tarmac area where the stewards waited, sparing them both a drawn-out scene, but the rasp of Connor's voice behind him stopped him.

"Edge?"

He turned back. Connor was leaning across the seat, looking up at him. "Yeah, Matt?" Reynolds said.

The older man grinned. 'You stay in touch now, you bastard. Okay?"

Reynolds grinned himself and nodded. "I will, Matt," he said, moving off towards the plane with a final wave

Connor watched him cross the tarmac and ascend the ladder, only starting the car again when Reynolds had disappeared inside the aircraft. He drove back to the entrance station and through onto the freeway in a dream, lost in thought.

He could see that Reynolds had meant it. At that particular moment he really did intend to stay in touch.

But Connor knew, equally, he would never see his former protégé again. *Too much water under too many bridges,* Connor thought, swinging the Buick through a lane change and accelerating up to fifty-five.

He'd been wrong after all. He had thought Myers's murder was God's way of bringing Reynolds and him back together, repairing the wounds of the past. But he could see now that was wrong. The ISS mission had been a special gift—a one-shot deal, out of the loop. A chance not to regain something.

But to say good-bye properly.

*Screw it,* Connor decided suddenly. *Good-bye ought to really mean good-bye.* Not just to Edge and the dreams of the past, but to NASA too. He would hand his resignation to the Director as soon as he got back. He'd done his part, seen the Agency through the crisis. It was time to quit, past time really. The forty-seven years he had given it ought to be enough.

Besides, didn't he have a woman to win?

His thoughts turned back to Carol sunnily. He started humming, unawares—some light refrain from one of those damn Grand Ole Opry tunes she loved so much. He would tell her tonight about his resignation. She wouldn't believe him, not at first. But he'd work on her, show her this time he meant it.

Who could tell? Maybe, if things went well, she might even move back in. The way he'd asked her to.

Connor settled back into the seat for the ten-minute run back to Johnson. He felt, as he drove, light-headed, almost giddy with optimism and possibility. A liberated man, freed now from even the encumbrances of memory.

9:17 P.M., 26 April 2005
Somewhere in New York

Aleks smiled as he felt Katya's hair brush his lip. She was clasped in his arms, the two of them sitting on the tiny fire escape, the closest thing to a balcony they had with this shitty apartment. A cool, early-spring breeze was coming up off the street—at least they got *one* benefit from being so high in a walk-up—bathing them in the smells of the city and waving Katya's beautiful red hair.

*Liliya's hair,* Aleks reminded himself.

He frowned. He couldn't afford to let himself slip like that. Not even in the privacy of his own mind.

*Aleksandr Grishkin and Yekaterina Kvatov are dead, stupid. Remember that.*

Now there was only Oleg and Liliya Yisotski.

Aleks rolled the unfamiliar names around in his mouth. Fuck your mother, they were hard to get used to! He hadn't realized how deep a name ran in you, how difficult it was to give up. But those were the names on the forged green cards the Chechen had provided, Oleg and Liliya Yisotski.

So Oleg and Liliya it had to be.

In time too, Aleks knew, there would be *Americantzi* names, and those would be even harder to get used to. He ran some of the few he knew through his mind, wondering which he would pick.

Would he be John? Or Neil? Or even . . . what was the other one he'd heard? William?

And what about Ka . . . Liliya? What would she be?

Elizabeth? Jennifer? Jane? Impossible—none of those were anywhere near beautiful enough for his little Liliya. Maybe by then it would be safe and he could just call her by her own *Americantzi* name.

Catherine.

He tried that out mentally a couple of times. He liked it. It was different, but that was okay.

*Everything* was different here.

The skyline was different—a bewildering maze of impossible, towering light, making him long for the flat, sparse landscape of Moscow with her mere seven "tallies" punching the night sky. Food was different, processed crap that lay heavy in your stomach and bound you up for days. Even the smells were different: still fetid, still *city* smells, but somehow instantly recognizable as something alien to the Moscow he knew.

Aleks nearly laughed out loud at that one. Fuck your mother! Who could have imagined he would one day find himself *missing* Moscow's foul stink?

Katya stirred nervously at his movement, and he hugged her soothingly in response. The trip had been hard on her, poor pet. Two weeks welded into that tiny space in the container, with just each other and those Kazakh prostitutes for company. Two weeks of nothing but the stale black bread that filthy Chechen had given them, hot, foul water and the overpowering stink of his shit and piss from the bucket that fell over every time the ship rolled.

And then, fuck your mother, as if that wasn't bad enough, three days out from docking one of the bitches up and dies! Aleks couldn't believe it. He had no idea what the poor bitch had had—he hadn't dared go near her. None of them had. They'd crowded into the far end of the space, as far away as they could, and tried not to look, or smell, as she started to bloat. The stink was indescribable. It was a fucking miracle the container had even got past the dock workers, let alone Customs.

And that any of them were still alive.

Aleks shook his head. The trip had been hard all right, on him as well as Katya. *But not as hard as on those poor fuckers sacrificed to the Turks,* he thought.

Four nameless souls, sent blindly to a death they had no idea was coming. Aleks wondered briefly who they'd been. Punks, the Chechen had said. Mongrel scum from the streets of Tblisi, deluded they were going to score big on a drug shipment, then thrown to the dogs. What do you care?

And he was right. Aleks didn't care, not much. They had died so that he and Katya could live. So that *all* of them could live.

Aleks wondered uneasily about the others. Gennady and Lyudmila. Had they made it out too? Gennady was right, of course. They'd *had* to split up. It was imperative. In case something happened—one of them died, or somehow didn't get through. Or got caught by NASA. But he missed them both already. Badly.

Would he ever see Gennady and Lyudmila again? Would the two of them make the rendezvous they had set together?

*Thirteen April 2007. At the foot of the Liberty Statue.*

Or were he and Katya really alone? The only ones left, sole repository of the people who were to come. That was an awe-inspiring thought. Frightening almost. Suddenly, the cityscape seemed to drop from Aleks's eyes, replaced by empty night sky that stretched dizzyingly out to infinity in every direction, terrifying in its lack of obstacles and infinite promise.

He pushed the thoughts away, suppressing a shiver. There was no call to be thinking of such things. *You have to be strong,* he ordered himself. *For Liliya's sake.*

But he felt the thoughts moving, as if by osmosis, into Katya. She stirred in his arms, her chest expanded, and sure enough, a moment later Aleks felt the first tear splash his hand.

He hugged her to him gently. "Shhh, Katya," he said placatingly, using her real name because he sensed she needed him to. "Don't cry, my *daragaya.*"

But the tears began to fall, and her body to shake. "I can't help it, Sasha," she sobbed, when she could catch her breath. "We are so alone here. We have *nothing.* Just like dust that blows in the street. And everything is so strange here . . ." Her voice tailed off, lost in another round of sobs.

Aleks squeezed her tight. "I know, Katya," he soothed, stroking her hair. "It is hard. But there is nothing of which to be afraid. This is a nation of immigrants, remember. The whole country is full of them."

Her sobs subsided, but she grabbed his hand tight and worked herself around to face him. Her voice, when she spoke, was tight and her eyes shone in the diffused city lights.

"I know, Sasha," she said fervently. "But not like us though?"

Aleks could feel the craving in the question, the yearning for affirmation. There was a world in it, a universe, of future hopes and future dreams. He bent to kiss her forehead in reassurance.

"No, Katya," he whispered, drawing her to him once more. "Not like us."

# Acknowledgments

A lot of people had a hand in *Cosmonaut* and deserve thanks. Clare Coney and Lyn McGaurr did bang-up jobs editing the manuscript. Clare Forster and all the staff at Penguin handled publication with enviable professionalism. Garth Nix, my imperturbable agent, was a steadying influence, as well as the man most responsible for *Cosmonaut* seeing the light of day.

Thanks, guys.

Some friends need special mention. John for edit sessions, the occasional kickback and the spur of his detestable boasting. And my muckracking mate Olav for his sheltering wing and sustaining friendship, twenty-eight years now and counting.

As for sources, the following people kindly volunteered time and information, and have my heartfelt gratitude: Adrian Flitney was a mine of scientific advice, any hour of the day or night; Dr. Roderic V. N. Melnik, and Enrique and Angelina Bismarck, helped out with Russian translations; Kazuyuki Takata of the University of New England and Professor Kwon of Griffith University did likewise with Japanese and Korean, respectively; Stephen K. Lorch of the Forensic Sciences Division of Michigan State Police was instrumental on forensic questions, as were Professor Jay Siegel of Michigan State University and the fabulous staff of the John Tonge Center here in Brisbane; Sergeant Patrick Henahan, ex–Special Assignment Squad of the Homicide Section of Detroit Police, was incredibly helpful on police procedure in Motortown, USA, as was Officer Kevin Bass of the same force; Leland Haynes, SR-71 Crew Chief at Beale AFB, California, patiently fielded crazy questions on the magnificent Blackbird; and the good people at Media Resources, NASA, did the same for Agency programs; the inestimable Lisa Phillips provided information on psych tests and a great FBI source book; and Brendan McCleary has my thanks for his help with IT info. None of them, of course, can be held accountable for whatever errors have crept, slipped or been deliberately inserted into the manuscript; I think we all know who's responsible for those.

# About the Author

**Peter McAllister** was born and raised in Brisbane, Australia. He has worked as a graphic artist and an ad salesman for a music radio station, studied anthropology and foreign language, and written numerous pieces for Australian magazines.